No Other Will Do

Books by Karen Witemeyer

A Tailor-Made Bride

Head in the Clouds

To Win Her Heart

Short-Straw Bride

Stealing the Preacher

Full Steam Ahead

A Worthy Pursuit

No Other Will Do

A Cowboy Unmatched from
A Match Made in Texas: A Novella Collection

Love on the Mend from
With All My Heart Romance Collection

The Husband Maneuver from
With This Ring: A Novella Collection

No Other Will Do

KAREN WITEMEYER

BETHANYHOUSE

a division of Baker Publishing Group
Minneapolis, Minnesota

© 2016 by Karen Witemeyer

Published by Bethany House Publishers
11400 Hampshire Avenue South
Bloomington, Minnesota 55438
www.bethanyhouse.com

Bethany House Publishers is a division of
Baker Publishing Group, Grand Rapids, Michigan

Printed in the United States of America

Library of Congress Control Number: 2016930769

ISBN 978-0-7642-1281-9

Scripture quotations are from the King James Version of the Bible.

This is a work of fiction. Names, characters, incidents, and dialogues are products of the author's imagination and are not to be construed as real. Any resemblance to actual events or persons, living or dead, is entirely coincidental.

Cover design by Dan Pitts
Cover photography by Mike Habermann Photography, LLC

Author is represented by Books & Such Literary Agency.

16 17 18 19 20 21 22   7 6 5 4 3 2 1

To one of the strongest women I know,

my grandma—Vera Burgess.

Nearly a century old and still ready to take on the world.
From her blackberry jam to her persimmon cookies,
she filled my childhood with sweet memories,
and her never-quit attitude has given me an example
of fortitude and perseverance I aspire to duplicate.

I love you, Grandma!

What doth it profit, my brethren, though a man say he hath faith, and have not works? can faith save him? If a brother or sister be naked, and destitute of daily food, and one of you say unto them, Depart in peace, be ye warmed and filled; notwithstanding ye give them not those things which are needful to the body; what doth it profit? Even so faith, if it hath not works, is dead, being alone.

James 2:14–17

Prologue

Malachi Shaw made the arduous climb back into consciousness with great effort. But everything Mal had accomplished so far in his thirteen years of life had required great effort. Not that he had achieved anything worth bragging about. Orphaned. Starving. And . . . cold.

That's what his senses picked up first. The cold. And not just the huddling-under-the-saloon-stairs-in-a-too-thin-coat-during-a-blue-norther kind of cold. No. This was a cold so harsh it burned. Which made exactly zero sense.

With a groan, Mal lifted his head and tried to draw his arms beneath him to push himself up. That's when the rest of the pain hit. His shoulder throbbed, his ribs ached, and his head felt as if it had collided with a train. Oh, that's right. It had.

Memories swirled through his mind as he slowly crawled out of the snowdrift that must have broken his fall. He'd hopped the train, just as he'd done a half dozen times over the month since his drunk of a father finally got himself killed—run over by a wagon while trying to cross the street. The old man hadn't been good for much, leaving Mal to scrounge for food in garbage bins while he spent whatever coins he managed to earn at the card tables on whiskey. But at least he'd kept a roof over their heads—a run-down, leaky roof supported by slanted, rickety walls that couldn't even hold the wind out, but a roof nonetheless.

The morning after they'd laid his father in the ground, the lady who owned the shack kicked Mal out on his ear. Barely gave him time to gather his one pathetic sack of belongings. A sack, Mal discovered as he frantically searched the area around him, that was nowhere to be found.

"No!" He slammed his fist into the frozen earth near his hip, then slumped forward.

What had he expected? That God would suddenly remember he existed and lift a finger to help him? Ha! Not likely. The Big Man had never cared a fig for him before. Why start now? Much better to sit back in heaven and get a good laugh watching poor Malachi Shaw fumble around. Taking his ma so early, Mal couldn't even remember what she looked like. Giving him a father who cared more about his next drink than his own flesh and blood. Then even taking that much from him. Leaving him alone. No home. No one willing to give him work. Leaving him no option but to ride the rails, looking for some place, any place, that would give him a fair shake.

And what had that gotten him? A run-in with a gang of boxcar riders who hadn't appreciated him infringing on their territory. Mal reached up to rub the painful knot on his forehead. There'd been four of them. All twice his size. Each taking his turn. Until the last fella slammed Mal's head against the steel doorframe.

Malachi didn't remember anything after that. Obviously,

they'd thrown him off. He could barely make out the tracks at the top of the long embankment. It was too bad God hadn't just let him break his neck in the fall. But then, where would be the fun in that?

"Gotta keep the entertainment around, don'tcha?" He scowled up at the gray sky that would soon be deepening to black. "Wouldn't want you and the angels gettin' bored up there."

Mal brushed the snow from his hair and arms with jerky movements and pushed to his feet. He beat at his pants, dusting the snow from the front and back as he ground his teeth. His fingers burned as if someone were holding them to a flame. His ears and nose stung, as well. He couldn't feel his feet at all. Not good.

He stomped a few steps until most of the white had fallen away from the laces of his boots. Cupping his hands near his mouth, he huffed warm air into them. Not that it helped much. The only thing that would keep him from turning into a boy-sized icicle was shelter. And a fire. And a coat. The thick flannel shirt he'd gotten from the poor box at the church did little to cut the wind. And now that it was wet from the snow, it chilled him more than protected him.

At least there weren't any holes in his shoe leather. The soles were thin but solid. If he were to count his blessings, like the preacher who'd given him the clothes advised, he'd at least have one. Better than nothin', he supposed.

If only those fellas had left him his sack. No sack meant no food, no dry clothes, no flint for a fire.

"Quit your whining, Mal," he muttered to himself. "Groanin' won't fill yer belly. If ya wanna get warm, do somethin' about it."

Straightening his shoulders, Malachi lifted his head and scanned the landscape, looking for any hint of a building in the area. A barn with animals heating the air would be best.

But there was nothing. Nothing but snow-dusted prairie grass with a few random post oaks sticking their heads up every now and again.

What'd he expect? For a closed carriage to show up with one of them fancy drivers who'd call him *sir* and ask him where he'd like to go?

Take me to the nearest barn, my good man, Malachi imagined saying. *And don't spare the horses.*

With a snort, Mal flipped up the collar of his shirt, stuffed his stinging hands in his pockets, and started trudging east. Gainesville shouldn't be too far away. That's where he'd been when he got the brilliant idea to hitch a ride in the third box-car from the end. Not his best decision. But the fellas already occupying the car had jumped on him pretty fast. The train couldn't have traveled too many miles from town before he'd been tossed. Surely there'd be a farm or ranch nearby with a barn he could hunker down in for a night or two. All he had to do was find it before full dark hit.

By the time he came across the first structure, Mal was shivering so hard, he could barely keep his balance. The wind pounding him from the north kept pushing him off track, making him fight to walk a straight line. But, hey, at least it wasn't snowing. That preacher man would be proud of him. He'd just doubled the size of his blessing list.

Mal chuckled, but the expulsion of air turned into a cough. One that made his chest ache. Hunching his shoulders, he ducked his head and turned full into the wind, cutting across a field to shorten his path to the barn.

Light glowed from the windows of the house that stood a short distance away. Smoke blew out the chimney at a sharp angle, as much a slave to the wind as he was. He usually took steps to avoid people, but in this instance, he was too cold to even consider looking for a more suitable hideout. If he could just bed down in some straw for the night and get warm, he could be away before the owners woke up in the morning.

Suddenly thankful for the encroaching darkness, Malachi flattened himself against the far side of the barn and inched his way around until he reached the doors at the front. Opening the one closest to him just enough to squeeze through, he slipped inside and held the door, fighting the tug of the wind in order to close it quietly. The last thing he needed was for the slam of a door to bring the farmer running. Farmers tended to carry shotguns, and Mal wasn't too fond of buckshot.

He peered through the crack he'd left open and watched the house, ready to make a run for the field, if necessary. But no one came out to challenge him. He released the breath he'd been holding and closed the door the rest of the way. Looked like his blessing list was up to three now. Mal grinned and trudged to the darkest corner he could find.

The smell of hay tickled his nose, but he was too happy to be out of the wind to pay it any mind. With numb, shaky fingers, he managed to undo the buttons on his flannel shirt. He removed it along with the long-sleeved wool undershirt he wore and stretched both over the empty stall door. He tried to undo the laces of his shoes, but his fingers were too stiff to pick the knots free. His feet would have to wait until he regained some feeling in his hands.

He huffed his breath over his cupped hands, then moved into the stall and buried himself in the pile of straw. He lay still for a long time, his bony arms curled in front of his thin chest, his knees pulled up tight. The dampness of his trousers caused his teeth to chatter uncontrollably. He closed his eyes and imagined everything warm he could think of. A roaring fire. A wool blanket—no, not one of those scratchy things. A quilt. A thick, soft, down-filled quilt with lace at the edges like he saw in a shop window once. A steaming bowl of barley soup.

The pang hit his stomach hard. *Great.* He knew better than to think about food. Now he wasn't gonna be able to think about anything else. Mal opened his eyes and squinted through the shadows. Maybe there was some feed in the corncrib he'd passed on the way in. It wouldn't be the first time he'd made a dinner of field corn pilfered from a bunch of livestock. Awful stuff. Hard and dry, and it always stuck in his teeth. But it would hold back the gnawing in his belly and maybe even let him sleep.

Reluctantly, Malachi unfolded himself and brushed off the straw. He clenched his jaw to still the chattering of his teeth and slowly made his way to where he recalled seeing the crib. One of the horses snorted as he passed and kicked at his stall door.

"Easy, boy," Mal murmured in a soft voice. "No reason to get worked up. I ain't gonna hurt nuthin'."

In the dwindling light coming through one of the windows, the horse watched him with big, brown eyes that made Mal's neck itch, but the beast quit his bangin'. Malachi eased past, keeping his gaze on the horse, not liking the way he stared at him. Down his long horse nose. All snooty. Like the shopkeeper's wife who used to shoo him with her broom every time she caught him going through the garbage bins behind the store. As if he were a rat or some other kind of vermin.

Caught up in his thoughts, Mal didn't see the shovel until his shoe collided with it. It toppled to the floor with a clatter that echoed off the rafters. Mal froze, his heart thumping harder than a blacksmith's hammer.

A hinge creaked. He spun to face the sound. On his left. Toward the front. Between him and the door.

Footsteps.

Malachi snatched the fallen shovel and pulled it back, ready to strike. He'd smash and run. As soon as the farmer showed himself.

12

A figure emerged from inside a front stall. A tiny figure with round green eyes and a halo of curly black hair standing out around her head. Pale skin. Plump, rosy cheeks.

Mal slowly dropped his arms and set the shovel aside. There'd be no smashing and running. Not when God had sent him an angel.

"Who are you?" the angel asked, her childish voice holding only curiosity. No accusation.

Mal couldn't say a word.

The angel didn't ask another question. Just stared back at him. Only then did Mal remember he didn't have a shirt on. He circled his arms around his middle, trying to hide his scrawny, naked chest. He didn't want to offend the angel. Or have her see the bones that showed through his skin. A man had his pride, after all.

"You must be cold," she said at last. Then she started unbuttoning her coat, and before he knew what she was about, she had the thing off and was wrapping it around his shoulders.

The heavy wool felt like heaven, still warm from her body. Heat seeped into his frost-nipped skin, thawing him until he thought he might melt like candle wax in an oven.

"Don't just stand there gawking like you've never seen a girl before," she demanded. "Put your arms in the sleeves."

His angel scowled at him, her lower lip protruding in an exasperated pout as she lectured him. Then, because he obviously wasn't moving fast enough for her liking, she reached out and did it for him. Peeled his arms apart and stuffed them in the too-short coat sleeves.

"You're near to frozen," she complained when her hand first touched his wrist, but the observation didn't cause her to slow down at all. She just reached for the buttons next, did them up, then started rubbing his arms up and down through the sleeves, the friction heating his skin even more. He stared down at the top of her head while she worked. She only came up to about his chin. Tiny little thing, his angel. Bossy, too.

She pulled away after a moment. "Hmm. This isn't good enough." She stalked over to a sawhorse situated near the tack wall, threw the bridle that had been sitting atop it to the ground, and grabbed hold of the striped saddle blanket draped across its middle.

"Sit down," she ordered as she dragged the thick blanket over to him. Once he complied, she flopped the blanket onto his lap. She stared at him again, all thoughtful-like. Her gaze hesitated at the ends of the coat sleeves, where his wrists and hands hung uncovered. "Oh! My mittens!" A grin broke out across her face and she bounded away, into the stall that she'd emerged from earlier.

She hurried back and thrust a pair of bright red mittens at him. "Here. Put these on." Her face clouded again for a minute, then cleared. "And my scarf!" She unwrapped the long knitted strip from around her neck and twined it about his, wrapping it up over his ears and head, as well. "That's better." The triumph in her voice made him smile.

She examined him again, the frown lines reappearing above her pert little nose. He was beginning to feel a bit like one of those snowmen the kids liked to build by the schoolhouse when the weather turned wintry. He half expected her to fetch a carrot and jab it against his nose. Not that he would have minded. A carrot would taste a fair sight better than cow corn.

"Your feet," she said at last. "There's still snow crusted in your laces. Aunt Henry is always fussing at me to get out of my wet boots and stockings before my feet shrivel. If you were walking around in the snow out there, though, we've got more to worry about than wrinkled toes."

Aunt Henry? What kind of person was that?

The girl glanced up at him. "Old Man Tarleton got lost in a

blizzard a couple years back, and his feet got so cold, they froze solid. Three of his toes turned black and fell off," She reported that grisly piece of news with a decidedly non-angelic degree of enthusiasm. "So we better get those shoes off."

She sat down in front of him and started picking at his laces.

Enough was enough. He couldn't let his angel touch his stinky feet. There was no telling what muck he might have stepped in.

"I'll do it," he groused. He tried to push her away and take off the fuzzy red mittens, but she wouldn't let him.

"Keep those mittens on!" She glared at him so fiercely he didn't dare argue. "I'll not have you catching your death on my watch."

Why was she doing this? Helping him instead of calling her father to send him away. Giving him her own clothing. Talking to him as if he were any other person. Not the piece of gutter trash he knew himself to be.

She finally got the laces undone and gently tugged his shoes off. He tried to pull his feet beneath the horse blanket before she saw the sorry state of his socks, but she wouldn't let him. She peeled the hole-riddled stockings from his feet one at a time, *tsk*ing over how icy his toes felt. He was just happy to see they weren't black like Old Man Tarleton's. They were filthy, though. Ugly. He pulled them away from her clean white hands and did his best to hide them under the saddle blanket.

She made no comment, just plopped onto the dirt floor in front of him and yanked her shoes off. What was she . . . ? His angel pulled the thick wool socks she wore off her feet and went digging under the blanket for his toes. Before he could react and scramble away from her, she latched on to his right foot, dragged it out, and pushed on the sock. She captured his left just as easily. 'Course he'd stopped trying to get away by then. His brain might be half frozen, but he recognized an unwinnable battle when he saw one.

The warmth of the socks brought a tingle of awareness to his feet that quickly expanded into a searing pain so deep, he wanted to kick her away so she'd stop touching him. But he didn't. Wouldn't. Ever.

He'd just encountered the biggest blessing his scrawny list had ever seen. No way was he gonna do anything to hurt her. So he gritted his teeth and sat still while she flopped the horse blanket down over his stinging feet.

"Now for the inside." She stood and pushed her bare feet back into her boots and disappeared into her stall again. When she emerged, she waddled, carrying a full pail of milk in front of her. He jumped up to help her carry it, taking it from her hands.

"It's still warm," she said. "I don't have a cup, though."

Malachi's mouth salivated at the thought of drinking fresh milk. "I don't need a cup." He'd just put his mouth directly on the pail and tip it until the creamy goodness slathered his throat. But no. He couldn't do that. Couldn't drink like an animal in front of her. Couldn't defile the milk by putting his mouth all over it.

He glanced around. There. On the workbench. A canning jar half full of nails and tacks and other odds and ends. Malachi rushed to the table, unscrewed the lid, and dumped the contents, careful not to let any fall onto the floor. He wiped the dust off on his still-damp pants and blew out the center. "This'll do."

Her nose wrinkled. "But it's *dirty*."

He grinned. "Little dirt never hurt me."

She smiled in return, and the action almost felled him. Never had he seen anything so beautiful, so *good*, aimed his direction. Smiles like that were reserved for other people. Deserving people. Never for him.

Clearing his throat, he pushed past her and strode back to the milk pail. He didn't want to dirty the rest of the milk by dipping the jar in so he set it on the floor and lifted the pail.

"I'll hold it," the girl chirped, still grinning as if this were some grand adventure.

Weakened from his ordeal, Mal's arms shook with the weight of the pail. Some of the milk sloshed over the sides of the jar. His gaze flew to the girl, his chest tight.

"Keep going," she urged, not angry in the least that he'd spilled milk on her fingers. "Fill it to the top."

The tightness eased. He followed her instructions, then set the pail down and took the jar from her.

He lifted the glass jar to his lips. His eyes slid closed as the fresh, creamy liquid rolled over his tongue. He savored the sweetness, drinking slowly, deliberately. And when a third was all that remained, he made himself stop and set the jar aside.

"Why aren't you finishing it? Aunt Bertie always makes me finish my milk before I leave the table."

Wasn't it Aunt Henry a minute ago?

Malachi shrugged it off. The aunt's name didn't matter. "I'm savin' it fer later." He'd learned never to eat everything he found all at once. He never knew how hard it would be to find something the next time. Better to squirrel some away while you had it.

"But we got plenty more." She tipped her head toward the milk pail.

"That's yours. Your family's."

The girl looked at him strangely, as if she didn't understand what he'd just said. "The aunts won't mind."

Mal shook his head.

"Suit yourself." His angel glanced around the barn, looking less than fully in charge for the first time since he'd met her. Then she hugged her arms around her waist and tried to hide a shiver.

"You're cold," Mal accused with more harshness than he should have, but doggone it, the girl should have told him she was getting cold.

He immediately threw her mittens back at her and stripped out of the coat. "You need to go back to the house, kid. Go sit by the stove or somethin'."

"I'm not a baby." But when her lower lip came out in a pout his resolve hardened. She was far too young to be shivering in a cold barn when a warm house was available.

"Scram, kid. I'll be fine."

She put the coat on and slipped the mittens over her small hands. "What's your name?" she demanded.

He glared at her then finally relented. "Malachi."

She smiled again, making him a mite dizzy. "I'm Emma."

"Good for you," he groused, still feeling guilty that he'd let her get cold. "Now, scram."

She did.

And all the light went with her. Leaving Mal alone. In the dark. Where he belonged.

He'd gotten used to the condition. It shouldn't bother him. Hadn't bothered him for years, in fact. But it did now. Because now he knew what he'd been missing.

Mal picked up the saddle blanket and wrapped it around his shoulders. Then he grabbed his jar and turned to go back to his corner and bury himself in the hay. The sight of the milk pail stopped him. She'd left it behind.

A little thrill coursed through him. Did that mean she'd be back? Or would the milk be left here? Forgotten. Like him. Maybe he should carry it up to the front stoop. To thank her for helping him.

He bent over to grab the handle. The barn door flew open.

"Good news, Malachi!" Emma stood in the doorway, the beam of her smile so bright he nearly had to lift a hand to shade his eyes. "The aunts said I can keep you!"

18

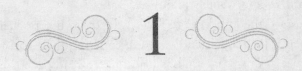

1

Emma Chandler yanked the hostile note free of the nail that had tacked it to the church door. She wadded the vile thing in her fist and shoved it into her skirt pocket, though what she truly wanted to do was hurl it into the street, run over it with about fifty horses, spit on it, throw dirt clods at it, and finally set it on fire and watch it wither into a pile of harmless ash that would be erased by the wind.

How dare someone threaten her ladies? The fiend had no right!

"He's getting bolder." The stoic voice of her friend cut through Emma's spiraling temper, reminding her that railing at injustice rarely solved the problem. Coolheaded planning. That's what they needed.

"Yes, he is." Emma scanned the countryside for signs of the coward, even though she knew she'd find nothing. She never did. And this was the third note he'd left in a fortnight. Each one in a place that penetrated the colony a little more deeply. "But at least it's still just words."

"We've no guarantee it will stay that way." Victoria Adams voiced Emma's greatest fear. "If words won't get him what he wants, he *will* escalate." Tori's voice rang with the certainty of one who had experienced such a lesson firsthand. "Let me see the note, Emma." She held out her palm.

Emma sighed and tugged the wad from her pocket. She dropped it into her friend's hand, knowing that Tori would recognize at once that an escalation had already occurred.

Victoria uncrumpled the note and scanned the page, a soft echo of the threatening words escaping under her breath as she read.

"Women of Harper's Station—

Clear out by tonight or I'll clear you out myself. This is your last warning."

"We have to call a meeting." Emma marched down the church steps and began pacing the yard.

Tori followed her down the steps but didn't pace. She simply leaned against the railing and waited for Emma to circle back around. "What will you tell them?"

The soft question stopped Emma in her tracks. She spun toward her friend. "I won't leave, Tori. I won't let a bully drive me away." She flung out her arm toward the handful of buildings that clustered around the old stagecoach station that had attracted the first permanent settlers to the area twenty years ago. "Harper's Station is supposed to be a refuge for women escaping this kind of intimidation. We've worked too hard building this place up, bringing the women in, giving them a fresh start. I won't scurry away like some timid little mouse just because some pigheaded man wants to flex his muscles!"

Tori, dear that she was, made no effort to interrupt Emma's impassioned ranting. She simply held her friend's gaze and waited patiently for the kettle to stop hissing. Which it did. Eventually. Emma might refuse to sacrifice her principles, but she'd never sacrifice the safety of her ladies. Not for any reason. Not even for the ideal that brought them all together in the first place.

She paced back to where Tori waited at the church steps, releasing her indignation a little bit at a time until her mind cleared of the haze. "I'll encourage all the mothers with children to follow the sheriff's advice and move—*temporarily*—to one of the neighboring towns." Emma's shoulders sagged as she met Tori's gaze. "Including you." How she hated to send her closest friend, her partner in starting the colony, away. But Tori had a four-year-old son, and if anything happened to Lewis . . . Well, such a thought didn't bear thinking.

Tori's eyes narrowed. "I'm not going anywhere." The steel in her tone brooked no argument. "I'm not leaving you to fight this battle on your own. Besides, where would we go? All my funds are tied up in the store. I can't exactly take the merchandise with me. And if I lose that, I lose everything."

"I'll keep an eye on things for you," Emma offered, but her friend cut her off with a firm shake of her head.

"You have the bank to run. You don't need the additional worry of tending my shop. I'll keep a tight leash on Lewis. We'll be fine." Tori fisted her hands at her sides, and Emma knew at once that she wouldn't be swayed.

Victoria never showed emotion beyond the affection of friendship and love toward her son. Nothing else. No fear, anger, surprise—nothing that could possibly give someone an advantage over her. If she was worked up enough to clench her fingers into a fist, her feelings on the matter must be strong, indeed.

"I want to show my son that when you believe in something, you fight for it, even when danger threatens. You don't hide."

A world of pain lingered behind that statement, a pain Emma could only imagine. Tori had been fighting since the day she discovered herself pregnant after being attacked by a man esteemed by her entire hometown. Fighting for a place to belong after her father sent her away. Fighting for a way to provide for herself and her child. Fighting the fear that she'd misjudge a man's character again someday and experience the nightmare all over again.

Emma stepped close to Victoria and took her arm. Only then did Tori unclench her fists and lay one of her hands atop Emma's.

"We stand together," Emma vowed.

Tori nodded. "Together."

Two hours later, just after noon, Emma stood at the front of the church, her back propped against the left side wall, watching her ladies file in. Her heart grew heavy as her gaze skimmed each familiar face. Which ones would leave? Which would stay?

Betty Cooper tromped down the center aisle, her stocky build and no-nonsense stride blazing a trail for the four younger women who followed in her wake. The middle-aged matron oversaw the laying hens that provided a large share of the income that the women of Harper's Station brought in. She'd been with Emma since the early days. Widowed, no children, but she had one of the biggest hearts Emma had ever encountered. She hid it well behind a gruff manner and an insistence on hard work, but she clucked over the ladies she supervised as if they were her own chicks.

The ladies of the sewing circle, several of whom had children in tow, chatted amongst themselves as they took their usual seats in the middle rows on the right side. They crafted exquisite quilts that fetched top price in Fort Worth. If half of them left, how would the remaining ladies meet their quota? The broker expected fifteen quilts every month, an easy enough order to fill with ten ladies plying their needles every day, but if their number fell to five . . . ?

Grace Mallory came through the door next, her head bent down as usual, her gaze fixed on her feet as she slid onto one of the back pews. The quiet woman had only been in town six months and liked to keep to herself, but thanks to her skill as a Western Union telegrapher, Harper's Station now had a working telegraph system. The county hadn't yet granted them a post office, so mail still had to be forwarded from Seymour, but any lady in town could send a telegram for less than a nickel a word. Losing Grace would be a blow, if she chose to leave.

Emma's attention flitted to the others already gathered. Those who worked the community garden and put up preserves and canned vegetables to sell. The ladies who ran the café. The boardinghouse proprietress. The midwife who served as the town doctor.

And, of course, the aunts.

Henrietta and Alberta Chandler sat on the front row, staunch as ever in their support of her. Aunt Henry's eyes glowed with a fierce, nearly militant light as she sat stiff as a board, flaunting her bloomers as she always did whenever anything that might possibly relate to women's suffrage came into play. Aunt Bertie, on the other hand, sported a much softer posture and more feminine garb as she sat next to her older sister. She turned to smile at Emma and gave her a little finger wave of encouragement.

The aunts had raised Emma since she was eight—Aunt Henry instilling in her the passion to stand against injustice, and Aunt Bertie teaching her to lead with her heart. They had been the ones to help her dream up the idea of a women's colony, a place run by women to benefit women. A sanctuary for those need-ing to escape, and a place of opportunity for those looking to better themselves.

Two years ago, when Emma came into her inheritance at age twenty-one, she'd heard about a small town of abandoned buildings being sold for pennies on the dollar. Residents had abandoned the old stagecoach town when the railroad came through nearby Seymour. The aunts had combined their funds with hers in an investment pool, and they'd purchased the land. Thanks to a few well-placed ads in area newspapers that first year and what some would call their growing *notoriety* since then, the colony boasted nearly fifty members—if one counted the children—women surviving and thriving by supporting one another.

And now some bullheaded, hateful man threatened to destroy all they had built. Emma clenched her jaw. *Not on my watch*.

As the women found their seats, Emma sought a last-minute dose of heavenly wisdom. *You can see what I cannot, Lord. You know what is best. Please don't let me advise these ladies poorly. Guide us in such a way that we might triumph over our enemy.*

"Emma?" Victoria touched her arm. The gentle understand-ing in the contact soothed and reassured her. "We're ready to begin."

Emma nodded and gave her friend a small smile. Then she straightened away from the wall, tugged on the edge of her tailored navy blue suit coat, the one she always wore when she wanted to project an aura of authority, and stepped up to the small pulpit the circuit preacher would use on Sunday to deliver his sermon. If they still had a town come Sunday.

The room instantly fell quiet.

Emma cleared her throat. "Thank you, ladies, for coming on such short notice. We have a matter of great urgency to discuss."

She glanced at the familiar faces, some visibly nervous, others curious, a few accusing, as if this current dilemma were somehow her fault. Emma immediately diverted her gaze back to her aunts. Henry nodded to her, her eyes blazing with confidence in her niece. Bertie just smiled, but the gesture was so obviously heartfelt and sincere that Emma couldn't help but be buoyed.

"I'm sure by now, word has reached most of you that a third note was found this morning. I'm afraid the author of said note has increased his demands. He has instituted a deadline, demanding we all leave by tonight."

A loud murmur swept the room as the women turned to each other with their questions.

"Ladies, please." Emma raised her voice to be heard. "I will be happy to answer all your questions in just a moment. But first, I want to make it clear that you are under no compulsion to stay. Everyone must decide for herself what is in her best interest. And know that I will support your decision no matter what it might be.

"Having said that, I think it imperative to confess to you that we still have no idea who this man is or why he wishes us to leave. Miss Adams and I visited with the sheriff after we received the first note. He did a search of the immediate area but found nothing suspicious. We wired him again today, just as we did after we found the second note. Due to the cattle rustling that continues to plague the ranchers in the southern parts of Baylor County, he is unable to lend us his protection. He reiterated his recommendation that we pack up and leave. That we remove ourselves from the threat and take up residence in Seymour or Wichita Falls or return home to our families."

"But I have no family," one lady shouted out from the back of the room. "That's why I came here."

"There's nothin' for me in Seymour," another called. "I done looked already. Without the egg money I earn workin' at Miss Betty's farm, I won't be able to feed my young'uns."

A chorus of panicked agreement rose, filling the room with desperation.

A lady in a brown dress shot to her feet. Flora Johnson, one of the newer women, who worked the garden. She'd shown up two weeks ago with a black eye and a midsection riddled with bruises. "You told us we'd be safe here." She crossed her arms over her rib cage. "Now you tell us we're on our own? That the sheriff won't even be bothered to lift a finger?" She glanced around to the crowd, all of whom had fallen silent. "I don't know about the rest of ya, but I've seen what happens when a woman tries to keep a man from gettin' what he wants. It ain't pretty. If I had someplace to go, I'd be packin' up right now." She turned back to the front, uncrossed her arms, and pointed an accusing finger at Emma. "You can't keep us safe, Miss Chandler. No one can."

Heart thundering in her chest, Emma faced her ladies, chin high. "You're right, Flora. I can't promise that you . . . that *any* of you . . . will be safe. I don't know if we are facing one man or many. Staying will entail danger, and the serious possibility of physical harm. What I can promise you, though, is that I will stay and fight.

"Harper's Station is my dream and my responsibility. My aunts and I own the land, and I refuse to be run off my property. What we face is no different than what the courageous families who settled this land faced before us. They had to fend off Indian attacks and raids from the warring Comanche. Some died. Some left. But some held their ground and prevailed.

"That is what I intend to do. Hold my ground, and do my best to preserve what we have built here. However, I will not ask anyone to fight this battle with me. Each of you must decide for yourself, but . . . I strongly suggest that those of you with children seek shelter elsewhere, if at all possible. The young ones must be protected. And be assured that if you leave, I will welcome your return once the danger has passed. You will always have a place here in Harper's Station."

"Unless the Station's no longer standin'," a very loud, very male voice boomed. The sound carried through an open window to Emma's right.

She caught a brief glimpse of a man in a heavy buckskin coat, a dark blue bandana pulled high over his face. Then she saw a flash of metal.

"Everybody down!" Emma dove off the stage toward her aunts. She swept them both from the pew just as gunfire erupted.

2

Glass shattered. Women screamed. Emma prayed.

Protect us, Lord!

Then all fell silent.

Emma cautiously lifted her head and looked toward the window where she'd caught a glimpse of the man in buckskin. He was gone. Or hiding.

Releasing her hold on the aunts, she crawled across the front of the church to get to the window.

"Mind the glass, Emma." Aunt Henry called out the warning in an overloud whisper.

Emma grinned. She should have known better than to think a little gunplay would rattle Henrietta Chandler. The woman's nerves were as strong as a gunslinger's. Emma heeded her aunt's advice and veered away from the window to avoid the broken glass. Once she reached the wall, she clambered to her feet and flattened her back against the whitewashed planks. Scooting the glass out of her way with the toe of her shoe, she eased closer to the window.

Was he still out there? Waiting for her to show her face so

he could take out the ringleader? Emma's corset seemed to shrink about her midsection, stealing her breath, constricting her movement. She closed her eyes and leaned her head back against the wall. *Calm yourself, Emma. You can do this. Your ladies are counting on you.*

Then, through the panic and the thunderous pounding of her heart, the hint of a sound tickled her ears. Hoofbeats. Moving away.

Emma spun toward the window and scanned the side yard. She craned her neck to check the road but saw nothing. Then she looked to the surrounding landscape. There. A rider. Disappearing into the scrub brush. Dark brown hat. Buckskin coat. Chestnut horse. Too far away to make out any other details.

"He's gone." She turned to face the women, who were slowly picking themselves off the floor, using the pews as support. "He rode off to the north. A single rider."

"Anyone hurt?" The gruff voice of Maybelle Curtis rang through the room. "I can run fetch my doctorin' bag if anyone's of a need."

A low murmur spread through the building as the women examined their children and each other for injury.

"Katie's got a cut on her cheek that will need attention," Betty offered, "but the rest of my chicks are in decent shape."

"Charlie knocked his head pretty hard on the side of the pew when we dove for cover," one of the young mothers from the sewing circle added. "I'd take it kindly if you could look at it for me, Maybelle."

A handful of others called out similar concerns. All minor, thank the Lord. Emma hurried back to her aunts. "Are the two of you all right?" she asked even as she examined them for signs of injury.

"Quit your fussing," Aunt Henry groused. "It'll take more than a topple from a church pew to do us in."

"We're fine, dear," Aunt Bertie confirmed in a softer tone. "Might be a little sore come tomorrow, but nothing to worry about. What about you, Emma? You were the most exposed when the shooting started."

"I'm unharmed." Emma took Bertie's hand and gave it a reassuring squeeze. "No need to fret over me. We Chandlers are made of stern stuff."

The woman beamed as she patted Emma's hand. "That we are, dear. That we are."

Convinced that her aunts were safe, Emma immediately searched the sanctuary for Victoria and her son. Finding her friend examining a hole in the far wall, Emma rushed to her side. "Tori? Are you and Lewis . . ."

Victoria turned aside to reveal a hale-and-hearty sandy-haired boy hiding among the folds of her skirts. "We're fine. Just examining these bullet holes." She reached above her head and ran the tip of her pointer finger over a divot in the white-washed wall. "Lewis was the one to bring it to my attention."

"Bring *what* to your attention?" Emma frowned up at the half-dozen dark circles marring the wall, indignation swelling inside her once again. The fool man could have killed someone.

"He aimed high." Victoria's matter-of-fact voice recited her observation as if she and her son hadn't just been under attack. "Even if we'd been standing, the shots would have sailed over our heads."

Emma pivoted to study the broken window glass on the opposite side of the building. Short, jagged teeth jutted a bare inch at most from the top of the window frame. It had shattered from the top. "You think he intended only to scare us."

Victoria nodded. "It seems so. But don't think I'm excusing his actions." Her eyes flared. "Anyone who fires a weapon into a crowded room deserves no sympathy. A bullet easily could have ricocheted and hit someone. As it is, the panic itself caused numerous injuries."

A pounding from behind Emma drew her attention—drew everyone's attention—back toward the pulpit. Aunt Henry's palm slapped against the podium twice more before she raised an imperious hand and jabbed a finger toward the broken window.

"The coward has finally shown his true colors. Opening fire on women and children. Such depravity is not to be tolerated! Those of you who feel you must leave, do so with all haste, but those of you who feel the fire of injustice burning in your bellies, prepare yourselves for battle. I, for one, pledge to stay and fight alongside my niece. Who's with me?"

"I am!" Victoria raised her hand in the air without a hint of hesitation. Emma's eyes misted.

Betty Cooper pushed to her feet. "I ain't about to leave my hens unprotected with a hooligan like that runnin' around and causin' mischief. Count me in."

"Harper's Station is my home." Quiet Grace Mallory stood next. Her voice wavered slightly as she spoke, but there was nothing uncertain about the determined set of her chin. "I'm done running. And I'm done being told what I can and cannot do. The Lord gave me as much free will as he gave that man outside, and I choose to use mine by not bending to his. I choose to stay."

Emma stared at the petite young woman. She'd never heard Grace string more than a handful of words together at any one time, and here she was addressing an entire room head held high and with a conviction that had Emma herself ready to sound the battle cry.

And she wasn't the only one so affected. All over the room, women pushed to their feet, committing to stay and fight for their home. The show of solidarity seeped into Emma's bones and infused her with strength, with purpose, and also with a touch of fear. These women were counting on her to lead them, to shepherd them through this travail. She knew how to fight financial battles, how to instill a spirit of independence in the women who came to her seeking aid, but how was she to fight a war of physical aggression and danger? Didn't the Bible warn against the blind leading the blind?

"I guess I better stay, too," Maybelle grumbled as she grabbed hold of one of the pew backs and pulled herself to her feet. "If all you hardheaded females are set on being soldiers, someone's gotta be here to nurse your wounds. And there *will* be wounds. Mark my words."

The practical reminder subdued the swelling current of partisanship, but Emma was thankful for the hefty dose of reality. Taking her skirt in hand, she ascended the dais and took her position beside Aunt Henry.

"Maybelle's right. As much as I would love for all of you to stay, there is every likelihood that we will be facing true danger. Each of you must prayerfully consider your choice and count the cost before making a decision."

Betty Cooper lumbered between the pews until she reached an aisle, then ambled up toward the front. "I'm all for countin' the cost, Emma, but if it's all the same to you, I think we ought to count a few other things, as well." She turned to face the group. "Those who plan to stay . . . how many of ya own a firearm?"

"Do we really need to bring weapons into this discussion, dear?" Aunt Bertie's usually pink complexion went decidedly pale. "Guns only breed violence."

Betty shook her head. "I don't like it none, either, Miss Bertie, but this fella has already proved himself to be dishonorable. He ain't above using force to push us outta our homes. If we plan to push back, we might have to do it in a language he understands." She scanned the crowd of assembled women. "Now, raise your hand if you own a firearm. I keep a shotgun by the back door to keep the vermin outta the henhouse. What else we got?"

Three hands went up. Three. Out of the entire colony, only four women owned a gun. And Emma couldn't even count herself among them. She could purchase some, of course, but they'd have to be ordered. Victoria didn't stock them in her store. There'd never been a need for them in Harper's Station. Until now.

"I have my husband's hunting rifle," the widow who ran the boardinghouse offered. "It's stored away in a trunk with the rest of his belongings. Don't know what kind of shape it's in. Haven't opened that trunk since I packed it up three years ago."

"All right," Betty said. "What else?" She pointed to the next woman with her hand raised. "Daisy?"

"I have my papa's old army revolver." Daisy was one of her aunts' dear friends and couldn't be a day under fifty. Which meant her papa's revolver was probably of a similar age. "I'm afraid I never learned how to fire it, though. I just held on to it as a keepsake after Mama passed. Along with Papa's confeder-ate uniform."

Emma bit back a groan. It was worse than she'd thought. But she hadn't really thought this through at all, had she? Her women's colony was designed to be a place of commerce, of belonging, of second chances. A place for women with nowhere to go to come together and support one another through hard work and camaraderie. A sisterhood. Never once had Emma considered that they might need a way to defend themselves against outsiders who wished them harm.

Yet here they were, in just such a situation. And thanks to her lack of foresight, they stood ready to defend their home with all the ferocity of a pack of newborn kittens.

The last woman with her hand raised, drew it down to her side as Betty turned her attention to her. Emma blinked. *Grace Mallory?*

"I carry a derringer in my handbag."

Shock held the crowd immobile. Soft-spoken Grace Mallory carried a gun in her handbag? Emma never would have guessed such a thing, not in a thousand years. But how well did she truly know the young telegrapher? Grace had always made a point to keep to herself. Why, Emma had learned more about her in the last few minutes than she had in the last six months.

Grace lifted her chin. "I know how to use it and would be willing to teach others. But it's only effective in close quarters. A weapon of last resort."

"Well, if you know your way around a gun," Betty announced, recovering more quickly than the rest of them from Grace's revelation, "that puts you a step ahead of most."

"I still think we should notify Sheriff Tabor," Aunt Bertie urged. "Perhaps now that a crime has actually been committed, he'll send deputies to protect us."

Emma shook her head. "I will, of course, report this incident to the sheriff, but he has made his position abundantly clear. He can't afford to assign men to Harper's Station. Not until the cattle rustlers are caught."

"He cares more for cows than women and children? Outrageous!"

Emma smiled at her aunt. Very rarely did Bertie get riled about anything. She was the sweet-tempered sister. But even Bertie had her limits.

"It's not as simple as that," Emma explained. "The rustling affects the three largest outfits in the county. If they continue losing stock, they will lose significant profit, which means men will lose their jobs, local businesses will lose sales, Seymour's economy will decline. Hundreds of lives could be impacted."

"Not to mention the physical altercations that cost men their lives." Maybelle Curtis added. "There've already been two casualties attributed to the rustling that I've heard about.

Good men, putting their lives on the line to defend the cattle in their charge. Sheriff Tabor is well within his rights to focus his energy there."

Bertie fell silent for a moment, her brow creased, but then something sparked in her eyes. She lifted her gaze to her sister, then turned her attention to Emma.

"If the sheriff is unavailable to assist us, what's to stop us from hiring a man of our own to see to our protection?"

"A mercenary?" Flora Johnson lurched to her feet, alarm turning her cheeks a violent red. "You can't! Men like that can't be trusted. All they care about is money. They're more likely to turn on us than help us. Once they see how defenseless we are, they'll empty the bank and run off, leaving us even more destitute than before." Her fingers visibly trembled. "No men. They can't be trusted."

"But what if we knew of one who *could* be trusted?" Aunt Henry proposed. She turned to Emma and peered at her with a pointed look. "A man who would rather sacrifice himself than bring harm to someone under his care."

Emma frowned slightly. What was her aunt suggesting . . . ? Then the answer came, and with it a fluttering in Emma's belly she hadn't felt in over a decade.

"Such a man doesn't exist," Flora snapped.

"Yes . . . he does." Emma lifted her face to survey the women who depended on her for guidance, for leadership. Hope swelled in her breast along with a surge of newfound confidence—for she now had a plan. A plan that was sure to succeed because the man Aunt Henry spoke of had been fighting against injustice since the day he was born. "His name is Malachi Shaw."

3

SOUTHERN MONTANA BORDER
BURLINGTON ROUTE CONSTRUCTION SITE

Malachi unwound the last foot of the fuse line, then examined the hole a final time. Depth looked good. Line was clear. No moisture. No debris to interfere with a clean run. Blast radius should be sufficient to break up the rock layers directly in line with the track path. He might have to lay a second charge to widen the area, but he'd make that decision after the rocks were cleared.

Scanning the area to make sure no one had ventured into the blast zone, Mal reached into his vest pocket and extracted a wooden matchstick.

"Fire in the hole!"

He struck the match head on the side of his boot, lit the fuse, and sprinted down the rocky incline as fast as the uneven terrain would allow. He counted in his head, knowing exactly how long he would have until the dynamite blew.

Five . . . six . . .

He zagged to the right to avoid the loose stones left over from a recent rockslide. Footing was everything.

Nine ... ten ... eleven ...

He located the tree that marked the edge of the safety area. Only twenty yards to go.

Sweat dripped in his eyes. The sting distracted him. He blinked to clear his vision. His toe stubbed hard against a chunk of sandstone jutting up from the ground. He fell forward, his momentum hurling his torso ahead of his feet. Mal fought against instinct. Instead of bracing his arms to catch himself, he tucked his arms into his body and curled his head into his chest to execute a bone-jarring roll. He couldn't afford to lose time with a sprawled landing. He had to keep moving.

Sixteen ... seventeen ...

The instant his feet came around, Mal popped back up and caught his balance even as he continued his wild descent. The marker tree loomed. Almost there.

Nineteen ...

Mal dove. The explosion detonated. The earth convulsed. A deafening roar reverberated through his body, vibrating his bones even before he collided with the ground. He covered his head with his hands. Dust and debris poured over him. But nothing bigger than a pebble. He'd survived. Again.

Blood thundered through his veins, invigorating him with an energy that buzzed with triumph. Mal jumped to his feet, a smile splitting his face as he turned to survey his handiwork. Never did he feel more alive than in the moment he escaped death's grasp.

Man, but he loved this job.

"You crazy coyote!"

Mal turned to see his gangly assistant running toward him. The kid was barely eighteen, an orphan—just like Mal—and far too eager to prove himself.

"I thought you were a goner for sure." Zachary laughed as he reached his mentor. "Shoulda known better. Dynamite ain't strong enough to take out Malachi Shaw. Nothin' is." He slapped Mal on the arm. "You gotta teach me how to roll like that."

"Sure, kid. But only if you remember that dynamite is strong enough to take out anyone who doesn't respect it. And even some who do."

Mal thought of his own instructor—Three Finger Willy. The old coal miner had taught Mal everything he knew about working with black powder, nitro, and dynamite, never missing a chance to remind him about the time he lost two of his fingers in an ill-timed blast. Willy had lost more than a pair of fingers a couple years back when a faulty fuse failed to blow. He went back in to check it, only to have the smoldering line reignite and make him a permanent part of the mine tunnel he'd been expanding.

Working with explosives might help a man feel alive, but it was only because he constantly flirted with death.

"I'll check out the blast site and give the all clear while you head back to camp to clean up." Zachary gazed up at him like a pup eager for a pat or word of praise. His open admiration made Mal itch. He doubted he'd ever get used to the feeling, even as he continued hungering for it.

Respect. It had only taken twenty-five years, but he'd finally earned a portion of the precious commodity he'd been starving for his entire life. All because he had a talent for staying alive.

Every time he finished a successful detonation, the men he worked with slapped him on the back and commended his bravery. He soaked up every ounce of their acceptance, like parched earth absorbing a gentle rain. Yet he hid the truth from them, knowing deep down that it wasn't bravery that allowed him to stay calm under pressure. It was a lack of caring. One didn't fear death if one had nothing to live for. Not that he wished for his own end. He'd been staving off that old devil too long to succumb without a fight. But sometimes he couldn't help wishing he had more than a company paycheck waiting for him at the end of each job. Something to give his life meaning. Purpose.

'Course, if he had that, he'd lose his edge in the demolition business. *Be thankful for what you got, Shaw, and quit your whinin'.*

He turned his attention back to Zach and thumped the kid on the back. "Watch where you step as you clear the area. Those rocks will be unstable."

Zach rolled his eyes. "Quit actin' like I never done this before, Mal. I know what I'm doin'." He pulled away and started trudging up the incline to the blast site.

Mal strode after him. "Hold up, Zach."

The kid turned, his face petulant. "What?"

Mal halted one step below him on the slope, making their heads equal in height. He lifted a hand, gripped the young man's shoulder, and gave it a squeeze. "You got a real knack for this business, Zach, but you're in a hurry, and that scares me. Demolition requires patience. Caution. Vigilance. When you hurry, you lose those things. I tell you to be careful because I want you to remember the importance of going slow, of double- and triple-checking the details. Not because I don't think you're capable, but because I want you to become a master at what you do."

Zach's jaw dropped, hanging so loose Mal could probably set it to swinging with a tap of his thumb. But then the kid straightened his posture, squared his shoulders, and tightened his unhinged jawbone.

"Does that mean you'll let me run my own demolition next time we get an assignment?"

Mal stared at the boy. Hard. "You've got the training. The

skills. If you can show me you've got the patience, then, yes, you can run the next demolition."

Zach let out a *whoop* loud enough to rival a dynamite blast, and for a moment, Mal thought the kid might try to hug him. Thankfully, Zach gathered his wits in time. Mal didn't do hugs. A slap on the back was affection enough between comrades. Anything more might make the kid think they were friends. Mal didn't do friendship, either. Friendship meant caring. It meant letting someone see beneath the surface. He'd only ever let one person see beneath his surface, and it had nearly torn his heart from his chest when he'd been forced to leave. Mal was no genius, but he was smart enough to learn from that mistake.

He liked Zach. But the boy was a colleague. Not a friend. Not a kid brother Mal needed to feel responsible for. Just a trainee.

So why did his chest thrum with satisfaction when the boy vowed to make him proud before setting off at a controlled pace toward the blast zone?

It didn't mean he cared. He was just glad the hardheaded kid was taking his advice for once. That was all.

Trusting Zach to do the job he'd trained him for, Mal trudged back toward the railroad camp, more than ready to clean off the dust and grime. The aunts would be glad to know at least one of their lessons had stuck.

On that first night in their home, when they'd forced him into a tub of steaming water and refused to let him out until he scrubbed every last crevice, he'd seriously considered making a run for the door. But then the warmth of the water penetrated his half-frozen skin. It relaxed his muscles. Made him feel safe and peaceful. In the end, he'd nearly fallen asleep in that tub.

That night he'd vowed never to be dirty again. Dirty defined his old life. Dirty, unwanted, afraid. Thanks to his angel, he'd escaped his past and been given a chance to plot a new course for his future. And the one he'd plotted included a copper tub large enough to accommodate a full-grown man. Even the camp laundress didn't have a tub so large. It would take a good thirty minutes to heat enough water to fill it up, but the soak would be worth it. Malachi could practically feel the gentle slosh of the water now. About as close to heaven as a man like him was bound to get.

Mal approached the section of track under construction and raised a hand in passing to the fellow carting water to the workers. Mules dragged railroad ties, Chinamen gabbed to each other in their native tongue, supervisors shouted orders, but it was the constant staccato beat of hammers on rails beneath it all that served as the heartbeat of the rail camp. The drive toward progress. A constant moving forward. Tearing down obstacles to obtain goals. The rhythm of his life.

He strode through the tents marking the outer edges of the camp so intent on reaching his own on the far side that he failed to spot the young boy running toward him until he nearly tripped over the lad.

"Mr. Shaw." The boy adroitly dodged to the side to avoid the collision, as if accustomed to such inattention by those older than he.

The action hit a familiar chord in Malachi. He stopped immediately and gave the boy his full attention. "Yes? What is it, Andrew?"

The boy smiled at hearing his name. Most men around camp wouldn't exert the effort to remember the moniker of an errand boy, but Malachi knew what it was like to be considered beneath another's notice and made a point to learn the names of all the young boys who worked around camp. Especially Andrew's.

The kid's mother had served drinks and other . . . things at one of the saloon tents that followed the rail camps. Mal recalled her being drunk more often than sober and had done his best to take Andrew under his wing, giving him permission to bunk in his tent if he wanted to steer clear of his ma's . . . *company* and teaching him how to stash the few coins he earned running errands in an empty soda-cracker tin stuffed with old socks to keep the coins from rattling. Parents with a hankering for drink had a tendency to develop sticky fingers.

Six months back, one of his mother's customers had caught her stealing money from his trouser pocket while he pretended to sleep. He took his anger out on her with his fists. One particularly brutal blow snapped her neck. She'd died instantly. Two weeks after Andrew's twelfth birthday.

With nowhere else to go, Andrew stayed with the railroad, running errands for the supervisors and whoever else had coin to spare. More often than not, he found his way to the pallet Mal left out for him near the foot of his bed, close enough to the tent flap so the kid could slip in and out on his own terms. Though Mal could always tell when he'd been there.

"A telegram, sir." Andrew held out a piece of paper to him, his smile fading. "It came in about an hour ago. Seemed important, so I been watchin' fer ya."

A telegram? Who would have . . . ? Malachi reached for the slightly crumpled paper. He scanned the words quickly, then started again at the top, focusing on each word while his gut turned to stone.

IN TROUBLE. NEED YOUR HELP. PLEASE COME.
EMMA

Mal clenched the paper in his fist, turned, and sprinted for his tent. Smaller footsteps, equally swift, followed.

"Want me to saddle your horse, Mr. Shaw?" Andrew huffed the question as he pulled up outside Malachi's tent. "I checked the schedule. There's a train leavin' out of Sheridan at three. You can still make it."

Malachi glanced over his shoulder as he threw open his tent flap. He should probably take the kid to task for reading his private correspondence, but he was too thankful for receiving the information to care. He dug out a silver dollar from his trouser pocket and tossed it to Andrew. "Thanks, kid. There's another dollar in it for you if you can have Ulysses ready and waiting in the next ten minutes."

Andrew nodded. "Yes, sir!" He shot off in the direction of the roped corral where the few saddle horses owned by the wealthier crew members were interspersed with the pack mules.

Malachi ducked into his tent and immediately dragged his saddlebags out from under his cot. Clean clothes. Food. Canteen. Money. Weapons. Only the essentials.

He stuffed two shirts and a pair of pants into one bag, then opened the small chest at the foot of his bed and grabbed the sack inside. Canned beans, soda crackers, and the leftovers he'd stashed after last night's dinner at the mess. Not as much provision as he usually preferred on a journey of such a duration, but it was enough to get by even if something went wrong on the way to Sheridan.

He removed his gun belt from the trunk next and buckled it about his waist, the holster heavy but comfortable against his hip. After casting a wistful look at the copper washtub standing in the far corner, Mal filled his canteen with the water from the ewer on his washstand, then opened the lockbox at the bottom of his trunk and pocketed the funds from last month's pay.

His heart pounding with purpose, Mal swung his saddlebags over his left shoulder, grabbed his hunting rifle and the ammunition pouch from beside his cot, and strode from his tent. He spotted Andrew leading his dun gelding toward him. He tossed the boy a second coin. Andrew snatched it from the air with one hand and handed the reins to Malachi with the other.

"I'll watch over your things for you while you're gone." Andrew jerked his chin toward Malachi's tent.

Mal nodded his thanks as he slid his rifle into the saddle boot. "Appreciate it." He fastened the saddlebags and canteen in place and mounted Ulysses.

"How long will ya be gone?" Andrew asked.

Malachi's gaze swung south. "As long as it takes." He blinked, then turned back to Andrew. "I'll stop by the boss's tent before I leave. Let him know where I'm headed. Tell Zachary he's in charge until I get back."

Andrew nodded.

Mal reined Ulysses around, but the kid's voice made him hesitate.

"Who's Emma, Mr. Shaw? Your sister?"

Mal's chest constricted. *Sister?* Some might think of a childhood companion in those terms. He'd never been able to, though.

As he touched his heels to Ulysses's flanks, the truth spilled from his lips in a quiet whisper. "She's my angel."

44

4

Malachi's knees bounced restlessly as he stared out the train window, ignoring the scenery blurring past. *Emma.* He hadn't seen her in ten years. Would he even recognize her? A dry chuckle escaped beneath his breath. As if he could ever forget even a single aspect of her features. They were etched on his brain as surely as if a branding iron had burned them there.

Of course, they would have changed. Matured. She'd been only thirteen when he'd left, on the cusp of womanhood. She'd be twenty-three now. A woman grown. Probably just as strong-willed and opinionated as ever. More so, even, since she'd been under the aunts' continued tutelage all this time. A grin tugged on his mouth, but he contained it. Mostly.

Those dark curls of hers wouldn't bounce along her back anymore when she skipped from place to place. They'd be pinned atop her head or stuffed under a bonnet. She'd be dressed in style, no doubt. Suit coat and long skirts. Maybe even one of those ties that looked like they belonged on a man. Only on her, it would look smart and respectable. Fitting for a career woman. A banker.

He still couldn't quite believe his little angel was running her own bank, taking after the father she barely remembered. But doggone, he was proud of her. He knew from that first meeting in the barn that Emma Chandler was special. Big heart. Big dreams.

And she'd kept him informed of her progress along the way. She'd written to him every month since he'd left. Newsy letters, nearly as exuberant as the woman herself. She'd kept him up to date with all the goings-on in Gainesville until she left to attend that fancy boarding school back east. Tears of homesickness had stained the first few notes she'd sent him from New York, but then her confidence grew as she fell in love with the world of finance. Of course, she wasn't supposed to be studying such improper subjects, but a little thing like propriety never stopped Emma.

She followed the stock market in the papers, attended lectures on investment strategies, and read nearly every book on finance held in the Astor Library. After graduation, she called in a favor from her late father's business partner, and sweet-talked him into allowing her to work in his bank as a teller while learning the details of the managerial side of things after hours. Her excitement about this new job had bled through the pages for the first few months, but then the tone of her letters changed.

Her male co-workers belittled her opinions, treated her as if she had no right to work alongside them, accused her of using her father's name to get on the payroll and her feminine wiles to remain there. After all, they knew she spent indecent amounts of time alone with the boss after hours. Mal had offered to come back to Texas and teach the cretins some manners, but Emma had made him promise to let her handle it. If she was going to survive in a male-dominated occupation, she'd have to learn to fight her own battles. And she had, though not without paying a price.

Her innocent optimism had been tarnished by harsh reality. And it changed her. Her letters grew bitter as she recounted tale after tale of how women were turned down for loans or dismissed as unintelligent when they came in with questions regarding their mortgages or accounts. She'd done her best to educate the women who were willing to listen to her, but more often than not, even the females looked down on her, questioning her morality for working outside the home or, worse, believing the rumors circulating about her and the boss who was old enough to be her father.

Thankfully, she'd gotten out and returned to Texas before irreparable damage had been done. Soon after, she'd met a woman named Victoria Adams, and the two of them had conceived the idea of a women's colony, taking men completely out of the equation.

Gradually, her natural optimism returned, along with a healthy dose of passion for helping women who were out of resources and out of options—women who'd been ill-used by men and those, like her, who longed to climb out from beneath a man's thumb to establish their own careers. She'd found her mission. Her calling. Providing down-on-their-luck females the same gift she'd once given him—a fresh start.

Yet her mission had not been without its risks. Had championing the less fortunate gotten her into the trouble she now faced? If the woman was anything like the girl he remembered, he could easily imagine Emma giving some dunderheaded man a tongue lashing without heed to the repercussions. She never seemed to care about the size or social weight of her opponent—only about what was right. Which was why he'd had to leave ten years ago.

He'd lived with the Chandlers for two years—two of the best years of his life. The aunts had fed him, clothed him, forced him to go to school. He hadn't been in a schoolroom for three years and had only gone sporadically before that. But Emma worked with him every night. Taught him to read, to write his letters so they didn't look like a five-year-old had scribbled them. Caught him up on history, grammar, long division. Ack. He still hated long division, though he had to admit, understanding the concept made calculating blast radiuses a lot easier. The teacher had lent him books to study when school wasn't in session, and by the second year, he'd nearly caught up to the boys his own age.

Not that they wanted anything to do with him. Which was fine with Mal. He'd been on the receiving end of snide comments and derisive looks his whole life. Didn't even put a dent in his hide. But when the oldest boy of the group, Oliver Evans, started taking an interest in Emma, Mal's hide got real thin, real fast.

Oliver's father owned the local drug emporium, and Oliver was used to winning the favors of any gal he pleased. At least girls who could be swayed by a bag of penny candy or one of them tiny bottles of toilet water. But Emma was too smart to be lured by such bribes. How many times had she taken one of the younger Swift girls under her wing to soothe hurt feelings after Oliver's cruel taunts about farm girls with patches on their skirts and chicken feathers for brains? Oliver would be the last boy to turn Emma's head. Which was probably why Oliver had been so determined to win her.

Mal kept a close watch on Emma every day at recess and walked her home after school. He made sure Oliver knew he was watching, too. Though the boy was a year older and three inches taller, Mal had been hardened by life on the streets. No pampered rich kid was going to lay a finger on Emma without her consent.

But during a potluck supper one Sunday after church, Mal let his guard down. A mistake that a decade later still rubbed his conscience raw. Emma and the aunts had been sitting on the family blanket. Aunt Henry had been up in arms about the preacher's sermon, insisting that there was no biblical basis for the traditional belief that Mary Magdalene was a harlot.

"Scripture records that Jesus drove seven demons out of her. Demons! Yet Christian tradition—a tradition perpetuated by men, I'll have you know—insists on linking her to the nameless woman caught in adultery. There is absolutely no evidence in the Bible indicating these two women were the same person." Aunt Henry tossed her napkin down as if it were a gauntlet. "Mary was a godly disciple. More faithful than the *male* followers who scattered at Jesus's arrest and crucifixion. It was the *women* who stayed by the Savior's side. And Mary Magdalene to whom Jesus appeared first after his resurrection. Not John. Not Peter. *Mary*. I dare you to name a more faithful disciple."

"I'm sure you're right, dear," Aunt Bertie soothed, or tried to. Aunt Henry seemed impervious to her sister's efforts.

"It's only because the male of the species feels threatened by the fact that the Lord chose a woman over a man for such an honor that they think to dishonor her good name with a past that wasn't hers. Shameful, I tell you. Absolutely shameful."

Aunt Bertie had glanced around nervously, then leaned forward to retrieve Henry's napkin. "I'm sure Mr. Horner meant no offense by his categorization. After all, that was only *one statement* in an otherwise excellent lesson." Bertie handed the napkin to her sister with a pointed look. "A lesson focused on the forgiving nature of God, and the importance of Christians extending that same forgiveness to their fellow man. Perhaps you could extend some to Mr. Horner for his error. The man is as kindhearted as they come and surely meant no offense."

Henry cleared her throat and dropped her gaze to her lap. "Yes, well. I suppose."

Then, because Bertie couldn't stand to see anyone uncomfortable, she'd suggested that Mal fetch her sister a piece of the lovely blueberry pie Bertie had made just that morning. Henry's favorite. Mal had immediately agreed, worried that if he hesitated, Aunt Henry would take note of his gender and set her tongue to flapping at him for the sins of his long-dead male forebears.

Emma had smiled at him with impish delight as he'd gotten to his feet, nearly letting the giggle he could tell was building inside her escape from behind the hand she raised to cover her mouth. She'd looked so happy, so carefree, he couldn't imagine anything bad ever befalling her.

But when he'd collected the pie from the food table some distance away and turned to head back to the aunts, his stomach clenched. Emma wasn't there. He picked up his pace, his eyes scouring the gathering for any sign of her. Nothing. His back had only been turned for a minute. How could she have disappeared so quickly? She couldn't have . . . unless someone had been waiting for him to break his vigil.

Oliver.

Mal dashed back to the aunts, uncaring that the slice of pie slid precariously close to the edge of the plate. He thrust the dessert at Henry and immediately demanded to know where Emma had gone. Flustered by his forceful tone, the aunts took precious seconds to gather themselves and answer. Abby Pierce had dragged Emma off to see a nest of duck eggs she'd discovered by the little pond behind the church. Some of the boys were threatening to stomp on the eggs, and Abby feared for the unhatched little ducklings.

Mal groaned and immediately raced for the pond. He dodged families, trees, girls rolling hoops, men tossing horseshoes. Dread built in his chest with every step.

Abby was no great friend of Emma's, her brother being one

of Oliver's most loyal cronies. Yet Emma would never allow a helpless animal to be harmed if she could do something about it. No doubt she had rushed to the ducklings' defense, not once considering it could be a trap. Mal clenched his jaw. There probably wasn't even a nest to defend.

He rounded the corner of the church and slid down the embankment that sheltered the pond. A flash of blue off to the left caught his eye. Had Emma been wearing a blue dress? Doggone it. He couldn't remember. He'd been more concerned about keeping track of where she was than what she was wearing. Stupid. Stupid!

He veered to the left anyway, and chased down the blue dress. Only to find it attached to a blond-haired female. Not Emma.

Mal grabbed Abby's arm and spun her to face him. She let out a squeal of distress, but he didn't loosen his hold.

"Where is she?" he snapped.

Tears filled the girl's eyes. "I didn't know. I thought they were just going to have some fun. . . . I didn't mean . . ." The girl was sobbing in earnest now, her broken sentences telling him nothing.

He shook her arm and bit out one word. "Where?"

Abby lifted her free hand and pointed toward a large cottonwood several yards back the way he had come. He released her and ran toward the tree.

He heard Emma before he saw her.

"Let me go. Please . . . stop. You're hurting me. . . ."

Her whimpers sliced through Mal's chest like a cavalry saber. He rounded the tree and stumbled to a halt. Every instinct demanded that he rush Oliver like a bull, take the fiend to the ground and pummel him until his face was too broken and bloody for even his old man to recognize. But Oliver was too close to Emma, bending over her while he held her pinned against a tree. Mal couldn't risk causing his angel pain. But Oliver? Oh, Oliver would be feeling lots of pain. Real soon.

"Just one kiss," Oliver demanded in a sickly smooth voice that turned Mal's stomach. "That's all. Then I'll let you go." His head lowered.

"No!" Emma jerked her face to the side. "I'll never kiss a pig like you!" Then without warning, she threw her head forward and slammed her forehead straight into Oliver's puckered lips.

The boy cursed and reared back, blood dripping from the corner of his mouth. Emma broke free of his hold for an instant, but Oliver recovered too quickly. Snatching her arm so hard she fell backward, Oliver raised a fist.

"I'll teach you to—"

Malachi let out a roar and charged. By all that was holy, he was going to tear the swine limb from limb.

But just as he came within reach, two of Oliver's cronies rushed him from behind. They tackled him, one throwing punches in his side as the other ground his face into the dirt. Malachi kicked and bucked, but they were too heavy. They twisted his arms behind him and forced him to his feet.

"I just wanted a taste of what you've already had, Malachi," Oliver taunted, his rage of a moment ago supplanted by smug superiority as he dragged a struggling Emma beside him. "It must be nice living under the same roof as her with no one but the crazy Chandler sisters to act as chaperones."

Malachi narrowed his gaze, silently promising retribution for the slur against Emma, but Oliver was too stupid to realize the danger he was in.

"Malachi would never!" In a flash, the fear in Emma's eyes hardened to indignation. "How dare you say such a thing? It's a vile lie!"

Oliver laughed. "What an innocent." He stroked a piece of her hair. Emma yanked it from his grasp with a twist of her head and a glare, only wincing slightly when the few strands tangled in his fingers tore out of her scalp. "Maybe he *hasn't* done anything, but that doesn't mean he hasn't wanted to. Right, Mal?" Oliver shot a knowing glance at Malachi.

Mal's gut clenched guiltily. He *had* imagined what it would be like to kiss Emma—she was too beautiful inside and out for him not to dream of such a treasure—but she was too young. And far too good for the likes of him. He'd sooner cut off his arm than take liberties.

"We've seen the way you watch her. Haven't we, fellas?" Oliver shared a look with his friends, his smirk fanning the flame of Malachi's rage. The boys holding Mal laughed and shouted their agreement.

Mal quit struggling. Let his arms go lax. Prayed his captors would instinctively relax, as well.

Oliver turned back to Emma. She renewed her struggles. "Do you suppose she tastes as sweet as she looks?" Then the dirty scum grabbed her head and brought his mouth down on hers. Hard. Staining Emma's purity with his foul touch. She whimpered, tried desperately to push him away with her free hand.

Malachi struck. Using his thin build to his advantage, he twisted free from his captors' loosened hold. Dodging their grasping hands, he threw himself to the ground, flipping so he'd land on his back. He kicked outward and upward, his bootheels jamming against the tender area of both boys, where he knew it would cause the most pain. As they howled and doubled over, Mal leapt to his feet and lunged for Oliver.

The boy's eyes widened. He released his hold on Emma in order to bring his fists up for protection, but Malachi didn't give him the chance to take a swing. Putting his head down, he rammed Oliver's midsection and carried him to the ground. Oliver punched wildly at Mal's back and shoulders, but Mal ignored the pain. All he saw was Emma's terror as Oliver forced his attentions on her. Mal straddled Oliver, pinning him to the ground just as Oliver had pinned Emma to the tree. Then he smashed his fist into Oliver's jaw. Oliver cried out.

"Say you're sorry," Mal demanded as he raised his fist, threatening another blow.

Oliver whimpered. Then his gaze darted to somewhere behind Mal. "Please, don't hurt me. Please. I didn't mean to . . ."

Didn't mean to? He'd held her down and attacked her!

Mal swung, but arms grabbed him from behind before the blow landed. Mal fought their hold. They were stronger than before. A man's arms.

"That's enough!" Abby's father pulled him off of Oliver and flung him aside.

Mal immediately sought out Emma. Tears streaked her face. Tangled hair stood out from her head, bits of bark clinging to her curls. But her bright green eyes locked on him, full of gratitude and of worry—for him.

She hurried to his side and immediately started fussing over his cuts and scrapes, as if they mattered.

"I'm sorry," he mumbled, peering down into her face through a rapidly swelling eye. "I should have watched you more closely. I should've—"

"Don't you dare blame yourself, Malachi Shaw." She scowled up at him even as she brushed the dust off his sleeve. "Oliver is the one in the wrong, not you." Then she smiled one of her magic smiles at him, the one that turned his insides to mush. "You protected me against three boys older and larger than you. In my book, that makes you hero material."

Hero material? Bah. A bunch of girlish fancy. But the words wormed their way into his bones, spreading their roots and vines until he couldn't escape them. A hero. Emma's hero. Him. Malachi Shaw. The idea was ludicrous . . . yet he longed so much for it to be true, that it infected him at the deepest level.

Unfortunately, Emma and the aunts were the only ones who considered his actions heroic. Harland Evans, Oliver's father, demanded that Malachi be charged with assault. The aunts insisted that Oliver be charged with the same crime against their niece. Abby's father could only testify to Malachi's attack on Oliver, not Oliver's attack on Emma, so since Emma was basically unhurt and Oliver sported a busted nose, bloody lip, and a nice assortment of bruises, the sheriff sided with the Evans family. Not convinced a boyish scuffle really warranted jail time, yet needing to placate Harland Evans, who insisted Malachi was a miscreant who never should have been allowed into their community in the first place, the sheriff gave Malachi a choice. Leave Gainesville or go to jail.

The aunts vowed to hire a lawyer and fight the injustice of the sheriff's ruling, but Malachi knew what a trial would mean. Emma would have to testify to what Oliver had done, relive the humiliation and fear. Her assault would be a matter of public record.

She wouldn't care one whit, of course. At least not on the surface. She'd march into that courtroom and defend him with all the fervor of a revival preacher fighting to save souls from hell. That's just who she was. But he wasn't about to let her recount Oliver's atrocities in front of a full gallery of witnesses—witnesses who would gawk and gossip and question her morals even though she was the innocent party in the whole ordeal.

So he'd left. Quietly. In the night. But not before Emma cornered him and made him promise to write to her. Often. She'd insisted that she'd worry herself sick if she didn't know where he was or what he was doing. She even thrust her writing box at him, stocked with paper, pen, ink, and postage stamps. And a coin pouch filled with her meager savings, he'd later discovered.

And since he'd never break a promise to her, and because he secretly longed to preserve his connection to her, even if he never laid eyes on her again, he'd written. And extracted a promise of his own. If she ever needed his help, she was to send for him.

Now she had.

Malachi refocused his gaze on the landscape outside his window, silently urging the train to greater speed. *Hang in there, Emma. I'm coming.*

5

Emma sat in her office at the bank, her head bent over her writing desk as she added the latest names to her ledger. Irene Booker and her son, Charlie, had left that morning, bringing the count up to thirty. Thirty women and children lost to Harper's Station. She'd expected such an exodus, but every departure still hit her like a blow to her midsection.

She replaced her pen in the black lacquered stand and lifted her gaze to the ceiling. *It's hard to believe you are in control, Lord, when a man with a gun steals our freedom and scatters our members far and wide. I thought this colony was your plan. Why are you allowing this attack?*

The ceiling offered no answer. Emma sighed and turned back to her ledger, or would have if Aunt Bertie's needlework sampler hadn't caught her attention. Hanging in a frame on the wall beside her desk, the colorful stitching radiated love and encouragement, just as Bertie herself always did. Yet today it also offered a pointed reminder.

"But the God of all grace," the brightly colored thread announced, *"who hath called us unto his eternal glory by Christ*

Jesus, after that ye have suffered a while, make you perfect, stablish, strengthen, settle you. To him be glory and dominion for ever and ever. Amen."

Emma bit her bottom lip, then bowed her head. "Forgive me, Father. I have no right to demand exemption from suffering when not even your Son was spared. No lives have yet been lost, and I thank you for that mercy most deeply. Please establish and strengthen us, and when the time is right, may those who have left us return to settle here once again, if it be your will."

Opening her eyes, she ran her fingers along the ledger page a final time, then closed the cover and set the book aside. Instead of dwelling on those who had been lost, she should be counting her blessings regarding how many had stayed.

The café had closed down, but the boardinghouse remained staffed and open, ready to serve meals to any in need of such service. There were two ladies to keep the garden watered, weeded, and harvested and three to keep the sewing circle in business. Other ladies had already volunteered to help the quilting group fill the current order, including the aunts, their friend Daisy, and Emma herself. Heaven knew there'd be little for her to do at the bank with over half her town absent. She'd operate the bank in the morning hours and quilt in the afternoons, assuming she could remember how to stitch a straight line. She'd never really had the patience for the task. But if plying a needle meant keeping the women of Harper's Station financially solvent, she'd gladly contribute her limited skill.

Besides, it was a sound investment strategy. If the ladies of the circle failed to get their quilts to market by the deadline, they wouldn't be able to make their monthly loan payments. And if Emma was going to be able to keep the bank open for business, she'd need those payments.

Reaching into the pocket of her skirt, she retrieved the gold watch that had once belonged to her father. She held it in her palm and flipped open the cover with a practiced flick of her thumb, her eyes, as they always did, finding the inscription etched inside the lid—*To William with love, Ann.* A gift from her mother on her father's forty-fifth birthday. He'd been a good deal older than his wife, but they'd been well matched in other ways. Father's philanthropy. Mother's volunteer work at the hospital. Their love for their only child. The stories the aunts had told Emma about her parents were what had spurred her to find her own way to help those in need. Yet, as much as she wished she were running a charity here in Harper's Station, the truth was, she was running a business—a business that offered hope and a fresh start to many. If the bank went under, the women would, too.

"What would you do, Daddy?" she whispered into the empty office, remembering all those times she would crawl into her father's lap and beg him to tell her about the bank. She'd idolized him. Wanted to emulate him in everything. Instead of tea parties, she had bank parties, having her dolls complete transactions with the money she'd made out of strips of brown paper and buttons pilfered from Mother's sewing basket.

"*Emma, darling.*" She recalled his cultured voice, could almost feel the hand he used to run over her hair. "*Banking is stewardship. We can't give to everyone who asks or we risk losing the ability to give to any. We must seek God's wisdom and direction, then work hard not only to protect but also increase what has been entrusted to us. Think like a five-talent steward, Emma.*"

Emma smiled. Daddy had loved Jesus' parable of the talents. Especially the part where the master condemned the single-talent steward for not at least putting his money in the bank to earn interest.

Emma circled her fingertip along the edge of the watch face. *Think like a five-talent steward. Take measured risks. Be wise. Don't let fear paralyze you.*

She'd built her business on that strategy. Invested the bulk of the inheritance her father had left her into developing the land and buildings comprising Harper's Station. Invested the rest with a New York broker who had worked with her father, one who had proven trustworthy and willing to take instructions from a woman. She invested bank funds with him, as well, though on a more conservative trajectory. Protecting her ladies came before profit. However, if her quilters failed to make their quotas and lost the income needed to make their loan payments, a few would be perilously close to defaulting.

The bank was solvent enough to let a couple months of missed payments slide for those in the direst need, but having such a small group of clients overall, the business wouldn't survive much beyond that. Hard decisions would have to be made—decisions Emma would rather avoid. Yet if it came to it, she wouldn't bury her talent in the sand. She'd make her father proud and do what had to be done.

The rattle of wagon wheels outside brought Emma's head up. Snapping her watch closed, she pushed to her feet and swiveled to get a better view. She slid the watch back into her pocket, then walked to the window and parted the lace curtains with her hand. Her pulse skittered. Benjamin Porter's freight wagon.

Had Malachi arrived?

Mr. Porter would be the one to direct him to Harper's Station when he showed up in Seymour. Except for the circuit-riding preacher, Mr. Porter was the only male allowed in the colony, and only because he carried their goods to market and brought supplies in from the outside. The man was courteous, dependable, and always fetched them an honest price. And upon occasion, he delivered passengers.

As the wagon drew nearer, Emma's breath caught. There *was* a passenger. A dark shape loomed next to Mr. Porter on the wagon seat, but Emma couldn't make out any distinguishing characteristics. She peeled the lace curtains back even farther, her stomach swirling about as if she'd swallowed a pitcher full of tadpoles. The wagon finally cleared the branches of the oak tree that shaded the café and revealed the passenger. Emma's breath leaked from her in a slow, silent sigh.

A female. Not Malachi.

She released the curtain and spun away from the window. What had she expected? That he had sprouted wings and flown to Texas? Even if he'd left Montana immediately after receiving her telegram, it would still take at least two days for him to reach Seymour, and only if he traveled through the night.

Ever since she'd made up her mind to ask him to come, anticipation had been swelling inside her like yeasty bread dough rising on a warm windowsill. She was in desperate need of someone to punch her down and knead her back into shape. Someone like the new lady who had come to Harper's Station. A lady who deserved to be welcomed by the colony's founder. Welcomed . . . and warned.

Emma smoothed the pleats of her shirtwaist and touched a hand to her hair. Then, forcing a cheerful jaunt to her stride, she exited her office and made her way down the street to Tori's mercantile.

Mr. Porter helped the newcomer down just as Lewis rushed out of the store. "Mr. Ben! Mr. Ben! Did you hear about the shooting? Some mean ol' fella shot up the church yesterday. And we was all inside!"

Oh, heavens. Emma picked up her pace. Wasn't that a lovely way to welcome a new sister to town?

Mr. Porter's pleasant expression hardened so fast, Emma nearly stumbled from whiplash. He jerked his attention from the boy to the shop. "Is your ma . . . ?"

Victoria appeared in the doorway. "I'm fine, Mr. Porter. Everyone is fine." Not quite meeting the freighter's gaze, she stepped into the street and offered her hand to the young—very young—woman at his side. "I'm Victoria Adams. Welcome to Harper's Station."

The girl—for she couldn't be more than seventeen—bobbed a quick curtsey, then took Tori's hand. "I'm Claire, ma'am. Claire Nevin." Her voice carried a bit of an Irish lilt. She smiled at Tori, but as Emma neared, she noted the girl's eyes carried the desperate, cornered look apparent in far too many of her ladies when they first came to town.

Emma finally reached the group and introduced herself. "Claire," she said, holding out her hand, "so glad to meet you. I'm Emma Chandler, director of the women's colony. We're delighted you came to visit."

Claire held tight to Emma's hand, refusing to release it. "I wish to do more than visit, ma'am. I wish to take shelter among ye." Her gaze darted from Emma to Tori and back to Emma. "Please, ma'am. I can't marry him." Her head wagged adamantly back and forth. "I just can't!"

Tori stepped forward and took Claire's elbow. She guided her to the bench sitting outside the mercantile. "Come along now, Miss Nevin. Have a seat. We'll get this all sorted out in no time. Miss Chandler is somewhat of an expert when it comes to granting assistance to young ladies in circumstances similar to your own. She'll know what to do." Tori met Emma's gaze, a wealth of meaning passing between the two.

How could they help the girl when they themselves were under attack? But how could they not? Young ladies with nowhere to go were the reason for the colony's existence. They couldn't simply turn Claire away.

Victoria steered Claire to the middle of the bench and seated herself to one side. Emma slid onto the opposite end of the bench.

"Lewis," Tori called to her son, "help Mr. Porter unload the supplies. The eggs and canned goods to sell are in their usual place in the back room."

The boy grinned up at the freighter, a sparkle in his eye. Emma had no doubt that the moment the two males disappeared into the storeroom, tales of yesterday's events would be flying from the lad's lips.

"And mind those eggs," Tori admonished. "I don't want a single crack in those shells. You hear me?"

"Yes, Mama." Lewis dashed toward the back of the wagon to help unload.

Mr. Porter stared at Victoria for a moment, then flicked a glance at Claire. He shifted from foot to foot, looking as if he intended to speak. Apparently he changed his mind, though, for he gave a quick nod and followed the boy.

"Now," Emma said, smiling her most reassuring smile as she patted Claire's knee, "tell us what has brought you here."

Claire dipped her chin. "I'm runnin' away."

Sympathy rose in Emma's breast at the defeat in the girl's voice. Young people should be filled with hope, their future filled with possibilities and promise. But judging by Claire's well-worn dress and pitifully small traveling bag, hope was in short supply for her.

"Who are you running from?" Emma gently prodded.

"My intended." Claire slowly raised her face, her eyes brimming with despair. "When I answered his advertisement, I told meself it didn't matter what he looked like so long as he was kind and a good provider. Anythin' is better than starvin' in the tenement, me sisters and brothers cryin', me da drinkin' and breakin' me ma's heart over and over again with his wastrel ways.

"I decided, with one less mouth to feed, they'd be better off. Eileen's old enough to tend the bairns. Polly's got a good hand with the cookin'." She sniffed. "They'd get along. And

I'd have a life of me own. Out here with the big sky, fresh air, and a man to provide for me. Only the man doin' the providin' ain't a man I can live with."

Claire turned to face Emma and grabbed her hand. Words tumbled out of her faster than water down a falls. "He's older than me da! He's got white chin whiskers and a belly that rolls over his belt. And meaty hands that make a mean-looking fist."

Emma winced at the telling description. Claire would have no idea what his fist looked like if she hadn't had cause to see it.

"He owns a store and can certainly provide for me right and proper, but he's far short o' kind. The minute I stepped off the train, he acted like he *owned* me. Started goin' over me duties as soon as we walked into the store. What I was to clean, when he expected supper, how I should address customers. It was insultin'. He left me feelin' like he'd just hired a housekeeper and clerk without benefit of wages. And then he had the cheek to show me the bedroom and brag about how quickly he got a bairn on his last wife, and how the woman had failed him by dyin' during the birthin' and takin' the babe with her. As if the poor woman had stolen his child from him apurpose. Then he laid his hands upon me hips and measured me with his eyes. He pronounced me a skinny twig but said me hips were wide enough to birth him the sons he wanted."

Emma's jaw grew rigid. "The bounder! What a despicable way to welcome a mail-order bride. Has the man never heard of wooing?"

"He didn't think wooin' was necessary," Claire said. "Not since he bought me."

Bristling, Emma stiffened her spine. "Mr. Lincoln outlawed slavery in these great United States thirty years ago. That man did *not* buy you."

"That's what I told him." Claire jutted out her chin, her eyes sparking with the first hint of spirit Emma had seen. "He tried to march me to the parson's house straightaway, without even giving me time to catch a breath or wash the trail dirt from me face, but I put me feet down. I told him I wouldn't say the words afore God, not until we'd had a few days to get to know each other."

Victoria nodded her approval. "Good for you."

Claire wilted. "He refused to spend the coin to put me up in a boardinghouse. Said I already belonged to him—that I'd signed a betrothal agreement. Threatened to bring me up on charges of breach of contract unless I either married him or paid him back for the train fare he forked out to bring me here. I told him I'd find work and pay him back, but I owe seventy-five dollars. It's a fortune, it is. And no one in Seymour would hire me. I spent all day yesterday askin'."

Claire reached out to Tori and clasped her hand as well. "You're my last chance, ladies. Mrs. Baker, the dressmaker, told me about Harper's Station, said I could find work here, maybe even a loan to pay off me debt and gain me freedom. If you turn me away, I'll be left with no choice." Her voice trembled as she twisted her head to entreat both of her prospective saviors. "I'll have to marry Stanley Fischer."

A jolt of shock shot through Emma. "Stanley Fischer . . . of Fischer's Emporium?"

"Aye." Claire's brow furrowed. "Do ye know him?"

He was only their most significant account. Having the largest dry goods store in Seymour, he took all the fresh eggs and vegetables they could sell. He stocked their canned goods, as well, eager to save on the cost of shipping items from more distant manufacturers.

Mr. Fischer had made it plain on several occasions that he disapproved of the women's colony. Called it unnatural, accused her ladies of being man-haters and defilers of God's design for woman to be man's helpmeet. Yet even as he spewed such vile sentiment, he recognized the quality of their goods and the fairness of their price. So in true hypocritical fashion, he accepted their business and turned a tidy profit in the process.

"We are acquainted with Mr. Fischer, yes." Emma shared a look with Tori. They both knew that if they took Claire in, Mr. Fischer would likely retaliate. He was in a position to strike a deadly blow to the financial solvency of their community, and he was just spiteful enough to do so.

What should she do? If she gave Claire the loan, it might mean dozens of other ladies would default on their own payments. But how could she turn her back on such a young girl, alone in the world? Such an action went against everything she believed in. But did the good of one outweigh the good of many?

"Tori?" Emma asked the silent question she knew her friend would be weighing in her own mind. Victoria had the most to lose if they took Claire in. She relied on Fischer's business to keep her own afloat.

Victoria only hesitated a moment before dipping her chin in a small nod. "We cannot send her back to him, Emma. No one deserves such treatment. We'll find new outlets."

Claire turned from one to the other, confusion lining her face. "What outlets? Does Stanley Fischer hold sway over you, too? He warned me that I'd not find haven with you, but I thought he was just blowing wind." She bit her lip and let go of the hands she held. She bowed her head and buried her hands in her lap.

"Ease yourself, Claire." Emma smiled, patting the young woman's knee. "No man holds sway in Harper's Station. We are independent women here. Hardworking women. Women who aid one another when a sister is in need. Mr. Fischer buys some of the goods we produce, but we are not fully dependent upon his business. There are other avenues we can explore." She pushed to her feet and tugged on the hem of her jacket. "Now, if I am to give you a loan to repay the fare Mr. Fischer purchased on your behalf, and if we accept you into our community, there are some stipulations you must agree to."

Claire jumped to her feet like a soldier reporting for duty. "Anything, Miss Chandler."

Emma schooled her features into her serious, banker mien. "You must work among us in a capacity that suits your skills, thereby allowing you to make reasonable payments on your loan at the end of each month, and you must abide by the rules of the colony."

"What rules are those, ma'am?" A cautionary crease lined Claire's forehead.

Good. It meant she was weighing the ramifications.

Emma listed the basic tenets of their society, ticking them off on her fingers. "You must attend church services every Sunday; you must not speak disparagingly about any lady among us; and if you see a sister in need, you must lend your aid."

Claire tipped her chin up as if waiting for more. When none came, she raised a brow. "Is that all of it, then?"

Emma nodded. "It is."

"Then I agree, ma'am." A smile beamed across Claire's face, making her appear even younger and prettier than before.

"Normally, this is where I would invite you to walk with me down to the bank," Emma stated, "but I'm afraid there is one other vital piece of information you need to know."

"What's that, ma'am?"

Emma met Claire's eyes. "Harper's Station is under attack."

6

After two and a half days of nonstop travel, Malachi stepped off the train in Seymour, Texas, bleary-eyed, unshaven, and weary to the bone. There'd been no sleeper berths available when he'd booked passage at the last minute in Sheridan, so he'd been forced to ride on a hard wooden bench in the second-class cabin for the duration of the journey. Though, truth to tell, it'd been worry, not the bench that had kept him awake. Anyone who worked in a railroad camp knew how to shut his ears as well as his eyes when his head hit the cot. Had to. Would never get any sleep otherwise. Yet every time he closed his eyes while aboard the train, all Mal could see was a young Emma staring up at him, pleading with him to help her.

Help her with what?

Wrestling that question had stolen his sleep. What kind of trouble was she in? What if he didn't have the skills necessary to help her? But she'd asked for him. She knew what kind of life he led. Shoot. Maybe she needed him to blow something up. Malachi grinned as he stepped from the train to the platform. If only it could be so simple. But Emma wasn't the simple type.

No, her problems ran from complicated to hopelessly snarled. She was too tenderhearted and too stubborn to leave any thread loose to flap alone in the wind. She always held fast to them all. It was her most endearing quality.

And the most frustrating.

Rubbing a hand over the dark stubble sprouting out of his cheeks and chin, Malachi strode away from the depot in search of two things—food and a horse. He could use a bath and a shave as well, but he didn't want to linger in Seymour any longer than necessary. His supervisor had only given him a week's leave, and he'd already used over a third of it getting here. Despite the sun hanging low in the western sky, he needed to press on to Harper's Station. If he hurried, he might manage to get there before full dark.

He followed the flow of passengers to the Washington Hotel dining room, but the man in the suit at the restaurant's reception podium took one look at Mal's rumpled clothing, still coated in dust from Wednesday's blast at the rail camp, and sniffed in displeasure.

"Table for one, sir?" he asked with eyebrow raised and nose slanted downward, his hoity-toity voice making it clear that the correct answer to the question was *no*.

Not in the mood to play the game of social niceties, Mal reached into his pocket and pulled out a five-dollar bank note. He slapped it down on the podium the fella stood behind with enough force to make Prissy Pants jump.

"I'm gonna save us both the discomfort of taking you up on that completely ingenuous invitation."

The man's second brow rose at Mal's use of the word *ingenuous*. Mal enjoyed leveling the playing field a bit by throwing a ten-dollar word into the mix. Men like Prissy Pants never expected it, which put them off their guard. Exactly where Malachi wanted them.

"Have the cook put together a box supper for me." Mal strolled around the side of the podium. Prissy Pants backed up a step. A few of the diners at tables closest to the front of the room turned their heads to stare. Casually dropping an elbow onto the corner of the lectern, Mal leaned in. "Whatever he's got on hand will suffice. I'll be back in ten minutes to collect it, then I'll be outta your hair for good. Work for you?"

Prissy Pants nodded as he edged away from the podium, trying to increase the distance between himself and Malachi. His eyes darted to the dining room patrons, then back. He swallowed. "I-I'll see to it at once, sir."

And he did, leaving his station to deliver Mal's order directly to the kitchen. *After* he'd pocketed the five dollars, of course.

Mal tipped his hat and smiled at the couple behind him. The lady shied away, skittish-like, but the cowboy escorting her nodded approval. Nice to know there were a few fellas who respected a workingman's dust more than a clean-shaven jaw.

Mal ventured down to Main Street and located a livery, where he made arrangements to rent a horse, saddle, and tack. Still having a few minutes to kill, he wandered down to the court-house square to get a feel for the town, then circled around and hiked the three blocks back to the hotel. When he returned for his meal, the line for the dining room had dwindled to nothing. Prissy Pants handed over his boxed supper without a word, but the censure still etched in the man's face got Mal to thinking as he stepped out onto the boardwalk.

He'd left Montana in such a hurry he hadn't packed more than the essentials, figuring he could buy whatever he needed along the way. Only, a place like Harper's Station wasn't likely to carry men's shaving gear in its dry goods store. Not much call for male toiletries in a women's colony. Showing up on Emma's doorstep scruffy and mangy because he was in a hurry to get there was one thing. Staying that way for the duration of his visit was another.

Malachi stuffed the boxed supper into the saddlebag he'd slung over his shoulder, then ran a hand over his jaw, the whiskers setting his palm to itching. Better pick up a razor and some shaving soap before he headed out. Besides, he still needed to get directions. Emma'd written him that the largest store in Seymour bought goods from her ladies, and judging by the size of the false front he'd spied across the street from the courthouse, Fischer's Emporium was the biggest store in town. Might as well take out two birds with one shot.

Cutting through the vacant lots behind the hotel, Mal headed back to Main Street. Jogging slightly to avoid the freight wagon rolling toward him, he hopped onto the boardwalk and made his way down to the large store on the corner. A stocky fellow with a white apron tied about his waist stood in front, sweeping the boardwalk with more vigor than the task required. His head bent, he muttered beneath his breath, stopping abruptly when Malachi's boots trudged across the boards he'd just swept.

The man's shoulders straightened as he met Mal's gaze, but the frown on his face stayed rooted in place. "I'm about to close up for the night, mister. If you got a big order, better come back in the morning."

"All I need is a razor and soap. Shouldn't take but a minute." Mal tried to soften him up with a friendly smile, but the fella's frown must've been carved from granite. It didn't budge. "I'm on my way out of town tonight," Mal explained. "I'd be much obliged if you could see your way to letting me make a purchase before you close."

The man sighed and turned his back as he opened the store's door. "Better my place than some other getting your coin, I suppose. Come on in." A bell rang as the door opened. "Just hurry it up. I got a meetin' with Sheriff Tabor in a few minutes to see about a personal matter."

"I won't take but a minute," Mal promised, "if you could just—"

"Razors're over there." Fischer gestured toward a middle aisle with a pointed finger.

Mal headed toward the shelves of soaps, breezing past the wide selection of ladies' bath goods, to find the razors. Bypassing the fancy pearl-handled ones more prominently displayed, he grabbed a plain one from the bottom shelf, a lather brush, and a round cake of shaving soap, then strode back to the counter and laid his items in front of the foul-tempered clerk.

"A dollar and two bits for the razor, fifty cents for the brush, and four for the soap. Comes to a dollar seventy-nine."

Mal handed him a two-dollar note and waited while the man counted out his change. "Don't suppose you could give me directions to Harper's Station?" he asked. "It's north of here, ain't it?"

"Harper's Station?" Fischer's hand balled into a fist, and red flushed his face. "You mean *Harpy's* Station? That bunch of man-haters. Harridans, all of 'em. Turning womenfolk against their men. It ain't natural. No man in his right mind would go to that godforsaken place."

A muscle twitched in Malachi's jaw. "Well, that's where I'm headed. Just thought since you did business with them, you'd be able—"

"Do business with them?" Fischer's teeth ground together in the back of his mouth. "Not anymore. Not after what they done. If it was up to me, I'd gather a posse together and clear them out. Good-for-nothing, meddlin' vipers . . ."

In a flash, Mal grabbed the shopkeeper's shirtfront. He dragged him halfway across the counter with a single yank. Coins clinked onto the floor, but Mal paid them no mind. He put his face nose to nose with the old cuss. "It's *not* up to you," Mal growled. "Got that?"

Fischer sputtered. "Hold on, there, mister." He held out his palms. "I-I didn't mean anything by it. Just blowing steam, you know?"

"Good." Mal released the slimy toad and shoved him back to his own side of the counter. "Because I don't take kindly to men who browbeat women."

"Yeah, well . . ." Fischer straightened his shirt and rolled his shoulders as if trying to erase the memory of Malachi's grip. "I don't take kindly to strangers who interfere in affairs that ain't none of their concern."

Mal scooped up his purchases, his hard-eyed glare never once leaving Fischer's face. "The women of Harper's Station *are* my concern. Anyone who threatens them will have to deal with me."

Then, leaving his change where it had fallen on the floor, Mal strode out of the store before he did something stupid, like knock a few teeth out of Fischer's head.

"What's your business at Harper's Station?" A tall, burly fellow stepped out of the shadows and blocked Mal's path to the stairs.

"My own," Mal ground out, tromping forward. What was it with these people? Couldn't a man buy a razor without being subjected to insults and inquisitions?

The fella stood an inch or two taller than Malachi and out-weighed him by a good thirty pounds of what appeared to be solid muscle, but Mal was riled enough to take him on should the gent want a fight.

The man made no move to stop him, but neither did he step out of the way. Mal tucked his purchases into his side and, leading with his shoulder, barreled his way past. The sturdy fella's arm felt like a slab of granite, but it budged enough to let Mal by.

"You defended the women in there," the man said as he followed Mal down the steps, "so I tend to think you don't mean them harm, but those ladies have suffered enough trials lately. I ain't about to let some stranger show up and harass them further."

Mal spun around to face his accuser, some part of his brain registering that the man was simply trying to protect the women, same as him, but his gut still ached for a fight. "I ain't a stranger," he ground out, even as he eyed the man's chin and balled his right hand into a fist. "At least not to Emma Chandler. She asked me to come." He bent toward the raised boardwalk and set his parcels down, then straightened. "I ain't gonna let that cretin in there"—he tipped his head toward Fischer's store—"stop me from answerin' her call. Nor you, either."

He threw a punch.

The burly fella caught it. With the flat of his palm. Not his chin, as Mal had intended. The man's fingers curled around Mal's fist in an iron grip. Mal drew back his left arm, determined to get the upper hand—he'd beaten opponents bigger than him before—but the man's friendly smile stopped his swing before it gained any momentum.

"Unusual way of shaking hands," the man said, forcing Mal's captured arm down to a more civilized level. "But I must admit, I'm glad to know you. I'm Ben Porter." He pumped Mal's fist up and down, his smile never dimming. "And if I'm not mistaken, you, sir, are Malachi Shaw."

Mal recognized the fella's name from Emma's letters. The freighter who transported their goods and brought in supplies. Glancing around, he spied the freight wagon pulled around the side of the building.

Slowly, Mal unclenched his fist and twisted his arm free, turning the forced handshake into an earnest one. "I am." He grinned at the larger man. "Sorry about taking a swing at you. Haven't slept much the last two days. Guess I'm a bit tetchy."

"Conversin' with Fischer will do that to a person." Porter slapped his shoulder with his free hand. "I can give you directions to Harper's Station, and if you can spare a few minutes, I can share what I know of the trouble they're facing."

Mal glanced up at the sky. The sun still blazed brightly. Summer hours afforded him more daylight to travel by. Surely he could spare a half hour. Getting some details about what he'd be facing was too good an opportunity to pass up.

"Know a quiet place where we can talk?" Mal asked, giving a significant glance toward Fischer's store.

Porter nodded. "My brother owns the livery a block north of here. We can use his office. Let me unload Fischer's order right quick, and I'll meet you there." Porter started walking toward the wagon.

"I think I just rented a horse from your brother." Mal took a step in the opposite direction. "I'll settle up with him while you finish here."

Fifteen minutes later, munching on a roll with a slab of ham tucked inside that he'd taken from his supper box, Mal followed Ben Porter into his brother's office. The smell of hay and manure clung to the place. Not terribly appetizing, but it afforded privacy. Mal swallowed the bite he'd been chomping and cautiously lowered himself onto a stool of dubious soundness as Porter took the single chair behind the desk.

Ready to get to the point so he could get on the road, Mal eyed Porter straight on. "So what am I up against?"

7

Daylight faded as Malachi neared Harper's Station, but he did his best to scour the landscape for any sign of the shooter Ben Porter had told him about. The freighter had no firsthand information. No description or hint of the man's identity. All he could offer was a young boy's account of a shooting at the church building. A shooting that could have taken Emma's life, exposed as she'd been, addressing her ladies.

A tremor coursed through him, just as it did every time he let himself imagine what could have happened that day. Which he'd done at least a hundred times since leaving Seymour.

Mal set his jaw. Emma was fine. Ben had seen her. Talked to her. There was no call to get worked up over what could have happened, not when there was so much more to get worked up about regarding what might still be.

Why did the fool woman insist on staying? Didn't she realize that a man who would shoot up a church wouldn't hesitate to shoot a woman if it meant getting what he wanted? She'd sent away the families with children, but what about protecting her own skin? Did she value her life so little?

His mount sidestepped, and Mal forced his hands to loosen their suddenly too tight grip on the reins. He knew the answers. Knew her. Emma was a fighter. He'd only be wasting his breath if he tried to convince her to leave. The best he could do was stand beside her and draw the enemy's fire until he managed to run the barbarian to ground.

Ben had no idea who was behind the threats. Stanley Fischer was the most vocal opponent of the women's colony, but his disapproval hadn't turned menacing until yesterday, when the mail-order bride he'd sent for had shown the good sense to flee her bridegroom and take refuge with Emma's ladies. If *he'd* had to choose between a lifetime with Fischer or facing the temporary dangers of a madman with a rifle, Mal would have chosen the madman, too.

Rustlers were stirring up trouble in the area, but it was unlikely one of them would attack Harper's Station. Other than a handful of milk cows and a passel of chickens, the women had no livestock to steal. Besides, the shooter had demanded they leave. Obviously, there was something there he wanted. Mal would have to check the water rights and soil surveys to see if there was anything of value to be gained from the land itself. If the shooter succeeded in scattering the women, it'd be a fairly simple matter to hire an anonymous agent to purchase the land on his behalf when Emma decided to sell.

The fella probably thought a few gunshots would be all it would take to scare off a bunch of unprotected females. Mal chuckled. He didn't know who he was going up against. Emma and the aunts had stubborn streaks a mile wide. Threats would just make them dig their heels in harder. Which meant . . . the attacker would have to either forfeit his game or take it to the next level.

Somehow Mal doubted a man unscrupulous enough to fire at unarmed women would hesitate to amplify the violence to gain the prize he sought.

Mal set his jaw and nudged his mount from a walk to a canter, wishing not for the first time that he had Ulysses with him. The gray mare he'd rented was sturdy enough, but she certainly hadn't been built for speed. She was female, though, so at least one of them would fit in.

The first buildings of Harper's Station finally came into view as Malachi crested a slight hill. Dark silhouettes of pointed roofs rose above the vegetation spread out on the flatland below him. His gut clenched. Emma lived under one of those roofs. Ben had said she lived in the one closest to the edge of town, the old stagecoach stop that had given the town its name.

An odd lightness danced upon his chest as he spotted the building he sought. He rubbed at the spot, then scowled when the itch failed to dissipate.

Mal slowed his mount and took stock of the rest of Harper's Station. A tight cluster of businesses lined one side of the road. A handful of other buildings scattered beyond. Not much there to covet that he could see.

A creak of a door focused his attention back on the station house. A young woman emerged from inside and stepped onto the covered porch. A sophisticated woman with dark hair pulled back from her face and wound into an intricate bun at her nape. A grown-up woman of means and mission.

Mal's heart thudded in his chest as he halted his mount. After all the letters they'd exchanged over the years, he'd thought he'd been prepared to see her again. He'd been wrong.

She curled her fingers around the railing post and leaned forward to look at him. Her brows arched slightly. "Malachi?"

The name fell from her lips so softly, he doubted he'd actually heard it. Must've just read the shape of it on her mouth. A mouth within a face achingly familiar yet changed.

Mal stared. He couldn't help it. His little Emma had grown into a handsome, well-put-together woman.

The long tan skirt she wore swept the porch steps as she slowly descended. Her ivory blouse puffed up slightly at the shoulders, nipped in nicely at her tiny waist, and swelled over curves he hadn't remembered being quite so . . . pronounced in the thirteen-year-old girl he last saw.

His collar seemed to tighten around his throat.

"Malachi? Is that you?" She'd reached the bottom stair, her hand falling away from the post.

"Yep." The short, scratchy croak of an answer wasn't much of a howdy after ten years, but it was all he could manage.

Then she smiled. No, it was more than a smile. Her entire face lit up with such joy it nearly knocked him from his horse. He'd forgotten. Forgotten what it felt like to have someone look at him like that. Like the world had suddenly gotten better because he'd arrived.

Unable to withstand her beaming a moment longer, Mal jerked his attention down to his saddle and concentrated on dismounting without doing something stupid like falling on his rear. He hoped his impassiveness would dim her enthusiasm enough for him to get a grip on his sputtering brain and allow him to think of something slightly intelligent to say.

He should have known better.

The instant his boots hit the dirt, she hit him. In a full-on, no-room-to-breathe hug.

Emma wrapped her arms around Malachi's waist and held on tight. He was back! After so many years, he was finally back.

It seemed to take forever, but his arms eventually lowered around her. Not that he actually returned her embrace. His arms circled her so lightly she barely felt the contact. If he hadn't given her back an awkward little pat, she might have thought him a block of wood for all the affection he showed.

But Malachi had never been one to admit he cared about something. Or someone. When he'd first come to live with them, she'd been determined to win him over. To make him like her so they could become the closest of friends. But after several weeks, his manner remained aloof. He never smiled, answered all her questions with either a shrug or a grunt, and on some occasions actively avoided her. It was enough to wear down even the cheeriest of dispositions.

Then one day when he was chopping wood, she came up behind him with the water bucket and dipper. He must not have heard her, though, for when she called his name, he whirled around, hatchet in hand. She'd had to jump back to avoid getting hit. He'd gone so pale, she'd worried he might topple over in a dead faint. Wanting to comfort him in some way, she set down the pail and opened her arms to hug him.

He'd slapped her arms away. Then he'd yelled. Awful things. Hurtful things. Said she had feathers for brains, then spat out a string of foul words she'd never heard before but could tell meant something horrible by the way his eyes sharpened into dark, pointed steel when he flung them at her.

She'd burst into tears and ran straight for her room, sure Malachi hated her. It had been Aunt Bertie who'd finally explained. As she'd held Emma in her arms and wiped her tears away, Bertie had told her a secret. Sometimes people who had lost too much in life were afraid to care. About anyone or anything. For caring meant hurting if they lost what they cared about. And if they did start to care, they fought against it. Hard. That's what Malachi was doing. Fighting.

Emma had decided then and there to fight, too. To fight for the frightened boy who didn't know how to be a friend because he'd never had a friend. She'd started not an hour later, when she caught him pilfering food from the kitchen with the clear intent of running away. With a straightforward assurance only a child of eleven could muster, she'd instructed him on the fine art of apologies. All he had to do was say he was sorry for yelling at her. She would forgive him, and all would return to normal. She even gave him an example just like Miss Pratt always did in school when teaching a new lesson, and apologized for startling him by the woodpile.

She still recalled the look he'd given her. As if she'd suddenly sprouted a third eye in the middle of her forehead. She'd grown truly fearful then, thinking he'd leave for sure. So she started bossing him, even though her aunts had told her countless times that people disliked being told what to do. But she'd had no recourse. He was going to *leave*. So she'd planted her hands on her hips and demanded his apology. She'd goaded him for good measure, too, pointing out that saying two little words was far easier than finding a new home that was anywhere near as lovely as hers.

Her boast had been sinfully close to being a fib. She knew there were finer homes out there. Homes with fathers that a boy like Malachi could look up to. Homes with brothers he could play with and no pestering little girls who were too bossy for their own good. But he must have believed her, for his eyes got all shiny and he dropped his chin to stare at his feet. Then he'd given her the apology she'd wanted to hear, and she'd given him the hug she'd longed to share. He'd been a block of wood then, too. Not moving a muscle when she'd enthusiastically squeezed his middle.

Not much had changed. He hadn't learned how to hug, and she hadn't learned not to force herself upon him.

Emma's face heated. *Good grief.* They weren't children anymore. What must he think of her throwing herself at him like that? Probably that she hadn't matured a bit in the past decade. Still the same leap-first-look-later girl she'd always been.

Emma released him at once and took a couple steps back,

covering her embarrassment with a chuckle. "Sorry. Guess I got a little carried away." She glanced up at him, and got her first true glimpse of the man Malachi had become.

Oh my.

In her excitement to see him, she hadn't actually *seen* him. If she had, she'd probably still be glued to the porch, clinging to the railing for support.

"It's good to see you, Emma." His voice resonated with a masculine depth far removed from that of the boy she remembered. He pulled off his hat and fidgeted with the brim. "You're looking . . . well."

"And you're much taller than the last time I saw you." And had broader shoulders. A more muscled chest. And the bearing of a man unafraid to face whatever challenge fate threw at him.

Yet he just stood there. Staring. At everything except her. His gaze flitted toward her in haphazard patterns, like a nervous bumblebee that couldn't decide whether to land or not.

The silence stretched. Why couldn't she think of anything to say? She'd never been at a loss for words around him when they were young. Of course, he hadn't looked like a rugged outlaw then. An extremely handsome outlaw with a gun on his hip, brown hair hanging past his collar, whiskers shadowing his jaw.

Good gracious. Her heart was pounding so hard against her ribs, she feared he would hear it if she didn't fill the silence with something. Anything.

"I've missed you."

Emma inwardly cringed. All right, maybe not *anything*. And definitely not something spoken in that breathy voice that sounded nothing like her usual take-charge self.

His gaze locked onto hers, though, and all regrets flew from her mind. For the briefest moment, she could have sworn she saw longing in his dark eyes. But then he cocked a half grin at her and looked up toward the heavens the way he used to do when she would pester him with too much jabbering.

"Seems you haven't changed much, Emma. Still getting into trouble."

Oh, she was in trouble, all right. But not because of the shooter targeting her town. Nope. Her real trouble had just arrived.

8

"Malachi Shaw, as I live and breathe."

Mal forced his gaze away from Emma and turned toward the crotchety voice that hadn't changed in all the years he'd been away. Henrietta Chandler, tall and thin, her dark hair still scraped back in the unforgiving bun he remembered, though with more gray streaked through it now than when he'd been a boy.

"Aunt Henry." He dipped his chin in deference, surprised by the emotion that swelled in his throat.

"Bertie!" Henrietta called over her shoulder. "The boy's finally deigned to pay us a visit. Better get on out here before he disappears again."

Emma leaned close—close enough that her side brushed against his arm. Mal forced himself not to react. At least not in a way she could see. Couldn't do much about the hitch in his pulse.

"She still hasn't quite forgiven you for leaving, you know." Emma's whisper sent a shiver over the skin near his ear and down his neck. It distracted him so completely, he never saw Bertie emerge from the house. She seemed to simply materialize beside her sister in a blink of the eye.

"Oh, Malachi." Aunt Bertie clasped her hands together

beneath her chin, her welcoming smile soft and warm, just like the rest of her. "It's so *good* to have you back. We've all missed you dreadfully. Haven't we, sister?"

"Hmmph." Aunt Henry's pinched lips gave no hint of relaxing, but Malachi recognized the stern look for what it was—a shield. Employed the same strategy himself on a regular basis. Probably why he'd always felt a stronger kinship with the elder, more strident Chandler sister than the younger one, despite Bertie's kind, nurturing, and gentle ways.

Henry sniffed. "Well, at least we don't have to wait until his next letter arrives to know he hasn't blown himself to bits." She waved with an imperious circle of her arm that brooked no argument. "Well? Get on up here, boy. It isn't polite to keep an old woman out on the porch in the night wind. I'll catch my death."

Malachi bit back a smile. The slight breeze that ruffled his hair still carried the heat of summer. She'd have to run pretty hard to catch death out here, though he had no trouble picturing her chasing down the Grim Reaper, taking swings at him with her broom as she harangued him for all his slights against womankind. Mal doubted the old fella would dare touch her, even with that long scythe of his.

Mal shoved his hat back on his head and gave a sharp nod. "Be right there. Just got to see to my horse—"

"You go on ahead. I'll take care of the horse." Emma's hand came down atop his as she reached for the reins. Her cheeks colored, but she didn't pull away. So he did. Slower than he should have, torturing himself with the feel of her fingertips trailing along the back of his hand.

"Thanks," he murmured, his eyes never leaving her face.

Emma lowered her lashes, then tugged the reins fully from his grasp and turned to lead his horse away. "Yes . . . well . . . You've had a long journey and must be tired. It's the least I can do."

Mal grabbed his saddlebags as she led the mare past him,

then lingered to watch her disappear around the side of the house. The gentle sway of her hips. The way she stroked the gray's cheek as she rounded the corner. The way she glanced back and caught him staring . . .

Shoot!

As if lightning had suddenly struck the ground between his boots, Mal jolted to attention, spun around, and hotfooted it toward the front door.

Emma's far too good for the likes of you, Malachi Shaw, he silently lectured himself as he scampered after the aunts. *You best remember that.* He was here for one purpose, and one purpose only—to clear out the scum threatening Emma and her ladies. It didn't matter how pretty she looked or how kind her manner. Or how impossibly good she'd felt pressed up against him in that impromptu hug. He just had to keep his head down and his eyes to himself for a few days and he'd soon be back to the safety of blasting tunnels in mountains.

By the time Emma rejoined the group inside, she had a firm grip on her senses. They'd not be taking leave of her again. So what if her girlhood crush had come raging back to life with all the strength of a woman's longing when she'd found Malachi watching her. The man had a life of his own. Probably even a woman of his own up in Montana, though he'd never spoken of one in his letters. Not that he would. Speak of one. In a letter. To her. After all, she'd never mentioned the clerk who'd paid court to her while she'd trained in the bank run by her late father's partner. Some things were just . . . private. And too embarrassing to admit to the young man who'd once been her champion and dearest friend.

Especially when that bank clerk had soft hands and an itchy moustache and never took her side in any discussion she instigated with the manager regarding the lack of loans granted to women. Poor Nathaniel. He just didn't measure up. Not against a boy who'd been willing to stand up for her and her aunts no matter how outlandish Aunt Henry's rhetoric became or how much the other boys ridiculed him.

A thought suddenly stopped her as Emma reached the back door. Did Malachi compare the women he met to his memories of *her*? How did she compare? Emma nibbled on her thumbnail, an unflattering picture painting itself in her head. He probably held her up as an example of what *not* to look for in a woman. Bossy. Opinionated. Stubborn. What was it he'd said? Oh, yes. He'd taken one look at her tonight and named her greatest failing. *"Still getting into trouble."*

Yep. Not exactly the sweet, biddable type a man looked for when searching for a bride. But then, she'd never really wanted a husband. The aunts had gotten along just fine without a man. Why couldn't she? She had her bank, her women's colony, dear friends to keep her from getting lonely. She didn't need a man to fulfill the ministry God had laid on her heart.

How many times had Aunt Henry quoted 1 Corinthians 7:34? *"The unmarried woman careth for the things of the Lord, that she may be holy both in body and in spirit: but she that is married careth for the things of the world, how she may please her husband."*

Men were a distraction. One she couldn't afford. She had a town to preserve, her ladies to protect. Emma squared her shoulders and yanked the back door open, Aunt's Henry's charge ringing in her mind.

Yet as she made her way through the kitchen, it was Aunt Bertie's voice that met her ears, bringing to mind all the times Bertie had countered her older sister's argument with other biblical truths. Like the fact that women were created to be a helpmeet to man. How countless godly women accomplished powerful ministries while being married. Deborah, Esther, Huldah the prophetess, Priscilla, and Jesus's own mother. Bertie had been adamant that Emma not be raised to believe that the path the aunts had chosen was the only one available. God could work through all women, married or single, young or old, rich or poor. All he required was a heart open to his leading.

"Where are you leading me, Lord?" Emma whispered as she slowed her step in the hall and peered into the small parlor. Bertie was plying Malachi with cookies and asking questions about his work while Aunt Henry shook his coat out over the entryway floor, away from the rug, wagging her head over the amount of dust that fell. And Malachi? Well, when Bertie turned to place the cookie plate on the small table between his chair and the sofa, he slid one of the two cookies he'd taken into his lap, covering it with his napkin.

Emma's lips trembled slightly. He still saved back food. The sight struck a chord deep within her breast. After all these years. A man grown with steady employment and a wage that reflected the danger of his work. Yet he hid food in his napkin as if he were still the half-starved boy she'd found in her barn.

The boy who'd first given her purpose. Now the man who'd left his job to answer her call for help.

Emma pressed her lips together and straightened her shoulders. Whatever feelings had stirred inside her upon seeing him again must be set aside. Malachi hadn't come all this way to renew an old acquaintance. He'd come to lend his aid. Aid that the women of Harper's Station dearly needed.

Time to focus on what was truly important.

Emma's light tread on the floorboards brought Malachi's head up, but he masked the rest of his reaction. A pretty remarkable feat given the staccato thumping of his heart against his ribs. He better get used to the grown-up Emma soon, or this was going to be an uncomfortable few days.

"There you are, Emma." Bertie bustled over to her niece and ushered her to the chair directly beside the one Mal sat in. *Great.* As if being in the same room wasn't bad enough, the woman had to sit within touching distance.

Mal glared at the large quilt frame shoved against the adjoining wall. There would have been more room to spread the furnishings out had it not been for the oversized wooden frame. What was it doing here, anyway? The aunts didn't even like sewing. Nor did Emma. But there the thing sat in their parlor, the red and tan squares stretched atop it, taunting him. Maybe he should go unpack his gear in the barn.

"Malachi was just telling us about his railroad work, weren't you, dear?" Bertie smiled at Mal, dashing his hopes for escape as she took her seat on the sofa. "It must be so exciting to see history unfolding right before your eyes. The wheels of progress continually turning." Her eager smile was so enthusiastic and genuine, Mal couldn't help but feel a touch of pride in his meager accomplishments. But then he remembered why he had come to Harper's Station.

Bertie might be acting as if his visit was nothing more than a long overdue social call, but he couldn't afford to pretend. Danger stalked these ladies. The very ladies who'd taken him in, seen to his needs, *mothered* him. And Emma, his brave little angel, the one bright spot in a childhood of darkness. She was counting on him to protect the colony she'd built. He'd not waste time playing house when he could be gathering the information he needed to stop the man threatening her.

"Now that Emma's here," Mal said, "I think we should discuss other, more urgent matters."

Bertie's smile tightened a bit but didn't fade. "Of course. It's just that we haven't seen you in so long, and—"

"Leave the boy be, Bert." Henry hung Mal's coat on a wall hook, then slid onto the yellow sofa cushion next to her sister. "There'll be time enough to get caught up on the pleasantries later. Malachi's obviously chomping at the bit to figure out what's going on here. Always was a worrier, that one." Henry arched a brow at him, her lips twitching ever so slightly at one corner, as if unwilling to admit to her teasing. He'd missed the challenge of ferreting out her subtle humor. "Emma," Henry said, "tell him about the church."

With nowhere else to look, Mal turned his gaze on Emma, and for the first time noticed the shadows beneath her lovely green eyes and the strain evident in the tiny lines around her mouth. As much as Emma believed in community and women helping women, she was still the leader here, the one people looked to for answers, for solutions to their problems. A heavy burden for one so young.

"I had called a meeting a few days ago to discuss the threatening note Tori and I found nailed to the church door."

Mal's brow furrowed. "Note? Porter didn't say anything about a note."

Emma tilted her head. "You've met Mr. Porter?"

Mal nodded as he leaned back in his chair and rubbed his palms along the length of his thighs. "Met him in Seymour after I got in today." No need to add to their worries by mentioning the altercation with Fischer. "I was looking for directions to Harper's Station. He overheard me asking a shopkeeper about the best route to take, then cornered me outside to ask what business I had here. Wanted to make sure I intended you ladies no harm."

"Always did like that brawny fellow."

"Henry!" Aunt Bertie gasped.

"What?" Henry shrugged. "The man's built like a grizzly. It's not like you haven't noticed."

Alberta Chandler blushed. "Good heavens. Benjamin Porter's been nothing but a perfect gentleman, going out of his way to help our Miss Adams with her supplies and shipping our goods at modest prices. He should be spoken of with respect."

"Oh, I respect him plenty. Told me himself he believed women had a right to decide their own futures. Should even be allowed to vote. He might be a muscle-bound giant, but his mama raised that boy right."

Mal could just picture Aunt Henry marching up to Porter on the street and demanding his views on women's suffrage before agreeing to his hire. Probably had him quaking in those extra-large boots of his. The fact that he'd won her over spoke well of his character.

"Well, once he learned who I was," Mal continued, "he offered to fill me in on what little he knew. Told me about the shooting and about Emma encouraging the women with children to leave town. At least temporarily." Mal leaned forward again, bracing his elbows across his knees. "Didn't say anything about a note, though."

"There were three of them, actually. The first was found nailed to a tree along the path to the river. The second on a fence post on the far side of Betty's farm. The third was on the church door. Each one a little closer to the heart of town. And each one a little more threatening."

Mal clenched his jaw. She recounted the details with remarkable straightforwardness, but she couldn't quite mask the fear in her eyes. This guy had rattled her. And he was intensifying the terror tactics.

He looked from Emma to the aunts and back again. "Did anyone get a look at him when he shot up the church?"

"I did." Emma pulled her arms in toward her stomach and folded her hands tightly together. "He hid his features behind a bandana, though, so I'm not sure what good it will do."

"You might be surprised." Mal twisted in his chair to face her more directly. "Tell me what you remember."

She glanced down at her lap. "He had a loud voice. A booming voice. And he wore a buckskin coat. There was fringe on the sleeves, I think." She closed her eyes and squeezed them tight as if trying to picture the man in her mind. "His hat was dark brown and his horse was a chestnut, with a black tail."

"That's good, Emma." And it was. She'd recalled a fair amount of detail when most people would be too overcome with shock to notice. "Was he tall? Short?"

She opened her eyes. "I don't know. I just had a couple glimpses of him. I'm sorry."

"That's all right. It's not that important. Was he alone?"

She tapped her fingers softly against the arm of her chair. "As far as I could tell."

"Have you had any further contact since the day of the shooting?" Mal's mind spun with plans. They'd need to set up a watch. Train the women how to protect themselves. None of them should walk out alone. They'd need to pair off, the larger the groups the better.

"No. It's been quiet since—"

"Fire!" A high-pitched scream from outside broke off Emma's answer. "Somebody help! The church is on fire!"

9

The church! Emma shot to her feet, her heart in her throat. "Henry. Bertie. Grab every pail or pot you can find in the house. I'll grab the ones in the stable and meet you by the garden. Malachi . . ."

But he was already through the front door. Gun drawn. "Stay in the house," he yelled over his shoulder as his boots pounded across the porch. "It could be a trap."

Stay in the house? While her ladies flocked to the scene and tried to extinguish the blaze on their own? Not a chance!

Emma ignored Malachi's command and sprinted through the house to the kitchen and out the back door. Trusting Aunt Henry, at least, to follow—Henry would never sit idly back and let a man fight her battles for her—Emma grabbed the milking pail and the one used for water and dashed across the length of the corral, making a beeline for the church.

The smell of burning wood assaulted her as she ran. Flames flickered in the distance, glowing with an orange light against the dark sky. But only on one side of the building. The side closest to the garden. If the fire reached the plants . . .

No. She wouldn't let it. They depended on that garden for food, for wages, for purpose. She'd not let it burn. Malachi could chase down the instigator, if he so chose. She had a town to save.

Ducking through the corral slats, Emma dragged the pails behind her, not caring about the dents and dings they gathered as they knocked into the fencing. Once on the other side, she hiked her skirts up again and ran toward the small group of women gathering at the garden gate. Someone had already pushed the gate wide and stood hunched over, working the handle of the pump they used to irrigate the crops.

Malachi, having taken the longer path down the main street, caught up to her just as she reached the road. He grabbed her arm and yanked her to a halt. "What are you doing out here? I told you it wasn't safe."

Emma jerked her arm free of his grasp. "Safe doesn't matter right now. I need to be with my ladies. Fighting the fire."

"Safe *always* matters, Emma." Malachi's gaze left hers to scan the area around them. "He could be lying in wait, planning to use the light of the fire to pick you off one by one."

"Well, if I hear a gunshot, I'll take cover. In the meantime, I have a fire to put out."

"Emma . . ."

Ignoring the plea in his voice, she spun away and sprinted across the road. "Form a line," Emma called, spotting Tori and Grace among the women. "We can take turns at the pump and pass the buckets down."

Tori nodded to her and immediately started organizing the women, some of whom were in their nightwear.

"I'll take over the pump. Let you young ones do the heavy lifting." Maybelle Curtis huffed up behind Emma. The poor woman must have run all the way from her home on the north side of town.

Emma patted her shoulder. "Thank you, Maybelle."

The older woman nodded, bent slightly to catch her breath, then straightened and started calling out orders of her own. "If the smoke gets too thick, tear a strip of petticoat and wrap it around your nose and mouth. Too much smoke in the lungs can take a person down. And mind your skirts. Especially those of you taking the front lines." She skewered Emma with a pointed look as she passed through the gate and took hold of the pump handle Flora had just released. "A stray spark can set the fabric ablaze before you know what's what. I don't want to be tending any burns that could have been avoided with common sense."

Emma nodded, grabbed one of the buckets Flora had already filled, and headed toward the church. Water sloshed onto her skirt and shoes as she scurried. The cold barely registered. The fire held her full attention.

Heat stung her face and hands as she neared the fire. Her eyes watered from the smoke. The acrid smell wrinkled her nose. *You will not steal our home!* The silent vow reverberated inside Emma as she tossed her bucketful of water on the first flames she encountered. The hiss of steam echoed loudly in the night, but the flames raged on, undeterred.

"Toss me the empty pail," someone called from behind.

Emma turned to find Grace waiting with open arms. Emma flung the pail across the three feet that separated them. Grace caught it, then spun around and repeated the motion, Tori's line well in place. And judging by the movement farther down, a full pail was already halfway to her.

Emma turned back to regard the church, a cough scratching at her throat. She walked a few steps along the wall, eyeing the damage already wrought. The flames seemed to be most concentrated in the center of the wall, though they licked upward as well. They hadn't reached either the front or back of the building. As far as she could tell, only this one section was ablaze.

She hurried back to where Grace was accepting the next

bucket. "It's not too bad," she yelled over the crackling of the fire. "We can do this."

Grace's lips pressed together in a thin line as she handed off the bucket. "I pray you're right."

Emma took the handle from Grace's hands. The weight of the bucket dragged on her arms, but she held tight and waddled back into the fray. With a strength born of determination, she took hold of the bottom of the pail and hurled the contents into the heart of the blaze.

Malachi shoved his revolver into its holster and stomped back toward the church. Nothing. That's what he'd found. Absolutely nothing. No hoofprints. No footprints. At least none of the male variety. There were a bunch of dainty female footprints around as one would expect, but nothing else.

How had the outlaw done it? Set the church on fire and left without a trace? Had Mal missed something? He'd gone over every inch of the ground leading away from the church. He'd searched the outlying scrub brush for broken twigs or bent branches and found nothing there either. But it was dark. Everything in shades of gray and black. All too easy for details to get lost in the shadows. He'd have to check the area again in the morning.

Some protector he was turning out to be. The male guardian brought in to ferret out the threat and shield the ladies of Harper's Station from harm, and he'd contributed absolutely nothing to their defense. Not only had he failed to find the man responsible, or even a hint of how the fiend had accomplished his task, he'd left the women to fight the blaze on their own.

As he strode closer, the scene brought into focus sliced the guilt into him even more deeply. Weary soldiers covered in battle grime. Bedraggled. Sodden clothes. Mud-caked shoes and hems. Faces drawn with fatigue.

All the remaining townswomen must have turned out. From one gal who looked like she was still in her teens, to a handful of females in nightclothes and caps, to the aunts who apparently listened to him as well as Emma did—they all worked together, their rhythm steady. Mal traced the line up toward the front, his scowl deepening. The women closer to the flames were streaked with soot. Their faces reddened from the heat. Emma, of course, was at the head of the line, tossing water onto the last ribbon of fire that licked up toward the roof.

Her fine white blouse had turned to gray, the untucked shirttail hanging shapeless behind her. Her hair hung in hanks around her face, but when she turned to accept the next bucket, focused green eyes glittered with purpose. Nothing short of collapse would keep her from fighting.

However, as she pivoted back toward the building and flung the water, her weariness became evident. The water only caught the bottom portion of the flames, leaving the top to continue its climb toward the roof.

A short woman rushed forward to collect the empty pail but then froze at the sight of him. Dropping the pail, she reached into the pocket of her skirt and pulled out a tiny gun. Her lips pressed into a tight line, her eyes hard, she cocked the weapon and aimed it at his chest.

"Stop where you are." Her voice was quiet, but it bore an intensity that carried above the sounds of clanking buckets and crackling flames. Her hand didn't waver, either. This one had grit—and a wariness in her gaze that spoke of past hardship.

Mal raised his arms out to the side, away from his gun, hoping to soothe her. Buckets started to pile up around the third lady in the line as she gaped at the scene.

"It's all right, Grace." Emma came up beside the gun-toter

and gently placed a hand on her arm. "This is Malachi Shaw. The friend I told you about. He just arrived tonight. I didn't have time to tell you. He's been out searching for the culprit."

"And now I'm here to help put out the rest of this fire," Mal said, keeping his voice as friendly as possible. "If you'll allow me to help."

Grace slowly lowered her arm. "Of course. Forgive me." She glanced down at her shoes as she uncocked the derringer and slipped it back into her pocket. "I didn't realize who you were."

"No harm done." Malachi grinned. "I'm actually glad to see that you carry a weapon. With all the trouble around here, the more protection you ladies have, the better."

With the gun now out of the equation, Mal lowered his hands and strode over to where another woman stood with what looked like a stockpot in hand. Her eyes wide, she made no move to stop him as he took the pot from her. He murmured a thank-you, then marched back toward the building and tossed the water high enough to douse the top edge of the flame at the roof's eave.

Emma slid into place behind him and handed him bucket after bucket. It didn't take long to extinguish the dying fire, but he doused the wood several additional times just to make sure no embers sprang back to life.

Once he called a halt, the women crowded around to assess the damage. Many turned their buckets upside down and used them as stools. All eyes rested on him. Or on the blackened wall behind him. He wasn't quite sure which.

Emma stepped in front of him, her hand smoothing her hair back from her face, her arm trembling with fatigue. "We did it, ladies. We saved the church!"

A cheer rose, and tired smiles broke out across the women's faces. A few even found the energy to raise arms into the air.

"It will require love and attention to restore the church to its former glory, but it is still standing. Just like us. We are still here. Still standing. And still strong!"

Calls of "That's right" and "Amen" rang out amid a round of applause and a score of nodding heads. Malachi's chest tightened, pride shooting through him. Emma was incredible. Was it any wonder these women flocked to her? She was a natural leader. A fighter. An inspiration.

She walked among the throng, stopping to speak to each woman there. All but one. The short one who'd pulled the gun on him earlier. Grace, wasn't it? The quick-draw female had wandered back over to the church, and was staring at the wall, her brow furrowed. She slowly paced the length of the charred area, her hand raised as if to trace some kind of pattern.

Curious, Mal moved closer, his boots sinking slightly in the shallow mud. "What do you see?" He was careful to approach from the side instead of the rear, not wanting to startle her again.

"There's something odd about this charring." Her eyes never veered from the wall. "Certain sections seem darker. Deeper. As if the fire burned hotter or longer there."

Mal squinted at the blackened wall. With smoke in the air and only a half moon, it was hard to make out the details. He cupped his hands around his mouth and called over his shoulder.

"Emma!" He waited for her to look his way. "Bring a couple of those lanterns up here, would you?" He pointed to the four lanterns someone had set up to help light the way for the bucket line.

Emma glanced back at the lanterns and nodded to him that she understood.

Mal studied the wall. There did seem to be darker strips. Some vertical. Some horizontal. It was odd. If he wanted to torch a church, he'd douse the interior with turpentine or kerosene and light it up from within. It would take longer for someone to notice the danger that way and therefore cause more damage.

But damage didn't seem to be the ultimate goal of this attack. The man had only lit one side of the building, the side facing town, the side most likely to be spotted. And it had been. Early. Before the flames had spread. So destruction hadn't been his aim. Was he trying to instill fear or testing the ladies' resolve? Mal frowned. Perhaps both.

"Here, Malachi." Emma handed him a lantern. Women crowded around, three of them carrying lights as well. "What are we looking at?"

Mal gestured with a jerk of his chin toward the wall. "There are lines burned into the wall."

"I think they might be letters," Grace said, tracing a pattern in the air with one hand as she stared at the church.

Letters? A cold knot twisted in Malachi's gut. He held his lantern aloft, shining the light against the charred wood. The other three ladies moved forward and held their lights up, the water-soaked wood glistening in the soft glow.

A gasp echoed behind him. Then a low murmur spread among the group. Mal clenched his teeth in an effort to tamp down the rage swelling from his gut up through his throat.

The man hadn't just splashed turpentine on the wall. No. He'd taken his time. Painted a warning meant to intimidate. To bludgeon. To terrorize.

For there in black, scarred letters blazed the message.

LEAVE or DIE.

10

"Well, if he wants me dead," Aunt Henry's disgusted tone cut through the low buzz of shocked murmuring, leaving silence in her wake, "he's going to have to come take care of the job face-to-face. I'm not leaving, and I'm not about to keel over just because he scored some shabby-looking letters into the side of the church."

Emma's lips twitched, wanting to smile despite the soot, the mud, and the taste of woodsmoke clinging to her tongue. Aunt Henry. Dear, indomitable Aunt Henry. Leave it to her to diffuse this awful situation with a barrage of plain speaking.

"Now, I don't know about you ladies," Henry continued, her voice growing stronger as every head swiveled to face her, "but I won't be giving that bully the satisfaction of standing around gaping at his vandalism and fretting over what might happen tomorrow. The good Lord taught that worrying about tomorrow is as pointless as milking a dry cow. Leaves you frustrated, frazzled, and with nothing to show for your effort. On the other hand, my mama, rest her soul, taught that a good night's sleep can shrink any problem down to a manageable size. So that's what I aim to do—get some sleep and leave the worrying to the Lord. I suggest you all do the same." She turned around, grabbed one of the stockpots Emma recognized as belonging to their personal stores, then waved an arm at her sister. "Come along, Bertie. Dry clothes and a warm bed await."

Bertie smiled at Emma—an everything-will-be just-fine type of smile that warmed her insides despite the soggy blouse plastered to her chest.

"Coming, sister." She swept past the other ladies as if nothing were amiss. "I think I'll put the kettle on as well. A cup of tea is just the thing to settle the nerves and warm the toes."

"Chamomile is especially soothing," Maybelle said, turning to follow. "Peppermint, too. I've got both at the clinic if anyone needs some." The midwife-turned-town-doctor reached across her body to rub her right shoulder, obviously sore from manning the pump.

Claire, who'd taken up residence with the older woman yesterday after joining the colony, hurried to Maybelle's side, lifting the lantern she carried out in front of her. "I'll be lightin' the way fer ye, Miss Curtis. My arm's strong, should ye be feelin' the need to lean upon somethin'."

And just like that, the crowd dispersed. Groups of two or three separated themselves and wandered toward their homes. Not one lady spoke of leaving. Not one fell into hysterics or fretful tears. Not one cast blame on Emma for failing to prevent the attack.

They'd banded together to fight the fire and had been victorious. Now they banded together again, unified in their resilience. They would not trade their victor status for that of victim. They were strong. Capable. Courageous. And Emma had never been more proud to be among them.

"Will you be all right, Em?" Tori came up beside her, two buckets in each hand, buckets still bearing strings with soggy, illegible price tags attached. "I need to check on Lewis."

Emma touched her friend's shoulder. "Go. I'm sure he must be worried."

"Daisy's watching him, but I . . ." Tori's attention strayed to the store down the street, a visible ache in her eyes. "I just need to see him."

"Of course you do." What mother wouldn't want to clutch her child to her bosom and reassure herself that he was well after such a disturbing event? Even a spinster raised by spinsters could imagine such a need. Could secretly envy it, too. Emma blinked back the mist forming in her eyes—infernal smoke—and gave Tori a gentle nudge. "Give Lewis a kiss for me."

As Tori started back, Emma glanced around to see who was left near the church. Those from the boardinghouse next door to Tori's store were already several yards ahead. Emma didn't want Tori walking back alone in the dark. She spotted Flora slumped against the garden fence near the corner farthest from the church and immediately waved to her. "Flora!"

The woman nearly jumped out of her shoes. Her head jerked up, the whites of her wide eyes glowing in the moonlight.

Emma silently chastised herself for startling the poor dear and bustled toward her, an apology written on her face. "Come, walk with Tori. Neither of you should go back alone."

"Yes, Flora," Tori urged, having drawn to a stop when Emma called out. "I'd feel better with some company."

Flora's gaze darted to the ground, to the church, to the garden. "I . . ." She made no move to straighten away from the fence.

Moving to her side, Emma gently took hold of her arm and helped her stand. Tori backtracked toward the garden and held out a hand to Flora.

"Come along, now," Tori said, using the same coaxing voice she used to lure Lewis into his evening bath. "I've got some of that peppermint tea in the store that Maybelle was talking about. How about I brew a pot and we all have a cup? Then you and Daisy can return to your rooms."

Flora glanced back at the garden once more before finally submitting to Tori's shepherding. The two walked off arm in arm, Tori chattering the whole way.

Emma studied the dark-haired Flora and sent up a quick prayer on her behalf. The message burned into the church wall must have truly spooked her. Understandable given the circumstances. Not everyone had the sturdy constitution of Aunt Henry. Besides, Flora had been on edge since the shooting at the church. She'd been the most vocal advocate for evacuation, encouraging as many ladies as would listen to leave. She would have left, too, Emma was certain, if she'd had anywhere to go. But she didn't. Flora had no family besides her husband, and judging by the bruised and battered condition she'd been in when she arrived at Harper's Station a few weeks ago, returning to him offered no safe haven.

The soft glow of lantern light in her right periphery alerted Emma to Malachi's approach, yet she couldn't look away from Tori and Flora to acknowledge him. She had to watch. Had to make sure they came to no harm. As if her watching over them ensured their safety. *Ha!* Her eyes on them wouldn't shield their bodies from a bullet should the shooter decide to enforce his threat. Nothing she did could stop the man—not from setting fires or shooting into populated buildings. What if he did start killing? How many would die because of her?

"You really are a great leader." Malachi's low voice caressed her ear even as his words unintentionally shredded her heart, letting all her doubts and insecurities escape in one fell swoop.

She twisted to face him. The weight of her responsibility pressed down on her with such heaviness, it nearly bent her in two. "Oh, Mal. You have no idea how *wrong* you are."

Malachi barely had time to brace himself before Emma slammed into his chest for the second time that night. He gritted his teeth against the contact. The closeness. Self-preservation demanded that he set her at arm's length, give himself a buffer so he could breathe, think. But he couldn't. He'd seen her eyes. Those glorious green eyes that had always seen the best in him had been filled with torment.

And now they were weeping against his chest, each teardrop scalding his soul.

Had he done this? Malachi stared into the night sky at the smirking half-moon, recriminating himself for opening his mouth. He knew he was rusty when it came to paying compliments to females, but he'd never dreamed he could reduce one to tears by making the effort.

Emma clung to his waist, her fingers digging into the damp fabric of his shirt at the small of his back. Her cheek pressed tightly against his chest. Her shoulders trembled with the force of her tears. She needed comfort. Needed someone to soothe her.

Why in the world had she chosen *him*? A rock probably knew more about comforting than he did.

Glancing back at the moon that seemed to be laughing outright at him now, Mal set his jaw and slowly curled his arms around her. Mercy, but she was a tiny thing. So delicate. Yet he knew her core was solid steel. She'd just forgotten for a moment. Forgotten how strong she was. He'd remind her. Somehow.

He patted her back once. Then, when she didn't stop shaking, he patted her again. She sniffed a little and let out a shuddering breath. That meant her cry was almost done, didn't it? Man, he hoped so.

Her fingers released their death grip on the back of his shirt, but her arms stayed circled around him. In fact, they squeezed him more firmly, her palms flattening along the line of his spine as her cheek burrowed deeper into the hollow beneath his shoulder. Mal swallowed. Sakes alive, but her holding him felt good. And wasn't he a blackguard for noticing? Here she was, in distress, and all he could think about was how good she felt pressed up against him.

Yet . . . if it felt good to him, maybe it could feel good for her, too. If he . . . just . . .

Ah, shoot. Malachi flattened his palms against her back and squished her close. She let out a little squeak as her nose mashed into his chest in an awkward fashion, but she didn't try to break away. He relaxed his grip enough to let her settle, then tried stroking her back like he did for Ulysses when his horse demanded pampering. Emma let out a little sigh. A rather soothed-sounding sigh.

Mal grinned triumphantly at the smirking moon. Ha! He *could* be more comforting than a rock. Wasn't so hard. Just had to imagine she was his horse.

Mal stroked her back again, making little circles with the tips of his fingers as he tried to conjure up a mental image of Ulysses. Then Emma shifted slightly, and all her softness moved to a slightly different position, bringing it to the forefront of his attention. The half-formed picture of his horse vanished.

Yeah. Should've known that wouldn't work.

But at least Emma wasn't crying anymore.

"They're all depending on me." Her tiny voice nearly got swallowed up in his chest. Mal loosened his hold and gave her room to breathe.

She sniffed a couple times, ran the edge of her sleeve beneath her nose—an action that brought to mind the little girl he'd once known—then turned her face up to look at him. Streaked with soot and tears, hair in a tangled mess, he shouldn't have found her lovely. Yet he did. So lovely his chest ached.

"They're all depending on me," she repeated. "They're

depending on me, and I have absolutely no idea what to do. I can't keep them safe. Can't protect their property, their livelihoods. This situation is completely outside my control."

"Leading ain't about controlling everything, Emma." Mal dropped his arms from around her and took a step back. "It's about helping the people around you succeed. Encouraging them to be their best selves." He kicked the toe of his mud-caked boot against the garden fence. "You've got that talent in spades. It's why they follow you."

It's why I followed you.

She shook her head.

He frowned. "Don't go arguin' with me."

She shook her head again anyway. Muleheaded female.

"A good leader would know what to do. I'm too young. Too inexperienced."

Malachi crossed his arms over his chest and leaned back against the fence. He scowled at her, too. He wasn't about to let her momentary doubts steal her confidence, her drive. He knew firsthand how hard it was to escape the mire of believing you weren't good enough. He'd been spoon-fed that drivel his entire childhood. Until Emma and the aunts had taught him differently. Time he returned the favor.

"So is that why you brought me here?" he challenged. "'Cause you needed a man to be the leader for you?"

Her brows scrunched downward. "No. I brought you here to help."

"To help, huh?" He pushed away from the fence and glared at her. "Okay. Then here's my first tip. Quit knocking yourself down. No one knows what to do when thrust into a situation they've never encountered before, no matter their age or experience. All anyone can do is take the information they've been given, weigh the risks and rewards, then make the best decision possible at the time. I'll help you gather that information,

Emma. I'll teach you and the others how to defend yourselves. Shoot, I'll even give you my advice—not that you'll take it." He gave her a meaningful look, recalling the way she'd disregarded his instructions to stay inside.

She jutted her chin out in response, that familiar spark of defiance returning to her eyes.

He had to work hard to hold back his grin.

"But you're the one these ladies respect," Mal reminded her. "You're the one they trust. Not me. You are their leader."

She glanced away, her face a mask of concentration as she silently battled to subdue her doubts. Mal watched her struggle for a moment, then, on impulse, grabbed her hand.

Emma blinked. She glanced at his hand on hers, then lifted her eyes to his face.

His throat suddenly tight, Mal fought the urge to drop her hand and turn away. She needed to know she wasn't in this alone. He tightened his grip.

"I'll be here for you," he vowed. "For as long as it takes. You don't have to shoulder the load on your own. I'll help you carry it."

And when she didn't need his help anymore? Malachi tried to ignore the insidious thought as he basked in the light of Emma's grateful smile, but the prospect lingered in the air between them, tainting the sweetness of the moment like rotted beef in a savory stew.

Leaving her once had left scars he'd yet to recover from. He wasn't sure he could survive the experience a second time.

11

Mal woke to the sound of roosters—*multiple* roosters—crowing to announce the coming day. The chicken farm stood far enough away that most townsfolk with closed doors and windows would probably sleep through the racket, but Malachi had opted for a pallet in the stable with the barn door wide open.

Emma had tried to shuttle him off last night to one of the homes in town that had been vacated after the first group of women left, but he'd refused to go. Some deranged lunatic was out there threatening the women of Harper's Station, and the females he cared about most were holed up together in the old station house. He wasn't about to leave them unguarded.

Besides, he wanted the chance to examine the area around the church in the light of day before anyone else could wander out there and disturb evidence he might have missed in the dark.

After tending the horses, milking the cow, and leaving the pail of milk on the back porch for Emma or one of the aunts to find, Mal grabbed the leftover oatmeal cookie he'd stashed in his coat pocket last night before the fire broke out and munched on the crumbled mess. Didn't look too pretty after being squashed every which way, but it was sustenance enough to keep him going. Had a roll and a little ham left over from the supper box he'd bought in Seymour in his saddlebag, too, but he'd save that for later, just in case he missed breakfast while out hunting clues.

An hour later, Mal's stomach was grumbling something fierce, but it was his mind that truly churned. He tromped through the paddock behind the station house, stomped up the back-porch steps, and pulled the kitchen door open.

"There you are, Malachi," Aunt Bertie exclaimed. "Just in time for flapjacks with my special recipe blackberry syrup." She winked at him, then bunched her apron up in her hand and reached for the coffeepot. "Have a seat, dear, and I'll bring you some coffee."

The sharp smell of the dark-roasted brew wafted toward him first, followed quickly by the fruity aroma of syrup heating in a pan of hot water on the stove. Stacks of fluffy golden-brown pancakes were no doubt waiting in the warming oven. Mal nearly groaned. He hadn't tasted Bertie's flapjacks in over a decade, but he remembered them. Oh, how he remembered. He'd once eaten seven in one sitting.

But as much as he would have loved to sit down and feast, he had a more urgent matter to deal with. A matter concerning the young woman placing napkins and forks at the four place settings arranged on the table.

Mal strode forward and deposited a canister in the middle of the table with a decisive *thunk*.

Emma eyed him askance, her nose scrunching a bit as she examined the dirt-encrusted can. "What is that?"

"Turpentine." He held up a dusty paintbrush and plopped it onto the lid of the can. "Found that with it, too."

Emma's gaze jerked back to his. Her face paled slightly. "Where did you find it?"

"Tucked out of sight behind the northeast corner of the garden fence."

The two forks she held fell to the table with a clatter. She gripped the chairback in front of her for support. "Why would he leave it behind? And by the garden, no less. Wouldn't it have been simpler to toss it in the bushes if he didn't want to take it with him?"

"I'm not sure *he* was the one who left it behind."

Her brow furrowed. "What are you saying?"

Mal worked his jaw back and forth before answering, knowing she wasn't going to take well to his conclusion. "I'm saying there's a chance he has an accomplice. Here. In Harper's Station."

"Of all the hog swill I've heard in my day, that batch smells the worst, Malachi Shaw." Aunt Henry burst through the kitchen doorway and pierced Mal with the same withering look she'd used the time she caught him in a lie about where the corn bread had disappeared to. That look had tugged so hard on his conscience, he'd spilled the whole story of taking the leftovers to his room and hiding them under his bed. She made him do dishes for a week after that. Not because he took the food and ruined her plans to have dressing that night with the baked chicken Bertie fixed, but because he'd lied to her. And drawn a colony of crumb-hunting ants into the house.

Her disapproval still made him squirm, but this time Mal held his ground. The Chandlers might not want to hear what he had to say, but he cared more about protecting their stubborn hides than offending their suffragist sensibilities.

"I wouldn't suggest the idea, Aunt Henry, if I didn't have good reason." He aimed his words in the elder Chandler sister's direction, but his eyes never left Emma's.

"Surely, you don't think one of my ladies . . ." She shook her head. "No. Absolutely not. You don't know them like I do. We help each other. Depend on each other. Besides, each lady took a vow when joining the community never to do another lady harm. None of them would ever . . . We're family."

Mal gentled his voice. "Family is no guarantee of loyalty." He knew that better than most.

"But you saw how everyone worked together to fight the fire. *Every* one. Why would someone set a fire, then work tirelessly to extinguish it? It makes no sense."

"Actually it's pretty smart." Mal rubbed an itchy spot on his stubble-covered chin. He really needed to shave. "Keeps others from growing suspicious."

Aunt Henry leaned across the middle of the table, blocking Mal's view of Emma. Henry grabbed the turpentine and brush, marched over to the corner of the kitchen, and dropped them on top of the pie safe. "Claptrap, I say. Nothing but a bunch of claptrap. A woman wouldn't burn a church. This is the work of a man. The man who shot at us a few days ago. That's who you need to be tracking down, not wasting time on a witch hunt."

His shoulders went rigid as his temper flared. "I ain't sayin' the man Emma saw isn't the one behind this. I'm sure he is. But you need to consider that he might have an accomplice." Mal paused to take a breath, then made a point to lower his voice. "You're the one always saying that women can do anything men can, Aunt Henry. But you can't just take the good without lookin' at the bad. Sure, women are capable of being doctors and bankers," he said with a wave of his hand toward Emma, "but they can also be criminals and deceivers. Excusing them all from guilt simply because they are female before you hear me out is as much an act of prejudice as those who assume men are the only ones capable of casting a responsible vote."

"He's got a point, Henry," Bertie said as she lowered a platter of flapjacks onto the middle of the table like a peace offering. A rather loud sniff was the only response she received to that observation. Nevertheless, Bertie continued bustling about as if nothing untoward had happened. She collected the syrup and butter crock, then deliberately pulled out her chair and took a seat. "Come along now. There's plenty of time to hash everything out while we eat."

Malachi bit back the argument that leapt to his tongue. Jaw tight, he removed his hat and tossed it on top of the pie safe next to the turpentine canister. His suspicions and conclusions clamored for release, but he swallowed them down. A few minutes' delay wouldn't hurt anything. Besides, people were less likely to be cranky after consuming Bertie's blackberry syrup. Himself included.

Emma slid around to the spot closest to the wall on his right, her demeanor quiet, subdued. Lines marred her forehead as she took her seat, her gaze locked on the emptiness of the plate in front of her. Henry had no such compunction. She glared at him as she perched ramrod straight in the seat opposite his.

"There we are." Bertie smiled, ignoring the tension in the air as she stretched her hands out toward him and Henry. "Would you say the blessing for us, Malachi?" She nodded at him, her eyes saying more than her words—*Don't forget what is most important.*

Mal cleared his throat. "Yes, ma'am." He reached for Emma's hand as he accepted Bertie's. Emma's fingers trembled slightly, so he gripped them tightly, trying to reassure her that all would be well. He'd see to it.

Then he bowed his head. "Lord, we thank you for the food before us, and for the people around this table." He ran his thumb over the back of Emma's hand. "Thank you for keeping everyone safe last night during the fire. Please continue to watch over the women of Harper's Station and protect them from harm. Resolve this situation quickly, Lord. In Jesus's name, amen."

No one spoke after that. The only sounds breaking the silence were the scrape of forks against plates and the occasional creak of wood when someone shifted in their chair.

The flapjacks were as light and fluffy as Mal remembered, and the syrup such a perfect blend of sweet and tart that, had his mind not been so occupied, he was sure he would have savored each bite with lingering care. Instead, he wolfed down six pancakes before the ladies finished their tea. Well, only five, really. One lay folded inside his napkin on his lap to be stashed later in his saddlebag. Mal glanced at Emma and the aunts, making sure none of them was paying him any attention, then slipped the napkin inside his vest, to the hidden pocket he'd sewn into the lining.

"I just can't believe one of my ladies could be guilty of helping this outlaw." Emma set her fork aside, abandoning a perfectly good half a pancake.

Mal was momentarily distracted by the leftover pieces, purple with absorbed syrup, and destined for the slop pail. Bertie's flapjacks deserved better. Then Emma turned to face him, and all thought of flapjacks, purple or otherwise, flew from his head.

"I know these women. Some are more prickly than others, but they all want this place to succeed. *Need* this place to succeed. Why would they sabotage their own future?"

Mal scooted his plate away from the edge of the table and leaned forward. "I don't know, Em. Maybe this fella offered enough money to tempt someone to secure her future in a faster, easier way. Or maybe he's blackmailing one of the colony members."

"But what makes you so sure that one of the women is involved?" This came from Aunt Henry.

Mal glanced her way before turning his attention back to Emma. "I found faint traces of footprints this morning when I searched the area around the church. A man's boot, a size or two smaller than mine, but larger than a woman's shoe."

"There's your proof!" Henry's palm slapped the tabletop. "He was there."

"Yes he was. Four days ago when he shot up the church. The tracks were too faded to have been newly made. And they didn't fit with what happened. They only led to the west side of the building, to the window where he shot into the church. Then they backtracked to where a horse waited. I found hoofprints in the grass that match Emma's account of the man riding off through the brush instead of on the road. No boot prints leading to the east side of the building where the fire was set. So unless he followed his previous tracks precisely and climbed over the top of the church, he can't be the one responsible."

The women fell silent again. Malachi felt like the worst sort of villain, casting aspersions on Emma's community, especially after their impressive display of unified purpose last night. But maybe that was the true benefit of bringing in an outsider. He could see things, or at least the possibilities of things, that Emma was too close to recognize.

"I know you don't want to believe that one of your own could be involved," Malachi said, his voice as gentle as he could make it, "but walking around with blinders on won't help your ladies, either. I'm not saying that we should start throwing accusations around. That would only rile everyone up and destroy the camaraderie that you've worked so hard to build, a camaraderie you'll need to defeat the skunk who's trying to drive you out.

"All I'm asking is that you stop assuming that everyone's motives are as pure as your own. Ask questions. Read between a few lines. We can start by finding out where that turpentine came from." He tilted his head toward the pie safe. "It looks like it sat in a cupboard or barn for a good long while. It belongs somewhere around here. If we discover where it came from, it might give us a clue to the identity of the person who used it. We should also determine who sent up the alarm. The first person on scene could have been the one to start the blaze. She wanted the fire to be caught early so the message would be decipherable. What better way to deflect suspicion than to be the one who sounded the alarm?"

Henry raised a brow at him. "You have a devious mind, boy."

He shrugged off her comment, but the action didn't stop the old guilt from swirling through his gut again. "I spent a lot of years deflecting suspicion in my youth, sidestepping the law in order to survive. I know how it's done."

Emma peered at him, her eyes finally sharpening, leaving behind the glaze of denial. "And that might be exactly what one of our ladies is facing—survival." She turned to the aunts and straightened in her chair, a new energy driving her movements. "Malachi is right. It's dangerous for us to naïvely assume that none of our ladies could be involved." She swung back toward Malachi. "But we must not be too quick to cast blame, either. There could be many innocent explanations for what appears to be suspicious behavior, and I won't have anyone badgered or unduly scrutinized as we struggle to piece the truth together. We will presume innocence even as we seek proof of guilt."

Mal nodded. "Agreed."

"We will also keep this discussion strictly between the four of us." She looked pointedly at each of the aunts. "You cannot speak of it to Daisy or anyone else. Understood?"

Henry gave a crisp nod.

Bertie's followed a bit more hesitantly. "Will you not tell Victoria? The two of you started this colony together. She's been with you since the beginning. Surely you trust her?"

Emma's eyes slid closed for a moment as if Bertie's words caused her physical pain. "I trust Tori completely," she said as she opened her eyes. "Perhaps I will share our findings with her once we have gathered some evidence, but at this point, the fewer people who know we are looking, the better. Less chance that something will be overheard that way."

Her spine straightened a bit more then, and her chin jutted forward the way it always had as a kid when she was about to start ordering him around. "Malachi and I will ask the questions that need asking. Henry and Bertie, you'll keep to your normal routine. No need to probe anyone for information. However, all four of us will keep our eyes open for anything that seems unusual. We'll report our findings back to the others here in the evenings, when we can be assured of privacy."

Mal bit back a grin. She'd found her bossy britches again, and they looked good on her. How this woman could have ever doubted her ability to lead was beyond him. She'd been made for it. Concern for those under her care—*all* those under her care—radiated from her. As did intelligence and foresight. She might be a bit impulsive at times, but she could also examine a situation with a banker's acumen, weighing future outcomes against current need. Oh, he had no illusions about her intent. She was bent on "saving" the woman he suspected had been dragged into this scheme, whoever she was. And for Emma's sake, he hoped the woman proved worthy of her efforts. If not, he'd take whatever steps were necessary to keep the people he cared about safe.

Done with her directives, Emma pushed back her chair and rose to her feet. A hint of a smile played at her mouth as she tipped her head at him. "Malachi, I think it's time you were officially introduced to the women of Harper's Station."

12

Deciding it was too early to call at the boardinghouse, Emma opted to take Malachi to the farm first. Betty always had her assistants up with the roosters and busy with chores. When they strolled up the path to the house, Emma spotted Katie scattering chicken feed. She lifted a hand in greeting.

"Good morning, Katie."

The girl twisted her head around then smiled and waved. "'Morning, Miss Chandler. Are you needing to talk to Betty?"

"Yes, please. And Helen, as well. I thought it best that everyone have a chance to meet Mr. Shaw, since he's going to be helping us out for the next few days."

Malachi tipped his hat, and Katie's gaze trailed over him in an appreciative manner. "Pleasure to meet you, Mr. Shaw. I'm Katie Clark."

"Miss Clark."

She giggled, the high-pitched titter grating on Emma's nerves. Katie sauntered over to where they stood, her basket of feed swinging unsteadily on her arm. Probably because her hips were swaying as wide as the pendulum on Aunt Bertie's grandfather clock. Emma raised her gaze to the sky. *Good grief.* Couldn't the girl be at least a *little* subtle?

Katie halted before them and reached a hand out to touch Malachi's sleeve. "'Miss Clark' sounds awfully stuffy. I'd much prefer you call me Katie." She batted her lashes. Twice. "It's such a blessing having a man like you around to protect us. I feel safer already." The lashes started to dip a third time, but Emma interrupted before they could make a full descent.

"Yes, well, you were going to fetch Miss Cooper for us?"

Katie's bat morphed into a startled blink at the sound of Emma's voice. She turned. "Oh, of course, Miss Chandler."

The way she said *Miss Chandler* made Emma feel like an old-maid schoolmarm. Which was ridiculous, seeing as how Katie was only a year younger than her. But Katie wasn't in charge of the colony or a bank or even her own daily schedule. Emma bit back a groan. Maybe she *was* old. She certainly felt it next to the bubbling, coquettish Katie.

Reluctant to leave, Katie tossed a coy glance over her shoulder at Malachi. "I'll be right back."

Malachi tried to smile, but the effort more resembled a grimace.

The girl scampered off, and Emma apologized. "I'm sorry. I've never seen her behave like that before. She's always acted quite sensible around me."

"Ha!" The shout came from behind them. Emma pivoted to find Betty Cooper marching toward them, dressed in trousers and a man's shirt, a shotgun propped backward across her shoulder. "That's because you ain't a man, Emma." Betty gave Malachi a stern, measuring stare as she strolled up. "And *you* best not get any ideas about my Katie or any of the other womenfolk around here." She poked her finger into the hollow of Malachi's shoulder. "You're here for one reason. To clear out the mangy coyote tryin' to break up our town. We don't need you for anything else. Flush him out, round him up, then hit the trail. Got it?"

"Betty. Really. Where's your hospitality?" Heat crept across Emma's cheeks as she snuck a peek at Malachi. The poor man looked as if he'd been skewered with a spit and placed over an open flame to roast.

"I'm just statin' facts. Best he know right from the start that I won't tolerate any hanky-panky goin' on with any of our girls. We keep men out for a reason, Emma. I agreed to let this one come because you and your aunts vouched for him and because we ain't got the firepower or experience to stop this outlaw on our own, but that don't mean I trust him in other matters. He's still a man."

"But, Betty—"

Mal placed a hand on Emma's arm, then stepped in front of her to face Betty. "That's all right, Em. Mrs. Cooper's right. Trust needs to be earned. I'll prove myself in time."

"I'd rather you not hang around that long," Betty grumbled. "Might not even need you after the new shipment of guns comes in. A rifle acts the same whether it's a male or female pullin' its trigger."

"True," Mal conceded, "but it does the shooter no good if he or she can't hit what they're aimin' at." He held his ground, meeting Betty stare for stare. "I understand my purpose here, Mrs. Cooper, and whether you trust me or appreciate my being here really doesn't matter. I won't be leaving until I'm sure Emma and the aunts are safe."

Betty held his gaze for a long moment. Mal never flinched. Finally, the woman seemed to make up her mind and gave a sharp nod before tromping past Mal to head for the house. Emma followed, offering an apologetic smile to Mal as she moved past him.

"What brings you to the farm?" Betty asked, her long no-

nonsense stride eating up the ground at such a pace, Emma had to skip a bit to catch up.

"I wanted to introduce Mr. Shaw around and ask a few questions about the fire. We're trying to piece together all the information we can to see if we can figure out exactly what happened."

"What happened was the church burned." Leave it to Betty to sum things up succinctly.

"Well, yes, but—"

"Were you walking a perimeter just now?" Malachi interrupted, jerking his chin toward the gun Betty carried.

"Yep." She made no effort to turn and face him, just kept marching. "Thought it a good idea after last night. Didn't see nothin' out of the ordinary, though. Was on my way back when I spied the two of you jawin' with Katie."

Malachi apparently had no trouble keeping up with Betty. His stride carried him past Emma with little effort and brought him abreast of the older woman. "I was thinkin' it might be a good idea to set up a watch rotation," he said. "Two ladies per shift, three shifts per night. Stationed in the church's bell tower for best vantage. That somethin' you might be interested in overseein'? Seems to me a woman who knows enough to check her perimeter would be just the sort I'd want to put in charge of the watch."

This was the first Emma had heard of a watch, but it was a sound notion. She just couldn't help feeling a little slighted that Mal was asking Betty to organize it instead of her. No one knew the town's women as well as she did.

It's not about controlling, Emma. The reminder scraped a raw spot on her conscience. Goodness. Was she really so full of herself that she thought she should be in charge of everything? How utterly impractical. There was plenty of work to go around without her getting her feelings hurt because Malachi thought someone else more aptly suited to a task than she.

And how better for Mal to prove that he wasn't one of those autocratic males who pay no heed to a woman's opinion? Even now, Betty was slowing her steps and regarding him with cautionary interest.

"I reckon I can manage that," Betty said. "My late husband and I were stationed at Fort Elliott for five years before an Injun got him. He taught me how to shoot and how to recognize signs of enemy encroachment. I can train the others on what to look for."

Malachi grinned. "Perfect. Consider yourself in charge."

Betty dipped her chin.

"I planned to get everyone together this afternoon for some weapons instruction," Mal continued. "I'd be grateful for your assistance with that, as well."

"I reckon I can manage that. You might think about askin' Grace, too. She's more familiar with handguns. We got a paltry collection of firearms at our disposal right now, but next time Mr. Porter comes through, we should have a better arsenal to choose from."

"When do you expect him?"

Betty hesitated.

Emma jumped into the conversation, thankful to finally have some information to contribute. "He should be here day after tomorrow. Monday."

"Good." Malachi eyed both women. "We can start the shooting lessons after he gets here. In the meantime, everyone needs to know how to load and care for the weapons. We can also inform the ladies about the watch. You think you can have a basic list ready by this afternoon, Mrs. Cooper?"

"Yep. I'll have it ready. I'll take care to mix ages and experience levels." Her gaze turned to Emma. "You know of any personal issues I should be aware of? Any gals that shouldn't be paired up?"

Emma thought a moment. "Flora can be a mite prickly. You might want to pair her with someone who has a more placid temperament. Oh, and I'm not sure Daisy can handle the stairs to the steeple. It might be better to have her contribute by watching Lewis when Tori is on duty."

Betty nodded. "Good thought. Do you think your aunts can handle the climb?"

"Yes, though they should probably only be assigned early shifts. They tend to doze off easily once the sun goes down."

"I'll pair one of them with my Katie. That gal can talk the skin off a turnip. She'll keep 'em awake."

"Better put her with Bertie, then," Emma recommended, a soft chuckle escaping at the thought of Henry being saddled with such a chatterbox. "Henry's liable to throw the girl from the ramparts."

Betty chortled. "Ha! Right you are." The sound of a door slamming had Betty's gaze lifting over Emma's head. "Speaking of . . ."

Emma turned. There was Katie, traipsing down the front steps wearing a different dress. One she usually saved for Sundays.

"There you are, Betty!" She bustled over to where the three of them stood and neatly slid her arm around one of Malachi's elbows as she insinuated herself into the circle. "I've been looking everywhere for you."

Apparently *everywhere* meant the wardrobe and bureau drawers. Not only had Katie donned a new dress, but she'd put her hair up. And Emma was pretty sure she smelled rose water, as well.

Betty frowned. Malachi fidgeted. Emma fumed.

Why was she fuming? She tried to tell herself she was angry at Katie's flirtatious manner because it would likely get Malachi into trouble, but she feared it was Mal's slowness in disengaging the other woman from his arm that had her hackles up. Which made no sense. She didn't have a claim on Malachi, at least not a romantic one. They shared a bond forged in childhood, a powerful friendship, but it was nothing more than that. It couldn't be. She had her work with the women's colony. He had his demolition job with the railroads. No two paths could be more divergent.

Katie scooted even closer, leaning in toward Malachi until her skirts pressed against his legs. In the process, she bumped against the burlap sack he carried.

"Careful, miss." Mal finally found his voice. And his feet, thank heavens. He sidled away from Katie and held the sack between them as a buffer. "I wouldn't want you to soil your dress."

Katie wrinkled her nose as if only just noticing the stained burlap. "What is it?"

"Turpentine." Malachi looked to Betty. "Wanted to see if you recognized the canister. We found it by the garden this morning. It might have been used to start the fire. It's possible that whoever lit the blaze stole the stuff from somewhere close at hand, then left it behind. We're hoping that figuring out where he got it from will help us track his movements."

Betty frowned, but made no effort to deny that the turpentine might be hers. "Well, let's take a look-see, then."

Malachi opened the sack and pulled out the dented, slightly rusted can. "This look familiar?"

Betty leaned closer to examine it. "Could be. Only one way to tell for sure. We need to check the supplies in the barn. See if ours is missing." Swinging her shotgun off her shoulder to clasp it across her body in a more ready position, Betty pivoted and started marching toward the barn. Malachi and Emma followed.

Katie hesitated for a moment, then hurried after them. "Wait," she called, her voice suddenly void of all flirtatious tones. "Are you saying that man was *here*? On our farm?"

Emma halted then retreated a few steps to intercept Katie while the others continued on. Hating the fear she saw etched in the young woman's face, Emma set aside her earlier frustration and laid a comforting hand on Katie's arm. "We don't know he was here, Katie. We don't even know that the turpentine we found came from Betty's farm."

"But if it *is* ours, that means he was here, right? Here. Where we sleep. Three women alone." The poor girl was shaking in earnest now.

Emma wrapped an arm around Katie's shoulders. "We don't know that. Someone else could have borrowed the turpentine and forgotten to return it. There are a hundred different explanations."

Katie looked directly into Emma's eyes. "But you don't believe any of those other explanations, do you?"

Emma sighed. "To be honest, Katie. I don't know what to believe right now. Mr. Shaw found that turpentine and is determined to learn where it came from. He believes it can help us figure out how the man is stirring up trouble in town without our being alerted. If we can unravel his methods, we can take steps to stop him. That's the plan, anyway."

Katie nodded. "I understand. I just . . ." She glanced past Emma to the barn and bit her lip. "His attacks always seemed to happen in other areas of the town. Not where I lived. It was easier to pretend the threat wasn't real when it was distant. Now it's here."

Emma rubbed Katie's arm, trying to reassure even as she battled her own apprehension. "I'm sure Betty would understand if you wanted to move into town until this is over. The boardinghouse is full, but there are rooms above the café that aren't in use. It's right next door to Victoria's store. You might feel safer there."

Katie started shaking her head before Emma finished. "No.

I'll not leave Betty and Helen out here alone." The change in her was swift. Gone was the panic-stricken girl, and in her place was a determined, loyal young woman. "Helen might be willing to come to town with me, but Betty will never leave her hens. She's too stubborn. We'll face whatever comes just like you're always telling us to do, Miss Chandler. Together."

"Good for you." Emma's chest swelled with pride. Perhaps she really *was* making a difference with these women. She gave Katie's arm a brisk pat, then turned to face the barn once again. "Shall we go see what they've discovered?"

Katie nibbled her lip again but nodded as she lifted her chin. "Yes."

13

It took nearly three hours for Emma and Malachi to make the rounds to all the residents of Harper's Station. By the time they'd made it back to the boardinghouse, most of the ladies there had already moved on to their usual duties—Grace to the telegraph office, Flora and Esther to the gardens, Daisy and her young roommate, Pauline, to the sewing circle. They'd spoken to the boardinghouse proprietress, Stella Grimes, and then worked their way through town, stopping at the store and the medical clinic before working back toward the garden, the station house where the quilters were working in the aunts' parlor, and finally the telegraph office.

Eager to get all the random pieces of information out of her head and down onto paper so she could organize them, Emma led Malachi to the bank and showed him to her office.

"So this is where you work," Mal said as he followed her through the doorway and walked about the office. He ran a hand along the scalloped corner of her desk and the base of the hand-painted desk lamp sitting there. His rough fingers looked strange against the delicate rose pattern, but this room had never anticipated hosting such a masculine guest.

Had he been the tailored sort she was accustomed to seeing in a bank office, men in striped suits with slender hands and short-trimmed hair, he might have fit in. But Malachi was no tailored dandy. His scuffed boots testified to the physical labor he performed. Broken-in denim trousers hugged slim hips that looked right at home beneath his holster and gun belt. His blue cotton shirt, black worsted vest, and black Stetson could have belonged to a hundred different cowboys, yet somehow they seemed suited only to him. Malachi Shaw exuded rugged masculinity in this lacy woman's room the way a cougar would exude sleek power standing in a field of wildflowers. Both seemingly out of place, yet both so confident in who they were that their surroundings held no sway.

Malachi strolled from her desk across the room to examine the bookshelf that stood out from the cream-colored walls papered in a faint scroll pattern. The shelves held her ledgers, several financial treatises she'd inherited from her father, a few newer books she'd purchased herself, and a trio of framed photographs prominently displayed on the second shelf from the top. The photograph on the left depicted her parents holding her as a baby. The one on the right showed the aunts as much younger women in front of their home in Gainesville. And the photograph she most prized . . . she and Malachi as children, standing behind the aunts, who were seated in matching parlor chairs—Henry looking so serious and stoic, Bertie with her soft smile, Malachi looking stiff and uncomfortable, and she . . . Well, she wasn't looking at the camera at all. She was looking at Malachi, a devilish gleam in her eye as if she were determined to goad a smile out of him.

It had been taken the summer before Malachi left, and it had kept her company all these years. Now seeing him pause to stare at it—his hand arrested in midair above it as if he'd been temporarily frozen by the memory of that day—Emma's breath caught. Dragonflies flitted about in her stomach, the tickling commotion making her light-headed.

"I have a copy, too," he said softly. "In my trunk."

In his trunk. Hidden away. Forgotten?

The tickling in her stomach dimmed, as if the dragonflies had suddenly been drenched with molasses. Their wings heavy. Their bodies falling.

"I keep it in that stationery box you gave me when I left . . . along with your letters." Malachi's back was to her, but his deep voice resonated through the room, through her. His near-reverent tone restored the tickle inside her and increased the fluttering tenfold.

He'd kept her letters. Dared she hope they were precious to him, preserved so that he might savor them on days he was feeling lonely? That's what she did with his letters, after all. Pulled them out of the old hatbox she kept on the top shelf of her wardrobe and read them late at night by the light of her bedside lamp. Remembered the boy he'd been. Imagined the man he'd become. Imagined him walking back into her life one day.

And now he was here. Here to rescue her, to be her champion, just as he'd always been.

No, not *her* champion. The colony's champion. He was here for Harper's Station, not for her. Dwelling on old girlish feelings and dreams would serve no purpose. She had a job to do. A colony to protect.

A heart to protect, too, a small voice whispered inside her head. *Remember, he'll be leaving.*

Just then, Mal turned. Determined to handle this as any other business deal, Emma pasted on her best banker's smile and waved toward one of the two vacant chairs sitting in front of her desk. "Have a seat. I'd thought I'd make some notes as we sift through what we learned this morning."

Mal shook his head. "No thanks. I think better when I'm moving."

"All right." Emma circled around to her own chair, sat down, and retrieved a few sheets of paper from the top desk drawer. Pen in hand, she dipped the nib into her inkwell and wrote the word *Turpentine* at the top left of the page. "So let's start with the turpentine. Betty identified the canister as belonging to the farm, which means she, Katie, and Helen all had access to it."

Mal paced toward the window. "But the women who work the garden stopped by a few days ago to collect a couple barrows full of compost for fertilizing. It would have been a simple matter for one of them to sneak into the barn, grab the turpentine, and hide it under the compost."

"But that's made with chicken droppings." Emma wrinkled her nose. She couldn't imagine concealing something in manure. One would have to actually touch the stuff.

Malachi chuckled. "You're such a girl, Em. Don't you see? That's what makes it the perfect hiding place. Guaranteed to repel inquisitive ladies."

"I can't argue with that." Emma twisted back around in her chair and inked her pen again. "All right. I'll add Flora and Esther."

"Any on the list so far you think we can rule out?" Mal asked as he paced along the inner wall. He paused to peruse the needlework sampler hanging near her desk, though she doubted he actually read the verse Bertie had stitched. His attention seemed too internal, too contemplative.

Emma glanced at her list of names and tried to be as objective as possible. Even though she'd lectured Malachi on assuming innocence, she knew she couldn't blindly trust her emotions. She had to examine every possibility, no matter how unpalatable.

"The only person I feel completely confident about removing is Betty. She's been with me nearly as long as Tori, and she seemed completely straightforward when we asked her about the turpentine. I would think a guilty person would try to avert suspicion by pointing the finger elsewhere or fabricating excuses. She did none of that.

"Besides, I can't imagine some outlaw manipulating her. She's as tough as they come. She doesn't have children or other family the man could use as leverage against her. That was the reason she joined us in the first place. She had no one left to care for after her husband died, no purpose. Taking in lost young women, teaching them to find their inner strength, and showing them they have value has become her mission. I can't imagine her jeopardizing that."

"Yeah, she didn't really strike me as the furtive type." Malachi rubbed a hand over his jaw. His still-whiskered jaw. He'd taken his turn with the bathing tub last night—they all had after getting covered in soot and mud while fighting the fire—but he'd foregone shaving this morning, too intent on examining the area around the church before the sun had fully risen.

What would he look like without the stubble? Less outlaw and more gentleman? Somehow she doubted it. Malachi had always possessed an edge, a touch of wildness that came from surviving on his own for so long. A shave and fancy clothes wouldn't tame him. Nothing would. Not completely.

Emma cleared her throat and ordered her thoughts back to her list. "Katie seemed genuinely upset by the prospect of our attacker nosing around the farm. I don't think it likely that she's involved, either, but I can't be certain."

Malachi walked around the front side of her desk and clasped the back of one of the chairs she had offered him earlier. His arms stiff, he leaned forward and met her gaze. "What about Helen? I didn't actually meet her when we were at the chicken farm."

Emma had to glance away from the shining chocolate brown of his eyes. Staring into them was far too distracting. "Helen goes out of her way to avoid men. She chose to work for Betty so she could be removed from town, from the chance of encountering Mr. Porter or any other man who might wander in unexpectedly. She only attends church because it is required of all the ladies who live in Harper's Station, but she sits sandwiched between Betty and Katie the whole time and leaves before the last amen fades from the rafters. I don't believe she's said a single word to Brother Garrett since she's been here, and he's about as harmless as they come."

Mal levered himself back up to a full standing position, though his hands still grasped the chairback. "So she's a viable candidate."

Emma frowned. "You don't think the fact that she's terrified of men precludes her involvement?"

Mal shrugged. "Maybe. But she's secretive. A loner. Skilled at avoiding people. That would make stealing the turpentine an easy matter. Besides, fear is a powerful motivator. Perhaps she's terrified of men because she's being controlled by one. Or maybe it's not men she's afraid of but people from outside the community. People who might recognize her and question her reason for being here."

Emma's stomach cramped. She hated this. Hated questioning the motives of women she considered family. Hated imagining the worst when her natural inclination was to hope for the best and do everything in her power to bring about favorable outcomes. But to find a favorable outcome in this situation, she had to suspect the worst of her neighbors, her friends. Only one morning in and it was already wearing her down.

"Hey." Mal's voice rumbled close to her ear.

When had he come around the desk?

His hand settled on her shoulder, the warmth from his fingers

132

passing through the edge of the puffed sleeve to travel down the length of her arm. "I know this isn't pleasant, Em, but I need a basic understanding of who the residents are. If it's too upsetting for you, I can ask the aunts instead."

"No. I'm fine. Really." She managed a small smile. "I want to do this. It's my responsibility. It's just disheartening to look at the people I love through such a suspicious lens."

"Until I met you, that was the only lens I knew existed." The soft words shot straight through her heart, but before she could respond, he patted her shoulder and stepped away. "Tell me about the garden ladies."

"The . . . um . . . garden . . . yes." *Good grief, Emma. Get your head on straight. He's going to think you a complete ninny.* "That would be Flora and Esther."

Mal looked at her a bit oddly but thankfully made no comment about her scatterbrained recital. Then he frowned slightly. "Didn't you tell me Flora was the one who encouraged everyone to leave after the shooting at the church? Seems her goal and the goal of the attacker line up pretty well."

"Perhaps," Emma conceded, "but she wasn't the only one eager for people to leave. Many others voiced the same concerns. And why wouldn't they? The man *shot* at them. Any sane person would consider leaving to be the safer option. I, myself, encouraged many of the women to leave."

Mal rubbed his chin. "Okay, but if you combine her desire to get people out of town with her familiarity with the garden area, which is where I found the turpentine, that give us more than ample reason to add her to the suspect list."

"I suppose." Emma underlined Flora's name, then moved her pen up to underline Helen's, as well. As she did so, another memory surfaced. "You know, Flora *was* reluctant to leave the site of the fire last night. And she was lingering around the garden fence."

"She could have been waiting for everyone to leave so she could retrieve the turpentine without witnesses," Malachi said. "You sending her back with Miss Adams foiled that plan."

"It's possible. But you didn't see her face, Mal." Emma thought back to her conversation with Flora. "Her eyes were dull, haunted, as if the fire had brought back terrible memories. I can only imagine what horrors Flora has seen in her lifetime." Emma glanced up to meet Malachi's gaze. "When she came to us, nearly three weeks ago now, she was bloodied and bruised and could barely walk.

"She stayed in the clinic with Maybelle for the first several days, too weak to do anything but recover. And that's not all." Emma lowered her voice even though no one was around to overhear. "Maybelle confided that she found evidence of old wounds. Scars and bones that hadn't been set correctly. You might have noticed the bump on Flora's nose and the way the little finger on her left hand is crooked at the end. Maybelle fears the woman has suffered abuse for a long time. Is it any wonder she spooks easily?"

Malachi blew out a breath and dropped his head forward. His knuckles turned white as his grip on the chairback grew forceful. "Any man who uses his fist on a woman deserves to be drawn and quartered." Slowly, he lifted his head. She sensed what was coming. His eyes glowed with apology. "As much as I hate what happened to her, I can't eliminate her as a suspect."

Emma nodded and tried to erase the acrid burn at the back of her throat by swallowing. Recalling Flora's battered body when she'd first stumbled into town always turned her stomach. Yet the reminder of her recent arrival brought another lady to mind. "Mal . . . we haven't discussed the other name that came up during our inquiries."

Malachi straightened, releasing the chairback as he paced a couple steps along the length of Emma's desk. "The first one on scene. The one who sounded the alarm."

Emma started a second column on her sheet of paper and underlined the name she'd just written. "Claire."

14

Mal paced the office as Emma went on to describe the newest addition to Harper's Station. He *had* to pace. Any time he settled too long in Emma's vicinity, he started thinking more about her and less about who the traitor might be. One would think that working with dynamite would teach a man better self-discipline.

He bit back a growl as he pushed a finger through the crevice in the lace curtains hanging over the window and pulled the right panel back. Everything looked quiet. The garden ladies were the only people outside, and even they would be breaking for lunch soon.

"Mal? Are you listening?" Emma's voice brought his head around with guilty speed.

"Sorry. Just wanted to check the street." He let the curtain drop back into place. "I heard you say Claire arrived the day before the fire, though. And since we don't have any evidence of a woman's involvement before then, her being the insider could make sense."

Emma nibbled on the end of her pen, her attention focused

on the ceiling, leaving him free to look his fill without being caught. Not that he would stare . . . Who was he kidding? Of course he would stare. He couldn't seem not to. The young girl he'd known had grown into a stunning woman—one he would only be with for a couple more days if he had any hope of making it back to the rail camp on time. So he stared. Memorizing the slender line of her neck, the way tiny tendrils of hair curled around the base of her skull, the way her nose scrunched around the edges when she disliked the direction her thoughts were leading her, as it did now.

"It's not just that Claire is young," she was saying, "it's that her story with Fischer checked out so completely. Mr. Porter confirmed that Stanley Fischer had indeed sent for a mail-order bride and that he threatened all kinds of retaliation against anyone who helped her back out of her obligation to him. The day after we took her in, Tori received a telegram informing her that Fischer's Emporium would no longer conduct business with the ladies of Harper's Station, nor would any other Seymour proprietor."

"And that same night, someone set the church on fire." Malachi strode past the bookshelf again, this time keeping his hands clasped behind his back so he wouldn't be tempted to finger the pictures she had on display there. Pictures of home. Or at least the closest thing he'd ever had to one. He cleared his throat. "Could be another level of revenge."

When he reached the front wall and pivoted to pace back toward the window, he caught Emma shaking her head. "Fischer has never approved of our colony, that's true, but if Claire is secretly working for him, that would mean he would have had to hire her to pose as his affianced bride, stage a big hoopla in Seymour about her rejecting him to get people to believe her dire straits, then send her here with a sob story and hope we would take her in. Yet threatening to cut off our business if we help her works completely against that aim. If he wanted Claire to infiltrate our colony, why would he take the risk of us turning her down in order to protect our current members' livelihoods?"

Mal paused a few steps from the window. "Maybe because he knows you're a woman of principle who will never turn away a female in need."

A laugh of disbelief burst through the room as if some little imp hiding under the desk had just popped an air-filled paper sack.

"Stanley Fischer?" Emma scoffed. "Believe me, the man doesn't consider women capable of high principles. Besides, he's not clever enough to pull off such an elaborate scheme. Especially when he could have suspended his business with us months ago without Claire even being in the picture. Not to mention the fact that I saw our attacker the day of the shooting, and he definitely was *not* Stanley Fischer."

"You said he wore a mask," Mal reminded her.

"Sure, but a bandana only hides the face, not the belly, and Fischer is rather well-endowed in that area."

Mal chuckled. Couldn't argue with that. The angry shop-keeper he'd tangled with back in Seymour had certainly had a hefty gut. And ego. He seemed more the type to bluster and growl than to coldly plan an elaborate subversion.

"Also . . ." Emma pointed her pen in Mal's direction, never one to let an advantage go unpressed. "Maybelle told us that *she* asked Claire to deliver Daisy's medication to the board-inghouse. Claire didn't volunteer to run the errand. She'd been busy washing their supper dishes at the time. So it was pure happenstance that Claire was the first one to discover the fire."

Turning around to face Emma fully, Mal reached behind him to find the windowsill and leaned back to use the edge of it like a seat. "I agree that she's not the most likely candidate, but her appearance right before the fire is too coincidental to completely ignore. I say we keep her on the list."

"Fine." Emma turned in her chair to face him, letting out a heavy sigh as she did so. "You know, this whole mess would be much easier to deal with if I just knew what the outlaw wanted. He obviously needs us gone for a reason, and I don't think it's simply because he feels threatened by a group of women living successfully on their own. He wants something here in Harper's Station. It's the only logical explanation for his persistence. But what is he after?"

"Is there anything special about the land itself?" Mal asked. "Water rights? Valuable mineral deposits? Any ore assays done by a previous owner?"

Emma shook her head, the toe of her shoe thumping the floor in a soft, staccato rhythm. "Not that I recall. The Wichita River flows along the northwest border of the property, but I don't own proprietary rights to it. I don't know of any ore or minerals that would be of particular value. We could check the county assay office to see if any claims have been filed for something in the surrounding area to be sure, but this is farm and ranch country, not mining country. And if what he wanted was the land, why not just approach me with an offer to buy?"

"Maybe he can't afford to pay full price. Maybe he's hoping that if he scares you and the others away, you'll be eager to make a deal so you can make a fresh start somewhere else." Mal crossed his arms over his chest and braced the heels of his boots out in front of him.

"But why does he want *this* land so badly?" Emma laid down her pen and pushed to her feet. "There is other property for sale nearby, undeveloped, but cheaper, if that is what he needs."

Apparently it was her turn to pace. He smiled until he realized her direction. Directly toward him. Leaving him trapped against the window. If he jumped to his feet and moved away, he'd offend her for sure. Willing his body to remain still even though every muscle tensed at her approach, he forced himself to continue breathing at a steady rate.

In. Out.

She came alongside him, close enough to touch if he unlaced his arms. Malachi immediately tightened his hold on his ribs.

In. Out. In . . .

Drat! He could smell her. Or the lilac bath salts she'd washed in last night. The smell had lingered in the small room off the kitchen when he'd finally taken his turn in the tub. He'd never washed so fast in his life, needing to get away from thoughts of Emma in a tub of scented water, wearing absolutely noth—

Malachi jerked away from the window. And Emma. "I need to go."

Emma's forehead crinkled. "Go? Go where?"

Where, indeed. He didn't have a clue. *Away* was at the top of the list. He could figure out the rest later. He didn't slow down to discuss possibilities, just made a beeline for the door.

"Did you think of something?"

He could hear the soft *click* of her footsteps. Following. His pulse flickered. His stride stretched.

Yet her question sparked an idea just as he reached the doorway. He grabbed the jamb with one hand and glanced back. "I'm going to wire the county land office. See if they have any assay records on file."

"Do you want me to co—?"

"Nope." Heaven save him. That was the last thing he wanted. Okay, it was actually the *first* thing he wanted. Wanted it so bad it made him ache. Which was exactly why he needed to get away.

But as he pivoted to make his escape, he saw her face fall. Saw the hurt in her eyes. It was the same look she'd worn the day he left ten years ago. A look that haunted him still. "I'll catch up with you in the old café building after lunch, all right?" he promised. "For the town meeting."

Her lips curved upward in a smile that didn't quite reach her eyes. "Sure." She nodded to him. "I'll just stay here and write up a few more notes while things are fresh on my mind."

Feeling like a heel but not trusting himself enough to stay, Mal slapped his palm against the doorjamb, fingered his hat brim in a show of respect, and turned tail and ran.

Right into an ambush.

They came from the east. Two riders. Masked. Armed.

Mal reached for his Colt. Gunfire erupted before he cleared leather. He ducked, instinct taking over. A bullet whizzed by his head. Another hit the ground near his feet. Another shattered the window behind him.

A woman screamed.

Emma! Had she been hit?

Hot rage seared through him as he scrambled for cover. They weren't shooting high this time. And neither was he.

Darting around the corner of the bank building, Malachi returned fire. Or tried to. The barrage of bullets slamming into the brick around him made it impossible to get a clear shot. He had to settle for aiming in the riders' general vicinity and firing blindly at the moving targets.

He emptied his revolver, pressed his back against the side of the building, and grabbed fresh ammunition from his gun belt. A couple more shots ricocheted off the brick as the horses passed his position. The rider closest to him turned around in the saddle. Dark eyes glowed above the mask. Hard. Determined. He raised his gun arm.

Ah, crud. Mal rolled to the side. The bullet struck the wall right where he'd been standing.

"Yah!" The outlaw spurred his horse to a gallop. His partner did the same, firing a few last shots into the air as he went.

Malachi shoved bullets into their chambers as fast as his shaking fingers would allow. He had to go after them. Had to stop them.

Gun loaded, he stepped out in front of the bank and took aim at the larger man's back. A woman's scream from somewhere up ahead rent the air just before he squeezed the trigger. The outlaw dropped low in the saddle. Mal's shot missed.

He took aim again, but the riders raced out of range, flying past the garden and the church and disappearing into the brush.

They were headed for the river. Mal's blood pumped through his veins with painful urgency. He had to get them back in sight. Now. He wouldn't be able to track them if they got to the water. He holstered his weapon and dashed in front of the bank, his gaze narrowing in on the station house behind the telegraph office. He needed his horse. He stretched his legs to run, but broken glass crunched under his boots, sending shards of another sort slashing through his chest.

How could he have forgotten?

"Emma!" The wounded roar rasped against his throat. He dug in his heels and changed direction. Fluttering curtains and jagged glass obscured his vision through the window, so he lunged for the door. Yet just as he reached for the handle, it swung away from him.

"Malachi! Oh, thank God you're all right." Emma stumbled through the doorway.

Malachi braced himself and even went so far as to open his arms a bit, but she didn't throw herself against him. Didn't rush to him for comfort. He should feel relieved that he didn't have to put up with the emotional display, the confining touch, the ill-practiced awkwardness that always beset him when someone tried to show him affection. Yet he didn't feel any of those things. What washed over him was disappointment.

142

She reached a hand out, as if to touch him. Tear tracks marked her cheeks, red rimmed her beautiful eyes. "I was so afraid."

Of course she was afraid. The fiends had shot up her office with her inside. It still scorched his hide to think of what damage they could have wrought. Mal grabbed on to her hand, squeezing it tight. "It's all right, Em. They're gone."

"But you . . . You're not hurt. Right?" Her gaze raked over him, searching for proof of his health. "I was so afraid you'd been shot."

That's why she'd been afraid? Why she'd been crying? For *him*?

Mal longed to examine that truth more closely. To examine *Emma* more closely. But he didn't have time. He had a pair of villains to track down.

"You're not hurt, are you?" he asked, his voice more gruff than it should have been.

She shook her head. "No. I . . . I'm fine."

He squeezed her fingers one more time then met her gaze. "I have to go after them."

Her shoulders lifted, and her chin came up. "I know." She released his hand.

Mal didn't hesitate. He couldn't. Not if he wanted to keep her safe. So he left her standing there and sprinted across the street.

"You better come back to me, Malachi Shaw," she ordered from behind him, her voice loud and strong.

Mal's feet churned up the dirt beneath him, but his lips twitched into a smile. His bossy little angel was back.

15

When Malachi reached the station house, he sprinted through the barn, grabbed a lead line, and jogged into the corral. As he strode toward the three spooked horses running back and forth along the far fence, he curled his tongue, tightened his lips, and let out the piercing whistle that never failed to bring Ulysses racing to his side.

Unfortunately, Ulysses was still in Montana. His rented nag paid no heed to the signal, too frenzied by the recent gunfire to do anything but buck and dance around the enclosure.

Malachi gritted his teeth. He didn't have time for this.

"Easy." As he approached the gray mare, Mal kept his voice low and his movements slow despite the urgency in his gut that screamed at him to hurry. "Time to take a little ride. You want to run, don'tcha?"

He opened his arms wide and stepped closer. The mare snorted and jerked her head but didn't flee. Mal said a quick prayer of thanks as he cupped a hand over the gray's nose. "That's my girl," he cooed.

The horse might not be as well trained as Ulysses, but she

knew her job. Her tail flicked and her withers trembled as she fought the remains of her distress and submitted to his touch.

Mal attached the lead line and, using the bottom fence rail as a step, swung up onto the horse's bare back. The nag sidestepped a bit but settled quickly enough. "Easy, now," Mal urged. He didn't have time to fetch a saddle or bridle. They were going to have to do this with a halter and one rein. Nothing he hadn't done with Ulysses in the past, but a daunting process with an untried horse. Directing was no problem. But getting the beast to stop? Well, Mal just hoped whoever had trained the mare had taught her to heed the rider's leg and seat signals. If not, he'd most likely be walking home. With a passel of new bruises.

"I've got the gate, Malachi!" Aunt Henry waved at him from the edge of the corral and swung the gate outward.

Thankful she'd had the gumption to leave the house and lend a hand, Mal scraped his heels against the horse's sides and lurched for the opening.

"Go get those scoundrels!" she called as he raced past.

He didn't answer. Just bent low over the mare's neck and galloped toward the river.

Two hours later, Emma stood at the café window, nibbling on the edge of her thumb as she watched for Malachi's return. Ladies trailed past her a few at a time, taking the seats she had set out earlier after she'd swept up the broken glass in her office and on the walkway outside the bank. Everyone was gathering for the town meeting. A meeting Malachi was supposed to run.

So where was he?

A hand touched her shoulder, and Emma twisted her neck to see Victoria eying her with sympathy. "I'm sure he's fine," her friend said. "Maybe he managed to trail them back to their hideout, and by this time tomorrow, it will all be over."

Emma tried to grasp the hope Tori offered, but it was like trying to capture a handful of water. All but the tiniest bit leaked out around the edges of her fist. She clung to the few drops that lingered behind, wanting desperately to drink them in. Yet they disappeared almost instantly in the desert of her worry.

Surely he wouldn't have tried to bring in two men by himself. Would he? She'd caught a glimpse of the masked outlaws through her broken window as they rode past the bank. The first man was the same rider she'd seen before. She was certain. A formidable foe on his own, but with a partner? A shiver danced along Emma's nape. Malachi only had his six-shooter with him. She'd spotted rifles in boots on both of the outlaws' saddles in addition to their revolvers. They had Mal outmanned and outgunned. When he'd gone searching for a trail after the fire, he'd told her he only intended to scout the location of the hideout so he could report back to the sheriff and bring in reinforcements. But if the outlaws discovered Mal on their trail, there was nothing to stop them from ambushing him.

"Come on, Em." Tori took hold of her arm and not-so-gently steered her away from the window. "Worrying won't bring him back any faster."

"No." Sudden purpose steeled her spine. "But going after him will."

She broke away from Tori's grasp, ignoring her friend's sputtering protests, and marched straight over to Betty Cooper, uncaring of the curious glances she collected along the way. "Did you bring your shotgun, Betty?"

The farm woman pushed to her feet and grabbed the double barrels lying on the floor beneath her chair. "You bet. After the shenanigans this morning, I think I might just sleep with this thing under my pillow." The women seated around her giggled, but their nervous glances to the window and back made it clear they knew the jest wasn't much of an exaggeration. Emma fully expected all the women would be sleeping with weapons close at hand this night, even if they had to resort to cast-iron skillets and hat pins.

"Come with me," Emma ordered. "We need to go after Malachi. He's been gone too long." Her teeth sank into her bottom lip as her gaze darted back to the open doorway. "He may need our help. He could be injured or . . . or . . . captured. I've got horses at the station house. We can be saddled and ready to go in fifteen minutes."

"No call to go hurrying off like some flibbertigibbet," Aunt Henry groused from her position at the front of the room. "The boy can take care of himself."

"Against *two* armed outlaws?" Emma couldn't believe her aunt could be so cavalier. This was Malachi's life they were talking about. "He risked his life going after those men. To protect *us*." She swept an arm out to encompass everyone assembled in the café. "Only a featherbrained coward," she said, borrowing one of her aunt's favorite expressions to describe females who didn't agree with her position on suffrage, "would sit by and do nothing when the man protecting her could be hurt or worse." Though Emma adamantly refused to think about what *worse* could mean. "I owe him better than that."

"He's *fine*, Emma," Henry insisted.

Emma fought the urge to grab the nearest unoccupied chair and hurl it at her aunt's head. "You don't know that."

"'Course I do."

How could she possibly . . . ?

"He just rode up," her aunt announced, a smug smile on her face that didn't completely hide the compassion lingering in her eyes.

Emma spun around, her breath catching in her throat as she glimpsed the truth of her aunt's words for herself. Malachi was striding down the road, the gray mare following obediently behind.

She rushed outside and leaned over the boardwalk railing. "Malachi. Are you all . . ."

His hat brim lifted, and her words died. She'd never seen such anger in his eyes. Such a hard, glittering determination. His jaw ticked as he flicked the mare's lead line around the hitching post and stomped up the café's stairs.

"Inside," he growled as he tromped past, leaving her gaping slack-jawed after him.

He'd never snapped orders at her before. Yet, their lives had never been in imminent danger before, either.

And truth to tell, deep inside, there was a part of her that sagged in relief at his taking charge. Just for a little while. These were still her ladies, her colony, but being responsible for their protection when she was facing an enemy she didn't understand and a fight she didn't know how to win had eroded her confidence until she was little more than a pile of ruins. Her pillar might continue to stand stalwartly in the wind, yet without roof and walls, it offered little shelter against the storm.

Malachi offered shelter. Strength. Protection. For all of them. So she trailed after him without a word and moved to stand next to Tori near the window at the back of the room.

"I apologize for my tardiness, ladies," he said, nodding at Maybelle and Claire, who ducked through the doorway just as he turned to face the gathering. Not waiting for them to find a seat, he plunged ahead. "But I have some information that you'll want to hear."

"Did ya find where them scallywags are holed up?" Betty's question boomed through the room. "My rig's hitched and ready. I'll gladly go fetch Sheriff Tabor."

Several of the ladies murmured assent, looking to one another with bright eyes filled with hope.

"I found evidence of two different camps," Malachi said, his deep voice rumbling with an authority that hushed the ladies at once and drew all attention to him. "Neither of which has been used in at least a week."

Emma didn't like the grim set of his mouth or the way his gaze found hers and seemed to impale her against the back wall, as if she should understand the significance of a pair of abandoned campsites. Straightening away from the wall, she raised her chin. Emma hated to admit ignorance, but this was no time to protect her pride. Protecting her ladies came first.

She took a breath. "What, exactly, does that mean?"

"It means," Mal said, "that the man is smart. He's moving his camp from place to place so he can't be pinned down. It also means he's been here a while. Most likely quite a while, planning, preparing . . . watching."

An icy shiver danced over Emma's skin. How long had he been out there? Watching. Plotting. Growing impatient.

"Unfortunately, the outlaws had too big a lead for me to catch up to them." He was focused on the seated females now, most likely searching their faces for a reaction to his news that the men had gotten away. Emma wanted to probe them, too, so she left Tori and meandered up along the edge of the room, keeping her back to the side wall. Profiles gave little away, though, and she didn't dare make her intentions too obvious.

"Once I got to the river," Mal continued, "there was no sign of them, either to the east or west. I combed the banks on both sides looking for fresh tracks. Found nothing but a single track on the west side. Which means they probably split up, and one is better at disguising his tracks than the other."

Emma watched the women on her list. Claire fidgeted in her seat. Flora stared at her lap. Helen reached for Katie's hand and squeezed it. All acted nervous, but none stood out. Not in a room where stress and anxiety hovered over the crowd like a swarm of angry bees.

A movement to Emma's right brought her head around. Tori.

Emma released a breath. Her friend had come up beside her while she'd been scrutinizing the seated ladies. She gave Emma a penetrating look, one that promised there would be questions to answer later, then turned to face the front. "Could there be more men out there that we haven't seen yet? Until today we've assumed the threat came from a single man. Now we've seen two."

That muscle in Malachi's jaw ticked again. "I can't say with certainty, but I don't believe there are more. The camps I found were small and spread out. If there were more men, the individual camps would be clumped together to enhance communication, not half a mile apart. No, I think we're looking at a small operation, but a savvy one. The fact that the man revealed the ace up his sleeve—a second man—means we're running out of time."

"Running out of time before what?" Betty demanded.

Malachi scowled, ran a hand over his face. "Before he decides he needs more than scare tactics to get what he wants."

A murmur arose in the room as the ladies turned to one another in shared concern, but Malachi's sharp voice cut them off with all the efficiency of a butcher's cleaver taking off a squawking chicken's head. "Stop!"

All tongues froze. All eyes zeroed in on the man at the front of the room.

"You don't have time to chatter and fret. Not if we're going to make a stand. Today he came after me, foolishly believing I was his only threat." Mal's hard gaze scoured each face in the room, then came to rest on Emma. "He was wrong."

Emma sucked in a breath, her heart fluttering in a way that had nothing to do with fear.

Mal turned back to the room at large. "We have an army that outnumbers his forces. An army of strong, capable women who are ready to fight for their homes. All you need is a little organization and training. That starts now." His voice brooked no argument, and none was forthcoming. In fact, several women sat straighter in their seats, squared their shoulders, and set their chins.

They were magnificent! Each and every one of them.

"Emma."

She snapped her gaze to Malachi at the sound of her name spoken in his commanding tones.

"Fetch my rifle and saddlebags from the barn." She started moving for the door as he turned his attention back to the women. "Betty. Grace. Come to the front. No female is going to leave this room until she can properly hold and load a weapon. And the minute the new shipment Miss Adams ordered arrives, we'll begin target practice."

Emma paused in the doorway, glancing back to catch Mal's eye one more time. Needing him to see her gratitude, her faith in him, her admiration as he single-handedly turned a gaggle of frightened geese into would-be tigresses.

He nodded to her, the movement of his jaw firm, convicted. "They won't catch us off guard again."

16

After retrieving the rifle, Emma retreated into the background, insisting that the other ladies be instructed first. Malachi's air of authority calmed their nerves for the most part, though it was his patience that kept them from getting flustered. He didn't allow them room for squeamishness but neither did he raise his voice when they made a misstep or heave a frustrated breath when he had to repeat himself, which he did . . . often. Even when Helen wanted no part in the training—or, more accurately, no involvement with Malachi—he kept a lid on his temper. He simply walked across the room to Betty, handed her the rifle, shooed the man-shy Helen toward her supervisor, and temporarily took over shotgun lessons.

By the time the café cleared out, each of the women had an idea of which type of weapon they would feel most comfortable using and which would be best suited for each situation. Rifles for longer distance, as when the newly paired partners would be on watch, and handguns for personal protection in closer quarters. After observing Malachi's instruction for several hours, Emma could easily recite the differences between the shells of a breech-loading shotgun, the side-feeding cartridges of the repeating rifle, and the bullets that fit within the round chambers of the Colt Army Revolver without error. She was doing just that, internally, when Betty and Grace took their leave. Anxious to prove to Malachi that she'd been paying close attention, she held her hand out to accept the revolver. Yet when he set it in her palm, the weight of it took her by surprise.

"Use two hands," Mal instructed, reaching for her left hand and positioning it beneath her right. "It will steady your aim and keep your arm from getting fatigued."

Emma nodded and firmed up her grip, but the moment his hand brushed hers, her insides started trembling.

For heaven's sake! What was wrong with her? He'd done the exact same thing with each of the other ladies he tutored this afternoon. The touch was purely instructional. Not personal.

There was no reason for her to feel shivery all over, or for her stomach to flip just because he moved behind her to help her take the proper stance. And her lungs had absolutely no excuse for running so shallow when his front pressed against her back and his arms stretched along the length of hers. Nor did her heart need to suddenly start throbbing in reaction to his warm breath fanning over her cheek while his bristled jaw scraped ever-so-lightly against her skin.

"Fit your finger to the trigger," he murmured low against her ear.

Was it her imagination, or did his voice sound huskier than it had a minute before? Probably her imagination. Heaven knew the rest of her other senses were going berserk. It would be a shame for her ears to be left out.

"Now . . . squeeze." The whispered command nearly melted her insides.

She obeyed and slowly moved her finger, but her eyes slid

closed at the same time as she leaned just the tiniest bit back against his chest. His firm . . . strong . . . warm chest.

Click.

The sound made her jerk. Malachi had emptied the chambers, so no bullet had fired, but the quiet tick shattered the silence . . . and the illusion of intimacy she had let herself sink into. *Good grief.* She was acting worse than Katie, leaning into Mal as if she were some man-starved flirt instead of a woman on a mission to learn how to protect herself and those she cared about.

She stiffened and straightened away from Malachi's all-too-pleasant physique, letting her arms drop in the process. Emma expected Mal to step away, give her one of those horrible I'm-disappointed-in-you looks, then lecture her on the importance of focusing on the task at hand.

He didn't. Instead, his arms lingered over hers, even as they hung at her sides. His hands did eventually move, but not away. No, they traced upward along her sleeves and then curled around her upper arms in a near embrace.

His face stayed bent against hers, as well, almost as if . . . Emma swallowed. Almost as if he was contemplating nuzzling her neck.

Her pulse stuttered even as she told herself she was mistaken. Malachi had been nothing but professional with all the other ladies. She was misinterpreting things.

But it didn't feel like a misinterpretation. Alone in the café. His hands holding her. His body close. His whiskers rasping gently against her sensitive skin.

"Next time . . ." His voice rumbled in a deep octave that did odd things to her midsection. "Keep your eyes open when you pull the trigger."

She should have been embarrassed, chagrined that he'd noticed her shameful lack of concentration, but she just couldn't summon a proper dose of regret. Not when he was so close.

Holding her. Nuzzling her neck. For he *was* nuzzling. She could feel the edge of his nose against her nape, his lips a hairsbreadth away from her skin.

If she turned her head a few inches . . . But she was afraid to move. Afraid to ruin the moment. The sensations flooding her were too extraordinary. Too wonderful.

"I will," she breathed.

"Will what?" he asked, his whiskers brushing against her earlobe and sending shivers dancing down her back.

"Keep my eyes open." Though at the moment her eyelids were drooping dangerously. She wanted nothing more than to let them slide closed and lean her head back against his shoulder. "When I shoot."

He froze. His lips hovered just above the sensitive part of her neck that clamored for his attention.

No! Emma could have bitten her tongue off in that moment. She never should have reminded him of the shooting lessons, of the gun. But she hadn't been thinking clearly. Her mind had been so deliciously fuzzy, thinking only of the man behind her, that the words had just slipped out. And now he was pulling away from her.

The warmth of his breath on her neck disappeared first, then the heat from his chest on her back as he stepped away. He released his hold on her arms and moved around to stand in front of her.

Wrapping his right hand around hers, he trapped the revolver between them. He raised the weapon slowly, his darkly intense gaze boring into hers as he placed the pistol's barrel flush against his own chest.

"What are you . . . ?" Emma struggled to pull the gun away, unable to bear the thought of Malachi being on the receiving end of a bullet. Especially one she was responsible for. She didn't care that the gun wasn't loaded. The horrible thoughts running through her head played havoc with that truth. What if he had missed a chamber somehow when he'd removed the ammunition? If the gun went off, he couldn't survive a shot at such close range.

"Stop it, Mal. This isn't funny." She tugged on the gun again, but his arm didn't budge.

"You need to be ready, Em." His voice came out hard, yet there was a sadness in his eyes that disturbed her far more. "If this man attacks you, you can't hesitate. Aim at the widest target, his torso, and pull the trigger."

Her heart thudded so hard in her chest it hurt. He squeezed her hand, and for a moment she thought her worst nightmare was about to come true—that he would force her finger back against the trigger. She shook her head. Tears leaked from the corners of her eyes. "Don't," she whispered.

He didn't. But neither did he let her release the gun. It was almost as if he thought she needed protection from *him*.

She narrowed her gaze and tipped her chin sideways. *What's going on in that head of yours, Malachi Shaw?* Did he think that what had happened between them a moment ago had proved him untrustworthy? A threat? Nothing could be further from the truth. Under his touch, she'd felt not only safe but cherished. As if she weren't alone in her mission. As if she had a partner to lean on. One who cared for her first and her responsibilities second.

No wonder she'd felt weightless and light-headed. It was a wonder she hadn't floated right off the floor to bump against the ceiling. For a few stolen moments, he'd released her from the burden of duty. It was a gift she needed to repay.

"I trust you, Mal." She held his gaze, urging him to see the confidence she had in him, not only in dealing with the outlaws but in dealing with what was flaring between them.

His brown eyes softened just a little, but then he blinked

and looked away. "I won't always be there, Em," he said, finally relaxing his grip on her hands and taking the gun from her.

Malachi stepped past to lay the pistol on the table behind her. An icy tremor coursed over her arms and shoulders, causing her to twitch and wrap her arms about herself for comfort. It was going to take some strong tea and an even stronger mind to keep from having nightmares about that gun pointed at Mal's chest. She prayed she never saw such a sight again.

"Here." Malachi handed her the rifle, the intimate huskiness gone from his voice. Nothing but cool, businesslike precision remained. "Show me how to load it, and then we'll work on your stance."

Emma swallowed her disappointment and gave him a quick nod. Time to take up the mantle of responsibility again. Collecting the first cartridge, she mimicked what she'd seen the other ladies do and fed it into the Winchester's receiver. She pushed it into the magazine with her thumb, ignoring the pinch both in the pad of her finger and in her heart as she reached for the next cartridge.

With grim determination, Malachi saw to the rest of Emma's training without a repeat of the disaster with the revolver. When she demonstrated sufficient capability with the rifle, he'd praised her efforts and then taken his weapons and left, using the same excuse he'd employed that morning. Sending a telegram. He'd never gotten around to wiring the county land office earlier, thanks to the outlaws' interruption, so it gave him a legitimate reason to leave—one more palatable than the truth—that he didn't trust himself alone with her.

He never should have held her so close, not while the scare of the gunfight that morning had still been fresh in his mind. A single stray bullet could have ended her life. The discovery that the outlaws had been stalking the ladies for weeks only added to his unnerved state. Imagining that coldhearted snake watching Emma, learning her routines, her habits . . . It chilled his blood.

So when she'd leaned back into his chest, thawing—no, heating—his blood, he'd been drawn in like a man craving a blazing hearth after fighting his way home through a snowstorm. That's what she'd felt like. Home. The way she'd lightly pressed against him, her body soft and pliant. Her voice dripping over him like honey. The smell of her hair, the pale column of her neck begging to be tasted. He'd nearly given in. He'd wanted to give in. Shoot, a part of him still did. Then she said she trusted him, her eyes green pools of sincerity—sincerity mixed with something deeper that grabbed his gut and twisted it into a knot he had yet to untangle. He'd been a breath away from grabbing her to him and kissing her with all the yearning he'd suppressed since the moment he'd arrived to find her a woman grown.

She was dangerous, tempting him to dream of things beyond his reach. He had a job. The respect of men he admired. A purpose in mentoring young pups like Andrew and Zachary. He didn't need her planting impossible ideas in his head. She would never leave her ladies. Her place was here with them. His was in Montana on the rail lines. He could never belong in a women's colony. One had only to note his gender to figure that one out. And Emma couldn't follow him to the rail camps. Living in tents, constantly on the move—it was a harsh existence, filled with rough men and even rougher women. Drink ran high. Morality ran low. She wouldn't be safe. Or happy. And he cared too much about her to subject her to that kind of life.

Best he just get on with the business at hand.

Malachi climbed the steps to the telegraph office and stomped inside. Grace glanced up from her position behind the counter and set down the long paper tape she'd been examining.

"What can I help you with, Mr. Shaw?"

Mal touched the brim of his hat and bent forward to prop his rifle against the wall of the counter. "Need to send a couple telegrams," he said, straightening. "One to the county land office and the other to my outfit up in Montana."

It was past time to check in with the rail boss and to remind himself where he belonged.

17

Emma didn't linger in the empty café. She needed company. The sensible, level-headed kind. The kind that could manage objectivity even while being fiercely loyal. She needed Tori.

Shoulders set, Emma marched down the boardwalk to Victoria's store and pushed open the door. At the sound of the bell jangling, Tori came out from the back room, a welcoming smile on her face. A smile that shifted from welcoming to penetrating in a blink of an eye. Emma's shoulders sagged in reaction—not in disappointment, but in relief. Here she didn't have to pretend to have all the answers. Here she didn't have to be in charge. Here she could be her weak, filled-with-doubts self, and no one would care.

"Go ahead and flip the *Closed* sign over." Tori gestured toward the placard hanging in the front display window. "I've already got some water heating for tea."

Emma grinned and shook her head. "How'd you know I'd be coming over?"

Tori gave her a disbelieving stare. "Private ammunition lessons in the café with the man you've pined over for half your life? Please. I put the kettle on the moment I spied Betty and Grace leaving."

Warmth infused Emma's face. Were her feelings so obvious? Heavens, she hoped not. What would people think?

Ducking her head, Emma pivoted away from the knowing look in Tori's eyes and flipped over the sign. She turned the lock in the door, as well, needing to ensure that the embarrassing conversation she was about to have with her best friend stayed between the two of them.

"Come on," Tori urged as she held up the edge of the curtain that separated her living quarters from the store. "I want to hear all the details." She pointed a finger at Emma as she neared, her eyes taking on a faux-stern expression. "And don't think I've forgotten about your odd behavior during the meeting, either. Time to spill your secrets, Emma Chandler. The juiciest ones first." She waggled her eyebrows, and Emma laughed.

"You know, it's not too late to kick you out of the colony," Emma threatened. She added a thump to her friend's shoulder for good measure as she passed into the small sitting room that adjoined the dining and kitchen areas farther back.

Tori didn't laugh at Emma's quip. She never laughed. But she did grin in good humor as she followed Emma into the chamber.

"Hi, Miss Chandler." Lewis scrambled off his belly, where he'd been playing with a miniature iron train set on the floor, and dipped his head to Emma. His gaze darted over to his mama as if to ensure she witnessed his fine manners.

Emma hid a smile. Tori was a stickler for gentlemanly behavior. When she nodded slightly to him, pride lit Lewis's features. He turned his attention back to their guest, his mannerly obligations fading under a burst of excitement.

"Did you know Mama's getting a big shipment of guns on Monday? She's even letting me have my own!" He danced around Emma, his nickel-plated train engine dangling half out of his fist. "A popgun that really shoots!"

"Corks," Tori clarified.

"How marvelous!" Emma bent down to address the four-year-old on his level. "I'm certain you'll be an excellent shot in no time."

"As long as he doesn't practice in the store. Right, Lewis?"

He nodded his blond head with admirable sedateness. "Yes, Mama." Then he turned his impish eyes toward Emma and winked—or tried to. Both eyes closed instead of just the one, but the conspiratorial air was sufficiently conveyed despite the misfire. "I've already started collecting targets to practice with. I've got a whole box of 'em under my bed."

"Do you?" Emma enthused. Lewis was such a darling boy. So full of life and adventurous spirit. And at the moment, the perfect excuse to postpone the awkward conversation that loomed on her horizon. "What kind of targets?"

"A curved piece of tree bark that'll stand up all on its own. A scrap of ribbon with a button on the end my mama made me from the leftovers in her sewing box. It'll dangle real good from a branch or fence post. She's been saving empty food tins for me, too. Wanna see?" He took a few eager steps toward the narrow staircase that led to the sleeping rooms upstairs, but Tori stopped him.

"Not right now, sweetheart. Miss Chandler and Mama need to talk."

His little face fell, making Emma want to go to him, scoop him up, and insist he show her all his treasures this very minute. But she didn't. Tori was right. They really did need to talk.

"Why don't you set them all up in your room," Emma suggested, "and when your mama and I are done, I'll come up and see if I can hit any of them." She reached in her skirt pocket and pulled out her coin purse. After opening the clasp, she pulled out a copper coin and held it out to Lewis. "With this penny. You can practice with it while your mother and I visit. If you end up hitting more targets than I do when I come upstairs, you can keep the penny. What do you say?"

His short fingers closed around the coin. "Deal!" Lewis fisted his hand around the money, then spun around and shot up the stairs like a squirrel scrabbling up a tree with a stolen nut.

"Nicely done." Tori quirked a half smile. "He'll be up there for hours now, determined to win that coin from you."

Emma chuckled softly. "Maybe not *hours*, but hopefully long enough for us to have a bit of privacy."

Tori moved toward the stove. "I'll get the tea."

"I'll fetch the cups." Comfortable in Tori's kitchen, Emma opened a high cupboard, stood on tiptoes, and pulled down two hand-painted teacups with saucers. Tori had kept the pair when the moss-rose tea set a customer ordered had arrived with a few pieces chipped.

The customer had refused three of the saucers and, as a consequence, the cups that went with them, one of which had a lost a handle. Tori had given her a discount, still managing to preserve a bit of a profit, then kept the remainders for herself. She couldn't sell damaged goods, after all. And being a practical sort, she wasn't one to let good china go unused. The handle-less cup held her thimbles and other small sewing notions atop her sewing cabinet in the parlor, and the worst of the chipped saucers was now a soap dish on her washstand upstairs. The other two perfectly whole cups and only slightly flawed saucers were used for company tea. Something Emma had missed in recent weeks.

Emma carefully set the china on the table and turned back for the sugar bowl. "It's been too long since we've just sat together and visited, hasn't it?"

Tori nodded as she added tea leaves to the kettle. "It has.

All this business with masked outlaws, shootings, fires . . . it certainly interferes with a lady's routine."

Emma smiled then sobered. "I wish Malachi had had better luck running them to ground, but the scoundrels seem to know how to stay out of sight. At least Mal found more than the sheriff did."

"Probably because he spent more than five minutes looking," Tori said, her displeasure with Sheriff Tabor no secret. "Mr. Shaw stayed out there for hours. Of course, he nearly had them stopped before they left town."

Emma turned, a brow raised in question. "He did?"

"Oh, yes." Tori nodded as she collected her tea strainer from the drawer left of where Emma stood. "Lewis had rushed to the window to watch, thinking it all some kind of grand game. Frightened me half to death, seeing him standing in front of the big shop window as if the glass would keep him safe."

Emma shivered, recalling the terror that had surged through her when the bullet had shattered *her* office window. If she hadn't been at the back of the room, staring through the doorway and trying to figure out what she'd done to send Malachi running, she could have easily been struck. The thought of such a thing happening to Lewis . . . No, she wouldn't even consider the notion.

"I pulled him away from the glass and made him duck down with me behind the wall closer to the counter," Tori explained. "Horses' hooves pounded as the riders raced past the store. I looked behind them, afraid for you, knowing that the bank and telegraph office were the only two buildings they could have been shooting at. That's when I saw Mr. Shaw. He stood outside the bank, gun raised. He had them in his sights. But then someone screamed. And the shot missed."

"Someone screamed?" Emma lifted one of the cups, holding it still while Tori poured the tea through the strainer. She placed the filled cup on its saucer and distractedly reached for the second, her mind paying little attention to the task. "Could you tell who it was?"

Tori gave her an odd look. "No. Not for certain." She stirred a spoonful of sugar into her tea and two into Emma's. "Flora and Esther usually work in the garden in the mornings, so I assume it was one of them." She took up her cup and saucer, handed the second set to Emma, and led the way to the table and took a seat. "Could have been anyone looking out a window, though. The sight of two armed men firing weapons as they gallop through town is enough to frighten a scream out of even the stoutest female."

Emma slid into the chair across from Tori's and set her tea down untouched. "True enough. I screamed myself when they shot my window out." She stared into the dark-colored liquid, a niggling thought bothering her. "But I thought the men had stopped shooting once they passed the bank. They seemed to have been taking direct shots only at Malachi."

Tori's brow wrinkled. "Hmm. That might be right." She closed her eyes a moment, as if trying to re-create the scene in her mind. "I remember hearing the hooves not gunfire as they passed the store. I figured they were making a run for it. That's when I turned to see what damage they'd left behind and saw Malachi taking aim." Her eyes opened and her gaze peered straight into Emma's. "The scream came from the opposite direction, from ahead of the riders."

As if *someone else* had seen Malachi, and that someone had shouted a warning. Giving the outlaw a split second to dodge the shot and spare his life.

Or one of the women could have glanced up to find two riders bearing down on her, weapons drawn, and screamed out of pure fright.

Emma sighed. There was no way to know for certain which

scenario was accurate. No way to judge if one of her ladies was guilty of collusion or simply afraid for her life. Emma picked up her tea and peered into the dark depths as if a solution might be hidden within. She blew gently across the surface, hoping to uncover some bit of wisdom in the process, but alas, inspiration failed to strike. Frowning, she placed her lips to the rim and took a sip.

"What aren't you telling me, Em?"

Emma glanced up from her tea into her friend's all-too-intelligent gaze. "Malachi thinks one of our ladies might be here under false pretenses. Might, in fact, be working with the shooter."

Emma expected sharp denials or scoffing, but Tori gave her no such reaction. She simply took another sip of tea and pondered the notion for several long seconds.

"I suppose it's possible," she finally said. "It would explain how the fellow managed to plant those notes of his so close to town without anyone ever spotting him. A spy could have done it for him. Though I hate to think of one of our own being guilty of such a crime."

"As do I." Emma groaned softly. "I didn't want to believe it. I still don't. But when Mal failed to find any evidence of a man being around the church when the fire was set, I had to consider that he might be right."

"That's why you were watching the ladies at the meeting so closely today. You were judging their reactions to Malachi's news that the shooters had escaped. Did you learn anything?"

Emma shook her head. "No. All I have is a pocketful of doubts and conjecture with no evidence to back it up."

Tori slowly lowered her teacup, the china clinking delicately against the saucer. "Who do you suspect?"

Emma hesitated, debating whether or not to give Tori the names. She didn't want to poison another mind against women who might very well be innocent. But there was a greater good at play here, too. And if ever a woman existed who could remain objective, it was Tori.

Having decided, Emma took a breath then took the plunge. "We've narrowed it down to three. Helen, Flora, and Claire."

Tori glanced past Emma as if to look out the small window that allowed light into the dining area. "I saw Claire walk down to the boardinghouse before the shooting started, probably to collect Maybelle's lunch."

Which made sense. Mrs. Grimes, the proprietress, paid for her rheumatism treatment by supplying Maybelle with three meals a week.

"So Claire could have been the one to scream."

Tori shrugged. "Or Flora. If she was in the garden. Of course, it could have been Esther or anyone else suddenly caught in the thick of things."

"Ugh! I hate all this suspicion." Emma shoved her tea away and fisted her hands on the tabletop. "It makes me feel like a traitor to the women who have put their trust in me."

Tori reached across the table and laid her palm atop Emma's fist. "You're not the traitor, Em. The spy is. If she does indeed exist."

"I know, but that doesn't make my job any easier. What if she's being coerced somehow? What if he's forcing her to act against her will? If I discover who she is, what am I supposed to do? Have her arrested? Ban her from the colony? I can't just abandon her if she's in need. If she's simply guilty of trying to survive the only way she knows how."

"And that's why God put you in charge." Tori squeezed her hand, her eyes full of understanding. "You have compassion even on those who mean you harm. Me? I'd kick her out without a second thought. Anyone who would knowingly put my son's life at risk, who would put their friends' lives at risk, isn't worthy of a second chance. I wouldn't care about her reasons, her motivation. I'd just want her gone. But you?" She shook her head, the hint of a smile curving her lips. "Emma, you see people the way Jesus did. You bend down to wash their feet even when they have thirty pieces of silver jangling in their pocket."

Uncomfortable at the comparison because she knew in her heart she didn't deserve it, Emma pulled her hand from her friend's hold and rubbed her arms. "That's not true, Tori. I wish my motives were so pure, but I fear it is my pride talking. My denial that I could misjudge someone so badly. How could I not see signs of deceit when this woman came to me for asylum? How could I have welcomed her into our family and put our entire colony at risk? That's why I seek out her motives, why I desperately want to believe that she is being forced to do something against her will. Because if she's not, then everything that has happened is my fault."

"God's in control, Emma. Not you."

The soft words shook Emma's soul. She glanced up to meet her friend's eyes. Conviction glowed in the bright blue orbs.

"You are not responsible for the attacks on Harper's Station," Tori insisted. "The people attacking us bear the blame. The only thing you can control is yourself—your choices, your actions, your thoughts. And if your choice is to believe the best about people, to extend kindness where others turn their backs, to offer hope where others offer only scorn, then I stand by my earlier assessment. You are following in the steps of Jesus."

Emma's throat constricted, and moisture pooled in her eyes. She stared at her friend, her vision blurring as the tears overflowed and ran down her cheeks. What could she say? She felt so unworthy of Tori's praise. Yet she wanted to believe it could be true. Wanted it with every piece of her soul.

Lord, help me to be the person she sees. To treat people the way you would if you were in my place. Grant me wisdom to see past the deceiver's tricks, and please . . . protect those around me who are caught in the middle.

Tori slid a handkerchief across the table to Emma. Smiling through her tears, Emma nodded her thanks and set about cleaning her face. Once she was done, she clutched the cotton square in her left fist and reached for her teacup with her right.

"Enough about troubling matters," Tori declared as Emma sipped her tea. Her friend leaned forward, her mouth quirked in an impish grin. "I want to hear all about Mr. Shaw. And you. In the café."

Emma nearly choked on her tea.

Tori's mouth stretched into a full smile, the cheeky minx. "And don't leave out *anything.*"

18

After sending his two telegrams, Mal busied himself the only way he knew how. With work. First, after assuring himself Emma wasn't at the bank, he boarded up the broken window in her office. Then he headed to the church and started tearing off the burned clapboard siding. No one wanted to come to worship and lay eyes on the despicable message—*LEAVE or DIE*—scorched into the wood. A church was supposed to be a welcoming place, a place where people came to be cleansed and encouraged, a place that offered eternal life. That abomination had to go.

He scavenged some planks from the woodpile near Emma's barn, pieces that looked as if they'd once been a stall wall. Some had a few rotted places that had to be cut away, but most were in decent enough shape. He set up a pair of sawhorses and planed the wood down on one long end so the planks would fit with the other clapboard, then sanded the worst of the rough patches from the ends. There was no time for perfection with the sun already hanging low on the horizon, so after testing a few by laying them on the ground to make sure they'd overlap well enough, he loaded the half-dozen boards onto his shoulder and trudged back to the church.

Once there, Malachi poured all of his pent-up frustration into the job. Yanking boards from the outer wall the way he'd wanted to yank that shooter from his horse. Pounding nails into the fresh wood the way he wanted to pound his fists into the smug devil's face. For stalking Emma. Driving away her ladies. Trying to steal her land. Shooting bullets into her bank. That memory still gave Malachi chills. It was only by God's grace she hadn't been injured or killed.

Pound. Pound. Pound.

Malachi reached for another nail from the glass jar at his feet, but it was empty. A growl rumbled in the back of his throat as the pressure built inside him. Not enough nails. Not enough guns. Not enough information to uncover the infiltrator. He'd come up short. Again. Just as he had this morning.

He'd had the shooter in his sights. And he'd missed. Mal spun around and kicked at the pile of burned scraps he'd torn from the wall. The charred wood splintered and cracked, but it didn't satisfy. Nothing could satisfy. Emma and the aunts were still in danger because he'd missed.

"You done toe-clobberin' that scrap heap, or should I sit back and enjoy more of the show?"

Malachi spun around, a geyser of heat erupting beneath his collar. "Mrs. Cooper! Ah . . ." He rubbed the too-warm spot on his neck. "I didn't expect to see you out here."

She raised a brow at him. "Why not? I told you me and Helen were taking the first watch at nightfall." Her gaze lifted meaningfully to the sky, and only then did Mal realize how little light remained. The sun must have set a good twenty minutes ago. "Night done fell, pardner."

Mal heard the laughter behind her tone and smiled sheepishly. "Seems so. Guess I was too absorbed in my work to notice."

"Mmm-hmmm." Betty stepped closer, her eyes suddenly serious. "Listen, Shaw. I don't care if you pummel those boards into toothpicks or grind them to sawdust. But some females around here won't understand that you're just working off steam. No, if they see you stomping around and kicking things, all they'll see is a temper out of control."

Helen. Malachi jerked his head up, looking for the timid woman. Had he scared her off?

"Don't worry. She ain't here." Betty pointed her shotgun toward the boardinghouse. "I sent her to fetch that ancient revolver Miss Daisy offered. Thing's as old as dirt, and we don't have any proper ammunition for it, but I figured it would be good for Helen to get used to holding a weapon. I can give her some pointers on aiming the thing while we pass the time. Then when the new guns arrive, she'll be more prepared."

"Good idea." And since Helen was still on Emma's list of suspects, he felt a bit better knowing she wouldn't have a loaded weapon tonight. Of course, pairing her with Betty was a boon, too. Not much got past the plain-spoken woman. "Who's set to relieve you?"

"We got the eight to midnight shift, then Grace and Maybelle have the watch until four. Figured we needed gals who owned weapons on duty the first couple nights before Tori's shipment comes in."

"Miss Mallory's tiny pistol won't serve much purpose up in the steeple," Mal said with a frown.

"That's why I'm leaving my shotgun with her. But I've warned the ladies not to shoot at shadows. We're here to watch and report, not start a gunfight. The last thing we need is for some nervous female to get spooked when something moves and end up hitting one of our own."

"Agreed." A bit of the tension that had coiled in Mal's shoulders dissipated. "Everyone knows where to find me, right?"

Betty frowned as if not altogether pleased with his presumption that he'd be the one they ran to if trouble erupted. "I told 'em if they spot something suspicious, they're to alert Emma at the station house." Her eyes narrowed on him. "You might be the hired gun, Shaw, but Emma's still the one callin' the shots around here. We report to her, not you. If she wants to bring you in, that's fine, but we aren't lettin' you take the place over just because you think you know best. We don't need a man to do our thinkin' for us. Got that?"

Mal was in no mood for the woman's hardheaded feminism. "Save your sermonizing for a day when two masked bandits haven't just shot up your town." He straightened to his full height and took a step toward her.

She didn't back up, but he hadn't expected her to. He just needed to make it clear that he wasn't going to let her or any of the women castrate him when he was the only one standing between them and a pair of gun-happy outlaws.

"I have no interest in running this town," Mal emphasized each word, praying they'd somehow penetrate the woman's stubborn hide and sink into her brain. "Emma is far better qualified for that role than I will ever be. But right now, your enemies have the skill, the training, and the weapons that you lack. I'm your best chance at evening those odds."

Betty harrumphed, obviously unhappy with his pronouncement, but she made no further argument. A good sign. The crotchety chicken farmer might just be warming up to him.

Thankfully, with Mal sleeping in the barn, he'd hear anyone who came to the station house looking for Emma, so he wouldn't need to countermand Betty's instructions, a chore that would certainly undo any goodwill he'd just scavenged for himself. Besides, he planned to cover the four-to-six shift every morning. Most people assumed that if they'd made it through the darkest hours of night with no incidents they were in the clear. But a canny attacker, like the one laying siege to Harper's Station, could easily turn such beliefs to his advantage. If Mal were the outlaw, that was precisely the tack he would take. Wait until vigilance was low, use the encroaching light of dawn to his advantage, and strike before the rooster crowed.

Mal spotted Helen approaching, the old revolver dangling loosely in front of her skirt. She glanced up and stuttered to a halt. Mal took that as his cue. He gathered his discarded tools and the empty nail jar and fingered the brim of his hat.

"I'll be on my way, then." He raised his voice and managed a small wave in Helen's direction without dropping the hammer tucked beneath his arm. "Have a good night, ladies."

He prayed they would. Have a good night. A quiet night. Free from attack or any malicious furtive activity. He doubted the men who'd ridden through town earlier today would strike again so soon. If they kept to their pattern, they would take a day or two to regroup before making another attempt to drive the women out. Perhaps they would wait for information to be passed from their spy before crafting their next move.

The thought had Mal pivoting back toward the women. "Mrs. Cooper?"

Both women's backs were turned. Helen flinched at the sound of his voice and made no effort to face him. Betty shooed the girl on into the church, then glanced behind to meet Malachi's gaze. "Yeah?"

"I want a report on *all* activity. Even the women. If you see Maybelle or Claire making a house call in the middle of the night or Aunt Henry lighting the kitchen lamp to get a late-night snack, I want to know about it. The better I understand the women's activities, the better I can protect them." *Especially from the traitor in their midst.*

Betty looked at him long and hard until something that felt like understanding zinged through the air between them. Finally she gave a sharp nod. "I'll make sure the second watch knows and tell the others after worship tomorrow."

"Appreciate it." Mal dipped his chin, then resumed his trek to the station house.

So far, the enemy had never truly attacked at night. The spy had set the church afire as evening fell, but the shooter himself had only made appearances during the day. Mal hoped that trend continued. He had a better chance of stopping an enemy he could see than one who used the cover of darkness. And heaven knew he couldn't afford to miss again.

Emma fought a yawn and lost as she sat at her office desk late Monday morning. Her mouth spread wide, and she made no effort to cover the cavernous expanse with her hand. Why should she? No one was around, and she was just too tired.

She and Flora had taken the second watch the night before, and she'd been so keyed up about having four hours alone with one of her suspects, that she'd not been able to sleep before her shift began. A fact she greatly regretted.

The numbers in the open ledger on her desk swam before her eyes. If only they would stay in the columns they were assigned and quit blurring into the others, maybe then she'd be able to finish her tallies.

Grace had brought over the telegrams from the New York broker who managed her investments. As on every Monday morning, he'd sent her the gains and losses she had earned the past week, both from her personal accounts and those for the bank. She needed to compile the figures, analyze trends, and decide whether or not to continue with her current investment strategy or make adjustments. But concentration seemed beyond her capabilities this morning.

Another yawn hit her, causing her eyes to water and her nose to run. Admitting defeat, Emma shoved the ledger away from her and retrieved her already dampened handkerchief from her skirt pocket.

It wouldn't be so bad if she'd actually learned something of value last night. But Flora had been tight-lipped. Emma's gentle probes into the woman's history had earned nothing more than vague generalities and evasive dodges. When she'd questioned her directly about the husband who had beaten her, Flora had practically curled into a ball in the corner of the small steeple area. Her eyes haunted and lost, she'd begged Emma not to ask any more questions. Emma had felt like the lowest of snakes. The poor woman had been abused and abandoned. Of course she didn't wish to relive that pain. What kind of monster would ask her to?

That left her with nothing of value to report to Malachi when he'd arrived to relieve them. Nothing. And with only two hours' sleep to fuel her now, she doubted she would accomplish anything of value today, either. She couldn't even total a simple column of numbers.

Maybe if she got up and moved around . . . splashed some water on her face . . . something.

Emma pushed to her feet and strode out of her office into the main bank building just in time to meet Maybelle as the older woman opened the door and stepped inside.

Forcing a welcoming smile to her face, Emma moved forward to greet the town healer. "Maybelle. So good to see you. You're looking well."

"And you're looking like death warmed over. You didn't sleep last night, did you, gal." The woman's eyes raked her from head to toe, missing nothing.

Emma wilted beneath the scrutiny. "Is it that bad? I'd hoped the burgundy shade of this dress would make up for my lack of vibrancy this morning." She ran a hand over the deep red

176

sleeve of her best suit jacket, the one she usually wore only to church. She'd even attached her indigo lace collar to her sensible ivory shirtwaist to liven her appearance. Obviously, it hadn't been enough.

"It helps," Maybelle said, her harsh tone softening to one of understanding affection, "but it can't hide the shadows beneath your eyes or the pallor of your skin." She stepped closer and took one of Emma's hands in her own. "I know you carry the weight of this town on those slender shoulders of yours, but you've got to take care of yourself." She patted Emma's hand, and the motherly gesture brought a slight sting to Emma's eyes. "The stress will eat you alive if you let it. Share your load, child. Get out from under some of that weight. It ain't good for you. And for heaven's sake . . . if you're scheduled for watch duty, get some shut-eye ahead of time."

Emma laughed lightly at the well-deserved admonishment. "You're right, of course. And I *am* sharing the load. Or at least starting to. Mr. Shaw has been a true blessing in that regard."

"I imagine so." The woman eyed her speculatively. "Not too hard to look at, either."

Warmth effused Emma's cheeks. Maybelle cackled. "Ah! There's the color we were looking for. Just keep thinking about your handsome Mr. Shaw and no one will notice the shadows under your eyes."

Emma smiled at the teasing even as she determined to steer the woman clear of any further discussion of Malachi. Leading the way to the counter where most customer transactions took place, Emma searched for a safer topic of conversation. "It was good to see Brother Garrett yesterday. I found his sermon on holding tight to faith amidst fiery trials particularly apropos."

Maybelle nodded agreement. "He told me afterward that he'd heard about the shooting incident but that he'd had no idea there'd been literal *fiery* trials until he'd seen the scorch marks on the outside of the church this morning. He commended Mr. Shaw for repairing the worst of the damage in preparation for services. Although, when he'd learned about the charred message left behind in the old boards, he'd been incensed. Promised to report the violation to Sheriff Tabor along with giving an account of the second shooting incident. Said he'd demand the lawman take greater steps to see to our protection. Don't think it will do much good, but I was sure to thank him for his concern."

"His advocacy can't hurt." Emma reached for the small set of keys she always kept in her pocket. She unlocked the door that separated the customer lobby from the more secure area behind the counter. After closing and locking it again behind her, she moved into the first teller window and fingered the key that would unlock the money drawer. Looking up at Maybelle through the protective bars, she smiled. "His prayers on our behalf will be much appreciated, as well." She slipped the drawer key into the lock and turned it until that catch popped free. "Now, what can I help you with this morning?"

"Thought I better withdraw some funds, what with the new shipment coming in today. Twenty ought to do it."

"Very well." Emma pulled one ten-dollar bill and two fives from her drawer, then counted them into the shallow divot carved into the counter beneath the barred window. Maybelle had a policy against buying anything on credit. Her late husband had been a wastrel who'd left her with a pile of debt after his death. If she didn't have the cash to pay for something, she did without. Thankfully, her midwifery skills had allowed her to recover her losses after a couple of lean years, and her stint as doctor for Harper's Station had only improved her lot.

Emma made a note in the account book she kept locked in the till. At the end of the day, she'd transcribe the transaction into the main ledger she stored in the vault.

"Anything else I can do for you?" Emma asked as Maybelle folded the bank notes and stuffed them into her purse.

"That should do me for a while, I think."

Emma nodded and slid the money drawer closed. She had just turned the key in the lock when Lewis burst through the front door.

His head swiveled from side to side, his wide-eyed gaze zeroing in on Emma. "Miss Chandler! Come quick. My ma needs you!"

Emma's stomach clenched. All tiredness fled from her bones, leaving a desperate energy humming through her. Grabbing the teller door key and forcing it into the lock with trembling fingers, she called out to the boy. "I'm coming!"

"What's happened?" Maybelle asked as Emma fumbled with the door.

For pity's sake, why would the stubborn thing not open?

Finally the key slid home and the lock turned. She threw the door wide and slammed it shut behind her. Taking precious seconds to lock it back, she nearly missed Lewis's answer.

"He's hurt," Lewis sputtered. "He's hurt real bad."

Emma's heart screamed a denial. *Please, God. Not Malachi.* But who else could it be? There were no other men in Harper's Station.

"I'll go fetch my doctorin' kit and meet you there," Maybelle said, already hurrying out the door.

Emma met Lewis's worried gaze, her own heart pounding so loudly in her chest she was surprised it didn't echo off the rafters. "Is he at the store?" she asked.

Tori's son gave a sharp nod and took off like a shot. Emma followed, barely pausing long enough to pull the bank door closed as she ran.

19

Emma's shoes pounded against the boardwalk. Lewis didn't dash through the main store entrance as she expected but sprinted around the far corner. Snatching a handful of skirt to keep from tripping on the stairs to the street, Emma followed without question. She had to reach Malachi. Wherever he was.

Wagon ruts in the dirt created an alleyway of sorts and then turned right, around the building. Lewis disappeared into the back storeroom. Emma increased her pace to catch up but twisted her ankle as her heel caught on the uneven ground. Wincing at the twinge, she recovered and continued on, keeping her gaze glued to the ground so as not to repeat her folly.

Had Mal been helping Tori with her merchandise? Had the shipment of guns arrived while Emma had been dozing at her desk? But no. The freight wagon would be here. And even as tired as she'd been, surely she would have heard . . .

Her imagination raced faster than her feet as she rounded the corner. Had he been cut? Had a pile of heavy boxes smashed his skull? Would he die?

She gained the doorway and rushed inside. Then stumbled to a halt. For there stood Malachi. Tall. Strong. Unharmed.

Or was he? Blood and dirt smeared the tan fabric of his shirt. Yet he was talking, giving orders.

"Stay here," he commanded. "I'll fetch them." He took a step toward the door, then growled and lurched back the way he'd come. "I swear if you get out of that chair one more time I'm going to shoot you myself."

Emma's exhausted brain struggled to make sense of the scene. Hard to do when her gaze refused to leave Malachi to see whom he might be speaking to.

"I'll keep him here, Mr. Shaw." Tori's voice. "You can go."

Malachi nodded and turned toward the door. He came up short when he saw her. His eyes warmed for a minute, then cooled to businesslike efficiency. "Good. You're here. It'll likely take two of you to keep the fool from going after his *pets*." Mal pivoted sideways to squeeze past her and out the door.

She had no idea what pets he was talking about. This whole episode left her feeling a bit like Alice, fallen down a rabbit hole into some kind of nonsensical world. All she knew was that she couldn't let her rabbit scamper off without answering one vital question.

"Wait!" she called, stirring from her stupor enough to dash after Malachi and lunge for his arm. Her fingers closed over his sleeve, and he stopped.

He tossed an impatient glance over his shoulder. "What, Em? I need to go before that stubborn cuss changes his mind."

She examined him from head to toe, not caring that a gentlewoman wouldn't ogle a man in such a way. The fear still spearing through her was far from gentle. She had to know for certain. "You're not hurt?"

His forehead wrinkled. "No."

"Lewis said to come quick. That *he* was hurt. A man was

hurt. I thought . . ." She cleared her throat and released her hold on his arm, realizing at last how silly she must look. Like some kind of dull-witted female who couldn't understand the most basic facts of biology.

Malachi's eyes softened. "You thought he meant me."

She nodded and glanced away. "But of course you're fine. And in a hurry." She smiled brightly—too brightly, she was sure, thanks to the embarrassment thrumming through her veins—and stepped back. "Go on with your errand. I'll help Tori."

He looked like he wanted to say more, but Emma didn't give him the chance. She spun around and hurried back into the storeroom.

Now that her brain was cleared of its panic fog, she recognized Benjamin Porter right away. Or what was left of him. The poor man was a bloodied mess. His shirt was torn in several places, his left knee—scraped raw—was visible through a hole in his trousers. He sat—well, squirmed was more like it—in one of Tori's kitchen chairs, unwilling to still enough for Tori to clean away the dirt and blood from his face.

Thankfully, Lewis was nowhere to be seen. Tori must have sent him into their living quarters, away from the grisly scene.

"I've got to get Helios and Hermes." Mr. Porter tried to rise, but Tori quickly set aside the basin of water she held and fit her palms to the large man's shoulders. "They're stuck in the traces." He batted at her hands. "Might injure themselves."

"You're staying right here." Tori's firm tone left no room for discussion. "Mr. Shaw will tend to your precious horses."

When Mr. Porter continued to struggle, Emma joined the fray, helping Tori press him back into his seat.

Suddenly his eyes went wide. "Bandits!" He wagged his head back and forth as if witnessing their approach on either side of him. "Can't let them get the shipment. Victoria needs it. She's counting on me."

Victoria? Since when had Tori and the freighter moved their relationship to a first-name basis? Or had they? To be fair, the man *was* spouting off about invisible bandits. Not exactly his most lucid moment.

Emma met Tori's concerned gaze over the man's head. "He's talking like he doesn't know where he is."

"I'm not sure he does. Mr. Shaw thinks he hit his head in the crash. There's a huge knot on this side."

"Helios! Hermes!" Mr. Porter cried out as if in pain, his gaze seeing something beyond Emma's shoulder, something only visible in his own mind.

"He keeps rambling on about his horses, fool man," Tori muttered, reaching again for the cloth floating in the basin sitting atop a nearby crate. "More worried about them than himself." She leaned her mouth close to the big man's ear. "Mr. Shaw went to fetch those great beasts of yours. He'll take care of them."

The freighter's hand lashed out without warning and latched onto Tori's arm. The cloth she'd just retrieved dripped water on his trousers, but he didn't seem to notice or care. His wild eyes searched her face. "Don't let him put them down. Even if a leg is broke. I might be able to mend it. Promise." He roared it the second time. "Promise!"

"I'll tell him as soon as I see him," Tori hurried to assure him, though Emma noticed she was careful not to promise something she couldn't guarantee. "He'll take good care of them. You've nothing to worry about."

Emma had never before prayed for the health of horses, but she did so now. Heaven knew this man had been through enough already, he didn't need to lose what seemed to be his closest friends, as well.

Mr. Porter released Tori's arm and settled, mollified at least for the moment. A red mark marred the skin below the cuff of her sleeve, but Tori ignored it and went back to cleaning his face.

Now that the big man had calmed, Emma couldn't help prodding her friend just a bit. "He called you Victoria," Emma whispered, curious to see her friend's reaction. Tori had always insisted on the strictest formality when dealing with men. It was one of the ways she held them at arm's length.

"The poor man's out of his head," Tori said, her cheeks admirably unflushed. "I never gave him leave to address me as such."

Emma smiled. "But he obviously thinks of you in such terms and cares about your opinion of him, if that outburst was any indication. The man's sweet on you."

There was the blush. Finally!

Tori gave her a sharp glare, though, so it could have been anger that spawned the pink in her cheeks. "You have better things to do than play matchmaker, Emma. You know my feelings on the matter."

She did. Tori had no intention of marrying. Or even being around men more than was necessary. And Emma understood why. A brutal betrayal like the one she'd endured would scare any woman off of marriage. Yet not all men were scoundrels. Mr. Porter had been serving as their freighter for nigh on a year, and he'd proven himself honorable and dependable and had never treated any of the ladies of Harper's Station with anything but respect and kindness. What if Tori was throwing away a chance at love simply out of fear?

And what if you're throwing away the same chance out of duty?

The thought snuck up on Emma, and insinuated itself in her brain, conjuring up memories of her and Malachi in the café. Of the way her pulse thrummed every time she saw him. Of the secret fear that watching him leave again would tear her heart to pieces.

Mr. Porter jerked against her hold right then and brought

her attention back to the matter at hand. Tori held the cloth to the man's head, where blood matted his hair. He hissed in a breath and pulled away from her touch.

Emma pressed him back into the chair. "Easy, Mr. Porter. You've been injured. You need to let Miss Adams tend your wound."

"Miss Adams?" He twisted his head toward Emma. "Where?"

"I'm here, Mr. Porter." Tori's voice seemed to soothe the giant of a man.

His gaze immediately sought hers. "Don't worry, miss. They're safe. In the wagon." He winced as Tori set the cloth to his head again. She couldn't seem to withstand his earnest gaze for more than a few seconds at a time. "I got a . . . a false bottom. Always carry valuables there. Just in case. There's un-scrupulous characters out there, you know."

Tori smiled slightly. "I know." She continued cleaning the blood from his hair. "I'm thankful you had the foresight to hide the weapons."

"Didn't want to let you down. Sold most of your goods, too. The ones Fischer refused. Got your money in my pock—" His words died off on another hiss when he lifted his hips and tried to bend his arm to reach into his trouser pocket.

"Just leave it." Tori laid a gentle hand on the small section of his sleeve that had no blood smeared upon it. "It'll keep." She glanced across him to Emma, her eyes bewildered, as if she couldn't imagine why this man had gone out of his way to do her such a significant kindness. "I never asked you to—"

"Wanted to," he interrupted, his eyes sliding closed, his voice slurring slightly. "You and the others need the funds. Deserve them for your labor." His eyes opened again, and for a second Emma swore she saw a twinkle of pride in them before the haze of pain covered it up. "Got a better price for 'em, too. Delivered to folks on the outskirts of town. Seems . . . people like

the convenience . . . of fresh eggs delivered . . . to their door."
His eyes closed again. "Might set up . . . a reg'lar route. I'd be
willin' . . . to run it . . ." His words died off, and he slumped
in the chair.

"Mr. Porter?" Tori tossed the rag aside and shook his shoulder. "Mr. Porter!"

A shuffling sounded behind them. "Step aside, gals, and let
an old lady through." Maybelle marched into the fray, Claire
close on her heels.

Emma backed away at once, relieved to have an expert in their
midst. Heaven knew she wasn't adding anything of value to the
proceedings, beyond keeping the giant of a man in the chair.

"Claire, fetch the smelling salts." Maybelle thrust her medical bag at the younger woman. "Let me guess. Head wound?"

Tori nodded, not taking her hand from the freighter's shoulder. "He has a gash on this side above his ear. It's swelling something awful. Even the lightest touch had him hissing in pain
when I tried to clean it."

Claire handed Maybelle a tiny vial. The midwife uncapped
it and waved it under the man's nose. He yanked his face away
from the stringent odor, and his eyes opened wide.

"What . . . ?"

"Mr. Porter." Maybelle grabbed the big man's chin as if he
were a ten-year-old boy and forced him to look at her. "Listen to
me. You've taken a hard knock on the head and already passed
out once. I need you to stay awake. Fight against the sleep for
me. Understand?"

"All . . . right," he croaked.

"Good." Maybelle released his chin, then scooted around to
the right side of his chair to examine the wound Tori had mentioned. "Scalp wounds bleed a lot, but the gash is not too wide.
Should only need eight to ten stitches. Swelling is significant."
She pressed gently against the area around the wound, drawing

186

a groan from her patient, but she continued probing without apology. "It'll give you a nasty headache, and you might not want to wear a hat for a few days, but having the swelling on the outside is better than the inside. We'll need to clean it real good, though, to stave off infection. Won't be too comfortable for a while, but a man your size should be able to handle a little discomfort without falling apart."

Mr. Porter straightened in his chair. He clasped the wooden arms and gave her a nod. "I'm ready when you are, ma'am." He sounded more like himself now. More lucid and in control.

Maybelle patted his arm. "No need to brace too hard yet. I'll need a minute to gather my things. You got any other wounds I need to know about? Shooting pains? Difficulty breathing? Deep cuts?"

He shook his head slightly, then winced at the movement. "Don't think so. Managed to walk here after the crash. Just sore."

"Good." Maybelle turned and caught Emma's eye. "Keep him talking," she whispered. "It'll distract him from what I have to do."

Emma bit her lip and took a moment to collect her thoughts before stepping closer to the chair again. "Mr. Porter." Careful to keep herself on the opposite side, out of Maybelle's path, Emma waited until his gaze met hers. "Were you attacked?" At his nod she asked, "Can you describe the men who attacked you?"

"There were two. One rode a big chestnut gelding, black socks and mane. The other rider was slighter of build and rode a sorrel. Weaker mount. Couldn't keep up with the chestnut."

"Figures he'd remember the horses better than the people," Tori grumped even as she stroked the hair off his forehead.

"Men wore masks," he gritted out between clenched teeth as Maybelle pressed a wet cloth directly atop his wound.

Emma hurried to ask another question. "Did they speak to you?"

"Said they wanted the guns. Seemed to be expecting them."

Emma hid her dismay. More evidence of a traitor in their midst. One who was still communicating with their attackers despite the start of the night watch.

Mr. Porter stiffened, his muscles flexing as he fought not to pull away from the women tending him. "Told them the shipment had been delayed," he ground out. "That I was only carrying foodstuffs. They didn't believe me. Forced me off the road at the top of Harper's Hill. Unhitched my team, then sent them racing off, the traces dragging the ground behind them." His face darkened as anger instead of pain etched his brow. "Didn't care that the lines could trip them up, could send them tumbling down the hill in their fright. Barbarians."

"What did the men do next?" Emma asked, eager to turn his attention away from his horses. It wouldn't do any of them any good if he got it in his mind to go after them. She'd never known him to use his strength against a woman, but all one had to do was look at his size to recognize that he could overpower all four of them with barely a flick of his wrist if he chose.

Thankfully, he took her cue and forced his grip on the chair to relax. His nostrils flared as he inhaled, and his jaw worked back and forth. "Took a knife to the flour sacks," he recounted, his voice steadier, more controlled, "and smashed the crates carrying the hams and bacon slabs. Might be able to salvage some of what's left once I retrieve my wagon. *If* I can retrieve it. Devils dismantled the brake, pistol-whipped me, and tossed me in the back before pushing the thing down the hill. I was too disoriented to realize what was happening until the wagon careened off the road. All I could do was grab the sides and brace myself. Crashed in an arroyo. Better than a tree, I suppose, though the impact felt about the same.

"Wagon's busted up, but it's still more or less in one piece. Shielded me from the worst of the collision." He paused. "Except for the crate that bashed my skull in the same spot the chestnut's rider had dented me with his pistol butt a few minutes before. Not sure how long I lay in the wreckage before I roused enough to pull myself up and climb out. Bandits were long gone by then."

"I'm so sorry this happened to you." Emma touched his hand. "The men who attacked you are obviously the same ones who have been threatening us. I can't help but feel responsible."

"Not your fault." Mr. Porter's eyes slid closed and tension visibly radiated through his jaw as he clenched his teeth.

Emma shot a worried glance at Maybelle, only to discover a needle in her hand and a long thread being pulled through the freighter's skin. Stomach roiling at the sight, Emma quickly shifted her gaze back to Mr. Porter's face. She curled her fingers around his large palm, offering whatever comfort she could.

After a moment, his eyes opened again. "With no wagon, I won't be able to make my runs for a while." He grunted and squeezed his eyes shut as Maybelle started another stitch. Once the needle was through, he continued. "Thought I might hang out here until I can find a replacement. Lend a hand."

Emma caught Tori vigorously shaking her head out of the corner of her eye.

"Need I remind you this is a women's colony, Mr. Porter?" Emma shot Tori a speaking glance. She'd be loyal to her friend and respect her wishes to a point, but she also had to consider the needs of the rest of the women in town. Having a second man around could make a world of difference.

When Emma returned her attention to the freighter, he was ready for her. His eyes burned with determination.

"A women's colony . . . plus Shaw. I'll bunk with him."

"I'll have to put it to a vote," Emma hedged.

Porter started to nod, then stopped when Maybelle fitted the needle to him again. "Take your vote, Miss Chandler, but know this—those men invited me to the fight when they crashed my wagon and endangered my horses. I'm involved now, whether you allow me to stay in town or not. I'll camp down by the river, if need be, but I'm not leaving."

20

Malachi found the wagon first, busted up in a ditch at the bottom of Harper's Hill, just as Porter had said. The horses were another matter. Judging by the flattened prairie grass, they'd gone off the road about a quarter mile past the end of the hill. Mal scoured the landscape for the big black Shires he recalled from his first meeting with Porter back in Seymour. The oversized draft horses stood at least sixteen hands, if not taller. White stripes down their faces. White, feathery socks at their hooves. Massive creatures. Much like their master. So why couldn't he find them? He saw nothing but prairie grass waving in the wind.

Until he followed the trail down a crumbling embankment. Turned out he'd been looking too high. The poor beasts had fallen to the ground about a hundred yards out from the road.

Mal dismounted and approached the downed pair cautiously. As strong as they were, one kick from a hind leg could take out his knee. Like most draft horses, Shires were docile and obedient creatures under normal circumstances. But these were far from normal circumstances.

The horses must have heard his approach, for the one that lay half on top of the other lifted his head and tried in vain to struggle to his feet.

"Easy," Mal cooed, worried the beast might do serious damage to his partner if he continued flailing. "I'm here to help. Just gotta see what we're up against." He crept around the pair, giving them a wide berth as he circled first past their hindquarters, then around to their heads.

He understood why Porter had been in such a tizzy. The geldings were still fastened together. Neck yoke hung intact beneath the collars. Crosslines over their backs. No wonder they'd been unable to get up. One had probably stumbled over the irregular ground and taken his partner down with him.

Holding his hand out in front of him, Mal took a step toward the fallen pair. The black on top—Hermes? Or was it Helios? Mal had no idea which was which—snorted and shook his head as if trying to fling the blinders away so he could better assess the threat and protect his friend.

"Whoa, Hermes." Mal decided using a name the horse had at least heard before, even if it was the wrong one, was better than nothing. The faster he could establish trust, the greater the chance they'd get out of this without serious injury. At least for the top horse. Mal hadn't witnessed much movement from the one beneath. But then, having nearly a ton of horseflesh pressed against you would make movement difficult for even the hardiest creature.

Mal shifted slightly to the left, putting himself in the horse's direct line of sight. He stretched his hand out toward the beast's nose. "Easy, boy. Porter sent me. He's real worried about you and Helios, there." Mal took another step, hunching low over his boots. "I can help you get free if you'll let me."

Almost there.

Hermes snorted again, his eyes wide, but his head settled to an occasional gentle bob. And when Mal cupped his open hand around the end of the horse's nose and crooned soft words, the black gradually stilled. Mal patted the horse's cheek with his free hand and stroked his forelock. Hermes's side heaved, but the shuddering sigh seemed to be one of relief, not fear.

"That's right. Just relax. Let me do all the work." Mal continued talking in low tones and stroking the frightened horse's neck as he worked his way closer to the yoke.

Not wanting to damage Porter's harness any more than necessary, Mal kept his knife in his pocket and worked at the buckle on the breast strap first. Hermes tried to get a look at what he was doing, and nearly slammed his horse collar into Mal's head.

Mal dodged, then patted the black's neck and gently pushed his head back down. "Lie still, big boy. If you knock me out, you'll have no rescuer. Then where will you be?"

Finally, he worked the buckle loose and tugged the breast strap free of the ring on the neck yoke. The martingale loop slid off next. Now all Mal had to do was find a way to climb between a pair of beasts weighing nearly two tons to cut the crosslines and any other tangles that held the animals together without getting squashed or trampled.

Not any more dangerous than blowing up mountains. Or at least that's what he told himself as he edged between the two massive heads.

Thankful for the blinders that obscured his movements from the horses' view, Mal eased a hand into his front trouser pocket and extracted his knife. He slipped the largest blade from its folded position and gently locked it into place. Then, folding the leather of the first crossline over the sharpened edge, he sawed through the strap. He paused to croon and pat both horses again. The gelding pinned beneath Hermes stirred, bringing a touch of a smile to Mal's face.

"What happened, old fellow? Hit a rock? A prairie-dog hole?

Probably expected your partner to right you like he would if you were still hitched to the wagon, huh?" Mal turned slightly and took his knife to the second crossline. "Ended up pulling him right down on top of you instead. Bet you're ready to get him off your back. Well . . ." Mal clicked his knife shut and slipped it back into his pocket. "Let's see if we can do something about that."

Keeping one hand on each horse as long as possible, Mal backed out until he was no longer between them. He moved to the outside edge and gently took hold of the halter straps near the top horse's cheek. "Ready, Hermes? One. Two. Three!" Mal pulled on the strap. "Up now, Hermes. Up!"

As soon as the animal started to move, Mal released the halter and jumped out of the way. Hermes rocked and snorted, and finally rolled to his feet.

"Oh, ho! Good job, old man!" Mal grinned and started moving toward Helios, but the second Shire needed no human encouragement.

The second black craned his neck upward, then surged to his feet. The half-unlatched neck-yoke bar flopped down at a sharp angle beneath his collar, one end dragging the ground. The horse kicked at it a time or two, as if not sure if it was something to be afraid of, but Mal moved in quickly to quiet him.

"You're a trouper, aren't you?" Mal praised as he worked the buckle on the breast strap and freed the beast from the dragging bar. "Now, I just need you two boys to stand still a little longer so I can get you untangled from the rest of this mess."

The obedient lads dipped their heads to chomp at the prairie grass while Mal set about unfastening the double yoke at the rear and tying up the reins that drooped behind them. He had to do some fancy hoof shuffling to get Helios untangled from the tug lines, but eventually everything was put to rights.

The team suffered several scrapes and cuts, and Mal was

sure they would discover many places where the harness had rubbed them raw once he got them back to the station-house barn, but they were whole and hearty for the most part. He ran his hands along each of their legs, found some inflammation below both of Helios's front knees, but Mal found no evidence of a break. Thank God. He didn't want to think of what Porter would do to him if he'd had to put one of the animals down. Hermes and Helios would need a heavy dose of rest, salve for their scrapes, and plenty of pampering, but they should make a full recovery.

He clicked his tongue and got his borrowed nag to follow him as he led the two Shires back through the grass toward the road. Helios limped a bit but trudged gamely on, keeping pace with Hermes's plodding as Mal walked between their heads, lightly gripping their bit straps. They'd nearly reached the road when the sound of an approaching wagon brought Mal's head around. He released his grip on Helios and reached for the revolver at his hip. But there was no need. The driver didn't pose a threat. At least not to the horses.

"Malachi! Thank heavens!" Emma dropped the arm she'd been holding up to shield her eyes from the sun and set the brake. Then in a flurry of deep red skirts that were far too fine to be traipsing through the dusty countryside, she clambered down from the high seat.

He tried not to notice the white ruffles of her petticoat or the flash of slender ankle momentarily exposed by her hurry, but such a feat was apparently beyond his heroic capabilities.

"What are you doing here, Em?" He resumed his stride, ducking his head to avoid the far too enticing sight of her, and led the horses up onto the packed dirt of the road. "Didn't Porter's episode prove it's not safe to be out here alone?"

"*You're* out here alone." She crossed her arms and gave him one of her I-dare-you-to-argue-with-*that*-logic looks.

Unable to pass up the challenge, he looked her dead in the eye. "I'm armed." He patted his holster.

She lifted her chin. "So am I." She glanced back over her shoulder toward the wagon. "I've got Betty's shotgun under the driver's seat."

"Doesn't count if it's not within reach." Mal smirked at her, then led the horses past, shrugging very unapologetically as he went.

"Malachi Shaw!" she sputtered, uncrossing her arms and storming after him just like she used to do the times he bested her in an argument when they'd been kids. "You know quite well that gun was within reach until I stepped down."

"Doesn't matter. It's not within reach now." He bit the inside of his cheek to keep from grinning. Man, she was fun to fluster. Her cheeks got all pink, and she dropped that oh-so-proper-banker demeanor.

"Well . . ."

He slid a sidelong glance her way and swore he could see the wheels spinning in her mind. Then all at once triumph lit her eyes. Before he knew what she was about, she dashed around Helios's head and planted herself right in front of Mal. He stumbled to a halt.

"*You're* within reach," she announced right before she snaked an arm around his waist and ducked beneath his outstretched arm. "And you're my greatest weapon of all." Her eyes met his. The competitive triumph flickered, then slowly gave way to something softer. Warmer. "And you'll never let anything hurt me as long as you are near." Her chin tilted up as she gazed into his face, her lips plump, her words a husky whisper.

"Never," he murmured, surprised he could find breath enough to fuel even that single word. Her faith in him, her absolute trust, terrified him. Yet at the same time, it made him feel invincible. After his failure to find the men who threatened her, to stop them, how could she look at him with those brilliant eyes—eyes that sported not one speck of doubt to dim their shine?

"I'm so glad you're here, Malachi." Her arm tightened slightly around his waist. Her lashes dipped. Her cheek turned.

Mal bit the edge of his tongue and drove his gaze heavenward. *Lord, have mercy. . . .* He could feel her fingers through the cotton of his shirt right beneath his rib cage. Then she leaned closer. The scent of her hair directly beneath his nose, tantalizing him. Then her face touched his chest, and her second arm wrapped about him. She nestled in with little movements, like a pup finding just the right place to nap. And oh, how he wanted to hold her to him, to claim her as his, to let her nestle up against him just like that every night for the rest of their days.

His arms trembled from the effort it took not to release the horses and cling to her instead. Could she hear his heart? He didn't see how she couldn't. The thing was driving against his ribs like a locomotive at full speed.

"Em . . . " he croaked, not knowing what he meant to say. *Em, you can do worlds better than me.* Or *Em, you don't know what you're doing.*

But he feared that what he really meant deep down in his greedy, good-for-nothin' bones was . . . *Em, I love you more than I love my own life. Hold tight, girl, and never, ever, let me go.*

21

Emma released her hold and reluctantly stepped away from Malachi. Who, she noticed, was looking prayerfully to the sky, jaw clenched tight.

Probably begging the Almighty for patience to endure the crazy woman who kept forcing hugs on him when she knew full well he didn't like to be embraced.

Where had her restraint gone? Just because they'd shared a moment in the café—a moment when, in her defense, he'd not seemed the least uncomfortable with holding. Touching. *Nuzzling.* Of course, *he'd* been the one doing the holding. Her hands had been occupied with the revolver. Still, his guard had lowered and given her reason to hope he might welcome some affection from her. But apparently not.

"Mr. Porter told us about a hidden compartment in his wagon," Emma explained breezily as she circled around one of the giant black horses to get to Malachi's mount. "One that might still be sheltering the weapons." She reached the gray mare and collected the reins. "After Maybelle took over the doctoring, I decided I'd be of more use fetching our goods before someone stumbled across the wagon." She summoned up the sunniest smile in her arsenal and flashed it at Malachi as she strolled past. He didn't need to see her disappointment. The man had enough on his plate to worry about. She needed to lighten his load, not add to it.

Besides, he was acting a bit odd. He hadn't moved a muscle since she'd touched him. Just stood on the edge of the road, arms stretched between a pair of massive draft horses, body frozen in place. Only his eyes moved. They followed her, their dark brown gaze making her stomach dance. An uninterested man wouldn't stare so intently, would he? Or maybe he was just trying to intimidate her into going back to town. Not that such a tactic would work. Which he knew from experience. He'd never been able to intimidate her. Not even when she'd been a slip of a girl. So there had to be something else in that stare. Something deeper she couldn't quite decipher.

Whatever it was, it brought an uncomfortable warmth to her cheeks. She lengthened her stride to pass him and turned her attention to tying the mare's lead to the back of her buckboard. "Did you happen to see Mr. Porter's wagon while you searched for his horses?" she asked without looking up from her task. "I plan to dig out the guns and salvage whatever else I can find before heading back. I was hoping you'd be able to assist, but it seems you have your hands full. No matter. I can manage. There are less than a dozen rifles, and the revolvers will be easy enough to carry." She glanced up, caught his scowl, and made a point to approach the driver's box from the *far* side of the wagon.

Grabbing a handful of skirt, she fit her foot to a wheel spoke and hoisted herself up. Then she had to scoot across the bench to reach the brake on the left side, making it all too obvious that she'd taken the coward's way out to avoid being near him. Which hadn't mattered anyway, because by the time she reached for the brake lever, the man she'd been striving to circumvent had released Porter's horses, bounded up the near side of the wagon, and covered her hand with his own. His hold was firm and unyielding, not tender in the slightest, yet the possessiveness of it had her pulse fluttering. Her gaze flew to his.

"If you think I'm going to let you roam around out here alone," he growled through a clenched jaw, "you're crazy. And for all your independent ideals, I know you ain't lost yer marbles." His grammar was slipping, a sure sign of his agitation. "Not yet, anyway." He muttered the last as he hopped down from the wagon.

He trudged back to Porter's draft horses and took hold of their halter straps again. Slowly, he edged them past the wagon, his attention focused on the ground in front of him in order to steer them around any uneven patches that might cause them discomfort.

"Porter's rig is about a quarter mile out. I'll lead you there, but you're gonna have to plod along at my pace." He cast a sharp glance over his shoulder at her. "And for the sake of my nerves, move that shotgun up to your lap. If trouble finds us, I want you to be ready."

Emma obeyed, too pleased to have his continued company to complain about his high-handed manner. Despite the fact that she'd traveled this very road without a man to guard her more times than she could count, she had to admit—at least to herself—that she'd not been looking forward to doing so today. The attack on Mr. Porter had rattled her. Her adversaries were unpredictable, their strikes calculated and always one step ahead. If she and Malachi had a chance at stopping them, they'd have to ferret out the traitor in the colony. Soon.

Salvaging supplies took less time than Emma expected. Flour, cornmeal, and sugar had scattered to the winds in the crash, thanks to the bandits' vandalism. Emma collected what little remained inside the sacks and tied off the slashed tops to keep them closed. Mal found the cache of guns right where Mr. Porter had said they would be, in a compartment hidden in the wagon bed directly behind the driver's box.

The freighter had built three wooden frames at the top of the wagon bed for carting smaller or more delicate objects, like the glass jars of canned goods the Harper's Station ladies sold. Emma had always thought the compartments terribly clever. Little did she realize that they served a second purpose— camouflage. For the box frames hid the seams in the wood of the wagon bed beneath. Anyone looking at the wagon would see nothing more than what showed on the surface. Mal had tugged on the boxes quite forcefully when trying to figure out the hidden compartment's location, and the wood had barely budged. It was only when she'd climbed up into the driver's box to help that she'd discovered the latches against the floor behind the bench. After she'd reached down to undo them, Mal tugged on the box frames again. This time the one in the center slid backward to reveal a rectangular opening. The guns and ammunition had been secreted inside.

She couldn't wait to tell Tori about it. Emma smiled to herself, swaying with the motion of the slow-moving wagon as she followed Malachi and the draft horses back to town. Her friend had always insisted that big men had small brains. It was why so many of them became brutes. Using their size to get what they wanted required less effort than thinking for themselves. It was why Tori had urged Emma to hire a different freighter to run her goods when she'd first met Mr. Porter. Once she understood that Porter was the only one willing to do business with a female store owner, she'd relented, but it had taken months for her to let down her guard around the man.

And now, Emma had proof that the man was not only kind

but intelligent. Clever enough to fashion an undetectable hidden compartment in his wagon. Wise enough to anticipate trouble and put said compartment to use. And well-read enough to name his faithful steeds after mythological beings related to his own profession. Who else but an educated man would name his horses Hermes and Helios? One for the Greek god of trade and border crossings, the guardian of travelers. The other for the Greek god of the sun who relied on mighty steeds to pull his golden chariot through the sky. No small intellect in that large man's head.

Unless it had been permanently damaged by the blow he'd just taken.

Emma's smile faded. Mr. Porter had seemed much less agitated and confused when she'd left, but head injuries could be tricky. She said a quick prayer on his behalf, asking the Lord to bless him with a full recovery.

"I see the station up ahead," Malachi called over his shoulder. "I'll take Porter's beasts there. Start rubbing them down and tending to their bruises and scrapes. If you'll untie my mare when we get there, she'll follow me into the barn."

Emma straightened on the seat, nodded, and then realized he couldn't see her assent. "All right. I'll take the supplies to Tori and check on Mr. Porter, reassure him that his horses are alive and in good hands."

"The stubborn cuss will probably try to come check on them himself. Don't let him leave if Maybelle thinks he's not fit. Tell him I'll give a full report as soon as I finish seeing to his team."

"I will. Betty should have the women gathered by now, too, so we can start distributing the weapons." Emma had explained the morning's events to Mrs. Cooper when she'd gone to borrow the shotgun. Betty agreed to round up the ladies as well as take a vote on whether or not to allow Mr. Porter to stay.

Emma hoped everyone saw the wisdom in letting the freighter

remain within the town limits. They'd accepted Malachi with a minimum of grumbling even though he'd been a complete stranger to them, having only her endorsement and the desperation of their circumstances to recommend him. Their circumstances were equally desperate now, if not more so, and they already knew Mr. Porter. Hopefully those factors would sway the vote in favor of letting him stay.

Now that Emma knew they faced at least two outlaws, it seemed sensible to have two experienced, trustworthy men on *their* side. Even with the training Malachi would be giving them, she and the other ladies wouldn't turn into a company of competent sharpshooters overnight.

Emma drew her buckboard to a halt at the station-house corral. Mal left the Shires standing obediently in the road long enough to open the gate. Emma scrambled down from the wagon seat, circled to the rear, and untied the gray mare. Mal met her there and took the reins from her. She tried not to notice the way his palm brushed along the back of her hand as he reached for the leather straps, but the resulting tingling sensation was impossible to ignore. Emma kept her chin down to hide her gaze from him, afraid he would see too much. She really needed to get her reaction to him under control.

"Once the guns have been distributed, take the ladies out behind the church," Mal instructed, his voice gruff. "Betty and Grace can supervise the ammunition loading and go over safety protocols. After I get the horses settled, I'll meet you there, and we can start the shooting lessons."

"All right." Feeling more in control of her emotions with a plan laid out for her to follow, she looked up. Directly into his eyes. He startled as if caught doing something he knew he shouldn't, which made absolutely no sense, for he hadn't been doing anything besides conversing with her.

Yet in the sliver of a moment before he blinked it away, she could have sworn she saw something in his dark-eyed gaze. Something stark yet tender. Something that resonated with the emotion pulsing in her own heart—longing.

Her stomach flipped in ecstatic little circles, but she held her facial expression carefully neutral. She had a job to do, a job that required her full attention. She'd wrap her discovery in brown paper and set it aside to ponder later. And ponder she would. For just like any investment that projected early signs of a great return, one still had to approach with a strategic mindset, calculating risk and evaluating proper timing. Make a move before the asset was secure, and an investor could be left holding an empty bag. Wait too long, and the opportunity could slip through her fingers to be capitalized on by another. Neither prospect was acceptable.

So for once in her life, she ignored the insistent impulses twitching inside her. She didn't blurt out her burgeoning feelings or lift up on her toes to touch her lips to his when the sudden craving surged through her. No. This time she'd plan. Analyze. Because this was one investment she'd not be able to recoup if lost.

Mal cleared his throat and backed away a couple steps. "I'll . . . uh . . . see you in about thirty minutes, then."

Emma nodded. "Behind the church. We'll be ready."

He held her gaze an instant longer, the contact playing further havoc with her heart rate as unspoken words seemed to hang in the air between them. Then he turned his back and led the horses through the corral gate. Emma did her part, as well, returning to the bench and driving her team over to Tori's store.

As she pulled up, a flood of women poured out of the café and immediately started digging through the contents of the wagon.

"Ladies." Tori swept out of the store with a large crate in hand. Her voice carried above the clamor as she descended to the street. "I've cleared off the yardage table inside. Let Miss Chandler and me bring in the goods and lay them out for you to make your selections. I have a price chart already prepared, so we'll be able to finalize your sales quickly. It will just take a moment to set everything up."

Emma hurried to meet her at the rear of the wagon and helped her shoo away eager hands. "Sorry," she murmured under her breath after the ladies retreated. "I guess I should have driven around to the back."

"I doubt it would have mattered." Tori layered rifles into Emma's waiting arms. "They would have followed you. Everyone is still worked up by the attack on Mr. Porter. They're eager to gain some means of personal protection."

"How is he faring?" Emma inquired as Tori filled the crate with handguns and ammunition boxes.

"Maybelle took him down to the clinic and is watching over him there." Tori dragged the crate to the edge of the wagon bed, climbed down, then turned to retrieve it. Gripping the handholds firmly, she grimaced slightly as the weight of the box pulled on her arms. But Tori had worked in shops her entire life. She was used to carting heavy loads. So with a straight spine, she marched up the stairs and into her store.

Emma followed.

"It took five stitches to seal that gash on his head." Tori turned down the fabric aisle. "The entire time Maybelle worked on him, he barely made a sound. Just sat there still as a statue."

Tori's voice held an undercurrent of wonder, possibly even respect. Emma couldn't help but grin.

"You should see the clever contraption he rigged in his freight wagon to keep his cargo safe. It was completely disguised. Quite ingenious, really. If he hadn't told me where to look, I doubt we would have found the cache, even knowing it was there." She reached the table and carefully dropped the rifles onto its surface. The clatter of steel on wood broke off their conversation for the moment.

Emma immediately started sorting the long guns into two piles, shotguns and rifles, while Tori organized the revolvers and ammunition.

"Do you know the outcome of the vote regarding Mr. Porter staying on for a few days?" Emma asked.

"Permission has been granted," Tori confirmed. "Nearly unanimously. Only two ladies voted against."

"Are you all right with that? I know you weren't eager to have Mr. Porter around any longer than necessary."

"I put my personal feelings aside." Tori stacked the last of the ammunition boxes, then reached for the price chart she'd written out and arranged it in the center of the table, never once meeting Emma's gaze. "Having another man around will improve our chances of winning this standoff. It would be foolish to put my own comfort ahead of the well-being of the entire town."

Emma touched her friend's arm. "Thank you."

Tori nodded, then stepped back from the table. "The display's not up to my usual standards, but it'll do for now." She glanced toward the shop door. "Go ahead and let them in. I'll fetch my receipt book."

Emma moved to the front of the store, opened the door, and waved the ladies inside. As they filed through, she found herself scrutinizing each one, wishing she could determine the identity of the two who had voted against letting Mr. Porter stay. One of them was most likely the traitor. Unfortunately, there was no way to know who cast the dissenting votes. In true democratic fashion, they always performed their elections by secret ballot.

Betty Cooper pushed her way to the front of the crowd and doled out advice and instructions to the ladies as they made their selections. Emma expected to see Grace there as well, but the telegraph operator was the last to walk through the door, and when she did, she stopped in front of Emma instead of proceeding to the gun table.

"Miss Chandler? Did Mr. Shaw return to town with you?"

"Yes." Emma frowned over the troubled look in the young woman's eyes. "He's at the station house, tending to Mr. Porter's horses."

Grace nodded and turned as if to leave. Frissons of disquiet prickled Emma's neck. She reached out and caught the young lady's arm. "Did something happen while we were away?"

Grace smiled as if to reassure, but the gesture failed to reach her eyes. "He received a telegram. That's all. I'll deliver it and return shortly."

"A telegram? From whom? The county land office?" Perhaps they'd found something of interest regarding Harper's Station's mineral or water rights.

"You know I'm not at liberty to say. All Western Union correspondence is held in the strictest confidence. If you want to discuss the contents, you'll need to talk to Mr. Shaw directly."

Why did Emma have the feeling that Grace was doing more than reciting telegraph regulations? It was almost as if she were trying to warn her somehow.

Emma bit her lip as she watched Grace cross the street toward the station house. What was in that message?

22

Malachi carted a second bucket of fresh water down the barn aisle and poured its contents into the half-barrel tub in Hermes's stall. Or was it Helios? He really needed to find out. Couldn't go around calling a horse by the wrong name. It'd be disrespectful. One of the Shires had a white belly, the other's underside was fully black. As soon as he figured out which belly went with which name, he'd be able to tell them apart. For now, he just had to keep guessing.

He gave old White Belly a pat on the shoulder, then sidled out of the way so the animal could drink. Mal had gotten the harness off of the pair and settled them in side-by-side stalls with a scoop of oats in each feedbox. Now, if he could just find some liniment and salve, he'd get them doctored and be free to catch up to the women. To Emma.

A pressure squeezed his chest. Mal rubbed at it absently as he made his way to the tack shelves. The ache was getting worse. Every time she touched him, it magnified, making it harder to recall the reasons he couldn't reach for her. Hold her. Claim her as his own.

Heaven knew he wanted to. But he'd learned early in life that wanting rarely led to getting. And if sacrificing his dreams allowed Emma to fulfill hers, well, he'd find a way to keep his mouth shut and his hands to himself. She'd accomplished so much with this place, with these women. Asking her to set her work aside in order to be with him would be a betrayal. He couldn't do that to her. Couldn't ask her to choose. Even if, by some miracle, she returned his feelings.

Mal lifted a brown tin from the shelf and squinted at the label at the same time a shadow fell across the barn opening. He glanced to his right and spotted a woman silhouetted in the doorway.

"Emma?" His traitorous heart leapt, but he reined his voice into stoic submission. "I thought we agreed I'd meet you at the shooting lessons." He purposely focused his attention on the bottles and tins on the shelf in front of him despite the fact that his mind didn't process a thing he was seeing. "I'm going to need a little longer to tend the horses."

"I'm sorry to disturb you, Mr. Shaw. It's Grace Mallory. From the telegraph office. You've received a wire."

Malachi pivoted to face the woman who was *not* Emma. He quickly masked his disappointment with a friendly smile and took a step toward her.

"Forgive me for mistaking you, Miss Mallory." He met her at the door. "I . . . uh . . ." Why was she giving him that odd look? So serious. Almost . . . resigned? "It was good of you to deliver the message with such diligence."

She extended her hand. A folded slip of paper peeked out from beneath her thumb. "You mentioned that you wanted to be notified right away if a reply came in. Today, one did."

He accepted the slip and tucked it into his shirt pocket, unwilling, for some reason, to read it in front of her, even though she would have to know the contents. He dug in his trouser pocket for a coin to tip her for her trouble, but she waved him off.

"I'll be with the other ladies at the store, then behind the church for the lessons. If you should decide to send a message in return, come fetch me, and I'll send the wire for you." Then she turned and walked away, leaving him staring after her with an unaccountable dread building in his gut.

Once Grace was out of sight, Mal turned his back to the doorway and strode deeper into the barn, his hand itching to dig out the telegram that sat heavily in his pocket. Why he felt the need to read it in the gloom of the barn's interior instead of under the full light of the sun streaming through the entrance, he had no idea. Yet that's what he did.

When he reached the tack shelf, he dipped his thumb and forefinger into his pocket and extracted the slip of paper. His eyes scanned the words quickly, like a kid trying to get foul-tasting medicine down as fast as possible, but as his gut knotted, he went back and read the words again.

NEARING BIGHORN CANYON
NEED EXPERIENCED BLASTER
REPORT BY FRIDAY OR BE REPLACED

Report by Friday. Four days. Two required for travel.

When he'd wired the rail boss after the shooting, he'd informed the man that he'd probably need a few extra days to wrap things up. The boss had given him one. One extra day and a deadline with zero flexibility. Mal's numb mind desperately tried to piece together a scenario that could possibly allow him to meet that deadline without leaving Emma in the lurch. Only one came to him. Catch the attackers by tomorrow.

Odds of success? A hundred to one. Mal rubbed the back of

his neck. More like a thousand to one. He hadn't even taught the women how to shoot yet. And he couldn't exactly leave them unprotected to go scouring the countryside for a camp that seemed to move to a new location every night.

So where did that leave him? In the middle of no-way-to-winsville, that's where.

Mal slammed the pad of his fist against the barn wall. Bottles and tins rattled on the shelves. Harnesses jangled. Pain ratcheted up his arm. He didn't care. He reared back and hit the wall again. This time Hermes and Helios took notice. They snorted and tossed their heads, their white eyes glaring at him for disturbing their much-earned respite.

"Mind your own business," he growled at them. "You're out of your jam. I'm mired chest deep in mine."

"Sounds like a sticky situation."

Mal jerked to the left, then spun toward the small side door that led to the house. "Bertie." He swallowed hard. Great. Just what he didn't need. "Why aren't you . . . ah . . . with the others at the store?"

She waved a hand in the air. "I've always been more of a pacifist than most. Drives Henry crazy." Her eyes twinkled. "I'll do my part to keep watch, but I'll not be purchasing a gun."

Somehow he wasn't surprised. He couldn't quite picture his gentle, bighearted aunt pointing a loaded weapon at another human being. He'd barely gotten her to hold the unloaded practice gun at the café the other day. It was only when Emma told her that she needed to set an example for the other ladies that Bertie had given in.

"I won't be showing up for shooting practice either, young man," she said when he opened his mouth to offer her the use of his rifle for just that purpose. She pointed her finger at him as if taking him to task for even suggesting such a thing. Which he hadn't. Yet. Because she shushed him before he could. The woman could read minds the way a schoolmarm read books. Or so it seemed to Mal. Ten years hadn't dulled her skills one iota.

She brushed past him and moved to the tack shelves. There she found a bottle that had tipped over during his little steam-letting session and righted it. "Someone's got to keep watch in town, after all, while everyone is out at target practice. I'll be up in the steeple keeping an eye on things with Lewis. We'll ring the bell if we see anything suspicious."

Mal stilled. She was right. The attackers would hear the gunfire. Realize they'd been tricked. But they'd also be able to scout the area and determine that everyone had gathered by the church, leaving the rest of town unguarded. They'd not take a chance straight on against so many weapons, but what would stop them from setting another fire or destroying property? The store. Emma's bank. The clinic. They could do serious damage to the women's livelihoods.

"That's a good thought, Aunt Bert. Think I'll put Porter on guard, too. He might still be under the weather, but another pair of eyes will be good to have around." Especially if those eyes were attached to a man who actually carried a gun and possibly even a grudge against the men attacking.

Bertie turned and smiled. "Yes. I'm so glad the ladies voted to allow that dear Mr. Porter to stay on until these difficulties are dealt with. I'll sleep better knowing we have another capable man about the place."

"Porter's staying?" Could this be the answer Mal sought? Could he turn the women over to Porter? The thought soured his tongue. Tasted an awful lot like quitting.

"Just until the unpleasantries are sorted out." Bertie sauntered closer and winked up at him. "He *says* he wants to stay because those bandits dragged him into our business by attacking him on the road. But if you ask me, he has another reason altogether. Two, actually. One with blond hair and a head for business. The other with short pants and a severe case of hero worship." She tapped Mal's arm and tittered, her eyes alight with merriment and some kind of hidden message that made his mouth go a little bit dry. "I do so adore watching young people fall in love. Some tumble as easily as a pecan dropping from a tree in the fall wind. Others fight against it with everything they have." She paused and stared up at him.

His palms grew moist. She couldn't know. Surely. He kept those feeling bottled up tight. She couldn't—

"Victoria's a fighter," Bertie continued, breaking contact with his gaze to turn her face toward the main barn entrance. "Benjamin Porter's going to have his hands full." She grinned then, her face nothing but sweetness and light. The weight on Mal's chest eased just enough to draw in a full breath.

Taking the offensive, Mal cleared his throat. "Better not be meddling in their affairs, Bertie." He gave her a stern look which she completely ignored. Instead she smiled and slipped her arm through his as if he were fifteen again and they were having "how to be a gentleman" lessons.

"I never meddle, dear." She tilted her head up to meet his eyes. "But I do make myself available to give advice. Should someone find themselves in a prickly predicament." She looked meaningfully at him. "Say, like the one that had you drumming the walls a minute ago."

Mal tensed. "Thanks all the same, Aunt Bert, but I can handle that one on my own."

"Yes. I heard you *handling* it all the way from the kitchen."

He tugged his arm free and turned to confront her about her poor definition of "never meddling," but she held up a hand to stop him before a single word made it past his lips.

"Don't give me that obstinate look, Malachi Shaw. I'm not going to wheedle anything out of you. We're all entitled to a few secrets. I just wanted to let you know that I'm available to listen should you need an extra pair of ears."

That shut him up. Apparently her definition matched his after all.

"Besides, there's someone else who can help you more than I ever could. One who already knows the details of what's plaguing you."

Grace? The telegraph operator seemed nice and all, but Mal wasn't about to discuss such a private matter with her.

"Someone imminently wise," Bertie continued, "who can be trusted implicitly. He'll help you discern the right path."

"But . . . Oh." Understanding finally dawned.

She's talking about you, isn't she, Lord? Of course she is. I'm a dunderhead for taking so long to figure it out. Probably 'cause I've been a bit remiss in visitin' with you lately. Might be a good idea to start up those regular chats again, huh?

"I'll leave you to your work now." Bertie patted his arm a final time and meandered back the way she had come. "Just be assured of one thing, Malachi."

He pushed his hat brim high on his forehead and scratched at an itchy spot above his left ear. "What's that?"

"No matter what choice you make, you will always be loved. By Henry and me. By Emma. And by the One who matters most."

A suspicious thickness clogged his throat and turned his voice hoarse. "Thanks, Aunt Bert."

She smiled in that motherly way of hers and disappeared out the side door.

He watched her go, still amazed that people like the Chandlers cared about a nobody like him. They'd stuck by him all these years, even after he left. Writing letters. Fretting. Praying. Why? He wasn't blood kin. He was just some kid who took shelter in their barn one night. Yet they felt like family.

And Emma . . . Well, Emma felt like more than family. From the moment his angel proclaimed she was keeping him, his heart had belonged to her. Distance had dulled the effect somewhat, but feelings were flaring at full force and in new, more adult directions these days. He didn't just feel devotion any longer, he felt desire. Longing. A soul-deep need that scared the wits out of him. Not because the situation they faced meant he might have to die to protect her. That'd be easy. He wouldn't even think twice. No. It was the living without her after all this was over that had him worried.

Mal pulled his hat from his head and lifted his focus to the barn rafters.

"Lord, if you got some extra wisdom up there you can spare, I'd sure be obliged if you'd throw some my way. I ain't got the first clue what I'm supposed to do."

As his gaze dropped, he glimpsed the liniment bottle Bertie had set aright on the shelf. A quiet certainty entered his mind. He shook his head and grinned.

He might not have the first clue how to handle his Friday deadline, but it was suddenly clear as a still-water pool what he was supposed to do at the moment. Finish the job at hand and worry about tomorrow, tomorrow.

He just prayed the wisdom bestowed on him tomorrow had a little more direct bearing on his main quandary.

23

By the time Emma and Victoria joined the gathering behind the church, Betty and Grace had the women organized into two lines facing the targets Malachi had set up after services yesterday. The scarecrow Betty contributed took center stage surrounded by several scrap boards with painted targets staked in the ground at varying heights and distances.

Aunt Henry was the first to step up to the shooting line, wielding her spanking-new Colt revolver with purpose. She didn't hit anything with her first round of bullets, but after reloading and accepting a few quiet suggestions from Grace, she managed to put a hole in the edge of the scarecrow's leg on attempt number ten. Her whoop of triumph spurred on a barrage of gunplay as the others vied to equal her success.

"C'mon, gals," Betty urged as she strode up and down her line of riflewomen. "Don't let Henrietta Chandler best you. If she can hit the target with that peashooter of hers, you can do it with a real weapon!"

Tori lifted her rifle and motioned to Emma with her free hand. "That's our signal."

Emma waved her on. "You go ahead. I want to observe for a while. At least until Malachi gets here. He'll want to know how everyone is doing."

"What he'll want is for you to practice," Tori chided. "Lead by example, remember?"

"Leadership also requires supervision," Emma quipped with a healthy dose of sass before turning serious. "I'm not trying to get out of anything, Tori. Honest. I'll take my turn." Even though the thought of shooting left her queasy.

Ever since Mal had pointed the barrel of that pistol at his own chest, the thought of firing a weapon made her ill. What if she accidentally wounded Mal or one of her ladies? Or a true innocent, like Lewis? She'd never forgive herself. Yet logic told her that the best way both to prevent an accident *and* protect those she cared about was to learn the skill. She just needed a couple minutes to settle her stomach first.

Tori stared at her, no doubt seeing past Emma's excuses to the truth beneath, but she didn't press further. "Don't wait too long," was all she said. "Postponing usually makes it worse."

Emma nodded, knowing Tori was right. She'd walk the line once, see how everyone was faring, then take her place with Betty's group. And if her stomach still churned? Well, she'd just have to ignore it. Or find a nearby bush to hide behind when she lost her breakfast.

"Hit the targets, Mama!"

Emma glanced up at the church steeple to see Lewis's short arm waving at them through the opening in the bell tower, a popgun grasped firmly in his hand.

Tori smiled and waved back at her son. "I'll do my best." She glanced meaningfully at her friend. "And so will Aunt Emma."

Rolling her eyes, Emma shooed Tori toward Betty's group on the left and made her way to the opposite end, where Grace was helping Claire balance her revolver in two hands, much like Malachi had demonstrated for Emma.

Remembering that particular lesson brought an altogether different swirling sensation to her belly. Which only worsened the churning.

Breathe, Emma. Walk and breathe.

Taking small steps and slow breaths, Emma made her way down the line, focusing on each of her ladies as she passed, desperate to take her mind off her nausea. Some were timid with their weapons. Others gripped them so tightly their arms shook from the force. None of them seemed able to hit the targets with any consistency.

It was early yet, Emma reminded herself. Like any skill, marksmanship required practice. Repetition. Time.

Unfortunately, time was in short supply.

She'd nearly reached the end of the line when she spotted Malachi jogging across the field behind the station house, rifle in hand, holster on hip. A little jolt of pleasure shot through her, though she couldn't tell if it was more from the prospect of spending time with him or the excuse he presented to postpone her lesson a few minutes longer.

She smiled and waved. He raised his chin in acknowledgment and angled his path to intercept her.

"How are the troops shaping up?" he asked, not the least out of breath after his little run.

"Aunt Henry hit the scarecrow." She decided to start with the good news. And to leave out the part about it taking ten attempts.

"Henry?" Mal chuckled and wagged his head. "Well, good for her. Anyone else connect with a target?"

And now for the bad news. Emma winced slightly. "Well . . . not that I've seen. But I'm sure they will by the end of the practice session."

Mal eyed her, one brow raised. "And you?"

Emma dropped her gaze to the dirt, her stomach immediately clenching. "I haven't . . . ah . . . taken my turn yet."

A warm hand circled her wrist. "No time like the present."

So much for him being her excuse to procrastinate. Emma bit back a groan as Mal dragged her over to Betty's group. She also pointedly ignored the I-told-you-so look Tori aimed her way as she stumbled up to the shooting line.

"Focus on the closest target," Mal instructed, gesturing to the painted board staked twenty paces away.

It might be close, but the thing was only a foot across and even fewer inches high. Its insignificant size instilled no confidence whatsoever.

Mal demonstrated the proper stance, took aim with his own rifle, and fired. The blast blended in with the rest of the shots echoing at random intervals along the length of the line, but for some reason, Emma flinched. The target flinched, too, taking the punishment of Mal's nearly perfect hit through the red circle at the center of the board.

"Now you." He stepped aside and urged her forward.

Emma swallowed hard, her insides roiling with greater ferocity. Her hands shook as she lifted the weapon to her shoulder. She tried to steady the barrel with her left hand, but her palm was too sweaty. Dropping her left arm, she rubbed her palm against the fabric of her skirt and bumped against the hard circle of her father's watch.

"You can do this, Emma." Her father's words rang through her mind, encouraging, expectant, gently pushing her past her fear of failure just as he had every time she'd tried something new as a child. Riding a pony, saying her lines in the school Nativity play, balancing a column of figures.

"Take a slow, deep breath. It will still your nerves."

It took a moment for Emma to realize the advice came from

Mal, not the memories of her father. Mal's voice was as steady as her father's always had been. Calming. Brimming with belief that she could prevail.

It was his belief in her that finally quieted the storm inside. The queasiness didn't abate, but after she followed his direction and inhaled a long, slow breath, the churning slowed enough that she could clear her mind and release her fear.

"Hold the grip. Tuck the stock into the pocket of your shoulder. Now reach out and support the barrel." His voice rolled over her like warm oil, soothing her remaining rough edges and greasing the cogs inside until everything ran smoothly. "Widen your stance a bit. Good. Twist at the waist and sight your target."

He didn't touch her, but she could feel him at her side. Feel his support. His strength.

"When you're ready, move your finger to the trigger, release your breath, and squeeze."

As if hypnotized by his voice, she followed his instructions as he spoke them. Her finger slid down to curve around the trigger. She exhaled, made a mental note to keep her eyes open this time, and squeezed.

The kick surprised her, shoving the stock into her shoulder with more force than she'd expected. Pulling a trigger for practice when the magazine was empty didn't exactly produce the same experience. Feeling a little bruised, she started to lower the rifle in order to rub the sore spot, but Mal's voice intruded again.

"Wide right. Try again."

She scrunched her nose. He was starting to sound less like a source of calm and more like a taskmaster. But she responded, fitting the rifle stock back into her shoulder. Couldn't have the man thinking her too delicate to continue, could she?

Not waiting for his instructions this time, Emma regained her stance, sighted the target once again, and shot.

High.

She glared at the target and adjusted the angle of her rifle, no longer caring about the ache in her shoulder. She was *going* to hit that plank of wood.

"Lower your cheek to the stock this time," Mal murmured close to her ear. "Use your dominant eye to sight the target. Don't try to look through both."

Emma pressed her cheek to the stock and focused on the sight at the end of her barrel then lined it up with the center of the target. She squeezed the trigger. The target wobbled. Her heart thumped a wild, excited rhythm. She lifted her cheek and stared at the old board in disbelief. She'd shot the top right corner clean off!

"Good job." Mal's hand rested on her left shoulder for a brief moment, just long enough for her pulse to ratchet up another notch. "Now do it again, and this time hit the paint."

Determined to prove to him she could do just that, Emma gave a sharp nod and lifted the rifle back into place. But just as she fit the stock to her shoulder, a muffled gunshot rang out behind her. *Far* behind her. She turned.

"That came from town." Malachi took off, sprinting toward the church even as the steeple bell rang out a warning.

Emma raced after him, not about to let him go alone. He slowed slightly at the front of the church and craned his neck up to peer at the bell tower.

He cupped his hands around his mouth and yelled a single word. "Where?"

Emma doubted Aunt Bertie would be able to hear a thing with the bell donging so close to her head, but she leaned out the opening and gestured across the street anyway.

The station house.

Emma leapt toward home, but a firm grip on her arm brought her up short.

"No." Mal scowled down at her, his eyes promising he'd give no quarter if she chose to disobey.

"That's my home," Emma protested, even as a touch of rationality cut through the haze of anger that had blotted out all else the instant she realized someone was in her house doing only God knew what. If she blindly rushed in, she'd no doubt play right into the outlaws' hands. Mal was right. She had to think.

But the next thought to enter her mind had her struggling against Mal's hold, desperate to do what she had just vowed not to. "What if he's setting another fire?"

She had to get inside, stop whatever damage the fiend had planned. Everything her aunts owned was in that house. All the heirlooms they prized, their family heritage. Bertie's needlework. Henry's suffrage-tract collection. Things that could never be replaced. And the quilt! If it was destroyed, there'd be no hope of the sewing circle filling their quota in time.

Yet Mal refused to budge. His grip on her arm only tightened. "You run in there," he growled, "you could get shot. *Leave or die.* Remember, Em? I'm not about to give him the chance to make good on that threat. Nothing in that house is worth your life."

She hated that he was right. Hated that she was useless as day-old toast with the rifle she carried. Hated that she was a liability instead of an asset.

Hated that, the longer she argued with him, the greater the likelihood that the outlaws would escape.

She ceased her struggles. "Fine. I'll stay."

He eyed her skeptically.

"I promise. Now go."

Mal had no choice but to trust her word. Thankfully, Emma was the trustworthy type. She hadn't lied to him in all the years he'd known her, and he didn't expect she'd start now. He prayed not, anyway.

"Keep the women back behind the church," he instructed as he released his grip on her arm. "For all we know, he could have staked out a sniper position upstairs in the station house and is just waiting to start picking you all off as soon as you get within range. I'll clear the building and let you know when it's safe."

Emma gave a sharp nod, then spun around and hurried back toward the growing crowd of females clustering along the edge of the church.

Mal headed the opposite way, not directly toward the station house, but veering into town. Someone had shot off a warning, and Mal's money was on Porter. Find the freighter, and he'd find the information he needed to rout the outlaws.

But when he found Porter, the information the man shared was not at all what Malachi wished to hear.

"He's gone," Porter announced without preamble when Mal caught up to him out by the telegraph office. He was leading a limping Helios back toward the station-house barn. Porter looked none too steady himself. "Lit out right after I fired the signal shot. I tried to give chase, but the canny devil drove all the animals out of the corral. Took the main road, too, so picking out his tracks will be a nightmare unless you noticed something distinctive about the chestnut's shoes the last time you went after the shooter."

Mal slammed the flat of his hand against the plank siding of the telegraph office. He'd spent hours staring at tracks in the dirt and mud around the river. No nicks, chips, or identifying marks. The shoes had been easy enough to track in the countryside with no other hoofprints to compete for attention, but they'd be impossible to pick out on a well-traveled road.

He had one day to find the outlaws. One blessed day. And they'd slipped in and out of town right under his nose. For pity's sake. He'd been in the barn not thirty minutes ago. They must have crept in the moment he left.

"One man or two?" Mal clipped out the question.

Porter answered just as abruptly. "One."

"Stocky build or slight?"

"Stocky."

Mal grunted. The leader, then. He'd figured as much since Porter had mentioned the chestnut.

Mal decided to head to the station house and assess the damage. Make sure the second man wasn't lingering behind somewhere. Mal recalled Emma's fears and started jogging toward the Chandler residence.

"I'm going to check out the house," he called to Porter over his shoulder. "I'll help you round up the stock when everything's clear."

The front door stood wide open, a casualty of the outlaw's hurried exit. Mal ascended the porch, drew his revolver, and pressed his back against the wall just outside the door. With a quick turn of his head, he glanced into the front room, then jerked his head back. No bullets flew in his direction. He tried again, taking a longer look this time. No one in his line of sight.

Mal caught his breath and bounded into the parlor all at once, leading with his gun. He sensed no movement. Keeping his back against the wall, he scanned the room. A lamp lay overturned and busted on the floor, oil seeping into the wood, but nothing else looked disturbed. Nothing smelled like smoke, either, thank the Lord.

Keeping his weapon drawn, Mal worked through every room of the house, one by one. The kitchen and upstairs bedrooms seemed untouched. The only places he found evidence of the outlaw's presence was in the parlor, hall, and basement. Dirty footsteps marred Bertie's clean floors, but it was what adorned the basement wall that turned Mal's blood to ice.

A note was tacked to the interior wall, a crude sketch of a woman lying on her back sat at the bottom of the page, Xs where the eyes should be. A message was scrawled above the drawing. *You're first, banker lady.*

Mal tore it from the wall and wadded it into his fist before shoving it inside the vest pocket he usually reserved for stashing food. No way would he be showing this to Emma. As soon as he found a moment alone, he'd burn the vile thing.

The outlaw was growing bolder. Striking even closer to home. Time for Mal to switch tactics. He'd had enough of being a step behind, of only being able to react after an attack. Time to go on the offensive. First thing tomorrow morning, Mal was going hunting.

24

Mal watched the sky grow pink from his post in the church steeple, determination building in him with every degree that the sky lightened. For the past two hours, he'd prayed for a sign, for some kind of confirmation that going after the outlaws was the right thing to do. Surely it wasn't too much to ask. God had given Moses a pillar of cloud. Gideon a soggy fleece. Joseph a dream. What had he given Mal? Nothing but a crick in his neck. So far.

"I know the Good Book says you're not slow in keeping your promises," Mal grumbled as he rolled his shoulders to get out the worst of the kinks, "but I'm feeling rather pinched for time. I need some of that wisdom you promised, and I need it soon." *Before I botch something up.*

Once the rising sun cleared the horizon, Mal climbed down the narrow, winding steeple staircase and exited the church. With no divine answers shedding light on his path, he had no choice but to make his own way as best he could. And that way entailed going after the men threatening Emma.

He had one day.

If he failed? Mal swallowed, his throat growing tight. If he failed, he'd have no choice but to forfeit one of the two things he loved most.

"Emma! Pay attention, girl. You're scaldin' the gravy."

Emma started. Her gaze jerked from the window to the bubbling beef stock in the pan she was supposed to be stirring. "Sorry, Aunt Henry." She immediately pulled the saucepan to a cooler part of the cookstove and worked her whisk through the thickened gravy, frowning as dark flecks worked their way to the surface. She glanced over her shoulder to where Henry was mashing the potatoes, thankfully with her back turned. Emma grabbed a spoon and tried to fish out as many of the charred flecks as she could. Maybe she'd get lucky and no one would notice. She certainly wouldn't be able to taste anything tonight—not when Malachi hadn't returned.

She sighed, her attention once again floating to the window. He'd been gone all day. All. Day. Chasing outlaws. Dangerous outlaws with guns and cleverly designed hiding places. Now dusk was falling, and there was still no sign of him.

He'd sworn to her that he'd take every precaution when he announced his intention to go "hunting," as he called it, yet something had been off. She didn't understand the odd desperation radiating from him. But he'd been acting strangely ever since that episode with the outlaw in the house yesterday. There was something he wasn't telling her.

She had to admit she'd found it difficult to sleep last night, knowing that horrible man had been inside her home. Malachi had assured her that the outlaw hadn't gone upstairs into the bedchambers, and she'd seen the truth of that when she helped Bertie sweep away the dried mud that had fallen off the man's boots. None of it had been found on the upstairs carpets. And while she found a small dose of comfort in knowing he hadn't violated her most personal space, his odd visit left too many questions swirling in her brain to allow her to rest.

Why the station house? What had been his intent? Another scare tactic that he hadn't had time to carry out before Mr. Porter interrupted him? Or had there been another plan altogether?

She thought of what Malachi had speculated about the man using one of the upstairs windows as a vantage point to take out the women one by one. But if that had been his intent, why had they found traces of him in the basement instead of the bedchambers?

Emma dropped her spoon back into the gravy and rubbed the spot that throbbed right above her left eyebrow. She was missing something. . . .

A motion outside snagged Emma's attention. She abandoned the gravy and moved closer to the kitchen window. There. A woman. Walking alone. Behind the church. Heading toward the river.

Pulse racing, Emma spun for the door. "Mind the gravy for me, Aunt Henry."

"Where are you . . . ?"

Emma sprinted out the door, leaving Henry's chopped-off question dangling in the air behind her. She couldn't think about dinner, her aunt, not even Malachi. Her mind was locked on one target. The traitor.

Hitching her skirts past her calves, Emma ran down the back steps, past the barn, and across the field that separated the station house from the church. She recognized the navy blue dress and severely styled dark hair of the woman venturing into the brush west of the church.

Helen.

Emma picked up her pace. She'd not let Helen escape her sight. She could be meeting one of the villains or stashing a note informing them of some piece of vital information. Emma had no idea what that vital information could be since the guns had already been recovered, but that didn't matter. Whatever Helen was doing, she had to be stopped.

Emma hit an uneven patch of ground and stumbled a bit. In the moment it took her to regain her footing, Helen disappeared. No!

Setting her chin, Emma kept running in the direction she'd last seen the other woman. She couldn't have gone far. The prairie would have had to swallow her up for her to disappear that quickly. Emma rushed through the scrub brush where she'd last seen Helen and nearly tripped over her quarry.

Helen shrieked and jumped to her feet from where she'd been hunkered over, some kind of metal blade in her hand.

Why hadn't Emma thought to bring along a weapon? All this training, and she'd just run off and left a kitchen full of cutlery behind. What had she been thinking!

"Emma! You gave me a start." Helen held a hand to her breast, her eyes wide. In genuine surprise, or in guilt over being found out? "Why are you running? Has something happened back in town?" Her gaze shifted past Emma's shoulder toward Harper's Station, her teeth biting into her bottom lip.

Such a convincing depiction of concern, but Emma wouldn't fall for it. She narrowed her eyes as she struggled to control her labored breathing. Hard to sound authoritative while gasping for air. "What are you doing out here, Helen? Alone."

The other woman returned her focus to Emma, her brow creased. "I was just—" The hand with the blade came up.

"Stop!" Emma thrust out her arm in warning.

"What?" Helen took a step back, her nostrils flaring in true alarm. "What's going on?" She twisted from side to side as if looking for an attacker.

At her jerky movement, the fabric of her skirt fell away from the half-concealed blade. Or what Emma had assumed was a blade. In truth it was a . . . . garden trowel? What was she using *that* for? To bury a secret message? To conceal pilfered goods?

"I'm sorry I frightened you, Helen." Emma lowered her arm. "But I need to know what you are doing out here. It isn't safe for you to be away from town."

Helen eyed her warily. "I just wanted to collect some wild onions. I noticed them growing out here during the shooting lesson yesterday." She gestured to the prairie.

Sure enough, a cluster of white flowers dotted the area. Onion flowers.

"Miss Betty said it would be all right as long as I didn't dally."

Emma hesitated. Had she jumped to the wrong conclusion? Helen appeared genuinely perplexed.

"I know this is going to sound odd, Helen, but I need to look inside your gunnysack. And have you turn out the pockets of your skirt." If she had writing utensils or something suspicious hidden away, Emma would know her story was an elaborate ploy. If not . . . Well, then she'd just made a fool of herself and frightened one of her ladies for no good reason.

Helen bent down to retrieve the burlap bag she'd brought along to carry the wild onions in and handed it over. Emma peered inside. Empty. As were Helen's pockets. Except for a completely innocuous cotton handkerchief.

Emma handed the bag back. "I'm so sorry. I made a mistake."

Helen's eyes sparked with defiance, but even that couldn't completely hide the hurt hiding in her gaze. "What did you think I was doing out here?" She lifted her trowel and forced a laugh. "Burying a dead body or something?"

"Nothing so gruesome, I assure you." Emma smiled, trying to piece together the trust she'd just shattered. "I simply grew . . . concerned when I saw you wandering off alone."

"Not for my safety, apparently." Helen frowned. "You would

have been more solicitous when you found me. No, you were suspicious about something." Her eyes widened, and she took a step back. Then another. "Suspicious about *me*."

"It was a mistake," Emma repeated. "One I deeply regret. Your safety *does* matter to me. The safety of all the women matters to me."

The lines digging into Helen's brow cleared. "That's it." She shook her head and staggered back another step. "You thought I was helping them. The men who are attacking us."

Emma followed, her arms outstretched in silent apology. But Helen warded her off. Backed farther away.

"How could you? What have I ever done to make you think I could be capable of such treachery? That I would be in league with two . . . *men*." She spat the word with such revulsion that Emma winced.

"You've done nothing, Helen. I swear. These attacks have me rattled—that's all. They have me seeing disloyalty where there is none. Please, forgive me." Emma sighed and glanced away, tears close to the surface as guilt churned in her belly. "I feel so helpless. This place is supposed to be a sanctuary. That's what I promised." She turned back toward Helen. "To you. To everyone. But I can't keep you safe. You're my responsibility, and I'm letting you down."

Helen ceased her retreat, but she said nothing. Emma couldn't blame her. She'd been so eager to find the betrayer, yet in her chase, she'd betrayed one of her own.

She inhaled a breath to apologize a final time when movement in the grass to the left of Helen's feet caught her eye.

Helen must have seen the change in Emma's face, for the other woman started backing away again.

"No. Stop!" Emma rushed forward even as Helen stepped backward onto the whipping tail of a snake easily five feet long.

The head came up with a loud hiss. Helen gasped and lurched sideways. Emma lunged forward. Directly into the path of the striking snake.

Fangs punctured her hand. The body wrapped around her arm and squeezed.

25

Malachi had already started for home when distant reverberations from the church bell floated out to greet his ears. The gentle sound hovered above him with all the dread-filled grace of circling buzzards. Instinct had him craning his neck to peer up at the sky just as the first vibrations faded. Then a second toll echoed, stronger than the first.

The *bong* slashed through Mal's stupor. Something was wrong.

"Yah!" He kicked his horse's sides and galloped for home.

He'd told Porter to ring the bell if anything happened while he was away. Mal had promised to race for Harper's Station like a runaway locomotive if he heard the signal. Now, even a train engine seemed too slow.

If something had happened to Emma or the aunts . . .

Mal leaned farther over the gray's neck, urging the mare to greater speed.

He never should have left. He'd abandoned the women for a fool's errand, leaving them vulnerable. Had the outlaws snuck past him while he'd been searching for their camp? Mal hadn't heard any gunfire, but men had other ways to hurt women, ways that didn't require bullets.

Mal clenched his jaw and drove his mount into the Wichita River. As he splashed across the shallow expanse, one truth echoed in his mind.

He'd chosen wrong. He'd put Emma's safety at risk in an effort to save his job. A lousy, dirty mess of a job that would never smile at him. Hug him. *Love* him. Shoot, more than likely the stinkin' job would kill him. Blow him into a thousand tiny bits. Why had he even debated? Nothing was more important than the people he loved. Nothing.

The mare climbed the east bank with three lunging strides, then picked up speed again on the flatland that stretched between the river and the churchyard. Uncaring that thorns grabbed at his soggy pant legs, Mal wove through the scrub brush, his gaze searching for Porter.

The freighter must have been watching for his approach, for the big man ducked out of the entryway to the church and waved to Malachi from the steps. By the time he made it to ground level, Mal was off his horse and demanding answers.

"You need to hustle down to the clinic." Porter moved to take the mare's reins. "Miss Chandler's been hurt."

Searing pain tore through Mal's chest. His mind screamed a silent denial even as his feet took off at a dead run.

Emma. Hurt. His fault.

Give it to me, he pled as he ran. *Whatever she's suffering. Give it to me. Angels don't deserve pain.*

She didn't deserve any of this. Attackers. Traitors. Him running off and leaving her unprotected.

You call yourself a just God? How is any of this just?

He sprinted past the boardinghouse. Victoria's store. The café. Turned the corner past the bank. Emma's bank. The front window boarded up. Desolate.

234

Please let her be all right.

His bootheels pounded up the three steps leading into the clinic. He threw open the door and lunged inside only to be smothered by a flock of clucking hens.

"Let me through." The sharp order guillotined the chatter. A half dozen faces turned as one to stare at him. Malachi didn't have time to play nice. If they wouldn't clear a path, he'd make one himself.

He twisted his shoulders sideways and started barreling through the overcrowded waiting room. Gasps and tiny, high-pitched grunts of displeasure echoed through the room. He bumped elbows, hips, even trod on one poor gal's foot—for which he mumbled a quick *sorry* as he pressed on, until a pair of hands clasped his left arm.

"Calm down, boy. Stormin' through here like a wild boar on a rampage ain't gonna help things."

Mal jerked his arm away before the familiar voice registered in his brain.

"Leave him be, Henry. He's worried about our girl. As he should be." Bertie moved directly into his path, her admonishment changing to reassurance as she turned from her sister to him.

He loved the aunts. He really did. But if Bertie didn't get her sweet, motherly self out of his way, he was going to pick her up and move her.

"It's all right, Malachi," she said, eyes soft. "Helen managed to get the creature off of Emma before any real damage was done."

Rage, hot and searing, blazed through Malachi. He grabbed Bertie's shoulders and gave her a little shake. "She was attacked?"

Horrible visions flashed like lightning through his brain. A masked outlaw chasing Emma. Her running. Screaming. The outlaw being too fast. Too strong. Dragging her down.

Pinning her beneath him. A desperate Helen fending him off from behind.

Mal steered Bertie aside. He had to get to Emma. Had to see for himself that she truly was all right.

" . . . didn't want to let go." Bertie continued yapping, shadowing him like an overeager pup. Her words faded in and out through the haze of his anger. "Strong bugger . . . They finally got Emma free . . . She stepped on his neck, and Helen chopped his head off with her garden trowel."

"Wait. What?" Mal jerked to a halt and spun to his left to face Bertie. "Helen took off his head? With a *garden trowel?*" Impossible. No way under heaven could shy, slender Helen take off a man's head with a tiny handheld spade. A Roman gladiator couldn't accomplish that feat with such a weapon.

Bertie raised an exasperated brow. "Really, Malachi. It's insulting for you to look so shocked. We're not helpless, you know. We might need a man's assistance to fight off another man bent on trouble, but any female who works on a farm, like Helen does, knows how to deal with a rat snake."

A rat snake?

Mal's knees quivered. He braced a hand against the wall, pretty sure his legs were about to buckle.

A rat snake. He shook his head and swallowed the laughter bubbling up his throat. To think he'd thought . . . Well, never mind what he'd thought. That mental picture would only ignite his rage again. Because it *could* have happened. Thank God it hadn't.

With his knees regaining a bit of fortitude, Mal pushed away from the wall and smiled down at Bertie. "I'm glad Helen was with her. She's a strong woman." He tipped his hat up to the top of his forehead as his pulse regulated. "Now. Can I go in and check on Emma?"

Henry came up behind her sister. "You got your head on

straight? She don't need you going off half-cocked once you get in there. The girl's been through enough already today." The look she gave him had him fighting the urge to squirm. Something told him she was talking about more than the snake.

"I'll not upset her, Aunt Henry. I promise."

She examined him from stem to stern, gave him one more good glare, and dipped her head in a sharp nod.

Mal reached for the knob and pulled open the door, his ears registering Henry mumbling something about Emma ruining a perfectly good skillet of gravy thanks to his thoughtlessness. Having no idea what she meant by that statement and no desire to figure it out, he left the waiting room behind and stepped through the doorway into the clinic office.

Claire Nevin stepped around a white curtain that divided the room in half and smiled at him. "She's in here, Mr. Shaw. Helen's sitting with her."

The gal turned and disappeared again behind the curtain. Mal tugged off his hat and followed. Emma sat propped up in a narrow bed, her head turned toward a second woman sitting in a chair on the far side.

Helen sprang up from her seat the instant he rounded the curtain edge, her eyes wide, her mouth pinched. "I better be getting back to the farm." She glanced at Emma. "I'll fill in for you during the watch tonight."

"You don't have to. I—" Emma protested before Helen cut her off with a shake of her head.

"Maybelle said to rest. You heard her same as me. I'm not due for another shift until Thursday. I'm taking your turn."

"All right." Emma nodded. "Thank you."

Helen offered a tight smile, then strode toward the end of the bed. She slowed when she neared Mal's position, her gaze growing wary. Mal sidestepped between the bed and the curtain to get out of her way, then watched her skedaddle like a mouse that had just found a clear path around a barn cat. Claire discreetly followed her out.

Once the other ladies were gone, Mal circled around to the opposite side and took up the chair Helen had vacated. That was when he noticed Emma's arm.

The sleeve of her blouse had been rolled up past her elbow. Her palm and wrist were wrapped in a bandage. The beginning signs of bruising darkened the skin in a spiral pattern along her forearm up to her elbow.

His chest ached. "Does it hurt?"

"Only a little. Maybelle assured me there's no venom to worry about. She treated the bite area with some salve anyway to stave off infection." Emma raised her bandaged hand from the mattress and turned the palm toward him.

He wanted to take that hand in his and kiss each fingertip. Tenderly. Lovingly. To cradle it to his cheek, assuring himself she was safe. But he did none of that. Just nodded and dangled his hat off the end of his knee.

"I shouldn't have left you, Em." He hung his head, then forced himself to meet her gaze. "I should have been here. Taking care of things."

Her green eyes stared back at him with no judgment. "I guess that means you didn't find the bandits."

Mal blew out a heavy breath and ran a hand through his hat-flattened hair. "Nope. Found a few traces but nothing substantial. Knew it was a long shot when I set out. Should've just stayed here. Maybe if I had . . ."

"You would have stopped that snake from latching on to my arm?" She gave him one of her don't-be-an-idiot looks. "Not even you could have stopped that, Mal. Besides, I'm glad you didn't. That snake healed a rift between Helen and me. A swollen arm and a banged-up hand is a small price to pay for that blessing."

Only Emma would call a snakebite a blessing.

"Oh, and . . ." She leaned toward him.

Mal bent his head to hers.

Emma glanced quickly toward the curtain, then whispered, "Helen's not the traitor."

Mal tilted his chin slightly in order to fully see her face. "You're sure?"

"Positive."

The tiny pucker on her lips as she formed the word drew his gaze to her mouth. A mouth he wanted to taste. To touch. To kiss again and again until they were both short of breath.

It was only inches away. All he'd have to do was lean forward a little. Turn his head.

She sat back.

And there went his chance. Not that he would have taken it with half the town only a room away.

The scratch of the curtain being pushed back brought Malachi to attention. Sitting as straight as a broom handle in his chair, he kept his gaze firmly away from Emma's lips as Maybelle walked in.

"Here's that salve I promised you," she announced, completely ignoring Mal as she strode up to Emma and handed her a small metal tin. "I've shown your aunts how to change the bandage and instructed them on what to watch for. Soak it in a basin of water with Epsom salts before bed and again in the morning. Then apply the salve and a clean bandage. If you see red streaks moving up your arm from the bite site or if the area starts to ooze and grows painful to the touch, come see me right away."

Emma nodded. "I will."

"Good." Maybelle's attention shifted to Mal. "Perhaps Mr. Shaw would see you home?"

Mal jumped to his feet, barely snagging his hat before it fell to the floor. "Of course."

"She's to rest." Maybelle's hard stare branded the instructions on Malachi's hide. "I want her using that hand as little as possible for the next few days. The cleaner she keeps it, the less chance infection will set in."

"Yes, ma'am." He plunked his hat on his head, scooted around to the other side of the bed, took Emma's good arm, and helped her to her feet. "I'll take good care of her."

Maybelle crossed her arms over her midsection. "See that you do."

True to his word, Mal escorted Emma from the clinic to the station house, though the trip took three times longer than it should have with the ladies swarming like honeybees to nectar in their eagerness to express their sympathy and well wishes. Emma handled it all with grace, of course, taking time to thank each one for her concern. By the time Henry and Bertie bustled her upstairs to her room, Mal felt as if he'd run a mile upstream in hip-deep river water. But he didn't stop to rest. Didn't even snitch a roll from the cloth-covered basket sitting in the middle of the kitchen table.

Nope. He walked straight out the door and didn't pause until he reached the telegraph office. He had a job to resign.

26

Four days later, a third male invaded the women's colony. A short, skinny boy with a big, ugly horse. Horse was probably male, too, Emma mused as she watched the odd pair meander past the station-house window. At this rate, her ladies were going to be outnumbered by the end of the month.

Emma tucked her needle into the fabric square she'd been quilting and stood.

"Is your hand paining you, dear?" Bertie asked, her brows arching in concern.

"No." She rubbed at the tender spot on the heel of her right hand. It did still hurt a little, but that wasn't why she'd stopped quilting. Emma smiled an apology to the women gathered around the quilt frame in her parlor for the afternoon sewing session. "I just saw someone I didn't recognize ride by the window. I'm going to check it out."

Needles paused in midair and faces turned to peer out the window across from where Emma had been sitting.

"Was it one of those awful men?" Pauline asked. The youngest lady in the sewing circle turned back to Emma with wide eyes as she nibbled her lower lip.

241

Emma shook her head. "No. It was a boy. And his horse was a different color than the ones we've seen the outlaws ride." She sidestepped around the quilt frame and crossed behind the sofa to the door. She claimed her rifle from the collection standing at attention against the wall—none of the ladies moved about without a weapon these days—then reached for the door handle as she glanced back into the room. "It's probably someone who wandered into town by mistake."

"Better take Malachi with you," Henry fussed. "Just in case."

"And if you can't find him," Bertie added, "Mr. Porter usually guards Main Street from the bench outside the store."

Emma had to fight a peevish retort. It was just a boy. Not that she'd make the mistake of underestimating him with all that had gone on. But, really—whatever happened to Aunt Henry's battle cry that a woman didn't need a man in order to be strong? She never would have doubted Emma's capabilities before. But, to be fair, the entire town had been on edge, dreading the next swing of the attackers' ax. One that hadn't come. Yet.

Emma tossed what she hoped was a confident smile at the aunts. "I'll be careful." Then she ducked out the door before the rising tide of her own worries dragged her under.

Clutching her rifle in her right hand so she could have it ready in a flash, she trotted down the road after the boy and horse. The pair traveled at an unhurried clip, so she caught up to them quickly.

The dun gelding—yep, a male, just as she'd suspected—snorted and tossed his head when she cut in front of him, but he didn't buck or rear. A well-trained beast, even if he was ugly as a shriveled potato coated with mud. He had a chunk missing from one ear, a charcoal-gray mane that had been chopped off to a ridiculously short length, a big blotch of white on the left side of his rump, and a body that could either be gray with brown specks or brown with gray specks depending on how much color came from road dust. The horse held his head up like a king, though, and looked down on her with effrontery for interrupting his jaunt.

But it wasn't the horse that concerned her. It was the rider.

Emma reached a hand up to stroke the gelding's nose while at the same time swinging her rifle up to her shoulder to make sure the boy saw she was armed.

"Welcome to Harper's Station, young man. What's your business?" Emma smiled at the boy, but she examined him, too. Searched for weapons, for lumps beneath his shirt that might indicate something hidden. Did a mental tally of how much gear he carried. And frowned. A lot of gear. A small trunk tied behind the cantle. Bulging saddlebags. As if the kid was planning on moving in.

"Well?" She raised a brow at him.

He held her gaze. "My business is my own," he said, his chest puffing up with bravado even as his fingers trembled ever so slightly around the reins he held.

The tremble softened her. The boy couldn't be more than eleven or twelve years old, yet here he was, traveling alone and putting up a brave front when confronted by a bossy female with a rifle. She knew all too well what it felt like to stand up to someone stronger with only one's wits and pride.

Lowering her gun, she came alongside him, still craning her neck to keep an eye on his face. "Don't worry." She warmed her tone to something almost friendly and patted the horse's neck, inches away from the boy's knee. "I'm not going to hurt you. It's just that we've been having trouble around these parts lately, and we're a little shy of strangers. However, that's no excuse for poor hospitality. Why don't you hop down, and I'll help you find whoever you're looking for."

He snorted. "I ain't gonna fall into that trap, lady. The minute I get off this horse, I lose my advantage. I'm not some fool kid who ain't got a clue how the world works. Who says I'm lookin' for somebody, anyway? I ain't." He sat up straighter in the saddle and sniffed loud and long. He raised his chin at a cocky angle as if thoroughly satisfied with his efforts to appear masculine. "I'm lookin' for work," he said, his gaze aimed somewhere to the left of her face. "I'm real good with horses. Got experience working at a forge, too. I'm a right handy feller to have around."

Emma bit back a grin. "I'm sure you are. But I'm afraid we have no livery in Harper's Station. Nor a smithy."

His blue eyes widened with incredulity as they found her gaze. "No livery? What kind of town ain't got a livery?"

"Harper's Station is a women's colony."

His brow scrunched. "A what?"

"A women's colony. Only women live here. We run businesses, farms, and manufacture goods to sell. Few of our ladies own horses, so we've no need of a livery. If we require a blacksmith or farrier for the horses we do have, we simply travel into Seymour to have the work done."

"I never heard of no women runnin' businesses. 'Ceptin' maybe a laundry. Well . . . and the pleasure houses." He eyed her closely. "You look too proper for that kinda work, though. And too sober. My ma used to say the drink made the entertainin' easier. 'Course, it couldn't have been too easy, 'cause she drank all the time and still ended up dead." He made the heartbreaking statement with all the pragmatism of a teller reciting his account figures at closing time. "What kinda business do *you* run?" Skepticism laced his tone. "Maybe I can work for you."

Emma smoothed the front of her bodice. "I'm a banker." Pride infused her words, as it always did. Yet this time she felt a great deal of gratitude as well—gratitude that she wasn't forced to make her living with backbreaking toil, or worse, on her actual back. Maybe she *should* find work for this boy. "Are you any good with sums?"

"A lady banker?" He scoffed. "Yer pullin' my leg."

Then again, maybe she should just push the chauvinistic man-child off his horse.

Emma sighed. No. It wasn't his fault he couldn't imagine anything as far-fetched as a lady banker. Most males couldn't. It was probably a defect in the gender as a whole. So instead of pushing him off the horse, she gave him the stare instead. The one that dared him to see past the expected to the possible.

The boy quit laughing. "No foolin'?"

"No foolin'." There was hope for this one yet. "My bank is just down the road a piece." She nodded her head in the direction. "I can give you a tour later, if you want." She held her hand out to him. "I'm Emma Chandler, by the way."

He'd started reaching for her hand but jerked back. "Emma? Mr. Shaw's Emma? The angel?"

Angel? Where had that come from? No matter. There was more important information to glean. "You know Mr. Shaw?"

The boy grinned and dropped off the horse so fast, Emma had to leap back to keep her toes from being smashed. "Know him? He and me are partners." There went the chest sticking out again. The manly display didn't last long, though. Boyish enthusiasm overpowered it in a blink. "We both worked on the Burlington up in Montana until Mr. Shaw quit four days ago. That's why I'm here. I brought his stuff."

Emma stepped backward, the sudden news throwing her off balance. "Malachi quit his job?" Why would he do such a thing? He loved working with the railroads. Was good at it, too. One of the most respected explosive expects in the field. Not that he'd ever made the claim himself. She'd learned of his prowess on her own. After Mal had written her about taking the railroad job, she'd had her broker check into the Chicago, Burlington & Quincy Railroad. The man provided her with glowing reports testifying to the savvy of their investors and the capabilities of their crew, including one Malachi Shaw, touted as the best blaster in the business.

The boy didn't seem to notice her distress. In fact, he grew increasingly more animated as his enthusiasm took over. "You should've seen the boss man's face when he got Shaw's telegram. His mouth got all tight, and his nostrils flared like an angry mule right before he starts kickin'. Then he let go with a string of curses that made even *my* ears burn, and I was born in the rail camps."

The boy chuckled. "Yep. He was none too happy, but it was his own fault for backin' Shaw into a corner like that. Tellin' him he had to report by Friday or be dismissed. I coulda told him that tack wouldn't work. But did he ask me? Nope. Anyone who'd seen Shaw's face when he got that telegram from you sayin' you was in trouble woulda known where to lay his bet. Shaw would never leave his angel until she was safe. Even if it meant givin' up his job."

The boy gave her a serious nod, his youthful enthusiasm fading into something more serious. "Mr. Shaw is the only one at the camps who treated me like a real person, not just some lackey to order about. That's why I watched over his things and brought them to him. What's important to him is important to me. And I reckon you, Miss Emma, are the most important thing of all."

Malachi had left his job. For her. Emma couldn't seem to think her way past that stark fact.

She had brought him into this mess, asked him to risk his life to help her protect her ladies, never giving thought to how long it might take or what kind of repercussions it might create for him. In truth, she hadn't cared. All she'd cared about when she sent that telegram was protecting *her* colony. The community *she'd* built. The things *she* cared about. There had even been a part of her, deep down, that had wanted to send for him just so she could see him again. Emma bit her lip. What a selfish creature she was. So concerned with her own desires, her own plans, that she never once considered what Mal might be forced to sacrifice. She'd banked on his loyalty, and he'd paid the price.

"Miss? You all right?"

Emma gave herself a mental shake and glanced back at the boy. "Of course. I'm . . . fine."

He didn't look like he believed her.

"When . . . when did your employer send his telegram?" An awful thought started piecing itself together in the fog of her mind.

The boy's forehead wrinkled. "Monday, I think. Why?"

"Monday," she whispered, then turned to peer in the direction of the river. The last pieces clicked into place. The message Grace delivered before shooting practice. Mal's sudden desire to search out the bandits the next day. It was his only chance to save his position with the railroad while still fulfilling his pledge to her. He'd wanted to keep that job. Wanted it so badly he'd hunted two armed gunmen. By himself. In their own territory.

Thank God he hadn't found them. A shiver coursed through Emma at the thought of what could have happened. Yet what *had* happened hurt, too. She'd stolen the one thing that had given him pride and respect. And what had she given him in return? Nothing but trouble.

Emma was so deep in her thoughts, she failed to hear the jogging footsteps approaching until the horse nickered and stamped his front hooves. Her head whipped around as she belatedly lifted her rifle.

Malachi.

His gaze searched her face for a brief moment before he turned his attention to the boy. "Andrew! You're a long way from Montana."

The boy straightened like a soldier coming to attention. "I

been watchin' over your things, Mr. Shaw, just like I told you I would. Brought Ulysses to you."

"So you did." Mal was grinning like a kid who'd had a long-lost toy returned. The gelding bumped Mal's shoulder with his nose. Mal chuckled softly and immediately started stroking the animal's mismatched ears, placing his forehead against that of the horse. "I missed you, old man," Mal murmured. "It's good to have you back."

"I brought your trunk and the rest of your stuff, too. Even your big copper tub. Had to leave that at the depot in Seymour, though. It was too big to tie to the saddle."

A deep rumble of laughter echoed in Malachi's chest, the sound warming Emma's heart even as it twisted the guilt deeper into her soul.

"I can just picture you trying to lash that big ol' thing to Ulysses's back." Mal glanced over to Andrew, then leaned back in to murmur to his horse. "You wouldn't stand for that, would you, old man?" Ulysses lifted his head and shook it as if in answer. Mal grinned, his own head pulling back even as his hand lingered. He stroked the gelding's cheek, a more thoughtful expression spreading across his features. Mal raised a brow at the boy. "Why did you leave the camp? I would have returned to collect my things eventually."

"I figured you might need some help," Andrew said. "Seemed to me that whatever trouble you got tangled up in was more complicated than you first thought. So I came down to lend a hand." The boy's cocksure voice couldn't quite conceal the pleading undertone. He wanted to stay with Malachi—likely the only man who had ever shown interest in him, who'd ever treated him with kindness, dignity.

But if he stayed, Emma's trouble could get him killed.

"No!"

Both males jerked their faces toward her.

"You need to go." Her eyes met Malachi's. "Both of you." She'd been selfish long enough. Yet the thought of him leaving her again ripped her heart from her chest. A sob welled inside her. She forced it back, the effort leaving her vulnerable to the tears cresting the rims of her eyes. "You've given me enough, Mal. Go back to Montana. To the railroad. You're the best blaster in the business."

The best man she'd ever known. The man she trusted above all others. The man she . . . loved. Yes, loved. Not with the girlish infatuation of her past, but with a mature ardency that urged her to set her own desires aside and do what was best for him. By keeping him here, she was slowly stripping away his identity and everything he'd built for himself. It had to stop.

"Em." Mal dropped his hand from the horse and stepped toward her.

She shook her head and backed away. The tears fell freely now, and the sob pressed against her throat, nearly choking her.

"I never should have asked you to come. It was wrong. Selfish. I'm so sorry."

He reached for her.

She bolted.

27

Malachi sprinted after Emma for three steps, then remembered Andrew. He skidded to a halt and turned back. "Sorry, kid. I gotta . . ."

Andrew lifted his chin. "I know. Go after your woman, Shaw. I'll get Ulysses settled."

Malachi's feet danced sideways, continuing in the direction he had started, even though his eyes kept contact with the boy. "I'm staying in the barn at the old station house you just passed. Tell the aunts you're a friend of mine, and they'll let you in. Probably feed you, too."

Andrew's face lit up like any twelve-year-old boy's would at the promise of food. He nodded and waved Mal on his way.

Malachi didn't hesitate. He spun around and churned up the ground. She was racing for the store. Probably thought to seek shelter with Miss Adams. Not happening. He wasn't about to let her hide from him. Not after that ridiculous little speech she'd just thrown in his face. They were gonna have words. A lot of them. However many it took for her to understand one thing clearly. He wasn't leaving. Not as long as she and her ladies were in danger. No matter what kind of nonsensical excuse she came up with.

Porter spotted Emma coming and lurched to his feet, rifle at the ready, eyes scanning the area for a threat. When his gaze locked on Malachi, he raised his chin in question. Mal pointed to Emma, then slammed his hand back against his own chest. *She's my concern. Don't interfere.*

Porter relaxed his stance. Even propped one booted foot on the bench he'd been sitting on moments ago. He braced the rifle stock against his thigh and leaned back to watch the shenanigans.

Mal didn't care if he was making a scene. Some things were too important to let polite manners get in the way.

What he didn't count on was another emotional female bursting into the mix. He was a step or two away from Emma when Victoria Adams threw open the door to the store and rushed onto the boardwalk.

"Emma!" she cried. "What's happened?"

Thankfully, Porter was a quick-witted man. Quick footed, too. At the same instant Mal latched on to Emma's arm, Porter grabbed the storekeeper around the waist and dragged her away from the steps leading to the street.

Tori screeched and kicked her legs, her feet waving about in midair thanks to Porter's excessive height. "What are you *doing*? Let me go, you big lout!"

Mal heard the freighter rumble something in reply, but he was too distracted by his own handful of squirming woman to give it any heed.

He spun Emma around to face him and nearly got whacked in the head with the rifle she still carried. But it was the tears streaming down her cheeks that rammed into his chest like an unseen blow.

Had he done this somehow? Hurt her to the point that she

would weep and run from him? The thought nearly weakened him enough to let her slip through his grasp. But then the same determination that had driven him to rise above his guttersnipe beginnings to excel at a profession that most men ran from exerted itself.

If he'd broken her, he'd just have to find a way to fix her.

Using instincts honed from a childhood spent dodging swiping broom handles and grabby lawmen arms, Mal ducked past the flying rifle, sidestepped the stomping shoe heels, and swept Emma up into his arms.

She protested at first, or at least, he assumed that's what those sobbing exclamations meant. He couldn't actually understand a thing coming out of her mouth. But as he carted her toward the vacant café, the oddest thing happened. The fight went out of her. She curled up against his chest. The rifle dropped, clanking onto the hard-packed dirt street behind them.

Mal didn't stop to retrieve it. Someone else could get it. Porter, maybe. Or one of the ladies. There were bound to be a gaggle of them watching from the store or boardinghouse windows farther down the street. He only had one concern at the moment, and nothing short of a full-scale attack by the bandits would alter his course.

Reaching the café, Mal managed to get enough of a hand on the knob to unlatch the door. He then used his foot to push the portal open. Not wanting to risk Emma running off again, Mal kept her in his arms and closed the door behind him with a second kick of his foot. He strode to the first chair he found and plopped down onto the seat with Emma in his lap.

She didn't boss him. Didn't lecture him on proper behavior. Didn't even lift her face to pierce him with a glare. All she did was burrow more deeply into him and let out a shuddery sigh that contained a hiccup left over from her weeping.

Mal looked to the ceiling, a silent prayer for help winging

upward from his mind. Then he set his jaw and got down to business.

"Tell me what I did, Em. Tell me what I did to hurt you, and I swear I'll put it to rights." Somehow.

"Oo it ur ob," she mumbled into his chest.

Well, that was less than helpful.

"I can't understand what you're saying, sweetheart." *Sweetheart?* Had that word really just come out of his mouth? Mal grimaced. As if he wasn't in enough hot water already. He didn't need to make things more complicated than they already were.

Yet he couldn't treat her like he didn't care, either. Right now, she needed to be soothed, and heaven knew he was about as soothing as a cactus. Perhaps an endearment or two wouldn't be so bad.

He took hold of her arms and gently eased her away from his chest. She ducked her head as if not wanting him to see her and quickly raised a hand to shield her from his view. A chill hit his chest. Not only because her warmth was no longer pressed there, but because of the damp spots she'd left behind.

Idiot. Offer her your handkerchief.

Leaving her propped unsteadily on his knees, Mal lifted his hips enough to jam his hand into his trouser pocket and pull out a—he gave it a quick inspection—clean handkerchief.

"Here." He shoved it under her nose.

She still didn't look at him, but she did accept his handkerchief. After wiping her eyes and giving her nose a delicate little blow that couldn't have been of much practical use, she folded the cotton square back up and fisted it inside her palm.

"Better?" he asked.

She nodded, still not looking directly at him, which was a pretty impressive feat since they were less than six inches apart. "Yes. Thank you."

"Good. Now tell me again what I did to upset you."

She nibbled on her bottom lip.

"Emma." He snapped her name like a general giving an order.

She flinched, then answered in a small voice. "You quit your job."

His job? How did she . . . ? Andrew. The kid must have told her. Mal had hoped to keep that little detail to himself, but apparently that was no longer an option. "There'll be other jobs, Emma. It doesn't matter."

"Doesn't matter?" Fire sparked in her green eyes, and for once he was glad to see it. He'd take an avenging angel over a crushed one any day of the week. "Of course it matters! That job is important to you, Malachi. I know it is."

He tried to shrug it off, but she was having none of it. She thrust her palms against his shoulders and pinned him to the chairback.

"Don't pretend it doesn't signify. It does. If someone tried to take my bank from me, I'd fight him every step of the way. Just like you fought to save your job. Don't think I haven't figured out why you suddenly decided to go outlaw hunting on Tuesday."

He should have known she was too clever not to make that connection.

"That's why you have to leave," she said. "You have to fight for the job you love. You've given me enough, Mal. More than I had the right to ask for. Take the boy and get out of here while things are quiet. The outlaws have probably given up, anyway. It's been four days without a sign of them. And Mr. Porter is here if we—"

"Porter?" Malachi surged to his feet, leaving Emma to slide off his lap. He grabbed her waist to steady her, then promptly set her aside. "You think I'm just going to walk away and leave your safety in Porter's hands? The man's still recovering from a cracked skull, for pity's sake. He'd probably have trouble withstanding a stiff wind, let alone a full-blown attack from a pair of ruthless gunmen."

Well, that might be overstating things a bit. Mal doubted a tornado would take the big man off his feet. But Porter cared more about the pretty shop owner than the others in town. It's why he stood guard on her front porch. That left Emma and the aunts vulnerable. A completely unacceptable circumstance to Malachi's way of thinking.

"Or maybe you think that since I've failed to solve your problem, you'll just give the job to someone else." He threw the accusation in her face even as he cringed inside, fearing that the statement was actually true.

"Of course not! You're the one I trust implicitly. Not Porter."

"Then why are you trying to get rid of me?" he practically shouted.

"Because I'm ruining your life!"

The bellow hung in the air between them for long seconds as Malachi tried to figure out what in the world she meant. Eventually he gave up.

Emma had turned her face away from him, but he gently took hold of her chin and guided her back around to where he could see her eyes.

"How, exactly, are you ruining my life?"

She tried to turn away again, but he wouldn't let her.

"Don't hide from me, Em. Tell me what you're thinking."

She let out a shaky sigh, then squared her shoulders and faced him head on. He dropped his hand from her chin, knowing she wouldn't need the persuasion any longer.

"I've been selfish."

He shook his head and started to interrupt, but she gave him one of those *don't you dare* looks that always stopped him in his tracks.

"You asked," she said, "so now you have to stand there and accept the answer."

He shut his mouth.

She nodded her approval.

"When I asked you to come here and help me, I never once thought about what such an action would cost you. I thought only of myself. Of my ladies. My town. And thanks to my selfishness, you've lost your job and nearly lost your life. I can't sit by and watch all you've worked for crumble around you, Mal. I care about you too much."

She cared about him? Like a friend? Like a sister? Or like something more? Mal's pulse leapt from a steady walk to a full-out gallop in a single heartbeat. Suddenly it wasn't his job he wanted to talk about.

"There'll be other jobs, Emma. But there'll never be anyone as important to me as you . . . and the aunts. You're the only family I've ever known. And family sticks up for family, no matter the cost. I'm not going to leave you to fight this battle on your own."

"Then maybe it's time I gave up the fight." Her shoulders sagged. "It's probably what I should have done in the first place. It was foolish to put my ladies' lives in danger for a piece of earth that can be replaced."

Mal drew back. "What? This can't be Emma Chandler standing before me. She never backs down from a fight just because things get hard. And she especially wouldn't back down from a pair of ill-mannered bullies picking on a group of defenseless women."

Emma slammed hands on her hips, a frown turning the corners of her mouth down. "We're not defenseless."

He chuckled. "Now, that's the Emma I know and love."

Again with the mouth malfunctions.

Maybe she didn't notice. It was just a turn of phrase, after all. It didn't necessarily mean anything. In his case it *did*, but she didn't have to know that.

Emma's gaze searched his face. He swallowed hard but brazened out the scrutiny. At least for a few long seconds. When the look in her eyes changed . . . softened . . . *invited* . . . he started to talk again. It was either that or pull her into his arms and kiss her with a hunger he wasn't sure he could completely control.

"We stand together, and we fight together," he vowed. "No matter how long it takes. No regrets. No blame. Agreed?"

"But what about Andrew? It's dangerous for him to be here."

Mal inwardly smiled. How could this compassionate woman ever think herself selfish? She was always thinking of others. Always.

"I'll fill him in on the facts of the situation, then give him the same choice you gave your ladies. Stay and fight, knowing the risks, or leave with my blessing and respect intact. He'll decide for himself."

"You're a good man, Malachi Shaw." Then before he could even think of dodging, Emma clasped his cheeks, raised up on tiptoes, and pressed her lips to his.

It lasted only a heartbeat—although, he was pretty sure his heart stopped beating in that moment, so that particular measurement was probably not very accurate. The only thing he knew for sure was that the kiss ended before his stupefied mind could respond.

Then she vanished. And all he could do was stand in the empty café and wish he'd chosen kissing over talking when he'd had the chance.

28

Lips tingling and mind awhirl with shock over her own boldness, Emma flew from the café to the store in such a fog of delight and embarrassment that she was nearly upon Tori before recognizing that the freighter had a grip on her friend's waist. And Tori was making no effort to escape. Oh, her posture was stiff, and her hands were braced against Porter's chest with her elbows locked as if trying to maintain the maximum distance possible. But none of that changed the astounding facts.

A man. Holding Tori. In broad daylight. And she was allowing it.

In fact, the two were staring at each other so intently, they didn't notice Emma's approach until her heel clicked on the bottom stair. The tiny sound elicited a reaction more in keeping with a gunshot.

Both parties jumped. Tori gasped. Porter whipped his head around, his expression fierce as he gripped Tori to his chest with all the might of a grizzly and instinctively twisted to put himself between her and danger. Tori's arms folded like a rag doll's as she collapsed against the big man's chest. Her mouth, apparently, worked just fine, however.

"Let me go, you cow-handed oaf. You promised to release me as soon as Mr. Shaw finished his discussion. Well, Emma's here now, so—"

His arms let go of Tori's waist so fast, she staggered backward and would have fallen against the store wall if Mr. Porter hadn't grabbed her elbow to steady her. Her face flaming pink, Tori batted away his help the moment she regained her footing.

"I'm fine," she insisted, though the blush on her cheeks told a different story. Emma couldn't remember the last time she'd seen her friend so flustered.

"Mr. Ben wasn't hurtin' her," Lewis chimed in as he popped up from his hiding place behind the bench, giving Emma a turn at being the one startled. "I checked."

He looked like such a little man making that proclamation that Emma couldn't help but grin. Which only made Tori's color deepen.

"He was just makin' her stay put."

"Yes, well . . ." Tori straightened her apron and stepped around the freighter, making a concerted effort not to look at him as she did so. "He had no right to hold me here against my will. It's . . . barbaric."

Lewis's nose scrunched up. "But you do it to me all the time, Mama. When I need a bath. When I'm squirmy in church. When—"

"Enough, Lewis!" Tori placed a hand on her stomach, closed her eyes for a moment, and inhaled a long, deep breath. When next she spoke, it was in the calm, rational voice Emma was accustomed to hearing. "Why don't you go with Mr. Porter on his rounds? He hasn't made his usual circuit around town and up to the steeple yet. Maybe you can help him spy an outlaw from the bell tower."

Lewis's face lit up and his feet started dancing in a tight little circle. "You mean it? You'll let me go on rounds with him?"

"Only if you promise to be careful and do precisely as Mr. Porter tells you."

"I will! I promise." Lewis jumped straight at the freighter, grabbed his hand and started tugging the big man toward the steps. "Come on, Mr. Ben. Let's go climb the steeple!"

Porter allowed the boy to drag him along, but his gaze pressed into Tori as he passed. Tori stared pointedly at the boardwalk beneath her feet. She might trust the man enough to let her son romp around in his company, but she seemed to be working mighty hard to discourage any personal entanglement.

The freighter apparently had a thick hide to go with those thick muscles of his, for he showed no sign of Tori's coldness affecting him. In truth, he acted the same as if she had met his gaze and smiled politely to him. He doffed his hat and rumbled the only words Emma had heard him say since she arrived. "I'll take good care of the boy, ma'am."

Then he nodded to Emma, ruffled Lewis's hair, and gestured for the boy to lead the way. Lewis set off for the church in a full sprint. Mr. Porter followed at a steadier pace, his long legs keeping the boy from getting too far ahead.

Emma climbed the stairs to stand beside Tori, who now couldn't seem to take her eyes off of the big man tromping behind her son.

"The two of them seem to get along well." Emma's observation broke Tori's stare. She immediately spun around, not quite glaring at Emma, but frowning for certain.

"Lewis is a young boy infatuated with the only man of his acquaintance. It's only natural for him to seek out a male influence in a town full of females." She crossed her arms beneath her breasts. "I don't see the harm in it."

"Neither do I," Emma assured her friend. "In fact, I commend you for allowing Lewis to spend time with Mr. Porter. He seems a dependable sort. Kind. Responsible. Capable.

There are far worse examples of manhood your son could emulate."

Tori pierced Emma with a sharp gaze. Emma held her stare, knowing Tori must be thinking of the man who had hurt her, reminding herself of all the reasons a man couldn't be trusted. But then she nodded once in belated agreement to Emma's assessment of Mr. Porter's character before raking her gaze over Emma, a new intensity lighting her eyes. She grabbed Emma's hands and held them out wide while she made a head-to-hem inspection.

"He didn't hurt you, did he? I saw him snatch you off the street and cart you away. You say you trust him, but no one really knows what a man is capable of when he's angry, Emma. I was worried sick. And then that brute of a freighter wouldn't let me go after you."

Tori released her hold on Emma and wrapped her arms around herself instead. "He said Mr. Shaw would never hurt you. But how would he know? They've been acquainted for less than a week. For all he knew, the man could have been beating you bloody in that café."

"Malachi?" Emma laughed softly. "Oh, Tori. Porter was right. Mal would never hurt me. Ever. He's too honorable. And too dedicated to my welfare and that of the aunts." Her smile dimmed. "Probably to his detriment."

Tori's brow creased. "What does that mean?"

Emma slid her fingers through the tight knot of her friend's arms. "Let's go inside and brew some tea. I'll tell you all about it."

Well, *almost* all about it. Emma didn't think she was quite up to confessing that she kissed the man. Not when her friend was bound to lecture her about the dangers of impropriety between the genders.

Besides, Emma wanted to savor that memory in private. Savor

it. Examine it. Memorize it. And perhaps, dream up a way to repeat it.

Malachi lingered in the café, waiting for his pulse to settle and for the haze to clear from his brain. Thankfully, he'd had years of training working with explosive materials and knew how to calm his mind. A few reminders about keeping one's focus usually did the trick. This time, though, it took more than a few. It took an entire lecture.

Emma was an emotional creature. Affectionate. She threw hugs around like they were handshakes. And kisses? Well, kisses were new, but not unheard of. She kissed the aunts on their cheeks all the time. It was a family thing, surely.

With her ill-placed guilt riling her up about his job, things had gotten out of hand. That's all. Her tears proved her delicate state. Even as a girl she'd rarely cried. Not even when he left. Her chin had trembled and her voice had wobbled, but she'd held fast. Yet today she'd been sobbing as she ran from him. So when he'd finally convinced her he didn't blame her for the consequences of losing his job, her relief had overcome her and she'd just reacted. His beautiful, impulsive angel had kissed him out of gratitude, nothing else.

That's what he needed to believe, anyway, if he hoped to keep his wits from scattering.

Two outlaws were threatening Emma and the ladies of Harper's Station. Wasting concentration on imagined motives for a friendly kiss would only put the women he cared about at greater risk. And that he wouldn't do. He was here as protector, not suitor. Best he snuff out that fuse at the source before it ran away from him and eventually blew everything up.

Head screwed on straight, finally, Malachi strode out the café door and back down the street to the station-house barn, intent

KAREN WITEMEYER

on finding Andrew. When he entered, a familiar nicker welcomed him. Ulysses. Man, but it was good to have his horse back.

Mal let out a low whistle, and his gelding answered with a snort and a bob of his head. "You're a sight for sore eyes, old man." Mal crossed to the stall where Andrew had set Ulysses up with fresh hay and water. His saddle and gear had been removed and he'd been given a quick rubdown, but the fellow could use a thorough brushing. Bertie had probably lured Andrew away with egg sandwiches and cookies. Mal patted his vest. Still had a couple cookies of his own tucked away. Gingerbread. Ulysses could probably smell them.

Even as the thought crossed Mal's mind, the horse bent his neck over the stall's half door and pushed his nose into Mal's chest, eliciting a chuckle. "All right, you beggar. We'll both have one."

He dug into the inside pocket of his vest and pulled out the treats. Holding his palm flat under Ulysses's nose, he offered the horse the one that was mostly whole. Then, after wiping his feeding hand down his trouser leg, Mal popped one of the broken pieces of the second cookie into his mouth.

The spices danced across his tongue, and the sweetness made him smile. The flavor reminded him of the ladies who had made them—spice for Henry, with her opinionated nature, and sweet for Bertie, the nurturer. The two made a perfect blend.

"It's good, ain't it?" Mal rubbed Ulysses at the base of his notched ear and threw the second half of the broken cookie into his own mouth. Dusting the crumbs from his hands, he stepped away from the stall to locate a currycomb and brush. "Let's see if we can get some of that trail dust off."

"I'll take care of that, Mr. Shaw." Andrew dashed through the barn doorway, coat flapping, cheeks bulging with an unfinished meal. The boy must have spied him through the kitchen window and come running. "I weren't neglectin' my duties.

263

Honest. Miss Chandler was just so insistent, I didn't think it'd be polite to turn her down."

"No one thinks you're neglectful, Andrew." Malachi stepped forward and clapped the youngster on the shoulder. "You've taken fine care of Ulysses for me over the last couple weeks. I can tell. I've just missed doin' for him myself. Like missin' spendin' time with an old friend."

"So you ain't mad?"

"Mad?" Malachi chuckled and gave Andrew's shoulder an extra squeeze before releasing him and walking back to his horse. "Hardly. I lived with these women for two years when I wasn't much older than you are now. They were always shoving food at me and demanding I come inside and eat at the table."

Andrew scrunched his nose. "And wash up. Not just yer hands neither, but yer face and neck, too."

Now that he mentioned it, the kid *did* look much cleaner than the last time he'd seen him. Mal grinned. "Yep." He pointed to the tack shelf. "I think there's a second brush over there. Why don't you give me a hand, and you can catch me up on what's been going on at the rail camp."

Andrew nodded, then jumped to retrieve the second brush while Mal started working the currycomb over Ulysses's side. When the boy joined him in the stall, Mal immediately asked about Zachary, his young explosives apprentice.

"Zach's fine," Andrew told him. "Boss man even let him run a few of the smaller blasting projects on his own while you were gone. Shaved off half of a good-sized boulder without blowin' apart the weight-bearing side. Zach strutted around the camp for two days after that, neck all stretched up like a rooster ready to crow. Oh, and he wanted me to make sure you knew he still has all his fingers."

Mal chuckled and shook his head. Leave it to Zach to get to the heart of a matter. He was proud of the boy. Handling a

KAREN WITEMEYER

man's job with a man's skill. He'd obviously been paying heed to their lessons.

"Who're they bringing in for the tunnel work?" Mal asked, moving down to the horse's flanks.

"Ted Osbourne."

Mal nodded to himself. That was one weight off his shoulders. "Osbourne's good. Zach will be in good hands with him in command." Though Mal would miss being the one grooming him. He was a good kid. Had a good head for the work—eager, at times a tad impatient, but never to the point of carelessness. Not working with him anymore was the only thing Mal truly regretted about losing the Burlington job. He was gonna miss that kid.

Mal cleared his throat and refocused on the kid here with him. "So what are your plans, Andrew? Will you head back to the rail camp?"

"Nah. I figured I'd hang out with you for a while." He sniffed and set his face in manly lines, though he didn't quite meet Malachi's gaze. "Get a job in the area. That lady of yours even offered to show me around the bank. Asked if I was good with numbers. You think she'd care if she knew I ain't learnt my times tables yet?"

Mal's mind was flooded once again with Emma. That's all it took—one simple question. And unfortunately, the images rushing in had nothing to do with banking or times tables or anything else that would be vastly less dangerous to contemplate.

Mal cleared his throat and tried to shift his mental picture of Emma from the café to the bank. From leaning in to kiss him, to leaning over ledgers at her desk. But, dad gum, if she didn't look just as fetching bent over a stack of papers as she did raising up on tiptoes. "I, uh, think banking has more to do with adding and subtracting than—"

Footfalls coming fast cut him off.

Mal jerked to attention, shoved the currycomb at Andrew, and strode out of the stall. His hand hovered above his holster as Porter came into view. The big man carried the shopkeeper's boy under his left arm like a sack of potatoes while his right held fast to his rifle.

"There's trouble at the farm." Porter shot a quick, suspicious look at Andrew, who had come up behind Malachi. "Spotted Mrs. Cooper driving that old wagon of hers like a cougar was on her trail. Them two gals are with her."

Betty Cooper never left the farm unattended unless there was a town meeting or church service to attend. If she had Helen and Katie with her now, something was definitely wrong.

Mal nodded once to Porter, ordered Andrew to stay put, then drew his gun and ran out to meet the wagon flying in from the north.

29

Mal heard the wagon before he spotted it. Horse hooves pounding against earth. Harness jangling. Wood creaking. Betty was coming in fast. Too fast.

Porter finally put Lewis Adams down and with a swat to his rear sent the boy running in to his mother. Which meant Emma would be out in a blink and squarely in the middle of whatever trouble was heading their way.

Mal set his jaw, ran up the store steps, and planted himself in front of the door. He knew he couldn't really expect to keep her inside, but he sure as shootin' could keep himself between her and whatever danger had Betty charging into town like a spooked herd on stampede.

Sure enough, the moment Betty's wagon careened around the curve past the clinic, Emma pulled open the store's door and pushed none-too-gently against his back.

"Get out of the way, Mal," she grunted, as if increased effort would make him budge. "I need to see what's going on." She gave up trying to shove him out of her way and swatted his shoulder instead. Not that it made a bit of difference.

"Do you have your rifle?" Mal snapped without turning to look at her. He knew she didn't. He'd picked it up from where she'd dropped it in the middle of the street earlier and taken it back to the station house for her.

"Nooo . . ." she hedged, and he could tell her mind was spinning to find a plausible reason why he should let her out despite her unarmed state.

She was probably clever enough to come up with one, too, which would make Mal's job that much harder. So before she could mount a counterattack, Mal pressed his advantage.

"No weapon means no exit. You stay inside until those of us who are armed determine it's safe to come out." He spoke harshly, giving her no room to argue.

"Fine," she grumbled, her frustration rolling off her in waves he could actually feel through the back of his vest.

Then all at once, she was gone. He felt the heat leave from behind him, even though Betty's call of "Whoa!" drowned out all sound of Emma's movements.

She'd return. Of that he had no doubt. He'd better move fast.

Mal didn't bother with the boardwalk stairs. He simply jumped down to the street, skirted far enough behind the rear of the farm wagon not to be blinded by the dust that was still settling, then scanned Betty's back trail for any sign of her being followed.

No other clouds of dust heralded pursuit. No suspicious shadows stood out from the surrounding scrub brush or prairie grass. No approaching hoofbeats caught his ear. 'Course it was hard to hear much of anything above the sniffling and hiccups of the two ladies in the back of the wagon and Betty's stomping as she climbed down from the driver's box.

Not able to make out any visible threat, Mal turned around and marched up to meet Betty as she reached over the side of the wagon and hoisted a gunnysack out. She spun around, spotted Malachi, and threw the sack at his feet.

Mal cast a quick glance down at the lumpy bag, then zeroed in on Betty's face. Mouth downturned. Eyebrows sharp. Unshed tears glimmering in her eyes.

Wait. Tears? Betty? The ex-soldier's wife was the toughest old bird he knew. *What could have—*

"They killed 'em," she spat, her voice quivering with a mixture of anger and heartbreak. "Ever' last one of 'em."

Mal looked back down at the sack, a sick dread swirling in his gut as he calculated the size of the lumps.

"All my best layers. Gone."

Her chickens. Mal clenched his jaw so hard, he nearly cracked a tooth. Who would do such a meanspirited thing? No. Wrong question. He knew who. What he didn't know was . . . "How?" he ground out. "How did they get to the hens?"

"Dogs." Betty turned her head and spat on the ground, her disgust palpable. "Two of 'em. Part coyote, I suspect."

"Oh no!" Emma pushed past Malachi, her skirts swirling around the sack that lay at his feet. "Not your chickens." Her voice broke as she reached out to touch Betty's arm with her left hand. Her right, he noticed, held an iron skillet.

Mal glanced heavenward, something between a chuckle and a groan catching in his throat. Well, at least she'd obeyed him. She hadn't come outside without a weapon, if one could call a frying pan a weapon. He wasn't inclined to classify it as such himself, but since there was no sign of outlaws bearing down on their position, he opted not to share his opinion.

"Betty, I'm so . . . so sorry."

Betty pulled away from Emma's hold. A wounded look flashed across Emma's features for a split second before she hid it away. A muscle in Malachi's jaw ticked.

"It ain't your fault, Emma. It's them no-good outlaws!" Betty kicked the wagon wheel with the toe of her boot and spat at the ground again. "What is so all-fire important about this town that they would kill a henhouse full of innocent creatures just to force us out? It don't make a lick of sense."

"I wish I knew," Emma said in a quiet voice. "I'd give it to them in a heartbeat, if it would mean they'd leave us alone."

"Well, whatever it is, I aim to see they *never* get it," Betty declared, bracing her legs apart and slapping hands on hips in a battle stance. "They killed my critters. I don't care what they throw at me. I ain't budgin' from my farm, and I ain't budgin' from this town. They'll have to shoot me dead and drag my ugly carcass down to the river to get me to leave."

"Betty, don't say that." Katie climbed down from the wagon bed and circled around behind her mentor.

Helen was only a step behind. "Whatever those horrid men want, it's not worth your life."

"We can replace the chickens," Emma said, trying to soothe, but it only turned Betty's face darker.

"Some things can't be replaced." Betty blinked. A single tear rolled down her weathered cheek. "My Robert gave me two of those birds before he passed. They were tough old biddies, kinda like me, but they reminded me of the sergeant every time I saw them pecking about the yard."

"Oh, Betty," moaned someone behind Mal. He glanced over his shoulder. Flora stood as still as a post, her eyes filled with tears.

On all sides, the street brimmed with women. Solemn, quiet women who had wandered out of shops and homes to gather around Betty. To grieve and mourn her loss and to offer what little comfort could be given. It made the backs of Mal's eyeballs itch a bit in sympathy even as it solidified his resolve.

Tomorrow he was going to ride to Seymour, return the mare he'd rented from the livery, round up as many men as were willing to make the trip back, and start beating the bushes for these two outlaws. Shoot. He'd pay the men for their time if he must. This had to stop before something besides chickens turned up dead.

"I need to know exactly what happened so I can report this to the sheriff tomorrow." Mal hadn't meant to bark the command, but if the disapproving stares aimed his direction were any indication, he'd spoken more harshly than he'd intended.

Betty wasn't offended by his tone. She barely even batted an eyelash. She'd spent too many years around army folks to let a little domineering behavior cow her. Yet her deepening scowl told him she didn't much care for his statement.

"Sheriff Tabor ain't gonna do anything. I got no proof that anyone set the dogs on my chickens. Never saw hide not hair of the bandits. The birds were safely inside their pen with the gate closed when I left to walk the perimeter. If it weren't for Helen's shot, I never woulda known something was wrong."

Mal turned a questioning gaze to the dark-haired woman at Betty's side. For once, the man-shy lady met his stare without ducking away. Head high and jaw set she described the incident. "Someone unlatched the gate while Katie and I were in the house cleaning the eggs we'd gathered that morning and packing them in straw. I didn't see who it was, but I know when I left the coop this morning, the latch was in place and undamaged. I always double-check."

"I heard the barking." Katie stepped forward to add to the telling. "A vicious, snarling sound." She shivered. "I rushed to the window and saw them run straight for the gate, as if they knew the difference between it and the fence. They stopped for a minute, sniffing at the ground, but when one of the dogs hit the gate, it swung open as if the latch didn't exist. The hens squawked and the dogs pounced." Katie covered her face with her hands. "It was awful."

"It was a slaughter." Helen frowned. "Even the ones in the coop didn't escape. Reminded me of fighting dogs. Bred to be killers. They didn't even pause to eat what they killed, just chased down everything that moved. I grabbed my gun and ran out to try to stop them."

"I didn't want her to go," Katie interrupted, tears streaming down her cheeks. "I was so afraid they'd turn on her. I held her back. If I hadn't, maybe some of the hens would still be—"

"You did nothing wrong, Katie." Helen's voice was firm, almost impatient. But there was a kindness to it, too, that seemed to reassure the younger woman. "Nothing was going to stop those dogs." She turned back to Malachi. "I shot in the air. Scared them off. They yelped and ran toward the river, leaving nothing but destruction behind."

Betty patted Helen's shoulder. "When I got back, I found meat scraps by the gate. Someone unlatched the gate but kept it closed so we wouldn't suspect anything. Then they laid out scraps to lure the dogs in." Betty turned hard eyes on Mal. "No man could've gotten that close in broad daylight without one of us noticing." Her gaze shifted to the crowd standing around the wagon. "One of our own did this."

Gasps and disbelieving murmurs spread through the crowd as ladies turned to look at their neighbors. Anger. Fear. Confusion. However, one face in the crowd registered nothing but determination. The face he admired most.

Without missing a beat, Emma hiked up her skirts, scaled the closest wagon wheel, and pulled herself up onto the driver's box. She stood tall. Resolute.

"Ladies!" She dropped her skillet onto the bench seat and clapped her hands twice to get their attention. Unfortunately, the commotion had grown too unruly in the brief moment it had taken her to climb into the wagon.

Mal lifted his fingers to his mouth to give a sharp whistle like the one he used to call Ulysses, but Emma beat him to it. Curving thumb and forefinger and placing them just past the edge of her retracted lips, she let out a piercing blast that had him grinning with pride. Mal leaned back on his heels. He'd taught her that. They'd been kids at the time, but still . . . no one could deny the woman's impressive pitch and volume.

Especially not the ladies milling about the street. The instant the whistle hit the air, their clamor died, and all heads jerked up to face their leader.

"Thank you." Emma nodded, satisfied that she had everyone's attention. "What happened at the farm is an abomination, and the fact that one of our own might have been involved is devastating. But hear me. We cannot afford to turn on each other, to allow suspicion and distrust to destroy our unity. We have an enemy to defeat, and if he senses that we no longer stand together, he will swoop in and tear us apart as efficiently as those dogs laid waste to Betty's hens. Our strength is in our solidarity. If that is lost, we have nothing with which to make our stand."

"But how can we stand together when one of the links in our chain is busted?" Betty challenged, her chin jutted forward, her eyes blazing.

Mal started to move toward the wagon, thinking to jump up beside Emma and make a tangible show of support. But a quick glance from her warned him off.

"You're absolutely right, Betty. We can't depend on a weakened link. But neither can we discard it into the scrap heap. We don't know her motives, what kind of hold our enemy might have over her. What if she is as much a victim as the rest of us? What if the outlaw is threatening the life of someone she loves in order to gain her cooperation? What if he's blackmailing her or forcing her to do his bidding by some other means?"

Malachi watched the faces of the women around him. Some softened in sympathy, others crinkled in confusion, while others hardened even further.

Betty's was about as soft as a slab of granite. "What if she's simply a Judas, getting paid to turn on her own? Or what if she's the outlaw's lover and has been in on the plan from the very beginning? We can't just look the other way, not when people—*sisters*—could die."

Murmurs of agreement rose again, but Emma held up a hand to silence them. "You're right. We don't know the true motives of the one who has aided our enemy. But every one of us came to Harper's Station with the hope of starting over. We all have things in our past that we wanted to escape or change or forget. None of us are in a position to cast stones. That's why I'm going to give whoever is involved the chance to make the right decision. To come to me. Privately. Tonight at the station house, I'll leave the front door unlocked, and I'll be waiting in the parlor. All night. There will be no blame given, no punishment inflicted. In fact, I will provide safe passage out of town before first light and funds for a train ticket to someplace new. An escape and a chance for a fresh start, no questions asked."

"And if the traitor don't show up?" Betty jabbed.

"Then we'll have to try something more drastic, like doing away with privacy and making sure no one is left alone at any time. There will be nowhere she can hide and no way she can aid the outlaw. Whatever consequences arise because of that will be on her own head." Emma scanned the audience, slowly, her gaze hesitating over each lady in the crowd. "So, please. Whoever you are. Come see me tonight. It is the best option, both for your safety and for ours."

After that final plea, Emma stepped to the edge of the wagon. Mal hurried forward to help her down. She offered him a small smile of thanks, then turned and walked back to the station house, head held high despite the fact that her tender heart must be throbbing with disappointment and grief.

He ached for her even as his chest nearly burst with pride

over the way she'd handled the situation. Strong yet compassionate. Fair yet filled with grace.

Although he had to admit, there was one thing he sided with Betty on. Emma couldn't know the true motives of the traitor. Her soft heart wanted to believe the best of people, but he'd seen the ugliness of evil too often to doubt its prevalence.

If she wanted to open her door in the dead of night to a woman who'd betray her own neighbors, he couldn't stop her. But he sure as shootin' wouldn't be leaving her to face her caller alone. He planned to lurk in a dark corner close at hand, armed and ready to do whatever it took to keep her safe.

30

The knock on Emma's door never came.

Mal sat in the darkened kitchen all night. Gun ready, ears perked for the slightest sound. But nothing came.

He watched Emma from a distance as sleep overtook her, head drooping, then shoulders, then her entire body sliding down the back of the settee to lie across the length of the seat. He crept into the parlor sometime after midnight to cover her with a knitted throw. He arranged her legs atop the cushion, slipping her shoes from her feet and bending her knees so that she lay tucked in a more comfortable position. Then he brought the afghan up over her shoulder. His fingers brushed against the softness of her dark hair and a nearly painful longing stirred in his soul.

She was so beautiful, his angel. So brave. Such a big heart. Always trying to save the world. Just as she'd saved him.

Malachi bent forward and feathered a tender kiss against her temple, one so soft he barely felt it himself, but one so full of feeling, his heart nearly burst as it pounded in his chest. His eyes closed as his lips touched her skin. He hovered, unable to pull away. So close to what he craved. To whom he loved. His angel. His Emma.

How he wished she truly was his. How he would cherish her. Guard her. Support her in all her world-saving endeavors during the day and hold her in his arms every night.

But such dreams were just that—dreams. In truth he had no claim to her beyond friendship. She was a woman of high ideals with a mission that required her full attention. He was a recently unemployed explosives expert who was better at destroying things than building them. The son of the town drunk who, despite his belated education and trade skills gained later in life, never fully escaped the stain of his past. She deserved better.

Although, the thought of anyone else claiming her set off a murderous impulse of such ferocity inside him that, before he knew it, his fingers were clenched into fists. Forcing himself to breathe, he relaxed his hands and slowly straightened away from her sleeping form.

"I love you, Em," he whispered. *And I vow to do whatever it takes to ensure your safety and happiness. Even if it means giving up my own.*

Backing away, Mal returned to the kitchen and his silent vigil—a vigil he kept until it was time for his predawn shift in the steeple. The change in location didn't alter his focus, though. Instead of watching for outlaws approaching from the river, he kept his gaze trained on the station house until the sky began to lighten in anticipation of the sun. No visitors paid a call.

Emma awoke to early morning sunlight teasing her eyelids as dawn broke. Disoriented at first, she stretched her cramped legs only to nearly topple herself from the parlor settee.

The parlor. The traitor. Had no one come?

Disappointment surged as she sat up and blinked away the

sleep from her eyes. Her messy topknot flopped halfway down the side of her head and one of Bertie's afghans fell from her shoulder.

How had that gotten there? She didn't recall . . . Or did she? There was something hazy and dreamlike tickling her memory. A warm presence. A gentle touch. Whispered words she couldn't quite make out. One of the aunts? Emma crinkled her brow in concentration as she tried to bring the memory into sharper focus. It didn't feel like one of the aunts. It felt different. Stronger somehow. Larger.

She glanced toward the kitchen doorway. A chair sat in front of the table. A chair facing the parlor entrance. As if someone had been watching her. Guarding her.

Malachi.

Warmth flowed through her. Comforting. Cherishing. She fingered the soft yarn of the afghan and pictured Mal bending down to arrange it over her. Did he feel the same heat in his veins that she did whenever the two of them drew close? Or was his affection merely brotherly? No. Not brotherly. It had to be more than that. A brother wouldn't look at her the way Mal had in the café the day he'd taught her how to hold a rifle. Or hold her with such bone-melting tenderness.

He felt something for her. He might not be able to admit it yet, but it was there. And as soon as this mess with the bandits was cleared up, she intended to confront him about it.

She was a Chandler female, after all. And Chandler women could do anything men could do, including propose marriage, if it came to that. Emma jumped to her feet like a soldier coming to attention, her back straight, arms stiff at her sides. Of course, she might have to convince him that he loved her first, but surely when she told him how much *she* cared for *him*, he'd see the truth.

Or run away again.

Emma frowned. Her posture sagged. Mal did have a bad habit of running when he thought leaving was in her best interest. Well . . . she'd just have to take that option off the table somehow. Prove to him that *he* was in her best interest.

She took a step toward the kitchen, thinking to march out to the barn and find him, but as soon as she started, her topknot completely unraveled and plopped against her shoulder before her hair spilled down her back in tangled disarray. Heavens. She couldn't go out there in this condition. She'd scare him off for sure. Hair of a wild woman. Rumpled clothes. Not to mention the likelihood of foul-smelling breath. *Ugh*. She'd have to freshen up first.

Tugging dangling hairpins free as she went, she dashed up the stairs, careful to keep her tread light so as not to wake the aunts. Henry was usually up with the sun, but she'd taken a shift on watch last night and would probably sleep another hour. Bertie rarely rose before seven.

Emma started finger-combing her matted hair as she moved into her room and gently closed the door. Stepping to the window, she took hold of the curtains, intending to close them so she could disrobe, but a movement near the garden grabbed her attention.

The ladies didn't work the garden on Sundays. Although, if Mrs. Grimes decided she needed something fresh to serve the circuit-riding preacher after services, she could have sent Flora or Esther to gather a few things. But the woman in the garden wasn't gathering vegetables. In fact, she didn't look to be moving much at all. Until Malachi came down from the steeple and passed by. Then she bent over the rows of plants and started harvesting, or pretending to. She positioned her back to him so he wouldn't be able to see her face. Not that he gave her more than a cursory glance since Porter had come up at the same time and said something to him while pointing back to the boardinghouse. Mal nodded and followed the freighter into the heart of town. Leaving the woman to her own devices.

Emma pressed her forehead to the window glass, trying to make out the woman's features. Who was it? She squinted through the glass, but the garden was too far away to make out more than the woman's outline. And her movements. No sooner had the men turned their backs than the woman sprinted through the gate and behind the church. Was she heading for the river?

Emma gasped and lunged for her door. She pounded down the stairs.

She had to catch her. Had to stop her from endangering the town. For she must be headed back to the outlaws, otherwise she would have taken Emma up on her offer of money and a fresh start.

"Emma?" Henry sleepily called to her from upstairs, but Emma didn't have time to explain.

"Get Malachi," Emma yelled back to her aunt, her pace not slowing. "Tell him I spotted the traitor running toward the river."

Emma grabbed her rifle from where she'd propped it against the parlor wall last night and raced out the back door.

"You can't—"

The door slammed, cutting off her aunt's protest.

Yes, she could. She had to. She had to protect her ladies. Besides, Mal would come for her. She'd not be alone for long. And this time she was armed.

Emma dashed through the corral, mentally railing at the time lost by having to climb through the fence slats. But when she caught a glimpse of a woman in a dark coat disappearing down the slope leading to the river, she found a new burst of energy. She ran across the field that stretched between her and the church, then cut across open country to the place where the woman had disappeared.

She crested the hill. Glanced right and left. Panic stabbed her gut. Her ragged breaths echoed loudly in her ears. Where was the woman? To the west, the river stretched fairly straight, but there was a bend to the right. Surely her quarry must have gone east around the bend. Otherwise she would still be visible. Praying she was right, Emma set out to the east, and before long, ran across a fresh set of footprints leading into the river. Small. Pointed toes. A woman's shoes. Triumph surged through Emma. She couldn't be too far behind.

Holding her rifle in one hand, she gathered up her skirts with the other and waded into the shallow river. Water ran over her ankles and halfway up her calves, dousing her stockings and the edges of her petticoats. She trudged on, doing her best to watch her footing even as she scoured the far shore for a glimpse of the lady she chased. No sign.

The traitor must be rounding the bend while wading in the water to hide her tracks. But Emma didn't want *her* tracks to be hidden. She needed Malachi to find them quickly. The woman she followed had to come out on the other side eventually. Emma could make better time, not to mention leave more visible tracks if she crossed the river directly. She eyed the far side of the river and found a sloping section of bank that would provide an easy exit. So she headed for it, pushing through knee-deep water in order to get there.

Once on the other side, she released her skirts, grabbed a quick couple of breaths to relieve her heaving sides, then forced herself into a slow jog along the river's edge, her gaze constantly swiveling between the river and the bushy mesquite to her left.

The bend in the river finally ceased its curving and began to straighten. Yet the improved view yielded no sign of Emma's quarry. Where had she left the river? Emma had seen no footprints. No trail of water droplets or flattened prairie grass from dragging hems near the river's edge.

Emma bit her lip. She couldn't lose the trail. Not now. Not when she was so close. She glanced toward the scrub brush but saw nothing. Heard nothing.

Frustration mounting, she jogged forward until she reached a pile of dead branches beneath a small cedar tree. Her attention was so focused on trying to spot her quarry that she didn't lift her back foot enough to clear the branches as she stepped over them. The toe of her shoe caught on something hard and immobile, nearly launching her onto her face.

Emma caught her balance and glared down at whatever had tripped her. Her eyes widened. A flat brown stone, almost completely hidden, lay beneath the leaves and twigs. A stone that had a dark spot in the middle. A wet spot.

Exhilaration shot through her. She looked for more stones hidden inside the camouflage of dead branches and found several, all about a man's stride apart. The branches and leaves meandered up the flat bank in a seemingly haphazard manner to a rocky section of ground where a trail would be next to impossible to find. No wonder Malachi hadn't been able to track the outlaws. They'd disguised their escape route perfectly. If she hadn't stubbed her toe, she would have completely passed it by without a second thought.

Instead of searching for a glimpse of the woman she pursued, Emma focused on the path. The stones hidden within the dead branches. The dry, rocky creek bed leading north into the densest patch of scrub brush. Emma pressed on, even as the vegetation grew from prairie grass to three- and four-foot shrubs, to mesquite and oak trees that stretched closer to ten feet. Only when she was completely surrounded with little or no visibility did she stop.

She'd been watching the ground for footprints, but had seen none. She could be three feet or three hundred feet from the precise route her quarry had taken. Since her eyes were of no help now, Emma closed them and stilled her body, focusing all her attention on the sounds around her.

There weren't many. No birds. No hum of insects. The breeze rustled leaves and cooled the perspiration on her forehead, but nothing else stirred. So Emma held her breath and listened harder. *Show me, Lord. Please.*

The wind stilled.

Utter silence.

Then a new rustling sounded to her left. A rustling with no breeze. It had to be an animal. Or a person.

Emma slowly turned her head to the left, careful not to make any noise that would give away her position.

Voices. Male. Female. Muffled and distant. But voices for certain.

Should she leave? Fetch Malachi and let him deal with the outlaws? Or would they simply disappear again? This might be her only chance to catch them unaware. She heard one male voice. Low. Growling. But that didn't mean the second man wasn't nearby. A shiver coursed down her back, but she willed the fear away. Her grip tightened on her rifle. She brought it around in front of herself, into a more ready position. Two hands. Finger hovering over the trigger. Hand beneath the barrel.

What should she do?

The female's voice grew louder. More agitated. Then a sharp clap. A cry of pain. Renewed rustling. Then a scream.

Emma lifted the rifle across her body and ran toward the sounds.

31

It didn't matter what the woman had done to betray the colony. That was one of her ladies out there. And no female was going to be battered by a brute of a man on Emma's watch.

But neither was she going to run blindly into a heated situation without first calculating her odds of success. So when the voices became loud enough to be distinguished, Emma slowed her step and crept forward with careful precision.

"I did everything you asked, but I ain't gonna be part of any more killin'. It ain't right, Angus. You swore nobody would get hurt."

Emma bit back a groan as recognition swept over her. *Flora.* She should have known. All the signs had been there. The way she tried to talk women into leaving early on. Her suspicious behavior after the church fire. Her reluctance to share any of her personal history with Emma when they'd served on watch together. Yet, the bruises and bloody gashes she'd worn the day she first came to the colony had been real, too. Why would she return to a man who abused her instead of taking Emma up on her offer of a fresh start?

"They're a bunch of chickens. Stupid woman."

The sound of a fist hitting flesh made Emma wince.

"And if I say it's time to up the stakes, it ain't your place to argue."

Emma crept alongside a large oak and peeked around the trunk. What she saw turned her stomach.

Flora had fallen to the ground and was cupping her jaw with her hand. Blood flowed from a split lip and one of her eyes didn't seem able to open fully. The man she'd called Angus stood over her and swung his booted foot into her ribs with such force Flora lifted a bit from the ground before flopping back down like a rag doll.

"A wife is supposed to obey her husband," he spat. "I don't care if they figured out they had a traitor in their midst, you should've stayed."

Emma's stomach roiled. She swallowed down the urge to retch and turned her gaze away to scan the area. She had to figure out if the second man was nearby.

"Let me take Ned," Flora pleaded, her voice raspy and broken as she struggled onto her hands and knees. "He's just a boy. Too young to be drawn into your schemes. They have men in town. Fighting men. And all the women are armed now. He could be hurt! Let me take him away from here, and you can do whatever you think you must."

The man growled and kicked his wife again. She sprawled back into the dirt. "You ain't takin' the boy from me. He's mine now. You had him all those years I was stuck in prison and you turned him into a milk-faced baby. Always whining. Askin' where his ma is. Fussin' about goin' home." Angus spat into Flora's face. She barely flinched and made no move to wipe the offensive liquid away. "The kid's got no backbone. This'll make a man outta him. Show him the value of patience, of planning and hard work. And if we gotta kill us a few womenfolk to get that stubborn bloomer brigade to finally clear out, well, that'll just harden him up. Teach him not to let anything stand in the way of his goals."

The second man was a boy? Flora's son? No wonder she didn't flee. She couldn't leave him to this monster.

On the other hand . . . Emma glanced around a final time . . . neither would Angus speak in such derogatory terms about his son if the boy was within earshot. That meant he was alone. Emma raised her rifle into position against her shoulder and eased a little farther around the tree.

"For the last five years I did nothing but plan and plot in that rotten hole, and nothin' is gonna stop me from gettin' that gold. Not you." He kicked her again in the ribs. Flora curled up in a ball and moaned.

Gold? That's what this was all about? Money?

"Not that pansy son o' mine." Another kick. "And not a pair of two-bit cowboys trying to be knights in stinkin' armor." He reared back for another kick, but Emma stepped out from behind the tree and aimed her rifle straight at his chest.

"Back away from her," she ground out in the meanest voice she could muster.

Malachi would have been proud. Her arms weren't shaking. Her aim was true. And she had so much anger and indignation swimming through her veins, she thought she just might be able to pull the trigger without experiencing a single morsel of regret.

The stocky man stilled his swinging leg and cocked a glance toward Emma. His yellowed teeth winked at her as he grinned in a way that was the precise opposite of welcoming. "Well, looky here. One of the bloomer brigade followed you, Flora. Pretty sure she's all on her lonesome, though." He casually scanned the area. "Aren't ya, honey?"

Emma gritted her teeth. She wanted to shout that she wasn't this foul vermin's *honey*, but something warned that getting riled would only give him reason to gloat. She'd not give him that satisfaction. She took a step forward, satisfaction zinging through her when one of his dust-laden eyebrows craned up in surprise.

"Flora needs medical attention. I'm taking her back to town with me." Emma took another step, stopping a few feet from Flora's fallen form, not wanting to get too close to the ham-fisted man standing over her.

Angus crossed his arms over his chest. "You ain't takin' her anywhere, sweet pea. That there's my wife. My . . . *property*. To do with as I see fit."

"She's a human being. No man's property."

The fiend leered at Emma, interest lighting his eyes. "You got fire in you, don't ya, sweeting?"

Emma choked down a growl. If that man threw one more of those disgusting endearments at her, she'd not be responsible for the reaction of her trigger finger.

"I like fire in a woman." He licked his lips and Emma nearly gagged. "Flora used to have spunk like that, too. Till I beat it outta her. Wonder how long it would take your spark to fade?"

You're never going to find out! Even as her mind screamed denials, her gaze remained cool, her aim steady.

"Flora," she said in a gentle voice. "Can you stand?"

Clothing rustled, punctuated by a small groan. Emma prayed that meant Flora was finding the strength to rise. Emma couldn't afford to take her eyes off the man in front of her to verify.

"Yer pretty, too," the lecher continued, showing no regard whatsoever for the wife lying broken and bleeding on the ground in front of him. "Dark hair. Shiny eyes. Uppity atti-tude. Hmm . . ." He grew thoughtful. His head leaned back and his gaze narrowed as he surveyed her more closely. "Stubborn. Controlling. Wanting to call the shots." His face cleared, and an awful smile parted his beard. "You're the banker lady that runs the town, ain't ya? I think you and me need to get better acquainted."

He lunged.

Emma pulled the trigger. The rifle kicked back into her shoulder, throwing off her balance.

He roared, aimed a quick glance at his left arm, where a red stain was blooming over the edge of his sleeve, but he never stopped coming. "You shot me!"

Emma stumbled backward, fumbling with the repeater's lever, desperate to get another cartridge in the chamber. Then her heel caught on a tree root. She threw out an arm to grab the tree, leaving the rifle unprotected. With one swing of his arm, Angus knocked the weapon from her hand.

Emma yelped. She turned to flee, but Angus was too fast. He grabbed her around the waist and hauled her up against his side. She pounded her fists against his arm, fighting to pry herself free, but his grip was as unyielding as iron.

"Let me go!" She kicked and squirmed, fighting desperately for her freedom. He laughed at her puny efforts.

Then she recalled his injury. Throwing her weight sideways, she flung her right arm across her body and slammed a fist into his bloodied left shoulder. A grunt of pain cut off his laughter. But he didn't drop her as she'd hoped. Instead his right arm tightened about her waist and his left rose in retaliation.

His fist slammed into the side of her head. Her body fell limp as her brain struggled to keep its faltering grasp on consciousness. Pain throbbed inside her skull. Her vision blurred. She heard a woman's cry of outrage, but she couldn't seem to get her head to turn to see what was going on.

"Stop, Angus!" Flora cried, a little more strength to her voice. "You hurt her, and Shaw will kill you."

"Shaw don't scare me. He can't even find me. Ha!" Angus shifted his hold on Emma, spinning her around to face him.

The sudden movement shot a host of tiny needles through her head. She moaned and squeezed her eyes closed. Then, just as the edges of pain started to dull, he tossed her up over his shoulder, belly down, head and arms thumping against his back as he clasped her legs. Her breath left her in a *whoosh*. Her head felt like it was splitting in two. Digging deep into her reserves, she found the strength to reach up and press the heels of her hands against her pounding temples. The motion lessened. The pain lessened. She pushed harder, trying to somehow contain the ache so she could think.

Angus stepped around his wife, who had managed to partially sit up, propping herself up with one arm. As he moved past, Emma raised up just enough to see Flora. The woman's face was battered and bloody, her body curled in on itself to protect her abused middle. Suddenly the pain in Emma's head didn't seem nearly as significant. Not when one of her ladies had endured so much worse.

The two women locked gazes. Flora's full of apology. Emma's with compassion. Then Angus's voice shattered the moment.

"If Shaw manages to find you before the animals do, Flora, give him a message for me." Angus paused then spun around to face his wife, swinging Emma away from her. "Tell him that if he wants to see his little banker friend alive again, he better clear out all them females from my town by tomorrow morning. Otherwise I'll clear them out myself with bullets, and the first one I fire will go into this one's heart." He smacked Emma's behind with the flat of his hand, then turned and strode with a fast pace deeper into the woods.

"I'm done playing, banker lady," he grumbled as he pushed through the brush. "Done panderin' to my wife's sensibilities and my boy's youth. I tried to clear y'all out the nice way, but you were too stupid to take the hint. So if Shaw don't do it for

289

me, I'll start pickin' off your pack one by one. They'll never even see me comin'."

"That's mur . . . der." The bouncing stride cut the moaned word in half. Not that her proclamation mattered. Angus just shrugged, jostling Emma even more.

"Nah. It's consequences. You were warned. Now you'll pay the price for your lack of cooperation."

A rustling to Emma's right shot hope through her heart. Had Malachi found her? *Please, Lord, let it be him.* It took her a moment to realize the sound was coming from the north, from deeper in the woods, farther from town.

Angus heard it, too. He froze, yanked a revolver from his left-side holster, then whistled a deep-toned birdcall. A second call, nearly identical, answered. Angus put his gun away.

Emma's hope faded.

A tall, thin man pushed through the trees to Emma's right. No, not a man, she realized as she caught a glimpse of his face. A boy.

"Pa! Everythin' all right? I heard a shot."

"Everything's fine, boy. It'll be even finer by tomorrow. Found me some insurance." He swatted Emma's rear again.

She gritted her teeth as disgust surged through her, but when the youngster walked over to examine her, his eyes unsure, almost apologetic, she knew she had one last chance.

"Ned," she whispered, recalling the name Flora had used. "Your mother's hurt back there. You have to help—"

Angus whipped around, separating her from the boy and renewing the torment in her head.

"Yer mother's fine, boy. I sent her to town with a message. Get on back to camp and start packin' up. We got to move again." As Angus spun around and trudged in the direction that must lead to his camp, Emma fought through the pain to lift her head and watch Ned.

He had turned to gaze off into the direction his father had come from, and he hesitated. She willed him to go after Flora. If the two could escape, Angus would have no further hold on them.

"Now, boy!" Angus barked.

Ned jumped and scurried to follow his father.

Emma flopped back down, a tear leaking from her lashes.

32

Malachi crouched down and traced the faint outline of a footprint in the earth on the far side of the river. Emma's footprint. The one he'd been tracking for the last twenty minutes. The one that disappeared after this final marking, as if the woman herself had sprouted wings and flown away.

"Where are you, Emma?" he whispered, his frustration and desperation mounting.

He'd tried to hold it together ever since he spotted Henry, still clad in her nightclothes, hurrying across the road toward the boardinghouse. Told himself Emma wasn't that far ahead. He'd track her down. But now that her trail had evaporated, his nerves were fraying with alarming speed.

Why had he thought the danger had passed just because the sun had risen? If Porter hadn't drawn him away to the boardinghouse, he might've seen Emma leave. Might've stopped her. If only . . .

Mal shook his head. Second-guessing his choices served no purpose. At least he knew who was responsible for leading Emma away. Porter had brought a distraught Esther to him and showed him the note the woman had found tucked into her Bible that morning. Mal had barely had time to scan the paper and read the signature at the bottom before Henry came flying across the street, her gray braid swinging wildly behind her. Mal had shoved the note at Porter and sprinted out to meet his aunt. When she'd told him what Emma had done, he hadn't taken the time to confer with the freighter. He just grabbed his rifle from inside the boardinghouse door and raced for the river, trusting Henry to inform the others about what had happened.

Emma's trail had been easy enough to read at first. He'd lost it for a while after she entered the river but picked it up on the opposite shore fairly quickly. Until it disappeared. He'd searched east and north, the two directions her path seemed to have been heading, but he'd found no trace of her. Not a single marking.

Which meant he was missing something. Again. Just like the two previous times he'd searched for the outlaws.

So he'd circled back to the last footprint he'd found. Now he stared at it, traced it, and prayed the Lord would show him what he was missing, because his own abilities were obviously not getting the job done.

"All right, Mal. A giant bird didn't swoop down and snatch her up, so her next step had to fall somewhere." He'd searched the far side of the branches that stood in her path, yet found nothing. So she either walked atop the dead brush back down into the river or she followed its path north. She'd already crossed the river, so returning that way made no sense. She must have headed north. Though why she would have chosen to walk upon such an uneven pile of dead branches and leaves when dirt and prairie grass offered much more stable footing, he couldn't quite wrap his mind around.

"Who cares if it make sense?" he muttered under his breath. "It's the only option left." Mal stepped atop the branches, taking a moment to dig in his bootheel to make his position more secure. Then he brought his second foot up. His heel sank, but something solid held his toe aloft. A stone. He hunkered down to examine it, brushing away the dried leaves and dirt with his hand. A flat river rock. The size of a man's boot. One that would allow a man to travel away from the river without leaving a trail.

Malachi surged to his feet, leapt off the brush, and started running again. Running along the outlaw's path of brush and stone, jaw clenched tight in disgust for missing what had been right in front of him all along, even as his heart rejoiced that he finally had a direction to search.

I'm coming, Emma. I'm coming.

Once the hidden path merged with a dry creek bed, the trail became harder to read. Mal lost precious minutes searching for clues in the prairie grass before he finally spotted one of Emma's shoeprints. No, not Emma's. Another woman's. Slightly longer from heel to toe, the impression a little deeper. Must be Flora's. Anger flared at the thought of the woman who'd betrayed them all, who might at this very minute be luring Emma into a trap. He'd seen her name at the bottom of Esther's letter. He'd not taken the time to read her excuses or apologies, if there were any. He didn't need to know the whys. All he needed was the where. Where was she? Surely if he found Flora, he'd find Emma as well.

Instead of wasting time searching for another set of prints, he followed Flora's trail into the thickening vegetation. Just as the scrub brush gave way to oaks and mesquites, a movement to his left brought Mal's head around. In a flash, he had his rifle aimed, cocked, and ready.

He froze in position, ears poised to catch any sound, eyes locked on the small space between the trees where he'd seen a shadow. A shadow that moved a second time. Low to the ground. Like an animal. A wounded animal. Limping. Scraping.

Mal raised his head from the barrel to widen his view yet

still kept his finger on the trigger. Whatever was out there was moving toward him. Slow. Deliberate. Yet it made no effort to move with any degree of stealth.

Then something slid out of the shadows. A pale hand stretched into the sunlight followed by a mud-colored sleeve. It stretched. Reached. Then pulled. A feminine head appeared. One Mal recognized. A grimace of agony twisted Flora's features as she dragged herself forward another few inches, her second arm curled protectively around her middle, her legs trailing behind. She reached again. Pulled. Dragged. Her battered face stirred Mal's pity. Her leaf-strewn hair and torn flesh ignited his anger. An anger that no longer focused on her, but on the man who could beat a woman so badly she had to crawl away to escape him.

Relaxing his hold on the rifle, yet still keeping it accessible and his senses alert, Mal jogged forward and dropped to the ground beside Flora. She immediately curled in on herself, covering her head as if bracing for more violence. A whimper escaped her.

Mal had started to reach for her but hesitated at her obvious terror. "I'm not going to hurt you, Flora. I'm here to help." He patted her shoulder once, then raised his hand to hover awkwardly in midair. She flinched at the touch, but didn't whimper again, thank heavens. He tried a second pat. Some of the stiffness left her posture and she began to uncurl.

"Where's Emma?" Mal asked, unable to keep the question bottled up a second longer.

"She tried to save me from him," Flora mumbled through swollen lips. "She shoulda left me there." Flora twisted her head around until her grief-filled gaze met Malachi's. "Shoulda run away the moment she spotted Angus. But she didn't." Flora shook her head, bewildered. "After all I done to hurt the town, she still stayed. Even shot him. Or at least drew blood." A hint of a smile cracked her lips. "He didn't expect that. Thought she'd be soft. Weak. Like me. Not Emma."

"Where is she?" It was all Mal could do not to shake the woman and end her rambling. While he wanted to hear an account of what happened, he wanted Emma safe first.

"He took her."

Mal sprang to his feet, rifle in hand, and ran toward the thicker trees where Flora's drag marks led. He had to find the outlaw's trail. Had to get Emma back.

"Wait!" a weak voice called after him. "You can't save her that way."

Mal ignored Flora's plea and ran deeper into the woods. He spotted Emma's rifle, fallen on the ground at the base of an oak tree. He snatched it up and held it tight while he scanned the terrain, as if somehow the connection she had to the rifle would lead him to her. But of course it didn't.

He found the place where the drag marks stopped. The place where Flora had lain. A chaotic pattern of footprints had displaced leaves and left evidence of a scuffle. A scuffle that ended with the smaller set of prints disappearing, leaving only the large prints to lead off to the west, prints that pressed deeper into the earth. Deeper because they carried a load. A load Malachi intended to retrieve.

Holding his rifle in one hand and Emma's in the other, Mal set off after the outlaw. About a hundred yards in, a second pair of prints joined the trail from the north. Nearly the same size but shallower.

Mal followed the trail, heart thumping, spirit praying for Emma's well-being. Then all at once the footprints vanished. Just like Emma's had when he'd trailed her from the river. But this time there were no hidden stones, no creek bed. A few large tree roots stood above ground. But on the other side of the roots, all Mal found were dead leaves and dry earth, neither of which had been disturbed.

The outlaws must have changed direction here and masked

their trail somehow. But which way had they gone? A growl of frustration rose in Mal's throat. Why must he always be a step behind? It was maddening.

Emma's captor had obviously spent years running from posses and lawmen to be so accomplished at hiding his trail. Mal would just have to be better. Smarter. He had a woman to find. A woman who meant more to him than anything else under the sun. So he picked a direction and started marching. When he'd gone about twenty-five yards with no sign of a trail, he backtracked and tried again at a different angle.

After five attempts, he finally stumbled upon the outlaws' trail on a nearly perpendicular path to where they'd been headed before. A path that passed near a tree sporting a broken branch with a scrap of burlap stuck in its bark. They must've had a sack of dirt, dead leaves, and other various ground scrapings waiting for just such an occasion. They made a sharp change in direction, then backtracked and covered the trail with debris to throw off anyone following. Mal had to give the man credit. He was a wily old fox. But tricks would only hold up for so long, and Mal was too invested to give up the chase.

Until he found the hoofprints.

He couldn't chase down horses. He'd have to return to town and fetch Ulysses. Following the trail on foot would keep him at too much of a disadvantage. Besides, Flora needed tending. He could practically hear Emma now, scolding him for leaving a battered woman alone in the woods, defenseless and unprotected. She'd never approve of his abandoning a female in need, even when her own safety hung in the balance.

So he begged the Lord to do what he couldn't—watch over and protect Emma—and then tore his gaze away from the trail and turned back.

Urgency continued pounding in his head, and a physical ache twisted his gut as his steps carried him away from Emma, but he set his jaw and forced his legs into a trot. The faster he took care of Flora, the faster he could return for Emma.

When he finally caught up to the other woman, she had dragged herself a few more yards toward the river. Hearing his approach, she swiveled her head around, her eyes wide with fright. Then recognizing him, the air whooshed out of her lungs. "Thank heavens you came back."

Mal hunkered beside her again and gently touched her back. "It'll be all right, Flora. I'll carry you back to town, and Maybelle will get you all fixed up."

She shook her head at him. "You don't understand. It ain't me you should be worryin' about. In fact, you should leave me here and run back as fast as you can go. They need to be warned. The entire town is in danger."

A coldness spread through Mal's veins like a ribbon of ice winding from his arms through his core and down to his toes. "What kind of danger?"

"Angus . . . my husband . . ." Flora's gaze dropped to the ground at that admission, but she quickly steeled herself and brought her face back up. One eye was swollen and red, but the other glittered with determination. "He gave me a message. Said to tell you that he's done waitin'. The women have until morning to clear out. If they ain't gone, he'll take care of the business himself—picking them off one by one." She swallowed hard. "Startin' with Emma."

No! The roar of denial screamed through Mal's head with such force he had to clench his jaw shut to keep it contained. Even then, an agonized moan rumbled in his throat as his hands trembled with helpless outrage.

"What does he want?" Mal forced the words through his tight throat as he balled his hands into fists to still their tremors. "The county land office wired me back a couple days ago. There's no record of valuable mineral deposits or water rights worth killing over. What could he possibly want with Harper's Station?"

"Gold."

"But there's no gold in the area," Mal insisted. "No silver, copper—nothing of that sort."

Flora shook her head sadly. "Not in the ground. In a U.S. Army payroll strongbox."

Mal rocked back on his heels, her words nearly bowling him over. "All of this is about a stash from a heist?"

Flora nodded. "From five years ago. Angus and a gang of no-good drifters he'd collected, ambushed a small army convoy headed for Fort Elliott, killing three soldiers and injuring several more. Angus told the gang to split up so they'd be harder to track, and fools that they were, they listened to him. He gave them each a piddling few coins to tide them over, then hid the rest. That way when the army tracked them all down, he was the only one with no evidence on his person. Talked his way into a reduced sentence. Probably would've gotten off completely if one of the injured soldiers hadn't recognized his horse."

Flora wilted a bit, the telling apparently taking its toll on her. Mal moved close and shored her up, lifting her so she could lean against his side.

"Angus spent the last five years in prison, obsessin' over that gold and making plans to get it back. And now he's forcin' our son to ride with him." She grabbed Mal's arm with surprising force. "Ned's only fifteen. He's just a boy. Too scared of his pa to stand against him. If you or the ladies challenge Angus on this, I'm terrified my boy will get caught in the crossfire. *Please*. You gotta convince the others to leave. It's the only way to protect my boy and Emma."

Mal didn't answer right away. He couldn't. Not when the truth of what would happen was churning his heart into mush.

Clearing out the town might appease Angus and keep Ned safe, but Emma had no such guarantees. If she stumbled across a family reunion between Flora and her husband, she had seen the outlaw's face—which meant she could identify him, testify against him, and send him back to prison. The minute Angus no longer needed her to assure the town's cooperation, Emma would be dead.

Mal swung his rifle strap over his shoulder and handed Emma's weapon to Flora. Without a word, he gently fitted his arms beneath the battered woman and lifted her off the ground, cradling her against his chest.

"First things first," he grunted. "Let's get you back to town so Maybelle can tend your injuries. Then we'll figure out what to do about Angus."

Malachi stood and carried Flora out of the woods. As his legs worked, so did his mind. There had to be a way to save the woman he loved. No other option was tenable. His angel would *not* be dying at that devil's hands.

33

Thanking God for hot summers that brought shallow rivers, Malachi slogged through the muddy, knee-high water with Flora in his arms. His legs strained against the river's resistance. His lower back throbbed. His arms burned from the effort of holding Flora as still as possible. But he kept on. One step. Then another. Not stopping. Ignoring the pain. Keeping Emma's face in his mind.

Climbing up the embankment on the opposite side of the river nearly did him in, though. The grade brought him to his knees. His weary muscles cried out for him to stop. To rest. To replenish his strength. But Emma couldn't afford for him to stop. Her life hung in the balance. So Mal gritted his teeth and grunted his way back to his feet. He redistributed Flora's weight, clenched his jaw, and took another step.

"You've carried me far enough, Mr. Shaw," Flora said, her voice as tired sounding as his body felt. "You can send someone back for me."

"Emma wouldn't want me to," he ground out, taking another step.

"It'll be faster," Flora insisted. "And I'll be safe enough on this side of the river. You can leave one of the rifles with me."

Malachi halted, torn. She was right. It would be faster. But would it be better? What if he handed over the rifle and Flora shot him in the back? His gut told him she was no killer, but her betrayal was too fresh for him to trust her completely.

So he took another step. Then another.

"Stubborn fool," Flora muttered.

Mal grimaced. She was probably right. He wasn't sure he could make it much farther. If he could just get around the bend, maybe he'd be close enough to town to fire off a signal shot. Two quick rounds from his rifle should bring help. If they were heard.

Two percussive blasts rent the air.

Mal blinked. Had he just thought those shots into existence? Of course not. He must have imagined . . .

"Over here! They're over here!"

Mal jerked toward the shout. He hadn't imagined *that*. He glanced back toward the water and nearly wept.

Ulysses was charging toward him, Andrew on his back. Water sprayed around them, catching the sunlight. Mal had been so focused on putting one foot in front of the other and getting around the bend, that he'd not noticed the horse and rider on the opposite side of the river.

And Andrew wasn't alone. Others now rounded the curve. Women running toward them, some in their Sunday-go-to-meeting clothes, others in more practical garb. All carrying weapons. All ready to do battle.

And Betty Cooper, bless her sensible heart and old knees, drove a wagon with Maybelle Curtis and her doctoring bag riding shotgun.

The Lord had sent the cavalry.

Flora tried to hide from the women, turning her face into Mal's shoulder, but it was an impossible task. Mal did his best to smooth things over by explaining as much as he could, especially to a hard-faced Betty as he neared the wagon.

"She's been severely beaten. By her husband. He's got control of her son." Mal met Betty's gaze. "That's why she did what she did."

"You don't gotta explain it to me, Shaw." Betty clambered down from the wagon and moved to the back to let the tailgate down. "I got eyes."

Mal sat on the edge of the wagon bed and carefully laid Flora on a pallet of blankets Maybelle had arranged. The midwife climbed into the wagon bed beside Flora and started clucking over the woman's injuries. Flora ducked her head and hid her face with her arm.

"None of that hiding, now, Flora," Betty said, gently taking hold of the injured woman's arm and peeling it away from her face. "Esther showed me your letter. We all know you were in a tough spot. Scared for your boy and unable to sway your man from his course. God never blessed me with a child, but if he had, there's no telling how far I'd go to protect him."

Tears rolled down Flora bruised cheeks. "But your chickens . . ."

Betty sniffed once and cleared her throat, her voice coming out a little thicker than before. "Yeah, well. I done forgave you for that when I read your instructions to Emma to use your bank funds to buy new ones. As much as I cared for them ornery birds, that's all they were. Birds. People are more important."

"Emma!" Henry's strident shout pierced the conversation.

Mal turned, dread weighing heavily in his gut. Henry and Bertie were running up to the wagon as fast as their fifty-year-old legs would carry them.

"Malachi," Henry huffed. "Where's Emma?"

He clenched his jaw and dropped his gaze to the ground.

How he hated to disappoint these ladies. But the truth was the truth, and dancing around it would only waste time. "The outlaw has her."

Bertie gasped and grabbed Henry's arm. Henry's eyes flared with fire. "Then what are you standing around here for? Go after her!"

"I tracked her to their camp. They left on horseback."

Henry snapped at Andrew. "You! Boy! Get off that horse and give it to Malachi. He's got to go after—"

"No, aunt." Mal stepped in front of her and laid his hands on her shoulders. "There is more to explain, and not much time to act. Organize the women while I give instructions to Andrew. I want everyone at the church in twenty minutes."

Then before she could find the breath to argue, he spun away from her and strode toward Andrew, signaling him to stop dismounting and stay in the saddle. He gestured to the telegraph operator, too, who had just caught up to the group.

"Grace, I need you to wire Sheriff Tabor. Tell him Emma Chandler's been abducted, and we have a witness who can describe the outlaw who took her."

"I will, but when I wired yesterday to report the attack at Betty's farm, the deputy sent a reply that the sheriff had been out of town the last three days chasing rustlers, and he didn't know when Tabor would be back."

Mal frowned. "Then tell the deputy to come." He turned to Andrew. "But just in case he refuses, I need you to ride to Seymour."

"But I want to stay with you," Andrew protested, revealing his youth more than usual. Then he caught himself and hardened. His jaw jutted forward, and his eyes shimmered with defiance. "You need all the help you can get if you want to get your woman back."

Mal didn't bother disagreeing. "That's true. But the rest

of the womenfolk need protecting, too. And you're the most capable rider I got around here." Andrew sat a little straighter in the saddle. Mal patted Ulysses's neck and peered pointedly at the boy who was in such a hurry to be a man. "Take Ulysses back to the barn for me and saddle the gray mare. There's money in my saddlebags. Take ten dollars and settle my account with the livery owner, then check on the deputy."

Mal glanced quickly over his shoulder to make sure Henry and Bertie still stood a distance away. He'd be telling them the rest of the news soon enough, but he couldn't afford to be slowed down with questions and demands at the moment. So he lowered his voice just to be safe.

"Tell him that the outlaw says, if the town isn't vacated by morning, he will kill Miss Chandler along with any person who remains behind."

Andrew swallowed slow and long, but he gave a sharp nod.

"If he still won't come, go back to the livery. The owner is Ben Porter's brother. Tell him Ben needs his help. And see if he knows of any other men in town who might be willing to assist."

"I'll send a wire ahead to Mr. Porter," Grace offered, "so he'll know to expect you. That will give him time to round up any others who might be willing to help."

Mal nodded. "Good." He turned back to Andrew. "Take one of the Chandler horses with you as a spare, in case you need it, but it'd be best if you stay in Seymour until this mess is over."

The boy's eyes narrowed. "I'll be back by this afternoon, Mr. Shaw. With reinforcements." Then, before Mal could argue the point, he reined Ulysses's head around and set off at a canter for the station house.

Stubborn brat. Mal's mouth twitched at the corners as he watched the boy weave around the women clustered at the wagon. The kid reminded him of himself at that age. Proud. Defiant. Desperate to prove his worth to anyone who would give him a chance. That defiance had landed him in hot water on more than one occasion.

Watch over him, Mal prayed. He'd do his best to keep an eye on the kid, as well, but the threat to Emma demanded his full attention.

Mal swept his gaze over the women Henry was herding back toward town. They moved at a quick clip. Even Betty had climbed back into the driver's seat of her wagon. She clucked to her team, and worked at turning them around while Maybelle and Bertie sat with Flora in the rear. Satisfied that everyone was following instructions, he backtracked a few steps to collect the two rifles Flora had dropped when the wagon arrived.

"Where's Porter?" Malachi asked Grace as he jogged back her direction.

"Keeping watch from the steeple," she called out as he loped past.

Picking up his pace, Mal left the females behind and cut across the fields for the shortest path to the church. Once there, he cupped his hands over his mouth and shouted up to the freighter. "Ring the bell, Porter. We need everyone gathered as soon as possible."

Without bothering to question why, the freighter grabbed the rope and pulled. The high-pitched metallic tone resonated through the air, sending vibrations along Mal's nape.

"It's a little early to be ringing the bell, son," Brother Garrett said, stepping out of the church door. "I only rode in about fifteen minutes ago. We don't normally sound the call to worship until ten o'clock."

"Sorry, Parson. We're going to have to forgo services this morning." Mal strode to the steps and planted his boot on the bottom stair. "An outlaw has taken Miss Chandler hostage and threatened the rest of the town. We have to make a plan, then get the womenfolk out of Harper's Station."

The circuit rider's indrawn breath was the only hint of his shock. His expression remained serene, though his eyes did warm with concern. He crossed the small porch to the steps and laid a hand on Mal's shoulder. "The sermon can wait for another day, but when everyone gets here, I insist we spare a few moments for prayer. If ever there was a time for divine direction, it is today." The preacher gave Mal's shoulder a squeeze, then stepped back. "'Except the Lord build the house, they labour in vain that build it: except the Lord keep the city, the watchman waketh but in vain.'"

Mal nodded. The old man was right. All his planning would be in vain if the Lord wasn't leading their efforts. "Thanks, Parson. An invocation would be much appreciated."

"Mr. Shaw!"

Mal spun around to see Victoria Adams running up to the church, dragging her son by the hand beside her.

"Mr. Shaw," she repeated as she neared him, her breath heaving. "Where's Emma?" Her gaze shifted from the church entrance to the yard to the station house behind them. "I heard the bell and thought she would be here. Is she—"

Mal held up a hand to forestall what was sure to be a torrent of frantic questions. "I'll explain what happened as soon as everyone gets here."

"Why don't you come inside with me, Miss Adams." Brother Garrett gestured for her to follow him into the church. "I was hoping Lewis might tell me some more about that rock collection of his. I picked up a stone a couple days ago that had some lovely quartz streaks running through it. I think I might have put it in my pack . . ."

Lewis bounded up the stairs, a grin on his face as he traded his mother's hand for the preacher's. "Is it white or pink?"

"But . . ." Tori glanced from her son to Mal. Her protest died away. She must have seen his torment. Heaven knew he was barely holding it at bay. She bit the edge of her bottom lip, then straightened her posture, lifted the hem of her skirt an inch or two to navigate the stairs, and marched past him. "I'll see you inside."

She didn't have long to wait. A steady stream of females filed into the church over the next ten minutes. Porter followed the last stragglers inside and posted himself by the door, rifle in hand. Mal did a quick count. Everyone was here. Well, except for Maybelle and Flora at the clinic. And Emma.

He swallowed hard to rid himself of the anguish that last thought conjured, tugged his hat off, stepped up to the podium, and cleared his throat. Instant silence blanketed the room.

"The outlaw has captured Emma," Mal said without preamble. "And he's threatened to kill her unless everyone vacates town by tomorrow morning." Ignoring the gasps filling the room, Mal set his jaw and continued. "So everyone will be leaving today." He stared pointedly at Betty. "No exceptions."

He took a deep breath and scanned the faces staring up at him. Friends. Neighbors. Women he respected. Admired. Women he'd been called to protect, a task he must accomplish no matter the cost. Before he could send them off to safety, however, he needed something from them. Something that could make the difference between saving Emma or losing her.

"But you are—*we* are—a community," he reminded them. "A community that thrives because you help one another. And you never abandon a sister in need."

"That's right!" Henry jumped to her feet and stabbed a finger in the air. "And if you think we're going to abandon Emma when she needs us most, you've gone plumb loco."

Head nods and murmurs of assent filled the room.

"Good," Mal said. "Because I need your help. There's only one way to ensure Emma's safety, and that's to shift the bargaining power in our favor. I don't trust this outlaw to keep his word. Emma can identify him, which means as soon as she outlives her usefulness, he has no reason to keep her alive. Our best chance is to find what he wants before morning and force him to negotiate a trade."

"But we don't know what he wants," Henry cried.

"Yes, we do," a timid voice said from the rear of the church.

Everyone twisted around in their pews to see Maybelle propping up a battered Flora. The woman's right eye was swollen shut, her face covered with bruises, her arm still wrapped protectively around her side, but she held herself with dignity, purpose, and determination.

Gripping the doorpost, Flora braced her feet and stood a little straighter. "He wants his gold."

34

Mal hurried down the aisle and swept Flora into his arms.

"Careful," Maybelle cautioned. "I think her ribs are broken. Fool woman should be curled up on a cot in the clinic, but she insisted on coming. Said she had to do all she could to help Emma."

Mal cradled the brave woman gently, giving her a nod of approval. "You're a strong lady, Flora," he said, meeting her gaze squarely as he recalled her earlier words about being weak when it came to standing up to her husband. "Don't let anyone ever tell you different. I'm glad to have your help."

Henry and Bertie, seated on the front pew, immediately scooted down to make room. "Set her here, Malachi," Bertie instructed. "Maybelle and I will see to her comfort as you continue."

Mal complied and lowered Flora softly to the pew. Maybelle slid onto the bench beside her.

Retaking his place at the podium, Mal faced the group. "Word has probably spread by now, but I think everyone needs to know the facts. Flora's husband, Angus, is the outlaw who's been

310

harassing Harper's Station. He's been in prison the last five years for robbing an army payroll convoy. Apparently, he stashed the gold somewhere here in Harper's Station before Emma purchased the property. Now that he's been released, he's set on retrieving the stolen gold. He's forced his young son, Ned—a lad of only fifteen—to work alongside him. He is the second outlaw. Fearing for Ned's safety, Flora has gone along with Angus's plan, trying to convince all of us to leave, in order to prevent her boy from being caught in any crossfire that might occur. Unfortunately, Angus has run out of patience. Which leaves the boy vulnerable, and Emma directly in harm's way."

Mal's fingers closed around the edge of the podium. The wooden corners dug painfully into his hands, and he struggled to tame the urge to run out of the church, jump on Ulysses, and race into the woods. To take down Angus and rescue the woman he loved. But this was no dime novel. He had no guarantee of a happy ending. Not in this world. He'd seen too many evil men in power and too many broken lives left in their wake to believe that good always won out over evil.

So he had to use every weapon at his disposal. And right now, the best weapons available were not the rifles and revolvers in this room but the knowledge and intelligence of the women who carried them.

Looking to the ladies seated in the front row, Mal started building his arsenal. "Flora, did Angus tell you where the gold was hidden?"

She shook her head.

Of course not. That would be too easy. But Mal was used to doing things the hard way. He'd been making do with scraps since the day he was born. A boy could make a right fine meal out of scraps with a little persistence and creativity. If the restaurant door was locked, he'd just have to go around back and start digging through the trash.

"He didn't trust me," Flora said. "Feared I'd steal it from him. The only clue I ever got from him was when I asked how he could be sure it was still there. 'It's secured in stone,' he said." Flora shrugged. "I searched for it myself, when no one was around. Dug under rocks in the fields, checked hearths in several of the town buildings for loose stones. I even climbed onto the roof of the café one night before we set up the watch and tried to look down the chimney by lantern light. I thought if I could just give him what he wanted, he'd give up this fool quest, and I could take my son home. But I never found even a hint of that money."

Victoria Adams raised a hand. Mal nodded to her.

"Several of the buildings had to be repaired when we first arrived. Some were enlarged. I know Maybelle added a room onto the clinic, and I expanded the back storeroom of my shop. Emma made some modifications at the bank, too, so it could support the large steel safe she special-ordered from Chicago. If this man hid his ill-gotten gains here five years ago, we'll only find them if we envision what the town looked like back then. I'm pretty sure Emma had to have the café's chimney rebuilt before it was safe for occupancy. If the masons didn't find anything suspicious, it makes sense that Flora wouldn't be able to, either."

"Good point, Miss Adams." Mal lifted his gaze to the rest of the group. "How many of you were here when the colony first started?"

The aunts both raised their hands. As did Betty Cooper, Maybelle Curtis, Victoria Adams, and Stella Grimes from the boardinghouse.

Mal released his grip on the podium and leaned his forearms on it instead as his mind started processing the possibilities. "I doubt he would have hidden the money outside. If he had, he could have just slipped into town on a moonless night when

312

everyone was asleep and retrieved it. So it has to be in one of the buildings. But which one?"

Betty thunked the stock of her shotgun against the floor. "It prob'ly ain't the church, since he set the place on fire a while back. Wouldn't be smart. Too much risk of the place burnin' to the ground and leavin' the payroll unprotected in the rubble."

"Agreed." Mal pressed his weight onto his elbows as he bent over the lectern. "Any other buildings we can eliminate?"

Grace Mallory slowly got to her feet at the back of the room. "There's no stone in the telegraph office. There's a single cast-iron stove used for heating. No hearth or chimney. The rest is made of wood."

One of the seamstresses, Pauline, Mal thought, raised a timid hand. She glanced at the woman seated beside her then turned back toward the front. "Our house is the same. No chimney. Just a cookstove and a stovepipe. It was really more of a shanty when we first moved in."

Her companion nodded emphatically. "All the smaller homes were. Only the larger, more established businesses have stone-work."

"All right," Mal said, straightening. "Show of hands . . . Which buildings have some type of stone feature?"

Stella Grimes from the boardinghouse raised a hand. As did Betty Cooper, the aunts, and Tori Adams.

The aunts . . . the station house. The one building they knew for sure the outlaw had been inside. Mal's heart thumped in a wild rhythm. Until he remembered that the muddy footprints they'd found had never approached the parlor hearth. Or any other stone feature in the house. Just the plaster wall in the basement where Angus had tacked his threatening note. Nothing but another scare tactic.

Mal cleared his throat and forced his mind back to a more logical, methodical plan. "I think we can eliminate Betty's farm," he said. "It's isolated enough that Angus could have attacked whenever he wanted." He looked to the aunts in the front row. "What about Emma's bank?" He thought back to the few times he'd been inside the building. "I remember wooden floors in her office."

"She paid a builder to reinforce the floors to ensure the interior room holding the safe would be supported," Aunt Bertie said, "and reinforced the walls with brick covered in plaster. But before that, the building was as simple as most of the others."

"So we have three main places to search. Porter . . ." Mal met the freighter's gaze at the back of the room. "You'll take the store. Tori, you and Lewis focus on packing up what you don't want to leave behind while Porter examines your chimney and hearth. I'll check out the boardinghouse, then move on to the Chandler home. Everyone else needs to pack their belongings and start heading out of town. We can't take chances with Emma's life. Angus is sure to be watching, and I want him to believe we are complying with his demands."

Mal paced to the left side of the stage, too antsy to stay behind the podium any longer. "Grace is going to wire the sheriff's office, and I sent Andrew to fetch additional support," he said. "I pray Tabor or one of his deputies will be here by the time we find the gold and can help us set a trap. If not, we'll find a way to manage on our own."

Because there was no way he'd leave Emma alone with Angus come nightfall. If they didn't find the gold by early afternoon, he'd have to abandon the plan and go after her without it. His chances of success would be greatly diminished, but now that he knew some of the outlaw's tricks, he prayed he'd do a better job of tracking.

Prayed . . .

Forgive me, Lord. I got so caught up in my own plans that I forgot to seek yours.

A few ladies started to rise. Malachi held up both hands. "Wait!" Everyone froze at his urgent tone. "Please. Be seated. There's one more crucial detail to see to before we depart." He twisted to the right and met Brother's Garrett's eye. "The most important detail. Parson?"

Mal stepped down from the dais, clearing the stage for the preacher.

"Thank you, Mr. Shaw." Brother Garrett approached the pulpit, set his well-worn Bible on the stand, and turned his compassionate gaze upon his parishioners. "I understand the need for brevity as lives hang in the balance, but as I listened to the unholy challenge you ladies have been forced to face, I couldn't help but be reminded of a passage from Psalm 18, one I pray will bring you hope as you battle your enemy." He fingered the ribbon marker on his Bible and opened the book to a place near the center.

"'I will love thee, O Lord, my strength. The Lord is my rock, and my fortress, and my deliverer; my God, my strength, in whom I will trust, my buckler, and the horn of my salvation, and my high tower.

"'I will call upon the Lord, who is worthy to be praised: so shall I be saved from mine enemies. The sorrows of death compassed me, and the floods of ungodly men made me afraid. . . . In my distress I called upon the Lord, and cried unto my God: he heard my voice out of his temple, and my cry came before him, even into his ears. . . .

"'He delivered me from my strong enemy, and from them which hated me, for they were too strong for me. They prevented me in the day of my calamity: but the Lord was my stay.'"

Silence hung suspended in the room. Women bowed their heads. Several closed their eyes. A few even nodded a silent amen. But the gentle minister wasn't finished.

"You are not alone in this struggle, brothers and sisters." The parson's attention zeroed in on Malachi. Mal felt the look go through him like a dart, piercing his soul.

How did he know? How had the man guessed that even while Mal actively solicited help from the ladies, he still felt alone? Alone in his efforts to save the town. To save Emma. Alone, like he'd been his entire life. Battling against those who expected him to fail. Battling his own fears that he'd prove them right.

"You have an ally who wields more power than any human foe. One who will stand beside you, or better yet, lead the charge as you face your enemy. Join me, beloved, as we call upon the Lord, as we cry unto our God."

Mal bowed his head and bared his soul.

"Almighty God," the parson intoned, "we beseech thee today for help in defeating our enemy. We cannot succeed without thy guidance, without thy strength. You parted the sea to rescue thy people. You made the sun stand still. You closed the mouths of lions. And best of all, you resurrected Jesus Christ from the dead, defeating the evil one for eternity. Thou art a God who saves.

"We ask thee to save thy people again today. To protect Miss Chandler from the one who holds her captive. To guard the life of young Ned, and to plant seeds of goodness in his soul so that he won't repeat his father's mistakes. To watch over the ladies as they leave their homes and to guide the men who defend them.

"Lord, only you know the wisest course. I pray that thou wilt give Mr. Shaw discernment, so this situation might be resolved without bloodshed. Thou hast taught that all things are possible to him that believeth. We believe in thee. Show us the way, and lead thy people to victory. In the holy name of thy Son and our Savior, Jesus Christ, amen."

Mal's head remained bowed, his heart aching and raw. *All I care about is getting Emma back safely. If finding the gold is not the best plan, show me the right one. And if I try to step wrong, throw a boulder in my path. I'm liable to miss a more subtle sign.*

When Mal glanced up, all the ladies were looking at him, their gazes expectant. Mal nodded to the preacher as the man collected his Bible and stepped down, then took up the vacated position on the dais.

"Well, until the Lord shows us a better way," he announced, "we're gonna stick to the plan we got. Ladies, start packin'. Harper's Station needs to be a ghost town by this afternoon."

35

Four hours later, covered with sweat and soot, Malachi leaned over the water trough at the station-house corral, cupped his hands, and sloshed water over his head. He repeated the action, this time taking a moment to rub the grime off his face and neck. Yanking his shirttail out of his waistband, he ran the marginally clean section of cotton across his brow.

His hand slowed as he ran the fabric over his eyes, his cheeks, and then the length of his jaw. His chin dropped, and his hand closed around his shirttail, wanting to ball it into a fist.

Nothing. He'd found absolutely nothing. And they were dangerously close to running out of time.

He'd set himself a deadline of three o'clock. If he didn't have the gold by then, he'd have to revert to tracking. Tracking required light. And time. And hopefully help. Mal glanced across the paddock to where the road from Seymour curved past the station house. No one had come. *Yet,* Mal reminded himself. No one had come, *yet.* There was still time. Less than two hours, but it was something.

After a preliminary inspection of all the hearths and chimneys had turned up nothing of significance, Mal and Ben Porter had combined their efforts to conduct a deeper investigation. Since Mal was the more slender of the two, he'd had the pleasure of wedging head and shoulders up through the hearths in order to feel around from the inside, while Porter banged a broom handle down each chimney.

Mal had gotten a description of Angus from Flora and was certain the barrel-chested, broad-shouldered man could not have reached up any higher than Mal into the fireplace openings. Unfortunately, nothing had jarred loose from Porter's thorough poking, either. So they'd moved on to checking all the exterior sections, climbing ladders and meticulously analyzing mortar for degraded places where stones could be loose. They'd found several, but none had yielded the prize they sought. Which meant either Angus's comment about stone had been a false trail and had nothing to do with his actual hiding place, or they were missing something.

The creak of door hinges pulled Mal out of his troubled thoughts. He turned to find Bertie bustling toward him, a half-wrapped sandwich in her hands.

Mal released his hold on his shirt, letting the damp cotton flutter down to cover his exposed belly. "You're supposed to be packing, aunt."

"Yes, dear. I know. But Henry and I have decided to only bother with the irreplaceable things. Papa's letters. Mama's tea set. The Chandler family Bible. Things of that nature. We'll be coming back soon enough. No sense in packing everything up just to unpack it again in a few days."

"But we're leaving Harper's Station unprotected while a thief rummages through the place." Mal couldn't quite believe she was making so little of all this. Didn't she realize that Angus was the type of man who'd be ornery enough to torch the place out of spite?

But the older woman just smiled at him and patted his arm. "You'll stop him before he gets that far. Don't worry." She pulled her hand back, frowned at the gray smudges on her fingers, then shrugged as she wiped them on her apron. "Even if you don't, there's nothing here that a man seeking gold will care about. If anyone has cause to worry, it's Tori at the store, but I'm sure that nice Mr. Porter will help her load up all her more expensive items."

She held out the sandwich to him, the bottom half wrapped in a napkin. "Here. You should eat something."

Mal glanced at his hands. His fingernails outlined with black grime, streaks of watered-down soot trailing down the backs, his palms little better.

"Just hold the napkin," Bertie urged. "The rest will wash out later. You need to keep your strength up if you're going to bring Emma back to us."

For the first time, a line of strain appeared across her forehead. She nibbled a bit on her lower lip as Mal took the sandwich from her. "I've been packing Emma's clothes," she said, her gaze dropping to the ground. "Henry went to the bank to gather up the ledgers. We decided to leave the safe as is. It's too heavy to move on such short notice, and Emma claimed it's fireproof. Hopefully, this Angus fellow will be so focused on his gold he won't want the trouble of trying to break in to a safe. Emma said that without the combination, a thief would have to use dynamite to get it open. And even then, chances are good that the steel construction would hold."

Mal took a savage bite out of the sandwich, ripping the bread with his teeth and gnashing the thin slices of roast beef with vicious strokes, desperate to obliterate thoughts of Angus touching Emma's bank vault. Emma's clothes. Emma's . . . person.

"Do you think she's all right, Malachi?" Bertie's soft-spoken question clawed like eagle talons across his heart.

He met his aunt's gaze and swallowed what was left of the mangled meat in his mouth. "She should be safe as long as she has value to him," Mal said, repeating the litany he'd been feeding himself the last several hours. "If he kills her, he loses his leverage."

"But there are other ways to hurt her besides killing." Bertie's chin wobbled just a bit, and the sight nearly shattered Mal's self-control. "She's a beautiful girl. Alone with two men."

"One man and a boy," Mal forced out through his clenched jaw. "Angus might get a little rough in his treatment of her, he seems to like to knock females around, but I don't think he'll do anything more severe with his son looking on."

At least that's what Mal prayed for with every breath.

Bertie's smile returned, subdued but optimistic. "I'm sure you're right, dear. Now, finish your sandwich, then come carry Emma's trunk downstairs for me." She turned and sauntered away, sure he would do as she bid.

But Mal didn't want to carry Emma's trunk. He wanted to carry Emma—to safety. Which meant he had to find the gold. Unless the Lord had devised some other plan. *Have you?* Mal glanced toward the sky. A disgustingly happy sky, blue and cheerful with a sun so bright it hurt his eyes and puffy white clouds that showed no hint of the evil raging on the earth below them.

Do you see? Or are you so far away that our troubles seem too small for you to bother with? I haven't found the gold, yet I haven't been inspired with any other ideas, either. Mal forced his clenched jaw to relax. He needed to be open to the Lord's leading, not angry and defensive. *Please. I need your help. I can't do this on my own. Show me what to do. I'm begging—*

A muffled shout had Mal dropping the remnants of his sandwich and grabbing the revolver at his hip. Heart racing, he tried to pinpoint the direction the sound had come from.

Another squeal. From the house.

Mal took off at a run, threw open the back door, and ran into the kitchen.

"Malachi! Oh, Malachi, come quick!" Bertie's excited voice came from somewhere to his right.

"Bertie?" He thundered into the parlor just as his aunt flew through the entrance on the opposite side of the room, the one near the stairs.

She wore the biggest smile he'd ever seen.

Flummoxed, Mal holstered his gun and strode across the room to her. "What is it? What's wrong?"

"Nothing," she enthused, her plump little body bobbing up and down in her excitement. "Something might be very, very right." She grabbed his arm and started pulling him toward the stairs. "Come see!"

Instead of heading up to the bedrooms as he expected, she dragged him through the doorway that led to the basement where they stored canned goods, storm supplies, and other random paraphernalia that had no other home.

"Bertie—"

"I didn't remember until I came down to fetch a crate." Excitement bubbled from her, an excitement he failed to share. This was taking too long.

"What did you remember?" Mal fought to keep his exasperation in check out of respect for the woman who'd been the only mother figure he'd ever known. But it wasn't easy.

Bertie reached the bottom of the stairs and smiled up at him as he clomped down the last two steps. Heavy, musty air filled his lungs, weighing him down even further until his aunt spoke again.

"The key to rescuing Emma, of course."

Rescuing Emma? Malachi leapt forward, the weight dissipating from his limbs and his heart. He grabbed hold of Bertie's hand. "How?"

She patted his arm, then pulled away from his hold, that unreasonably cheerful smile still etched on her face. Reaching overhead, she took down the single lantern illuminating the basement from its hook in the ceiling. Then she pivoted, took a handful of steps past a shelf full of canned goods, and held the light aloft so that it shined against the far wall.

"I'm certain the gold you've been looking for is behind there." She pointed straight ahead.

The hope Bertie's overactive imagination had spawned inside him withered as he stared at a perfectly normal, non-stone wall. The same non stone wall where Angus had left the threatening note about Emma. A threat he would carry out by morning if Malachi didn't find the gold.

"It's plaster, aunt."

She didn't appear fazed by his observation. "On this side, yes," she said, stepping forward and running her free hand over the smooth, whitewashed wall. "But on the other side is the remainder of the stonework from the chimney on the floor above. Stone that reaches all the way down to the floor of this basement."

Mal's gaze bored into the wall, as if he could find the stone if he just stared at it hard enough. Could it be that the note hadn't been a scare tactic, but a misdirection, like the sack of leaves Angus kept on hand in the woods to cover his trail? He'd broken in to the station house to claim the gold, but when he'd found the stonework covered in plaster, he knew he'd not have enough time to bring down the wall and retrieve it. So when Porter's shot warned him time was up, he'd left the note to throw anyone who searched the house off the scent.

And it worked, until Alberta Chandler figured out the truth, thanks to some heavenly guidance.

Mal rushed forward and placed his hand on the wall, his fingers trembling slightly.

Bertie chuckled, her faith so complete it spilled out in joy. "I completely forgot about this section until I came down here looking for a crate I could use for packing Emma's books. I know in my heart, the gold is here."

Listening to his aunt's chattering with half an ear, Mal scoured the basement for something he could use to . . . There. An old sadiron. That should do the trick. He strode over to the work-table, clasped the handle, and swung the hefty laundry tool around. In three strides, he was back in front of the wall. While Bertie nattered on about Emma hiring the same builder to shore up the basement that she'd used for the bank, Mal reared the iron back and smashed the pointed tip into the wall.

Plaster cracked and crumbled.

He struck again.

A chunk fell to the floor. White dust puffed into the air.

He struck again.

More plaster fell, revealing brick behind it. Brick that needed to come down.

Mal spun around and made for the stairs, taking them two at a time.

"Where are you going?" Bertie called after him.

"To get a sledge."

"I don't think we have . . ." The rest of her words died away as he cleared the last stair and raced for the barn.

Unfortunately, she was right. All he found in the barn was a measly nail hammer that he doubted would be good for much more than hanging pictures. Mal growled and threw the worth-less hammer back onto the workbench. It bounced off a glass jar of nails with a loud clatter, but even then, the jar didn't break. Just tipped over and spilled its contents.

Where was he supposed to find a sledge strong enough to break down a brick wall in a town full of dainty ladies with delicate tools? Betty might have something out at the farm, but riding out there and back would waste precious time. So what else could he use? What was strong enough to knock down brick and stone?

Suddenly, Mal grinned. He ran to his bunk, yanked out his saddlebags, and pulled out a fresh box of rifle cartridges. Tucking that under his arm, he ran back to the workbench and grabbed a chisel and the puny hammer he'd thrown down in disgust a moment earlier.

Confidence surging, he sprinted for the house.

The Good Book taught that with a grain of faith, a man could move a mountain. Not only did Mal have rapidly renewing faith, but he had a few hundred grains of something else.

Gunpowder.

36

"He's going to do what?" Aunt Henry screeched.

"Blow up the basement, dear." Bertie answered in such a matter-of-fact tone that she could have been describing the supper menu.

Mal swallowed as he focused on creating his fuse line. "I'm not blowing up the entire basement. Just the wall."

"It's going to be so exciting!" Bertie enthused. Mal swore she must be bouncing again, the way her voice jiggled. "He said we can watch from behind the support pillar at the back of the room if we want."

"And wait for the house to come crashing down on our heads? No, thank you." Henry huffed out an offended-sounding breath, most likely crossing her arms over her chest in that snippy way of hers. "I can't believe you gave him permission to blow up our home."

"Stop being so dramatic, sister. He's an expert, remember? He earns his living creating explosions."

"I never did approve of that." *Sniff.*

Mal had to bite the inside of his cheek to keep from responding.

He didn't have time to get into a long-winded argument over the merits of his chosen profession right now. He needed to finish making his fuses.

He'd already scraped the heads off a dozen matches and ground them into a fine powder with the handle end of his chisel. After dunking his finger into the glass of water Bertie had brought him earlier, he dripped a small amount of the liquid onto the match-head powder and stirred it into a paste. Then he rolled the paper fuses he'd twisted into tight little lines through the mixture until they were evenly coated.

He should only need one fuse, but it was always good to run a test first to make sure the homemade mixture didn't burn too fast or too slow. Having a couple spares didn't hurt, either, so he set up four six-inch fuses on Aunt Bertie's cooling rack to dry and started in on the next project—chiseling a hole in the wall's mortar.

When he pounded on the wall, Henry mumbled something about needing to make sure all the essentials were out of the house before Mal brought it down around their ears and clomped up the stairs. Bertie lingered. She stood against the back wall, out of his way, and watched. After a while he forgot she was even there.

Once he was satisfied with the size and depth of the hole he'd whittled, he moved back to the workbench and started taking the cartridges apart and extracting the gunpowder. He emptied cartridge after cartridge until he had a small bowlful of black powder. Then he spooned it into the crevice and packed it tight, careful not to use so much that he risked doing permanent damage to the house. Yet he needed an amount capable of knocking a hole into the wall large enough to weaken the structure and allow him to get at the stone beneath. A delicate calculation.

Mal tested the fuses, found them dry, and took one in hand for a trial run. Moving to a clean spot on the workbench, he took a glass jar of canned string beans and used it to weigh down the edge of the fuse, leaving the rest jutting out from the bench at a right angle. Mal poured what remained in the drinking glass over his palms and fingers and cleaned off any gunpowder residue. He dried his hands thoroughly on a clean rag, then struck a match and lit the fuse.

It sizzled and hissed and burned fairly quickly, reaching the glass jar in about four seconds. He might have used a bit too much of the matchstick paste, but no matter. It worked.

"Should I warn Henry?" Bertie asked, her voice closer than he expected. He'd been so absorbed in the test, he hadn't heard her approach.

Mal turned. "Yes. You might want to accompany her out of the house, too," he said, rethinking his earlier position about letting her stay. The amount of powder was minimal, and the explosion would be small and well-contained, but debris could be unpredictable. He'd hate for her curiosity to result in an injury, no matter how minor.

"Don't you dare light that fuse without me, Malachi Shaw. If you cheat me out of the chance to see you in action after reading about the excitement of your job in your letters for the past several years, I'll never forgive you."

The corners of Mal's mouth twitched upward. Henry was usually the militant one, but it seemed Bertie had her fair share of bossiness, too. Reminded him of Emma. Which tightened his mouth back into a hard, serious line.

"Hurry back, then," he said as he shooed her toward the stairs. "We're running out of time without a guarantee that this will work. If the gold's not there . . ."

Bertie paused on the second step and glanced back at him. "It's there, Malachi."

He jerked his chin down in a stiff nod and went to work arranging the fuse in the hole.

Over the next fifteen minutes, while he waited for a loudly complaining Henry to vacate the house with the necessary belongings, he carefully moved all the glass jars that could possibly be in the blast zone to safer locations against the far wall. Then he draped a pair of quilts over the remaining shelves to keep out the dust and small shards that the blast would send flying.

When he was finished, he stepped back and examined his handiwork, double-checking to make sure he hadn't missed anything. The room looked secure. All he needed was Bertie to get back so he could light the fuse.

This would work. It had to.

You're in control, Lord. Not me. Protect us in the blast, and grant us success.

It was the prayer he prayed before igniting any charge, but today the words felt different. Deeper. More desperate. So much more than a paycheck or a reputation rested on this job. The life of the woman he loved was at stake, completely redefining success.

He pulled a new match from his vest pocket and held it between his thumb and forefinger. A creak on the stairs told him Bertie had returned, but he didn't turn. He never looked away from a fuse before he lit it.

She must have sensed his intensity, for she didn't speak until she'd taken up her position in the place behind the support pillar that he'd pointed out to her earlier. Even then, she whispered. "Everything's ready, Malachi."

He stepped up to the wall, set his left palm against it while a final wordless prayer groaned through his soul. Then he bent his knee and with a flick of his wrist, dragged the match head against the sole of his boot. *Scratch. Hiss.* Then a tiny *whoosh* as the matchstick flared to life.

"Fire in the hole!"

Mal touched the flame to the fuse, and waved out the match. *One.*

He ran to Bertie's position, grabbed her about the waist, and bent his taller frame over hers.

Two.

He jerked her fully behind the pillar to ensure her protection. *Three.*

He tightened his grip and braced for the explosion.

Four.

The concussive blast echoed through the basement, shaking the rafters and setting the canned goods to clinking and rattling on the shelves. Mal didn't wait for things to calm, though. He released Bertie and darted forward.

Plaster dust filled their air, creating a thick, white haze that threatened to choke him. Chunks of brick and plaster covered the floor. Yet all Mal cared about was the jagged hole in the center of the wall. A hole as big as his head. And behind it? Glorious gray stones. Crumbling, weak stones loosened either by the explosion or from age.

Mal snatched up the hammer from the workbench and used the back side of the head like a pickaxe, stabbing inside the hole and yanking until entire bricks pulled free and pounded to the floor beside his feet. *Slam. Yank. Slam. Yank.* Over and over. Faster and faster. His urgency building with each swing.

As soon as the hole was as wide as his shoulders, he stopped swinging at the brick and started swinging at the stone. Pebbles rained down behind what was left of the wall.

Mal swung again. And again. Harder each time. Needing to hit the hollow. To reach inside and search for a thief's treasure. For Emma's ransom.

The hammer connected with a particularly large stone. Reverberations jolted his wrist, his elbow, his shoulder and neck. The rock didn't crumble like the rest. So Mal swung again, but at a slightly higher location. Solid. Unyielding. Supported by something?

He chose a third spot, a few inches higher and slammed the hammer against the stone. This time, rocks rained down again, only the pebbles that fell inward clanked against something. Something metallic. Something that could be a strongbox.

Mal flew at the higher-level stones in a flurry of strikes. When the stone was decimated as high as he could reach, he tossed the hammer to the ground and leaned forward into the hole. But it was too high to get the right leverage.

"Get me something to stand on," he shouted, hoping Bertie was still in the room. His focus had been so intent on the wall, he had no idea if she was there or not.

A wooden step stool appeared at his feet.

"Thanks."

He kicked bricks and stones away to clear an area, then set the stool against the wall and jumped straight to the top step. He reached into the chimney again, shoving his head and shoulders into the space. This time his palms came to rest against a hard, flat surface. *Please let it be the gold.*

Letting out a grunt that expanded into a full-out roar, he pushed against the box with everything he had. All at once it gave and plummeted down the flue with a crash. Mal nearly followed it down, but the lower section of brick braced his thighs and kept him on his feet.

Mal righted himself, hopped down from the stool, and kicked it out of his way. He retrieved the hammer and tore into the brick with a vengeance, slamming and wrenching until he could finally see the small hearth opening at the floor and the steel box stamped *U.S. Army* lying at a lopsided angle inside.

His fingers closed around the handholds, and he hoisted it up, the heft of the box sending silent cheers of victory clamoring through his brain. *The gold. Praise God! The gold!*

Mal dropped the heavy box onto the workbench and rubbed at his suddenly watery eyes. Stupid things wouldn't stop leaking. Dratted plaster dust.

He swiped a final time at his eyes and gave a good long sniff before grabbing up the box again and turning to face his aunt. "Time to get Emma."

37

"They're leavin', girlie." Angus lowered his field glasses long enough to cast a superior smirk over his shoulder at Emma before turning back to watch the parade of wagons rolling out of Harper's Station. "Looks like that man of yours ain't as big a fool as I thought. Turns out he knows when he's beaten." He cackled as he fit the binoculars back to his eyes, enjoying the spectacle far too much.

Emma glared at the back of her abductor, wishing she could scald his hide with all the righteous indignation boiling inside her, but her jaw still ached from the last time she'd lit into him. He'd shut her up with his fist. Going another round would only weaken her chance of escape. She needed to be strong. Alert. Ready to seize any opportunity that presented itself.

Unfortunately, her escape options were limited, seeing as how she was tied to a tree. Of all the times for a man to respect her intelligence and abilities. She'd gladly exchange her suffragette card for a captor who believed her too dull witted and timid to bother guarding. But she was stuck with Angus, a man whose paranoia had him anticipating trouble five steps ahead.

Which meant he'd never keep his word about letting her go once the town had been emptied. Not when he knew she'd run straight to the authorities with his name and description the instant she was released. He planned to kill her, one way or the other.

"No sign of the law, either," Angus gloated. "Not that I expected there would be. Last time I sent Ned into Seymour, he told me the sheriff was out with a posse chasin' down them rustlers that've been stirrin' up trouble to the south. Them fellers have plagued the sheriff for months. Nearly as slippery as I am." He barked out a laugh. "Tabor won't be back for days yet. You won't be getting help from that quarter." Angus shot her a taunting look.

Emma lifted her chin and schooled her features into a completely bored expression. It was the best she could do to thwart him. He'd not gain the satisfaction of seeing her fear, her worry, her anger. Not anymore. She might be tied to a tree with rope securing her waist and arms, but she wasn't conquered.

Her captor scowled at her, then turned back to his spying. Emma felt a tiny surge of victory and smiled.

"Greater is he that is in you, than he that is in the world." The familiar verse rose to bolster her spirit. She had allies. Powerful ones. Neither God nor Malachi would abandon her. One was with her now, and one was coming. She felt it in her heart of hearts. Malachi was coming for her, and when he got here, there'd be a reckoning.

The reckoning came less than an hour later.

"What's that fella doing?" Angus shifted to a different vantage point and resituated the field glasses against his face. "He's supposed to be leavin' like the rest of 'em. What's he doin' headin' to the church?"

"You think he plans to make a stand, Pa?" Ned glanced from Emma to his pa and back again, his forehead lined with worry.

"Be right foolish of him, but it wouldn't cause me much trouble if he did. All I'd have to do is distract him for a few seconds, then take him down from behind. He ain't got any backup. Saw that big fella driving the store lady's wagon outta town a while back."

Ned shuffled his feet through the dirt, his hands shoved into his trouser pockets. "He don't seem like the kind to be distracted easily."

He's not. Emma met Ned's gaze, tried to give him courage to make a stand of his own. But he just looked away.

"Every man can be distracted, boy. You just have to know his weakness." Angus turned to his son and grinned with such malevolence, Emma half expected to see fangs protruding from the viper's mouth. "We got Shaw's weakness right here." He nodded toward Emma. "Put a bullet in her, sling her over a saddle, and send the horse galloping into town . . . Shaw won't be able to help himself. He'll leave his cover to chase her down, try to *save* her . . ." Angus gave a snort of disgust, then twisted fully around to smile at Emma. "And that's when I'll shoot him in the back. He'll never even see it comin'."

"You animal!" Emma struggled against her bindings, desperate to get free so Angus couldn't use her as a weapon against Malachi. She wanted to pounce on the fiend herself and scratch his eyes out for even voicing such a horrible plot.

But the ropes held fast, and all her struggling managed to accomplish was bruising her forearms and ribs while entertaining the beast. His laughter crawled over her skin like a family of scorpions, poking and stinging and making her want to weep.

"That got your back up, didn't it, girlie? Seems you ain't so indifferent, after all." Angus took a step toward her, his right hand balled into a fist.

"Pa," Ned interrupted, squinting into the distance. "Shaw ain't climbin' into the steeple. He's hangin' something from the roof. Looks like a sheet smeared with something dark in the middle." The boy pointed toward town.

"What?" Angus stomped away from her, pushed his son out of the way, and brought his field glasses back up to his eyes. "A white sheet," he scoffed. "The mark of surren . . ." The word died away, replaced by a string of curses. "He can't . . . It has to be a bluff."

"What, Pa? What's happened?"

Angus shoved the field glasses hard into his son's chest, then started pacing, muttering vile invectives against Malachi under his breath.

Ned held the lenses up to his eyes. "'Found your gold. Time to trade.'"

Emma knew better than to let her triumph show while Angus tramped about in an agitated state. The man was volatile. But now he was also vulnerable. Thanks to Malachi.

Seemed the outlaw had been right—every man *did* have a weakness. Even Angus.

Malachi stood in the churchyard, his back against the north wall, listening to the wind whip against the sheet he'd nailed to the roof twenty minutes ago. How much longer? He scanned the landscape between the church and the river, searching for a sign, any sign, that his message had been received.

He hadn't wanted to stumble through the woods, calling out to Angus and giving away his position and tactical advantage. All the man would have to do was shoot Mal from a covered position then search out the gold for himself. And without Mal to stand in his way, Angus would dispose of Emma with equal speed.

No, he'd needed to lure the man into the open, someplace where they would be on equal footing, someplace where he had more power to bargain for Emma's life. So he'd *borrowed* a can of black paint and a brush from Tori's store and used one of Bertie's old sheets to create a message for Angus. One the outlaw would be sure to see . . . as long as the man had been watching the exodus of the townsfolk.

Mal had been so certain that Angus would park himself in a place where he could watch all the comings and goings. But what if he hadn't? What if he truly was waiting for morning to make his move and didn't see the sign?

Mal shifted his position, tightening his grip on the rifle he held. No time to second-guess himself now. God had led him to this point. He just had to have faith. To stay strong and trust that if the Lord wanted him to change plans, he'd find a way to let Mal know.

Five minutes passed. Then another five. The sun dipped lower in the sky, slanting light beneath Mal's hat brim, impeding his vision. He raised his left hand to shade his eyes, more concerned with spotting the enemy than in having both hands on the rifle.

As if that movement had been a signal, in the next heartbeat, two horses cantered out of the woods and across the brush-laden prairie. The first was a big chestnut with black socks and mane, the markings etched in Mal's memory with keen precision after the shootout by the bank. It carried two riders. A large, barrel-chested man and a slender, black-haired angel. The angel rode in front, her body shielding the man who held a revolver to her temple. Mal barely even glanced at the second horse. The small sorrel and its youthful rider didn't pose much of a threat, though Mal did a quick scan, anyway, to ascertain that the boy did not have his weapon drawn.

Angus reined in his chestnut a good twenty yards from the church. "If this is a trick, Shaw, your woman's gonna be the one to pay the price. If I don't see my gold in the next two minutes, you'll see my bullet blow through her pretty little head."

Mal tamped down the searing rage that churned in his gut and lifted his rifle with cool precision. He didn't aim the barrel directly at Angus, not with Emma in the way, but he had it up and ready, his finger steady on the trigger.

"It's no trick. I found the strongbox in the basement hearth of the old station house. Wedged in the flue about five feet from the floor. Sound familiar?"

The chestnut danced restively to the side, a sure indication his rider was agitated. Mal narrowed his gaze. Good. Time to even the odds a little more.

"Let the woman go, and I'll tell you where I've hidden it."

Angus tightened his hold on Emma. "Not a chance. I let go of the skirt, and you take a shot at me. I ain't a fool, Shaw. You tell me where the gold is . . . then I'll let 'er go."

Mal slowly shook his head. "Nope. Soon as you know the gold's location, Emma's as good as dead."

"What d'ya propose we do, then, cowboy? Stand here and jaw all evenin'?" he scoffed. "I ain't exactly the socializin' type."

"I propose that we set aside our weapons and handle this trade like gentlemen. You and the boy dismount and send the horses on their way, then you and I lower our weapons and kick them aside. Once that's done, send the boy over, and I'll give him further instructions."

"How do I know you won't attack him or take him hostage?"

Like you did with Emma? But Mal kept the accusation to himself and simply shrugged. "He can keep his pistol—can train it on me the whole time, if he wants."

Mal knew he had to appear to give Angus the upper hand or the man would never agree to the terms. Besides, he could afford to be a little generous, seeing as how he had strategically placed a few extra weapons of his own.

Angus mulled it over, shifting in his saddle. He clearly wanted to agree. The restless energy flowing from him into his mount was a sure indication of his being torn. The moment Mal had accurately described the gold's hiding place, Angus had been salivating over how to reclaim it. Hopefully his greed would win out over caution.

After a long, heart-stopping minute, it did.

"Ned! Get off your horse, boy, and do as he said. Aim your gun at his chest. Don't give him an inch."

The boy obeyed. Dismounted. Gave his sorrel a slap on the rump to send it trotting off into the field between the church and station house. Then he drew his pistol and aimed it straight at Mal's torso. The kid had a steady hand—steadier than Mal had expected, making him a little uneasy. Perhaps the boy wasn't as unwilling a participant as Flora had led him to believe.

Angus had to holster his revolver in order to maintain his grip on Emma while dismounting. Mal breathed easier the instant the gun disappeared from Emma's temple. He met her gaze across the churchyard, promising her with his eyes that he would take care of her, keep her safe. Her chin lifted and her shoulders straightened. She was ready. Mal bit back a smile. His angel was a fighter.

"All right, Shaw." Angus slapped the hindquarters of his own horse, sending the rifle in the saddle boot safely out of reach. "Let's see that rifle of yours hit the dirt."

Malachi complied. He slowly lowered the weapon to the ground, then used the toe of his right boot to kick it out of reach.

"Now the holster." Angus gestured with a jerk of his chin.

Mal unbuckled the gun belt, folded it over, and tossed it in the same direction as the rifle. Then he raised his hands in the air to show himself unarmed. In truth he still had a knife in his boot and a second revolver in the waistband of his trousers against the small of his back, but he figured his opponent would be similarly armed during their *truce*.

Holding Emma tight with a beefy arm across her midsection, pinning her hands to her sides, Angus slowly worked the buckle loose on his own gun belt and let it fall to the ground. Instead of kicking it away, he dragged Emma three paces to the left.

"Go on, boy," the outlaw ordered his son. "Get me my gold."

Ned marched forward, his pistol never wavering. But as he neared, Mal saw all the fear and uncertainty playing in his eyes. Flora had been right. The kid was in over his head. He put on a good show, probably learned that skill early on in order to avoid his pa's temper, but he hadn't yet learned how to deaden the truth from his eyes.

When the boy stood two paces away, Mal whispered to him in a voice barely loud enough to carry between the two of them. "Your ma will tell you where the gold is. She's in the church."

Ned's eyebrows arched so high they disappeared behind the shaggy hair hanging over his forehead. The gun gave a little wobble.

"What's he tellin' ya, boy?" Angus demanded. "Where's my gold?"

Like a good little solider, Ned kept his gaze trained on the target and never looked away as he called out to his father. "I-I don't know. He said there . . . there'd be a message inside the church."

"Well, get after it, then."

"What about him?" Ned asked, tipping his head toward Mal.

Angus grinned and moved his left hand up to Emma's throat. She shook her head vigorously from side to side in an effort to escape his grasp, but he was too strong and she had nowhere to go. "Don't worry 'bout him, boy. He won't try nothin'. Not while I got his woman. If he does, I'll just squeeze. Shouldn't take long for the little lady to suffocate. Such a delicate creature. Ain't that right, Shaw?"

Angus tightened his grip beneath Emma's jaw, forcing her chin up toward the sky. Mal seethed but held his position. As long as she was still breathing, he had to let this play out.

38

Tension coiled like a spring inside Emma, her senses on high alert even as the outlaw's hand tightened on her throat, making it difficult to breathe. She knew Malachi must have a plan, but she couldn't see him. Not with her head tilted so far upward. If he gave a signal, she wouldn't see it. And she couldn't risk making a move before he was ready. Not if she wanted to ensure his safety.

Angus had another gun. It was jabbing her in the back. Not only was she shielding the outlaw from gunfire, but she was also blocking Malachi from seeing the weapon Angus had tucked into the front of his trousers. A weapon he had every intention of utilizing as soon as he got what he wanted.

"What's takin' so long, boy?" Angus shouted, his booming voice so close to her face her ears rang. "Is my gold in there?"

Ned didn't answer.

Emma's already pounding heart thumped a little faster. Was this part of the plan? Getting Ned away from his father? But why would he stay in the church? What had Mal told him?

"Ned! Answer me, boy!" Angus's grip on her throat tightened.

She winced at the pressure and rose up on her tiptoes in a vain effort to open her airway.

"You ready to see your woman die, Shaw?" Angus shoved her forward a couple steps as he advanced toward Mal. "If I don't see either my boy or my gold in—"

A loud *bong* cut off his words. Angus jerked his gaze toward the steeple. His grip loosened a fraction. Emma struck.

She thrust her elbow backward into his belly as hard as she could. Air whooshed from his lungs. His hold faltered as he dropped to his knees. She twisted away and fell to the ground, knowing Mal would never defend himself if she was in the way.

At the same time her back collided with the hard earth, Angus's hand closed around his pistol. Emma drew up her knees. Focused on the gun. Kicked out with all her might. Her right heel connected just as a shot rang out. The gun went flying, but so had a bullet.

Malachi!

Emma frantically rolled to the side, her gaze searching. Had he been hit?

No. He was running toward her. Shouting her name. A revolver miraculously in his hand.

Brutal arms grabbed her and tried to lift her from the ground, but she refused to be the outlaw's shield again. She rolled to her back and kicked savagely at his knee.

He groaned. Stumbled. Reached for something inside his boot.

A knife!

Mal's footsteps pounded close. Too close. He wouldn't see the knife. If he tackled Angus, the outlaw would gut him like a fish.

Emma could think of only one thing to do. She rolled toward Angus and grabbed his wrist with both hands, trying to pin the knife to the ground. But Angus was too strong. He flung her off of him with enough force to send her through the air and crashing into Malachi. Mal's gun clattered to the ground as he tried to catch her and break her fall.

"Knife," she managed to croak out as Mal pushed her aside and yelled for her to get to the church.

The church? She wasn't about to hide away while her man battled a maniac. She stumbled toward the first weapon she spied, the rifle Mal had tossed aside at the start of this negotiation.

Once she had the gun in hand, she spun back toward the two men and lifted the stock to her shoulder. Malachi straddled Angus on the ground, his hands around the outlaw's wrist as he struggled for control of the knife. They were too close together, moving too fast. She couldn't shoot without chancing injury to the wrong man.

Mal pounded the outlaw's wrist into the ground. Once. Twice. He lifted it for a third blow, but Angus grabbed a handful of dirt in his left hand and flung it into Malachi's face. Blinded, Mal couldn't see the blow that followed—a left jab to the side of his head.

Mal crumpled. Emma whimpered. But in a blink, he rolled to his feet like a cat, having pulled a knife of his own from somewhere. With a swipe of his sleeve, he wiped the worst of the dirt from his eyes as he circled his opponent, his gaze one of fierce concentration. He was faster, lighter on his feet than Angus, but the outlaw was bigger and surely more adept at fighting dirty.

Or maybe not. Even as the thought formed in Emma's mind, Mal proved it untrue by making a mock knife throw. When Angus flinched and dodged to avoid the fake toss, Mal charged. Brought his knee up into the outlaw's groin and slammed his elbow into Angus's face.

Something cracked. Angus's nose? Blood gushed. But the outlaw wouldn't go down. With a roar, he slashed at Malachi with the knife. Mal blocked with his forearm, bringing his own knife down into his opponent's thigh.

Angus cursed and shoved Mal backward. Mal stumbled. Angus hurled the knife. It sank into Mal's shoulder. Emma gasped.

Mal turned at the sound. "Get out of here!" He glared furiously at her as he yanked the blade free. A large crimson stain spread over his shirt and vest.

She turned to obey his order, then froze. While Mal had been yelling at her, Angus had grabbed one of the fallen revolvers. She'd unwittingly been his distraction after all.

The outlaw's arm lifted. His narrowed gaze homed in on Mal.

Emma lunged toward the church. But not for safety. For a clear shot.

Remembering everything Mal had taught her, she took quick aim at the widest part of Angus's body and pulled the trigger. The rifle's kick knocked her backward, but it was the sound of a second shot and the glimpse of Mal dropping to the ground in her peripheral vision that sent agony stabbing through her.

"No!" She ran to him, not even taking the time to see what had happened to Angus.

But in the same instant, Malachi sprang to his feet and grabbed her about the waist. Emma was so shocked by the unexpected action, she gave a little shriek and fought him for a heartbeat when he reached for the rifle in her hand.

Not that it stopped him. He snatched the weapon from her half-numb fingers and shoved her behind his back as he took aim at the man still standing in the churchyard.

"Make a move, Angus," Mal snarled, "and I'll put the next bullet between your eyes."

Angus's gun arm hung limp at his side. A stain nearly matching the one on Malachi's shirt seeped from his bicep down to his elbow. Emma bit her bottom lip. Apparently she'd missed her target. Though, by the look of his arm, she'd done enough damage to keep him from harming Malachi. That's all that truly mattered. Angus's pistol fell from his hand and dropped to the ground with a *thud*. His disbelieving gaze followed it, then slowly lifted.

"She shot me. Again."

"About time a woman took a pound of flesh from your mangy hide," Mal spat. "I saw what you did to your wife. You should be horsewhipped for that crime alone."

Fire ignited in Angus's eyes. "Flora's mine to do with as I see fit. She's none of your concern, Shaw."

"Maybe not," a young, masculine voice said from somewhere behind Emma, "but she's my concern. And you've hurt her for the last time."

Ned strode around the corner of the church and marched past Malachi, his pistol and his fury aimed directly at his father.

"Put that gun away, boy," Angus blustered, even as his nostrils flared as if catching the scent of danger. "What happened is between your ma and me. It don't concern you."

"Don't concern me?" Ned shouted the words like an accusation. "She's so busted up she can't even stand without help. The lady was right, wasn't she." He nodded his head in Emma's direction. "You beat Ma and left her for dead in the woods, like an animal shot for sport and left to rot. But *you're* the animal. A rabid animal that needs to be put down."

Emma's heart lurched. So that's why Ned had stayed in the church. Flora was in there. Knowing the extent of the damage Angus had wrought against the woman, it was no wonder the boy was spitting mad. But if he let his anger rule him, his actions would haunt him for the rest of his days. She couldn't let that happen.

"You can't shoot him, Ned." Emma tried to step around Malachi, but he shifted to keep himself in front of her, his rifle still trained on Angus. "He'll pay for his crimes. We'll make sure of it."

Ned shook his head. A tremor entered his voice. "I should have protected her. I have to make it right. Make sure she never has cause to fear him again."

Emma's heart thundered in her chest . . . No . . . the thunder came from outside. From the south. Riders. From Seymour.

Ned took another step closer to his father, his gun steady, his finger on the trigger.

"You can't protect your ma if you're not around." Mal's voice rumbled low. Calm. Logical. "You shoot your pa in cold blood, you hang. Then who will provide for your ma? See to her protection?"

Ned's gun hand trembled just a touch.

"Listen to him, Ned." Flora's voice.

"Ma?" Ned glanced behind.

Emma twisted around, too, and found the woman hobbling forward, a resolute Claire propping her up. "I need you, son," she pled. "More than I need anything else. The next time your pa gets out of prison, he'll be old and weak, and you'll be a full-grown man in his prime. I'll have nothing to fear."

Ned's gun lowered a few inches but remained locked on Angus.

"I know he deserves killin'," Flora said, her face hardening as she swept a disgusted glance at her husband, "but he ain't worth your life. We just gotta trust that God and the law will see to his punishment."

The ground vibrated beneath Emma's feet. The riders were getting closer.

"Please, Ned." Flora reached for him. "Take my hand. Let's go back inside."

After a hesitation that felt like an hour but was surely only a few heartbeats in length, Ned uncocked his pistol and slid it into the holster at his side. He was halfway to his mother when Angus sneered at his back.

"Told ya, you turned him soft, Flora." He spat onto the ground. "That pansy of yours will never be a real man."

Mal lurched forward, swung the rifle around, and before Angus could blink, slammed the butt into the outlaw's head. The snake crumpled face first into the dirt. Exactly where he belonged.

39

The moment Angus slumped unconscious to the ground, Mal spun around and grabbed Emma's upper arm.

"Are you all right?" he demanded. His blood still pumped through his veins at lightning speed.

"Yes." She nodded, but he didn't believe her.

There were red marks along her slender throat from Angus's fingers and a darkening bruise along her chin about the size of a man's fist. The jackal had laid hands on her. Hurt her. A muscle ticked in Mal's jaw. He wanted to slam the rifle stock into the fiend again. Lord knew he deserved it. But Emma was his main concern now. She looked as though she'd been through a war. Her dress was filthy, one sleeve torn at the shoulder, another tear leaving a gash down the left side of her skirt. All from rolling around in the dirt battling Angus . . . *Heaven above!* She'd been fighting—no, defending *him*—when she should have been running for cover. Mal didn't know if he should shake her for acting so rashly or crush her to him in appreciation.

He opted for the latter.

Dropping the rifle to the ground, Mal grasped her upper

arms with both hands and yanked her to him. Anger, leftover terror, and sweet relief all swirled through his chest as he pulled her near, but it was the love thrumming through his heart that brought his mouth crashing down upon hers.

He could have lost her. Forever. He held her tighter. Closer. Not ever wanting to experience that kind of scare again.

But wait. He was being too rough. After all the violence she'd suffered at Angus's hands, he didn't want to subject her to unwanted attentions. He should stop. But he couldn't. Heaven help him, she tasted too sweet, and he'd hungered for this for so long. Maybe he'd find the strength if she pushed him away.

She didn't. Instead, she melted against him.

A sigh-like moan escaped her throat, and just as he started scraping together the wherewithal to release her, she launched up on her tiptoes, clasped his shoulders, and kissed him back. Deeply.

Mal shuddered. The wound beneath his right shoulder shot a twinge of discomfort through him at her enthusiastic response, but he ignored it. Who cared about a little pain when the woman he loved was kissing him?

His hands gentled their grip on her arms and traveled around to her back, cherishing her. Caressing her. Replacing Angus's mark of brutality with one of tenderness.

His palms skimmed their way up to her nape. His thumbs stroked featherlight touches over the slender column of her throat. Soothing. Erasing the ugliness. Then he cupped the back of her head in one hand, adjusted her face to the perfect angle, and poured all the love he'd stored up in his soul for the past decade into their kiss.

She met him stroke for stroke, reaching up to bury her fingers in his hair. Tiny shivers of awareness danced over his scalp, down his neck, and along his arms. His gut tightened. His hold tightened. He flattened his right palm into the hollow between her shoulder blades and drew her so close to him that not even a breeze could have slipped through.

"I see you . . . ah . . . have things well in hand, Shaw."

Emma gave a little jump in Malachi's arms, then tore her lips from his and hid her face in his chest.

Mal glared up at Benjamin Porter, who was trying not to smile and failing miserably. And the freighter wasn't alone. The man's brother, Bart, stood a few steps behind him along with half of Harper's Station—Andrew, Betty, Grace, Tori, and some young fellow Mal didn't recognize.

Not only had he lost his head and kissed Emma, but he'd done it with an audience. Claire and Ned must've born witness, too, but were probably too concerned about Flora's condition to stay and enjoy the show in its entirety.

"That the outlaw?" Betty stepped around the gawkers and marched over to examine Angus's crumpled form. "He dead?"

With great effort, Malachi forced his arms to uncurl. He stepped away from Emma, hating the feel of her hands slipping away from his neck, his chest. He wanted to grab them back, to maintain the connection. It felt as if she was slipping away for good. No doubt she was. Despite all they'd been through, the core of their circumstances hadn't changed. She still lived in a women's colony and he still lived the rough-and-tumble life of a railroad man. Or would as soon as he found another position.

"Shaw?" Betty turned to stare at him, impatience lining her practical face. Either unfazed by what she and the others had interrupted, or attempting in her own way to smooth things over by getting down to business, she stood over Angus and waited for Mal to respond.

He cleared his throat and tried to ignore the flush of heat rising up from his collar. "He's not dead. He's got a knife wound in his thigh, a bullet in his arm, and a knot on his forehead from where my rifle butt ran into his skull. Someone should probably tie him up and carry him back to Seymour along with the army payroll he stole five years ago. The strongbox is inside the church."

"That's what we brought *him* along for." Betty jerked her thumb back toward the stranger.

Porter gave the fellow a little push. "Get to work, Deputy. Tie him up and charge him with kidnapping, assault, arson, extortion . . ." He looked at Mal. "Anything I'm missing?"

"He already did time for thievery, but attempting to take the money a second time could be a new charge. Not sure."

Betty nudged Angus none-too-gently with the toe of her boot. "Murder," she announced. "Eighteen counts. The weasel killed my chickens."

Technically, Flora had done the deed on Angus's behalf, but Mal wasn't about to split hairs with the woman.

As the deputy and Porter moved to take care of Angus, Mal watched Emma enter the company of the other women. Tori and Grace surrounded her, cutting her off from him, leading her around the corner, out of his line of sight. A feeling akin to panic clutched at his chest. But what could he do? She belonged with them.

Emma allowed Tori and Grace to lead her away, still embarrassed—and in truth, a bit light-headed—from being caught so thoroughly kissing Malachi. Thankfully, neither of her friends felt the need to comment upon her public display. They were both chattering on about how Sheriff Tabor had been nowhere to be found and Andrew had been unable to convince Deputy Lang to leave his post in Seymour to assist.

"If it wasn't for Mr. Porter's insistence, we'd have no lawman with us at all," Tori said.

"Insistence?" Grace scoffed. "The man used every inch of

height and muscle the good Lord gave him to intimidate Lang into compliance. I swear, for a man who's been nothing but gentle and kind around us women, he looked like a grizzly when he took on that deputy."

"Yes, well . . . I'm just relieved to find you safe and well, Emma," Tori said, neatly turning the conversation. "We've all been worried sick. Your aunts, especially. They made me promise to ride back to Seymour the minute the ordeal was over and convey what had happened. Since I left Lewis behind with them and Daisy, I gladly agreed. I've never spent a night away from my son. Mr. Porter and his brother agreed to escort me back, no matter the time."

"I'll be staying to help out with things around here," Grace said as they climbed the front steps to the church entrance. "See if Claire needs a hand with Flora. I'd wanted to stay behind in the first place, to offer my gun to the fight, but Mr. Shaw insisted I leave with the rest. He hadn't wanted anyone to stay behind. He was afraid of what might happen to you if Angus thought we weren't complying with his demand. But Flora was adamant that she wouldn't be leaving as long as her son was in the line of fire."

"And Claire was in no hurry to return to Seymour, what with Stanley Fischer still upset over his mail-order bride running out on him." Tori gave Emma a knowing look. "So Mr. Shaw agreed to let the two of them stay as long as they stayed out of sight."

"Oh, speaking of Claire . . ." Grace said as they crossed the threshold into the back of the sanctuary.

"Is that my name, I'm a hearin'?" The redhead stood up from where she'd been helping Flora settle onto a pallet of quilts in the corner. "Oh, but it's good to see ye ladies." She bustled forward and hugged each one in turn. "Now, tell me, why were me ears burnin' when ye came in?"

Grace laughed. "I had just remembered that Maybelle sent

me back with the key to her medical cabinet. She meant to leave it with you but forgot to take it out of her doctor's bag." Grace reached for the chain around her neck and pulled it from beneath her dress. A small key dangled from the end. She lifted the chain over her head and handed it to the younger woman.

Claire took it and tucked it into her skirt pocket. "I'll be needin' that, I'm a thinkin'. That scoundrel outside will require some patchin' before they carry him off to the hoosegow."

Patching . . . "Oh my stars!" Emma exclaimed. "Malachi!" She turned to Claire. "You have to see to him right away. He took a knife to his shoulder, and there's blood all over his shirt."

Emma grabbed Claire's arm and started pulling her back out of the building even as she silently castigated herself. Just because the man had held her in arms that felt wondrously strong and kissed her with a passion that felt more vibrant and alive than anything she'd ever experienced didn't mean he wasn't hurting. How much blood might he have lost by now? What if the wound got infected?

He should have been her first concern, but she'd been too worried about what her ladies would think of her kissing him in broad daylight.

"Hurry," she demanded, dragging Claire behind her as she rushed down the steps and around the corner.

At first she didn't see him, and her chest tightened in alarm. "Malachi?" The cry was loud even to her own ears.

"Over here." Betty Cooper called to them from the shadows of the church wall.

Mal tried to stand when Emma ran over to him, but Betty forced him back down onto the empty crate he'd been using as a seat.

"Sit still, Shaw," Betty groused, "or you're gonna mess up my bandage."

She'd wrapped a long strip of white cloth over his shoulder

354

and across his chest. His *bare* chest. His very fit and well-defined bare chest. Emma's mouth went a little dry. "Is . . . is he all right? I brought Claire to help with the wound. The loss of blood—"

"I'm fine, Em," Mal muttered, not meeting her gaze. "The leather on my vest kept the blade from going too deep. It'll heal up in a few days."

"Might need a couple stitches," Betty said, speaking more to Emma than the stubborn man sitting on the crate. She finished wrapping the bandage and tied off the ends. "You should have Maybelle take a look at it when she gets back tomorrow."

"Fine. Are we done?" Mal pushed to his feet before she could answer, grabbed his shirt from the ground, and yanked it over his head as he stalked off to join the other males tending to a rousing Angus.

Emma frowned after him. He hadn't even looked at her. Not once. Perhaps he was uncomfortable having three women staring at him when he wasn't properly dressed.

Or maybe . . . Her stomach clenched. Maybe he was shutting her out. Distancing himself, just as he'd done the last time he'd gotten ready to leave.

She might have accepted his leaving without a fight ten years ago when she'd been a child, but she wasn't about to let him get on his high horse of nobility and ride away from her again with some flimsy excuse about it being for her own good. Not after he'd kissed her like a starving man who'd finally been offered a place at the table. She might not have been kissed more than three times in her lifetime, but she knew the difference between polite interest, brotherly concern, and a soul-deep need that matched the longing of her own heart.

Emma straightened her shoulders and set her chin. Mr. Malachi Shaw had better brace himself. He was in for the battle of his life. And she wasn't afraid to fight dirty.

40

Two days later, Mal tied down his saddlebag with a heavy heart. He was going to miss Harper's Station. All the women with their quirky personalities and independent spirits—he had no doubt they would flourish just as Emma had predicted.

They'd flooded back into town first thing yesterday morning, as soon as they were assured Angus was behind bars. None of the men had accompanied them. A not-so-subtle message that it was past time for him to be hitting the trail.

Porter had stayed in Seymour to get caught up on overdue shipments as well as to oversee the building of his new freight wagon. He'd also convinced his brother to give Andrew a job at his livery. The kid was a natural with horses, and since his pay included meals and a place to sleep, Mal figured he'd make out just fine. Trail might be a tad lonely without the kid along, but the boy needed stability, something Mal couldn't offer right now. Even if he found work quickly, a rail camp was no place to raise a kid.

Taking hold of Ulysses's reins, Mal led the animal out of the barn and around to the front of the station house. No voices echoed within. No pots and pans rattled, no shoe heels clicked on the wood floors. Deserted. Empty. Downright depressing.

Well, at least the ladies had made the rounds yesterday to say their good-byes.

Maybelle had added a couple of stitches to his shoulder and given him a sack of clean bandages and salve along with strict instructions on how to tend the wound. Betty had ordered him to keep a sharp eye out for bandits while he traveled. Grace offered to wire his former employer on his behalf, but he'd turned her down, wanting to start somewhere fresh. Tori had gifted him with two new boxes of cartridges for his rifle and a leather satchel for carrying his additional belongings, which he needed after Henry loaded him down with a thick stack of writing paper, pens, and ink, and Bertie heaped more food on him than he could possibly eat in a week.

The only person he hadn't said good-bye to was Emma.

Mal clenched his jaw and forced his boots to keep walking, one foot in front of the other. He wasn't looking forward to this last farewell. Saying good-bye to the aunts had been hard enough this morning. They'd both put a good face on things, but if they felt even a fraction of the tearing pain he did at the prospect of being separated from the only family he'd ever known—again—they'd hidden more hurt than they'd let show. Of course, they might've already made peace with his leaving. He'd been gone for ten years, after all. Easy enough to slip back into old habits.

Ulysses snorted as he clomped along. Mal sighed, as well, then forced his chin up. He had plenty of lonely miles ahead to wallow in the doldrums. He needed to put on a cheerful face for Emma. Show his support of her work. Let her know how proud he was of the woman she'd become. Not to mention drinking in the sight of her one last time, memorizing each line and curve so he'd be able to carry her image in his mind.

Pulling up to Tori's store, he tossed Ulysses's reins over the hitching post and leaned his back against the railing to wait. All the women had congregated inside the café next door for a meeting or planning session or some such gathering. He hadn't been invited.

He'd barely settled in when the café's door creaked open. Emma stepped onto the boardwalk and descended to the street. She was so beautiful. Her prim banker's suit with the dark blue jacket and matching skirt showed off her slim waist and delicate figure. The white shirtwaist drew his gaze up to the slender line of her throat, the curve of her cheek, and the few tendrils of black, curly hair blowing in the breeze that refused to be tamed by her topknot.

He straightened away from the railing, his arms aching to hold her one last time, his lips starving for another taste of her sweetness. He locked down the impulses but could do nothing to slow the racing of his heart or the twisting in his gut.

She stopped two steps away from him, just out of reach. "So you're really leaving." Her green eyes accused him, making his gut clench tighter as guilt tangled around the knot already there.

He tried to shrug it off, to make some flippant comment about it being time since he'd done what he came to do, but he couldn't. Not with her eyes flashing green fire at him—fire that couldn't quite hide the pain lingering behind the sparks.

She deserved the truth from him. It might not change anything, but he'd not tuck tail and run with so much unsaid between them.

"You should at least wait until Sheriff Tabor gets back," she said before he could find the words he sought. "Deputy Lang mentioned there was a reward for finding the gold. That money belongs to you."

Mal shook his head. "Nah. The gold was in your house, and I destroyed most of the basement to get to it. Keep what you need to make repairs and give the rest to Flora. She and Ned need a chance to make a fresh start."

"But what if I need you again?" Something broke in her voice this time, as if her control was as much of an illusion as his was.

His gaze flew to hers. Moisture glistened. *Not tears, Emma. Please. I'll never make it if you cry.*

Even as the thought ran through his head, she blinked the moisture away and straightened her shoulders. His brave little soldier once again. Somehow that made his heart ache all the more.

Stepping closer, he took her hand and clasped it between both of his. "I'll come whenever you call, Em. You know I will. I . . ." He glanced down at the dirt, then forced his gaze back up to her face. "I love you. I think I have since the day you found me shivering in your aunts' barn and told me you were gonna keep me." Mal shook his head and ducked his chin. "I want to keep *you*, Em. More than I ever wanted anything in my life."

She gave a little gasp, and her free hand flew to cover her mouth as if reliving the kiss they'd shared . . . and the truth it had revealed.

He stroked her fingers, surrounding their coolness with the warmth of his palms even as his heart cracked straight down the middle. "But you have a life here. An important life ministering to women who need you. It's your calling. Your God-given purpose. I'd never ask you to leave that. It's who you are."

Her hand fell away from her mouth, revealing a bottom lip that trembled. "Oh, Malachi. I love you, too. With all my heart."

Joy, bittersweet and sharp, stabbed through him at her words. If only there was a way . . .

She reached out and caressed his jaw, her touch sending shivers over his skin. "You're the best man I've ever known, Malachi. I owe you more than I can ever repay."

Mal slowly wagged his head, careful not to shake off her

touch. "You don't owe me a thing, Em. You saved my life. Gave me a family. Made me believe I was worth more than the gutter trash everyone always compared me to. Fighting off a no-good outlaw doesn't even make a dent in that debt."

She shook her head at him and dug her teeth into her bottom lip. Then she twisted away from him and crossed her arms over her chest. "Do you promise?" she blurted.

At this moment, he'd promise her anything if it was in his power to grant. "Promise what?"

"To come. If I need you."

He sagged with relief. *That* he could promise. All day long. "Yes. I promise." He cupped her upper arms. "All you have to do is send word, and I'll be here. I swear it."

"You better."

He grinned and bent close to touch his lips to her forehead. Man, but he loved it when she got all bossy on him.

He started to back away, sure that if he didn't leave now, he'd never find the strength to do so. But Emma reached out and clasped his arm.

"Malachi?"

He swallowed and turned to face her. "Yeah?"

"I need you."

His heart thumped an awkward beat. What was she saying? She said it again. Louder this time. Imperious. "I. Need. You."

"Em, I don't understand. . . ."

She closed the distance between them with one long step, released his arm, and grabbed him around the waist, holding him as if she planned to make him her prisoner. Then she tipped her head back and glared up at him. "You promised you would come if I needed you. Well, I need you. Today. Tomorrow. The next day. I'm going to need you forever."

"But what about your ladies? You can't just abandon your work." Though in that moment he wanted her to. Wanted her to choose him over her ministry, God forgive him. But that wasn't right. It was selfish. Greedy. Mal reached for her arms and tried to pry them away from his midsection. "You belong in Harper's Station, Em. I belong in a railroad camp. There's no way for us to be together."

"What if there *was* a way?" She threw the words at him like a hunter taking down a buck, and heaven help him if he didn't feel the blow straight through his chest. "Would you stay, then?"

Letting go of her arms, he traced a path up to her face and lightly stroked the edge of her cheek. He couldn't quite meet her gaze, so he watched his fingers move back and forth along the soft skin.

"Yes, angel." The words hitched in his throat. "I'd stay. I'd marry you and spend the rest of my days loving you. We'd have children and raise them to follow their dreams and passions, making sure they knew their parents believed in them and saw them as people of value and worth. We'd grow old together, and sit on the porch in matching rocking chairs and watch the sun go down while we reminisce about how an ornery outlaw brought us together."

Moisture trickled into the path of his fingers. She was weeping. Biting back a groan, he dragged her into a hug and tucked her head into the crook of his shoulder. For once, *he* was the one instigating, a fact that should surprise him but oddly didn't. His barriers had crumbled. No more holding back, no more protecting the hidden places inside him.

She loved him. If she could bear up under the uncertainty of the future, so could he.

He ran a hand over her hair as her brow nestled against the side of his jaw. "Maybe someday, when things change . . . But for now, your place is here. And as much as I believe in your work and in this place, I don't belong in it. There's no permanent place for a man in a women's colony."

She pulled back from him and gazed into his face with tear-filled eyes at odds with the smile curving her lips. "Don't you see, Malachi? Your belief in this work is exactly why you *do* belong."

Emma took another step backward, so much energy vibrating through her, she couldn't stand still. "This place was never created to keep men out. It was created to give women power over their own destiny. Omitting men just seemed to be the easiest way to accomplish that feat. But our ladies voted, Mal." She clasped his hand and beamed up at him. "They voted to accept you as a permanent resident of Harper's Station. Unanimously, I might add. You've earned their trust, their loyalty. You're family now."

Mal reeled, not quite able to absorb what she was saying.

Emma winked and squeezed his hand. "Even Helen voted to let you stay."

Hope surged to such fierce heights inside him, he balked. Afraid to believe he could finally regain what he'd lost a decade ago—a home.

"But what would I do?" Mal tugged his hand from her grasp and rubbed the back of his neck. "I can't exactly stitch a quilt or put up vegetables. A man has to work, Em. I can't stay if there is no way for me to provide for you, for a family."

Her smile never dimmed. "That's what we met about today," she said. "We fully expect the town to start growing again. Grace will be sending telegrams out to those who left us at the start of all the trouble, letting them know it is safe to return. And others will come, too. Especially if we can promise them protection.

"Some of these women come to us seeking sanctuary from abusive fathers or husbands but are afraid to stay because they don't feel safe with only females standing between them and their abusers. But if there was a man, a good man—say, a town marshal—willing to guard them, they'd be more likely to stay and eventually to thrive as the strong women God always desired them to be."

A marshal? Mal nearly laughed at the irony. How many times had he evaded the law during his youth? And now she thought him worthy of being the law, himself?

"Think of Lewis and Ned and the other returning families with children," Emma continued. "They need godly men in their lives. Boys need an example to emulate, and girls need a way to recognize a man of character who will respect and honor them.

"The pay wouldn't be what you're used to at first, but as the town grows, so will your salary. We've already voted in a city tax ordinance. Of course, it's with the understanding that when things are quiet, you'll make yourself available to assist with things that require heavy lifting or repairs. Betty said if you'd help her build on to her henhouse, she'd donate a percentage of her profits from the additional chickens to the law enforcement fund.

"Mr. Porter convinced Tori to expand her business, as well, by starting a delivery route to area farms and ranches, saving the owners from having to travel into Seymour or Wichita Falls for supplies. If that partnership proves as lucrative as they expect, that will mean increased sales of all our products—quilts, canned goods, eggs. The more the economy grows, the more we can afford to pay—"

"Slow down." Mal chuckled, holding up a hand. His stunned mind could barely keep up with her rapid-fire explanations.

The woman was amazing. While he'd resigned himself to the fact that his dreams of a life with her were unattainable, that banker's brain of hers had been busy plotting a perfectly feasible plan to make the impossible possible.

He grinned at her, took her hand, and lifted it to his lips. "I don't need a big salary, Emma. Just enough to provide for you and our children." He pressed his lips slowly to the back of her hand, gratified when a tremor passed through her that matched the one dancing around in his belly.

"So you'll stay? Oh, please say you will." She leaned her head against his chest in a quick hug, then turned her face back up to look at him. Her cheeks flushed pink and her eyes glowed with love. "You're the only man I've ever wanted, Malachi Shaw. No other will do."

He nodded. "I'll stay."

With a squeal of pure happiness, Emma threw herself into his arms. He swept her around in a circle, laughter gurgling up inside him as her feet dangled in midair. As he lowered her back to earth, he bent his head for a kiss—one not born of desperation, but born of love, a love they had years to explore.

"That better mean you're staying, young man," Aunt Henry shouted.

Mal lifted his head but didn't release his hold on Emma's waist. Not only was Henry looking on, but the entire town had stepped out of the café to watch, each lady with a smile on her face.

He pushed his hat up off his forehead and grinned. "Just try to get rid of me!"

Then he bent right back down and resumed his kiss. The onlookers cheered. Emma barely lasted a heartbeat before she dissolved into giggles, not that Malachi cared. He simply held her close and reveled in feeling her heart beat in time with his.

With his angel in his arms, he'd always be in heaven.

More From
Karen Witemeyer

Visit karenwitemeyer.com for a full list of her books.

A teacher on the run. A bounty hunter in pursuit. Charlotte Atherton and Stone Hammond will have to decide whether to trust each other before they both lose what they hold most dear.

A Worthy Pursuit

Nicole Renard is on a mission to find a *suitable* husband. But when her plans are waylaid by a dashing yet eccentric researcher, can she stop her heart from surging full steam ahead?

Full Steam Ahead

When Crockett Archer is forced off a train and delivered to an outlaw's daughter for her birthday, is it possible this stolen preacher ended up right where he belongs?

Stealing the Preacher

⬧ BETHANYHOUSE

If you enjoyed *No Other Will Do,* you may also like . . .